Make You Sorry

Christine Rae-Jones

Cliffside House Publishing

This paperback edition published by
Cliffside House Publishing 2020

Copyright © Christine Rae-Jones 2020
Cover design by ©TheCoverCollection.com

ISBN: 978-1-8380863-0-5

www.christinerae-jones.com

Chapter 1

The silence of the house bore down on him.

A lived-in house has background noise, even when the occupants are asleep. Here, there was nothing. No gurgling radiators, no snoring, no clock ticking. Just his heartbeat.

And the drip.

He squinted in the direction of his alarm clock before remembering he wasn't in bed at home. Reaching down from the lumpy sofa, he patted the floor for his phone. Ten to six. His mouth was parched and he needed to pee. Had he dreamed that dripping noise? Was it the pressure of last night's beers in his bladder that had woken him?

He put his feet on the floor and sat up, massaging the stubble on his face. When he arrived yesterday, he'd found the house cold and unwelcoming, much like his mother-in-law who owned it. Dorothy Cooper had moved out two years ago but he could feel her presence and her disapproval. In her world, a man wouldn't spend the night fully clothed on her velour sofa. And he wouldn't wake up with a hangover, especially on the day his family's removal van was arriving.

He laced up his trainers and stood, gripping the sofa to keep his balance. Along with the gas and electric, the water supply had been cut when Dorothy moved out so he would have to pee in the garden. Her favourite rose bed was just the place. The thought pleased him.

But first, that drip. It seemed to be coming from the

1

hall, but that wasn't possible, was it? The house had been drained down.

Oh God, don't let it be a leaking roof. What would that cost?

Coming into the hallway, another drip, louder this time. More of a splat.

He pointed the beam from his phone down to the black and white tiled floor. It reflected off a dark pool. The tinted light might have disguised it but the sweet, coppery smell could not. He diverted his light up to the chandelier and watched droplets of blood trickle through its complex structure. Each hung at the tip of a crystal icicle until weight overcame surface tension.

Drip.

Keeping to the inside edge of the treads, he made his way up the stairs, heart and head pounding. Halfway up, he paused to listen.

Nothing.

He slowed his steps, aware that at any minute he could face an armed opponent, hell bent on escape.

The first door he tried was stiff, but yielded to his shoulder. Light from the streetlamp at the end of the drive, cast shadows across the room. An upturned chair; two wardrobes; a dressing table; a body.

He looked behind the door before making his way around the perimeter of the room. He needed to check for vital signs. He pointed the phone light at the body.

Young; gaunt; and male, underdressed for February, in worn, black jeans and a dirty red T-shirt. Eyes open and face contorted by the grimace which showed he had fought for his life. Dark staining on the parquet tiles surrounding outstretched arms.

He bent down and touched two fingers to the neck. No pulse. He studied the face. Nobody he knew.

He straightened up and dialed a number from his contact list. The Operations Room answered after two rings.

'Hi, it's DI Nick Morgan here. Look, I don't officially start with the Major Crimes Unit until Monday, but there's a body in my master bedroom. I'm going to need a full team here ASAP.'

<u>Chapter 2</u>

Friday 7th February

When DS Dave Spence got the call to attend Cliffside House he was already showered and dressed in one of his favourite suits. He liked the way the navy three-piece made him look tall and thin, especially when teamed with the blue shirt and silver tie.

'"Body in my master bedroom!"' His tone was angry as he sat on the bed and laced up newly polished black shoes. 'I'll bet that's bollocks. When we arrive, he'll be standing there with a stopwatch, timing how long it takes for us yokels to mobilise a crime scene team. You know what the Met's like… all statistics and targets.' He paused. 'He's not even meant to start until Monday.'

Penny Spence sighed. Friday was the one day of the week she didn't have to be up early to attend school assembly and the call had woken her. Now she was sitting up in bed, arms crossed. 'It's not going to be like this every morning, is it?' She plumped her pillows. 'It's not his fault he got the job. You couldn't be promoted because you hadn't sat the DI exam.' She waited for him to look at her. 'I'm still amazed he applied. Wasn't he one of the Met's golden boys? What's he going to do in a quiet place like Gullhaven?' Spence shrugged. 'Whatever's going on, he's here now and you need to get on with him because he's going to have an input on any future promotion you go for. Have you put the kettle on?'

'Kettle's boiled and I'll bring you a cuppa before I go, as usual.'

He stopped when he reached the bedroom door. 'He can't expect to run the investigation, can he? Not when the body's turned up in his own house. We should be investigating him.'

Penny turned away and snuggled under the duvet. 'I expect you'll be late home again? I'll leave something out for you.'

Traffic was light and Spence reached Cliffside House by seven. He had known the property all his life and always thought it looked intimidating. When he was four, his two older brothers told him it was haunted and even now, it would not surprise him. He stopped the car a few houses short of his destination and opened a window. The sea below was calm but he could still hear the noise of the waves at the bottom of the cliffs. He composed himself and took a few breaths before completing the journey to his new boss's house.

Spence parked on the road and scrutinised the building. In contrast to the neighbouring properties which were symmetrical and neat, this one had inappropriate extensions and a dilapidated, east-facing balcony. A large entrance porch made it impossible to park near to the front door.

The streetlamps went out and he waited for his eyes to adjust before getting out of the car. The figure sitting on the doorstep started to rise as Spence walked towards him.

'Sir?' He spoke softly, although he didn't know why. 'I'm DS Spence, sir. Under the circumstances, I don't suppose it's appropriate to say "Welcome to Gullhaven Cove?"'

As he got closer, Spence struggled to suppress surprise at Morgan's appearance. They had met only

5

briefly when Morgan was being shown round the department, prior to his transfer. In sharp contrast to the erect, smartly dressed, and confident man whose hand he had shaken, this version was a wreck. His jeans and rugby shirt were creased, his hair was tousled and he was in need of a shave. What had once been expensive trainers were grubby and scuffed. As Spence got closer, he had to resist recoiling from the smell of stale beer which carried towards him on the slight sea breeze.

Morgan apologised. 'There's no water in the house and I haven't been able to brush my teeth yet.' He pointed up to a bay window above the front door. 'He's up there. There's no light but as far as I could tell from this,' he pointed to the phone in his other hand, 'he's bleeding from the back. Stabbed or shot, maybe? No visible exit wound on the front.'

Spence stepped past him, making for the front door.

'You'll have to go round the back, then through to the hall and up the stairs. I've not been trusted with a front door key.' Morgan's voice was raw with resentment. 'I'm supposed to be moving in today. That's not going to happen, is it?'

As Spence struggled for an appropriate reply he heard what he was sure would be the first of the crime scene team's vehicles approaching. That was one of the advantages of living in "retirement-on-sea." Early morning traffic was light. There was no 'rush hour.'

Morgan looked towards the road, 'Circus has arrived then.'

'Yes, sir. And I think you should come with me to the station. At the very least we'll need a statement and I'll see if I can rustle up a toothbrush, coffee and a shower.'

Morgan turned and looked up towards the window. 'What was he doing here?'

6

The question hung in the cold morning air, but Spence guessed a response wasn't expected. He pointed to the end of the drive. 'My car's just on the right, sir.'

They crunched their way down the shingle drive, Spence remaining a step behind Morgan, watching him, making no attempt to conceal his suspicion.

<u>Chapter 3</u>

Friday 7th February

Dorothy Cooper was also up early. The weather was dry so she hoped her joints would not be too painful today. She wore her black, high-waisted Italian trousers and a crisp white shirt. She didn't always bother with jewellery, but today she chose the pendant and earring set, a present from her daughter, Samantha. Swollen fingers made it difficult to use the clasp, but she managed at the third attempt. Excitement brought colour to her normally pale cheeks and it took careful application of makeup to tone it down. She leant closer to the mirror and ran fingers through her white hair. The short style suited her sharp features and impatient temperament. She could step out of the shower, comb it into place and be done.

She would breakfast in the residents' dining room this morning. In the two years since moving into Silver Sands Supported Living she had never done this, but today was special. Today, her daughter and grandchildren were moving into her house. And Plod too, of course.

Soon after her husband's funeral she had fallen and broken her ankle, forcing her to leave Cliffside House and move to Silver Sands. It was only meant to be for a few months, but she soon realised that living alone in that large house with only memories and spiders for company wasn't an option. That was when she started to plan for Samantha and the grandchildren to come and live there with her, even if that meant her policeman son-in-law, would have to come too.

She accepted that it wouldn't happen overnight, but a plan was a plan, and she was determined to see it through.

Plod had proven to be a powerful adversary. Every time Dorothy tried to make Samantha feel guilty for neglecting her poor mother, Plod talked her round. He had phoned Dorothy a few times and told her that he knew what she was trying to do. It hadn't stopped her.

But nothing had worked; not the inconsolable tears, refusing food or being disruptive with the other inmates, as she called them. She drew the line at bedwetting but had been reaching a point where nothing was off limits. Each ruse resulted in a flying visit from Samantha. Her daughter would explain patiently why the time was not right for Nick to transfer from the Metropolitan Police. She would hug her mum, tell her she loved her and return to her own life in London.

Ironically, it was Plod himself who was making it possible. Cliffside House had swung it. In the two years the building had stood empty, its condition had deteriorated and now it would take serious work to make it habitable again. Dorothy knew that before he joined the police, Plod had worked with his father renovating properties. He had the skills to bring Cliffside back to life.

She slipped her swollen feet into black patent leather shoes and smiled at the simplicity of her plan. During a rare family visit, she had offered the house, rent and mortgage free, on condition that they carry out any required works at their own expense. She may have omitted to mention that she planned to move in with them when all creature comforts were restored, but she'd deal with that later. Anyway, she didn't expect it to be a problem. Once installed with the family, she would be ideally positioned to influence Samantha's future. She would start by getting her back into the family business. Then she would work on replacing Plod with Graham Fletcher, Samantha's first serious boyfriend. He was now a respected partner in the local solicitors' practice and a much more suitable husband for her daughter.

She checked her teeth for stray lipstick and nodded, satisfied with her appearance. Today, she would be the centre of attention in the dining room. Today was going to be a good day.

<u>Chapter 4</u>

Friday 7th February

During the drive to the police station neither Morgan nor
Spence spoke. Morgan thought that the roads seemed
quiet for a working day, but then he was more used to
London traffic. He noticed cars queuing for what must
be the cheapest fuel in the area and then a few short
parades of shops. Narrow roads leading off the trunk
road had traditional houses and bungalows with cars
parked on drives or, he presumed, tucked up in garages.
As they reached the outskirts of town the demographics
changed. Here he saw people waiting at bus stops
wrapped up against the cold and staring hopefully into
the distance. Some of them were warming their hands
around cardboard coffee cups. He envied them.

They passed a large shopping mall where bright
floodlights drew attention to an empty car park. On the
other side of the road he saw a few blocks of sixties
flats. Kerbside parking on the narrow roads leading off
their route was dense here, suggesting that the larger
houses had either been turned into flats, or that there
were multicar families living here.

Spence's driving was meticulous; always in the
correct lane; right on the speed limit; and using the pull-
push steering method he had learned in tactical pursuit
training. Morgan was aware of receiving regular
sideways glances, but continued alternating his attention
between his phone and the view through the windscreen.
He was trying to judge the right time to ring his wife.
Sam would be up early to walk the dog and get the twins

organised before the arrival of the removal men. Her stress levels would be high and nothing he had to say would help with that. Their furniture could not be delivered to Cliffside and they had nowhere to sleep for the next few nights. She would be upset and she would want an explanation he wasn't able to provide. Would she understand that his drive to Gullhaven had been a strain and that, when he arrived, he'd driven straight to the local pub on the cliff top road for a pint and a steak? He wasn't sure, so he probably wouldn't mention that he'd been there long enough to get on first name terms with many of the regulars. Had he been out when the attack happened, or had he slept through it? He couldn't tell her. He didn't know. When he closed his eyes he saw the body lying in the centre of a circle of blood-stained oak parquet flooring. He looked at his phone again. He'd call her later.

Morgan was comfortable with the silence in the car. He had enough on his mind without making polite conversation. He thought that Dave Spence looked tense. His lips were tight and there was a muscle twitching just above his left eye. Maybe that was Spence's normal facial expression? Traffic started to edge forward and Spence eased the car into gear without returning Morgan's glance.

When they arrived at the station, Spence swiped his pass at the barrier and reversed into a space two rows back from the wall and opposite the staff entrance. It was done with such ease that Morgan knew this must be his preferred spot. When they got to the door, Spence pushed the button and alerted the officer in the Ops Room that he was bringing DI Nick Morgan into the building. Morgan was surprised. Surely Spence's pass would have given them both access? Was it necessary to alert everyone to his arrival, particularly in this disheveled state?

Spence led Morgan to the office recently vacated by DI Bradley, who had taken early retirement. He went in first and switched on the lights. They paused, simultaneously aware of the hierarchy dilemma they faced. This was an office for a DI and so Morgan should sit behind the desk. But Morgan was at the station to make a witness statement and would not be joining the team until Monday, so maybe Spence should sit there.

Morgan spoke first. 'Let's get on with it because I've got a lot to sort out today, including where my family's going to sleep tonight. So, if you fetch me an MG11 form and a pen, I'll write the statement myself.' He pulled one of the visitor chairs up to the desk and sat, scraping his fingernails back through his short graying hair. 'You mentioned coffee and a toothbrush?'

Spence left the office without replying.

<u>Chapter 5</u>

Friday 7th February

Samantha Morgan cursed her luck. Ten minutes before the removal van was due, the rain started and the dark sky predicted it wasn't likely to stop.

Nick had set off yesterday to sort out reconnection of all the services, leaving her with the last stages of packing. When the twins returned from school having said goodbye to all their friends, Victoria was in tears and Alexander had run straight upstairs and banged his bedroom door shut. She couldn't be sure but thought she might have caught a waft of alcohol as he pushed past her in the hallway. At twelve years old? Really?

This morning, when she returned from walking Truffles, their Springer spaniel, the three of them had breakfasted in silence. The dog had retired to his basket and gone back to sleep.

Samantha knew it made sense for Nick to go to Gullhaven a day early but she was tired and there was still a lot to do. She was eagerly anticipating the few days they had booked at the Riverview Hotel. After a sauna, a dip in the pool, a couple of gin and tonics, and a restaurant meal with decent wine, she was going to put this whole nightmare behind her.

She heard the low vibration of the diesel engine as the Hardy and Wynn Removals van reversed as far as it could on to the drive. 'They're here,' shouted Victoria and immediately burst into tears again. Samantha's mobile rang.

'What is it Nick? I'm busy, and the van's just arrived.

Have you not got anything to do?'

She wasn't really listening to his reply as she waited for the doorbell to ring. Then she heard words which focused her attention on the call. Nick said 'So we can't move the furniture in until CSI release the house.'

'What? What do you mean? Answer the door, Victoria, and for God's sake, stop crying. Go and brush your teeth Alex. Stop there, Nick. I don't understand. What do you mean we can't move in?' She was holding three conversations at once and it made her feel dizzy.

Ricky, the van driver, came into the kitchen. He waved to attract her attention then pointed across at the kettle. His accent was from somewhere between east London and Essex. 'I see you've remembered not to pack the most important item in the house. Two teas with two sugars and one with only milk. Thanks Mrs Morgan. We'll start again upstairs.' She heard heavy footsteps followed by laughter and loud singing from one of the bedrooms.

Samantha told Nick to wait then turned to the twins. 'You two. Go and get Truffles sorted while I talk to Dad. Take him with his basket and all the stuff I've left on the draining board to Mrs Gifford across the road. She's going to look after him until I'm ready to pack the car. Quickly now. And brush your teeth first, Alex.'

At a little over five feet two, Samantha had to step up on to the foot rest to reach the seat of the breakfast bar stool. She plonked herself down before giving the call her full attention. 'I swear to God, Nick. This had better not be your idea of a joke.'

Morgan kept his description of finding the body to the bare minimum before continuing. 'CSI are there now and I'm at the station. I'm waiting to write a statement but the DS who went to fetch the form has disappeared.

I'm gasping for a cup of coffee. Oh, and Riverview have cancelled our booking. They say their boiler has burst so I need to find somewhere else for us to sleep tonight.'

'I don't understand how there can be a body in our house when you were there all night. It can't have been there that long, can it? You said it's still bleeding.'

There was a long pause before he replied. 'I went to the steakhouse on the cliffs to get something to eat. It could have happened then.'

Samantha's jaw clenched. 'Bleeding bodies don't just walk in and lie down on a bedroom floor. How did he hurt himself? I assume it is a he?'

'Yes, it's a he. And Sam, love, I don't know what happened, and it's too early to jump to conclusions. Can you ring round and find storage down here for our furniture for a while? Let's say a week. I'll need you to bring a couple of my suits in the car and a few shirts and ties so I have something to wear for work. You and the twins will need more of the basics too. I'll find us somewhere to stay for a few nights. I need to go now but I love you.' He ended the call before she had time to say any more.

As she went into the hall, a large clothes hanging box tumbled down the stairs and landed behind the front door. She looked up to see Ricky's grinning face. 'Don't worry, love. It's just bedding, nothing fragile. Any sign of that tea?'

Chapter 6

He first noticed Abigail Slater at Club Europium as last summer merged into autumn. That shiny silver dress barely covered her arse and when she reached up to punch the air, he caught glimpses of panties, reflecting the purple strobe lighting. Did she know? Of course she did. He saw other lads watching her, mesmerised; their girlfriends, stony faced. Occasionally, she would glance around to see who was looking before throwing her head back and picking up the beat, her long fair hair swinging like a bright curtain in sunlight.

Out of his league, he thought and went back to his overpriced beer.

His next sighting of her surprised him. She was wearing a business suit and white blouse and her hair was tied back into a neat ponytail. Her black skirt covered her knees but, from his seat four rows behind her, he could see it was tight enough to define both cheeks of that backside. Her jacket fitted neatly before flaring out from the waist into a short frill and her white blouse was unbuttoned to her cleavage.

She was standing in front of three unsmiling magistrates summing up the case for the defence. Her client had taken the purse out of an elderly lady's bag while she picked through the reduced shelf at a supermarket. Abigail Slater's passion was as evident as it had been on the dance floor and he saw her ponytail swish left and right as she tried to engage with each magistrate.

They found him guilty and one of them said they were going to ask the Probation Service to prepare a report on the defendant who was then taken away by the security staff. Abigail Slater chatted amiably with the prosecutor as she gathered her papers. Then, she slung her handbag over her shoulder and made her way towards the back of the court. As she passed, she smiled at him and he knew he had to have her.

Chapter 7

Once he had ended his call to Sam, Morgan left the office. He walked along the corridor and through the open plan CID area to the far end where there were desks allocated to the Central & Southern Major Crimes Unit.

He sensed he was being watched although nobody made eye contact. Some were concentrating on a computer screen or deep in conversation with a colleague. Others were on the phone, gesticulating with their hands as if emphasising what they were saying. He was looking for a coffee machine or a water fountain. Finding neither, he paused to look at the whiteboards which showed the status of on-going investigations.

'DI Morgan?' It was a loud, deep voice calling from behind. 'I wasn't expecting you until Monday. Couldn't you wait?'

Morgan turned to see Detective Chief Inspector Richard Johnson striding towards him with an outstretched hand which he shook. He said, 'I received an unwelcome housewarming present last night and I've come in to make a statement.'

Johnson closed his eyes and nodded a few times. 'I saw it on the overnight log. Cause of death unknown and deceased unidentified. How are you coping?'

Morgan thought it was an odd question to ask an officer with over twenty year's service. He had lost count of the bodies he'd encountered in that time, most of them in a much less presentable state than his current tenant. He replied 'I'm coping well, sir, but it's causing some difficulties for my relocation.' Johnson smile was sympathetic and Morgan continued, 'As I said, I've come in to make a statement. DS Spence went to get me a coffee and an MG11 but that's the last I saw of him.'

'I met him in the car park and sent him back to the scene. We're a bit thin on the ground at the moment so he'll have to do his best as SIO until I can get hold of DI Patel.' Johnson pointed vaguely to one of the boards which had pictures of three young women pinned to it. 'She's gone to West Midlands to arrest a suspected rapist who's been hunting round the student accommodation. She'll be back later today. Anyway, come with me, I have my own supply of coffee and I'll get someone to fetch the statement form. I can also update you with what we had going on before you brought your own case to bugger up my crime figures.' Morgan fell into step behind the taller man. So Spence had been in the car park, had he? He'd never intended returning with the coffee and form. That was useful to know.

The two men walked to the stairwell. Johnson's office was a couple of flights above the CID floor and he bounded up the stairs two at a time. Morgan followed and passed through the fire door which his boss was holding open for him.

When they got to his office, DCI Johnson busied himself making two black coffees using a machine and pods which Morgan guessed he'd brought from home. He accepted a cup gratefully, inhaling the aroma and savouring it before he took his first sip. God it tasted good. He wanted to gulp it down but he didn't want to make a bad impression.

Sitting in his high backed chair Johnson began, 'I've

never liked bad coffee or even instant coffee which is a completely different drink. It's sacrilege to give it the same name. Bad tea is even worse. My wife bought me this after we started using one at home and I find it makes the start of another day actually bearable.'

'Thank you sir, I completely agree. Thank you.' As soon as he said it, Morgan thought it sounded grovelling but it couldn't be unsaid. 'You wanted to talk through some cases?'

'One case, Morgan, just the one. It's a tricky one and it's caught the attention of the local media. We've got a missing person. A solicitor actually, from a local practice.'

Morgan took another sip of coffee and waited for Johnson to continue, but he seemed in no hurry. Morgan glanced down at his watch.

'She's not been with them all that long - a year perhaps? She deals with a lot of the cases that get to the Magistrates' Court but that could be because she pulls a lot of the out of hours shifts. Her name's Abigail Slater although I understand she prefers to go by Abi.' Morgan felt Johnson's eyes on him. He was trying to pay attention but was also conscious of everything he needed to organise and the limited time available. 'The flatmate didn't come to us straight away. Apparently, Abi has disappeared before. But eventually, this same flatmate came in and reported it. It seems that she'd taken advice from a missing persons' charity. The girl's been gone a little over two weeks now and the local papers and TV have picked up on it. Her work laptop and phone are missing but we got her personal phone. That's only because she forgot it when she left work in a hurry.'

Morgan felt his investigator instinct twitch. He'd been in Gullhaven less than twenty-four hours and was already aware of a possible murder and a missing person. He'd expected life here to be quieter than London. Maybe not.

Johnson was still speaking. 'Of course, we've done all the usual. Phone log, emails, social media, the works. We've spoken to the fiancé, the flatmate, friends and neighbours. I'm told we're still waiting for bank and credit card statements.'

Morgan frowned. When it came down to it, nothing Johnson had said hinted at any suspicion of foul play. He glanced again at his watch. 'You said she'd gone missing before, sir?'

The DCI had been staring into the distance and now looked back at him. 'We believe so, but not for longer than two or three days and certainly not under these circumstances. It's the human interest angle that's got everyone hooked. You see, she's due to marry tomorrow and she disappeared on the way back from collecting her dress. All the witnesses say she was really excited. Talked of nothing else from the minute she got engaged, so nobody believes she would disappear of her own volition. That's why we think something has happened to her.'

Chapter 8

Friday 7th February

When Morgan returned to his office he found a small pile of statement forms and two cheap pens on the desk. He hesitated before starting to write. He should balance the amount of detail he provided with what he preferred not to disclose. Surely details of his alcohol consumption were not relevant to the investigation? When it came down to it, he didn't know anything about the body on his bedroom floor or how it got there.

When he finished writing, he put the pens in the desk drawer and turned his thoughts to his other problems. Johnson had suggested an alternative four star hotel for the night and Morgan hoped it might go some way towards making amends with Sam. When he rang to book, the receptionist told him that they didn't allow pets. He was mid-explanation of his predicament when she ended the call. Truffles was a member of the family and since the move would already be unsettling for him, he decided against putting him into kennels and set about finding another solution.

He returned to the open plan office to find someone he could leave his statement with. This time, he observed the photos of children, thank you cards and brightly coloured mugs containing coffee which had gone cold. He caught the attention of two young women who introduced themselves as DCs Lynn Greenfield and Jennifer Smart, members of the CID Major Crime Unit. Both looked to be in their late twenties and were wearing black trousers and low heeled black shoes.

Greenfield was smaller than Smart by about two inches and completed her outfit with a grey jumper and black jacket. Smart was wearing a white blouse and was holding her jacket across one arm. Morgan couldn't tell if she had just arrived or was about to leave. He noticed that she was more heavily made up than other female officers he had worked with and, as he got closer, he saw that her cheeks and forehead were scarred from adolescent acne. He wondered how much bullying she had suffered in her teen years.

The women commiserated with his accommodation plight and Morgan was about to turn away when Smart put out her hand to detain him. 'Have you considered a park home?'

'You mean like a caravan?' Morgan asked, and imagined his wife's reaction. Samantha had inherited her mother's snobbery gene.

Smart smiled politely. 'A lot of people make that mistake, but park homes couldn't be more different from caravans. When my parents visit, I don't have space to put them up, so I book them into Gullhaven Park. It's on the outskirts of East Gullhaven, just past the country club and golf course. The locals would prefer it not to be there of course, but it was a park home site long before the NIMBYs moved in, so they have to put up with it. Some of the properties have two and three bedrooms and all mod cons. You'll be comfy there and it's quiet in winter so I don't think you'll struggle to book. If you can, try to get one overlooking the lake and the woods.' Smart asked for his mobile number and sent him a text with the contact details. He thanked her and returned to his office to make the call. East Gullhaven was where his mother-in-law's supported accommodation was, but he couldn't remember ever noticing the site.

The friendly female voice which answered his call confirmed that there was a home available by the lake which had three bedrooms. She told him that if he secured it with a credit card immediately, she would drive up there and turn on the heating so it would be cosy for everyone's arrival. Morgan asked about sheets, pillowcases and towels as, somewhere in his mind, he thought that caravan sites expected you to provide your own. The woman's laughter was throaty and deep and he could hear that she was still smiling when she answered. 'They're provided. This isn't the fifties, you know. It'll all be set up and ready for you by three o'clock. You'll have to bring your own food, or eat out. Our restaurant is closed. And this is low season so I'm afraid the pool and recreation areas are off limits too, while they are being prepared for Easter re-opening. Sorry.'

'That's okay,' said Morgan. 'I'm just pleased you can fit us in.'

'See you soon, then. Bye.'

Replacing his phone in his jacket pocket, Morgan wondered if he should have looked harder for a hotel. If Sam wasn't happy there would ultimately be a price he would pay.

Chapter 9

Dorothy Cooper was sitting at her window overlooking the grounds and drive of Silver Sands. She liked to know who was coming and going and it was busy today. Delivery vans bringing food for the weekend and medical supplies; a taxi for one of the inmates – hospital trip probably – and the grey van used by Danny Easton, the maintenance man. She liked Danny. He reminded her of her errant son, Steven, except he was taller, and more respectful.

Breakfast had been a disappointment. The inmates were more excited to hear that Betty Andrews had got a date for her hip replacement. What was wrong with these people? She hoped that Plod would get on with the house renovations quickly so she could move back in and not have to waste her time with them anymore.

She looked at the clock. If she put her smock on now, she would be in good time for Helen Talbot's art class in the activities room. Her mobile rang and she squinted at the screen to see if it was someone she could be bothered speaking to.

'Hello, dear. I'm surprised you've got time to ring me today. How's the packing going and how are the twins? Is the van there yet? I'm really looking forward to knowing you'll be just down the road.'

She heard Samantha exhale. 'It's chaos in the house, so I'm in the shed. It's pouring with rain and I've just served the removal men their umpteenth round of tea and biscuits so I'm ringing to update you.' Dorothy waited for her to continue, sensing she wasn't going to like what was coming.

'There's a bit of a problem with the house.' Her voice dropped. She was reluctant to continue. 'It's a crime scene and we can't move in.'

Dorothy was confused. 'Speak up, dear. What do you mean? Do you mean burglars? There's nothing left in the house that's worth taking. And why didn't Plod fight them off? Wasn't he supposed to be there last night?'

'Please don't call him that, Mum. You know I don't like it.' She chose her words with care. 'He got there late and may have slept through whatever went on. And it's not burglars... Nick says there's a body upstairs.'

Dorothy frowned as she took in the information. She would have to book breakfast in the dining room again tomorrow as this news would definitely trump Betty's hip replacement. But what if the family decided they didn't want to live in a crime scene? That would upset all her plans. Samantha was still speaking and she just caught that the hotel booking had been cancelled.

'Where are you expected to sleep tonight then?' she asked. 'And what about the furniture... and the children?'

'And the dog,' said Samantha. 'Nick is sorting out accommodation and my next call is to a storage company. That's why I'm ringing. Who did you use when you went into the home?'

'It's not a home, dear, it's supported accommodation. I'm more than able to look after myself as you know. I'll send a text with their number as soon as I get off the phone. And be sure to bring the lovely twins to see me as soon as you arrive.'

Samantha agreed before she ended the call although Dorothy suspected it wouldn't happen. Sometimes, Samantha said yes, just to avoid an argument.

Chapter 10

At half past eleven, Nick Morgan sent his wife the postcode of Gullhaven Park for her satnav describing it as "a late availability holiday let." He programmed the same information into his phone and set off to find a taxi to take him back to his car, which he hoped was still in the pub car park. That had been a stroke of luck. If he'd left it at Cliffside House, it would have been included as part of the crime scene and who knows when he would have got it back.

The taxi driver, an overweight white man in his sixties was chatty and to Morgan's dismay, refused to take the hint to be quiet. He took out his phone and busied himself with the task of sending texts and emails, but the verbal assault was relentless. He heaved a sigh of relief when they got to the pub and he was able to surround himself with the silent security of his white Volvo hatchback. It was a short drive to Cliffside House and he parked on the other side of the road to watch the activities of the crime scene.

There was a PCSO standing with a clipboard on the drive. Beside him, a white bin overflowed with the coveralls, gloves and overshoes discarded by investigators who had left the scene. The officer looked cold, tired and bored. Beyond him, Cliffside's front door was open and above it, in the upstairs bay window, Morgan saw the bright light of the investigators' lamps. He wondered if the body was still in situ. It felt odd to be present at, but excluded from, a crime scene.

A woman appeared from the side of the house. She was talking on her phone whilst trying to strip off her protective clothing. Morgan watched her get increasingly frustrated before she handed her phone to the officer and stepped out of the white suit – right leg, left leg. She was still wearing gloves, and she rested her fingers on the garden wall for support. Once all the items had been disposed of, she put out her hand for the return of the phone and smiled her thanks. When she turned towards him, Morgan could see that she was Asian, possibly Indian, although from this distance, he couldn't be sure. He estimated that she was about the same age as him; five feet five or six and medium build. She was wearing a navy trouser suit and he saw a V-shape of something yellow at her neck. Was this DI Patel, he wondered? He started the Volvo engine and checked the navigation app on his phone. With Friday traffic, it would be dark by the time his family arrived and he was going to be in enough trouble without dragging them across acres of mud trying to find which door fitted the keys. He planned to familiarise himself with the Gullhaven Park Estate before they got there.

Arriving at the site reception, he met the woman who had taken his booking on the phone. She had red hair, green eyes and a ready smile. Her voice was husky with a hint of a West Country accent. 'I'm Maisie,' she said. 'Last minute plans for half term is it?'

His smile was sardonic. 'You wouldn't believe me if I told you.'

'Maybe not, but you look like you could persuade me, if you tried.' Both her eye contact and smile were steady as she held out two sets of keys and it occurred to him that she might be flirting. There had been a significant absence of flirting in the Morgan household for a long time and he felt his body respond. He ignored it. He was in enough trouble. Anyway, she must be at least fifteen years younger than him.

Taking the keys, Morgan concentrated on the paper map secured to the desk with yellowing sticky tape. Maisie's fuchsia-painted fingernail pointed at the reception building where the map was completely worn through to the wood underneath. His eyes followed the route down narrow roadways which passed blocks of colour, each representing an area of park homes.

'Yours is A-20 in Lakeside sector. It's secluded and quiet, although most of the estate is quiet this early in the year. The weather hasn't helped us much. When it's nicer, we get some hardy souls but not this year.' She paused and looked up at him. 'Please make sure you park in the designated space on the left of the sector only. It's wet out there and if your car sinks, you might have to leave it there forever.' She laughed that deep throaty laugh again and Morgan smiled politely. He didn't feel much like laughing today.

'Is there space for two cars? My wife will be arriving later with the children and the dog.'

Maisie nodded. 'She can park in the space for A-19. We usually only allow one car per home on the site, but we're not busy. Wouldn't want to cause a domestic... well, not over parking anyway.' He thanked her and returned to his car. It was raining heavily now and he hoped Sam would be careful. On motorways, she was inclined to exceed the speed limit and drive too close to the vehicle in front. Everything that meant anything to him would be in that car.

He tried to remember Maisie's directions and started by turning right out of the reception car park. The roads around Gullhaven Park were narrow and edged by high hedges. There were a few signposts, but he made two wrong guesses before arriving at the Lakeside sector. Once there, he spotted A-20 and parked in the designated space. Approaching it, he saw how unlike a caravan the structure was. The glazed door was about three feet off the ground and the wooden steps up to it had sturdy handrails on either side. It opened into a wide living and dining area with a fitted kitchen along one wall. The room was bright, clean and modern and led into a short hallway with four doors leading off. The first was a double bedroom which wasn't huge, and opposite, a room with twin beds. The next door led to a toilet and shower room with no window and a noisy extractor fan which came on when he pulled the light cord. Opening the last door, he was anticipating a room the size of a cupboard and the resulting argument which the twins would have over the sleeping arrangements. To his surprise, this room was the master bedroom, bright and spacious with an en-suite shower and a great view of the lake and woods.

Everywhere was warm as Maisie had promised. The beds were made up and there were fluffy, blue bath and hand towels as well as tea towels and a tablecloth piled on the dining table.

He looked at his phone. Still no message to say his family were on the way. He saw he had missed two calls from his mother-in-law and realised he must have left it in the car when he picked up the keys. Dotty would have to wait because he needed to find a supermarket.

Chapter 11

Dave Spence stood in DCI Johnson's office waiting for him to finish his phone conversation. When at last he put the phone down, Johnson held up a forefinger.

'Give me a second to make a quick note,' he said, scribbling on a pad. 'Right then. Where are we with Cliffside House?'

'When I went back to the scene, I went upstairs and I knew him straight away. It's one of the advantages of being local,' Spence could not resist the jibe. 'I must have nicked him ten times over the years. It's Carl Raynor.'

'I don't think I know him.' said Johnson.

'No? He's one of our regular druggies. Pages of previous for possession and served time for possession with intent to supply. Latest offences are all shoplifting.'

'How long does the pathologist think he'd been there?'

Spence cringed. He had been so excited to recognise the body that he'd forgotten to ask Doctor Mackenzie about time of death. Sod it! Now he looked like a rookie. 'The blood was still dripping at six this morning, sir. He can't have been there long.'

Johnson gave him a knowing look but let the omission pass. 'We obviously can't have DI Morgan on this case so DI Patel can pick it up when she gets back. You'll need to write up the decision log so far. You can get her up to speed as soon as she arrives.'

'She's back, sir. I met her at the scene and handed over what I already had. She was pleased I'd been able to give her a name. I told her I'd find the next of kin for a formal identification.'

'Good,' said Johnson. 'That's good.' He looked back down at the pile of papers on his desk. Spence cleared his throat. 'Was there something else, Spence?'

'I wanted to ask if I could be assigned to the case, sir. As I said, I know the victim and DI Patel asked me if I would attend the postmortem.'

Johnson took off his glasses and placed them on his desk with exaggerated care. 'That'll be down to DI Patel and DI Morgan to decide between themselves on Monday.'

Spence was persistent. 'It's not often we have a murder in Gullhaven, and I think the experience would benefit me. I'd really like to be on this one, sir.'

'Every case is important, Spence. Never forget that. DI Morgan is joining us at a bit of a quiet time but I've discussed the missing solicitor with him in case it turns out... well... not as we want it to turn out. I know it's a CID case rather than MCU, but the media are all over it. DI Morgan has a lot of experience in handling them, so he's a good fit. And we'll see what else comes in over the weekend.'

'Won't CID feel that DI Morgan is trespassing on their territory, sir?'

'With their caseload, I don't foresee a problem.'

Spence was smiling when he left the DCI's office. He'd provided the breakthrough in a major case by identifying the body while Morgan was going to be bogged down in an enquiry into a woman who'd gone missing for the third or fourth time and who always reappeared. Welcome to Gullhaven, DI Morgan. Not so golden now, are you?

Chapter 12

Friday 7th February

With rain battering on the roof and wind whistling round the walls of A-20, Morgan only just heard the alert of a text from Sam to say they had stopped for petrol and were about five miles away. He replied to tell her to come through the estate gates and that he would meet them in the reception car park.

He looked around, mentally crossing his fingers that everything would meet with Sam's approval. He'd stocked up on booze, music and films as well as a selection of pizzas, garlic bread, olives and crisps. It wasn't the restaurant meal they had planned for their first night at the coast, but it was better than queuing for a takeaway in the rain. He had also bought a packet of cigarettes which he'd put in a drawer in their bedroom. He knew that Sam still turned to her old vice for comfort, even though she thought it was her secret. He didn't approve, but it wasn't worth picking a fight over. Satisfied that he had done everything he could, he grabbed his keys and left.

The windows of Nick's car were misted over by the time he saw Sam's headlights appear in his rear view mirror. She parked next to him, and he got out and walked round to her window as she opened it an inch.

'I'm not getting out,' she said.

'Do you mean here, or do you mean ever?'

'I'm tired Nick, and we're hungry. Can we just get to where we're staying?' She closed the window again to prevent further conversation and Nick retreated to his car.

They drove slowly in the rain, his windscreen wipers squeaking across the glass at double speed and Sam following. When he parked, she pulled into the space beside him. Morgan retrieved the umbrella he had found in the kitchen, unfurled it, and ran back to Sam's car. Rain was bouncing off the wooden steps and a large puddle had formed at the bottom of them. There was a distant rumble of thunder.

'Wait here please, kids. I'll get you all in one by one. Mum's first.'

Nick held out his arms to carry Sam into the home, but she shook her head and took the umbrella. He went with her and repeated the process for Victoria and then Alexander who carried Truffles in his arms. There were three more trips for luggage, and dog paraphernalia and when he had completed the last, he shut the door, braced himself, and faced her.

'Best I could do at short notice,' he said.

'Well, it's hardly The Riverview Hotel and Spa, is it?'

'I think it's cool,' said Victoria, 'And I want the double bed.'

Everyone looked at her brother who held up his hands in resignation.

'Whatever,' he said, and Morgan thought he looked pleased. He must have preferred the room with the twin beds.

After years of living in south London the Morgan family were accustomed to the constant hum of traffic, planes and neighbourhood activity. That evening, the silence of the lake and woods, broken only by noise of the storm, felt oppressive. The twins lifted their heads from their phones barely long enough to select more pizza or diet cola. Nick assumed they were texting friends back in London saying how much they were missing them and bemoaning their parents' choice to bring them to "planet wherever." He was glad there was enough of a WiFi signal to keep them occupied.

The open plan living area discouraged any mention of the body at Cliffside House until the twins had gone to bed. He and Sam washed up and sat on the brown corduroy sofa, each with a replenished glass of red wine.

'Are you going to tell me what happened?' she said.

'I don't know what happened. The drive down was crap and I was tired and pissed off when I got here. I went to the pub at the end of the cliffs, had a meal and a few beers. I left the car, walked back, slept on the sofa. And you know the rest. He was upstairs, on his back, in the big bedroom. I'd never seen him before and all I remember is that he was young, male, skinny and dead. I don't know what else I can tell you.'

She sipped her wine before continuing. 'What are we going to tell the kids?'

'Well, we're not going to be able to keep it a secret, that's for certain. If it's a murder, and I don't see how it can be anything else, it'll be all over social media by now, and headlines in the local news tomorrow. It'll go on for days too. It's not like London here. They haven't had a murder since forever ago.'

'You really think it's a murder? Sam asked.

'From what I could see, he was bleeding from his back. That injury's not likely to be self inflicted, is it?' He took a sip of wine. 'If he was stabbed in the back, we should arrest your mother. She's good at that.'

Samantha would not normally let a negative comment about her mother pass without some form of rebuke but she was tired and the wine had mellowed her. 'But, what are we going to tell the twins? In a week's time, they'll be starting at a new school where everyone is going to know that they live in a murder house. We'll have coach loads of kids coming for tea so they can sneak into our bedroom to see where it happened. I don't know if I can live like that.'

Nick reached his arm along the top of the sofa and she stretched her neck backwards until her head lay on it. 'For what it's worth, I think Alex will be fine with it,' he said. 'He'll have a bit of notoriety from day one at that school and we both know he'll milk it. Vicky's harder to predict. I'll speak to her tomorrow.' He leant forward and put his wine glass down. 'I'll nip out with Truffles for his last pee break, then why don't we finish the bottle in bed?'

'If you're thinking of starting something, let me tell you, I'm way too tired.'

He sighed. 'Sam, I'm not starting anything. I'm finishing something: the wine. That's all. I've had a hell of a day too so let's draw a line and hope it all looks better in the morning. At least we know things can't get any worse'

Chapter 13

Saturday 8th February

Nick Morgan was woken next morning by Truffles whining at the door and he saw that they had all slept much later than usual. 'No wonder he's upset,' he said to Sam, 'he must have been crossing his legs for the last hour.' He got up and dressed in yesterday's clothes before remembering that they were really the clothes from the day before yesterday. He cautiously sniffed under his arms before going out into the hallway where Truffles greeted him eagerly.

'Sorry, mate,' he said as he clipped the lead to the dog's collar. He made a mental note to find out how to change the address details for his microchip.

They went out into bright sunshine and a biting cold wind blowing from the north. Nick changed his planned route to a shorter one. When he started to head back towards their home, Truffles followed without complaint. Nick thought they must both be looking forward to breakfast.

In the time they were out, Sam and the twins had got up, dressed, and were waiting. The aromas of coffee and toast were a welcome greeting and, having measured out the dog's food, Nick was able to join them for a rare family breakfast.

'Are we going to see grandma today?' asked Victoria.

'Oh, God,' Nick put his knife down. 'She rang me yesterday and it completely went out of my mind. I never got back to her. Sorry.'

'Why would she ring you, Dad?' asked Alexander. 'Was it about the house? Do you need help at the house today? I'd rather help you than see her. Can I Mum?'

Nick's glance at Sam was met with a tiny nod. Alexander had presented them with the opportunity they needed to explain why the family did not have immediate access to Cliffside House.

'Something happened at the house that you need to know about,' said Nick. He recounted his discovery with as little detail and drama as possible. The twins listened with wide eyes and open mouths.

'Cool,' said Alexander when Nick had finished. 'Will there be blood on the floor when we move in?' Victoria squealed and grimaced. She brought clenched fists up to her mouth and closed her eyes.

'Stop it, Alex,' said Sam. 'This lad has died and you need to show some respect.' Having been brought up in the family funeral business, she believed that whoever they were, and however they had died, clients were to be shown solemnity and respect at all times.

'We can't live there now, can we?' Victoria's voice was pleading. 'Can't we just go back to London?'

Alexander got up, went to his sister, and put his arms around her. 'I'm here. Don't be scared.'

Sam and Nick exchanged surprised glances. They were accustomed to Alexander's dismissive behaviour towards his younger twin so this was a revelation. Nick was moved and he cleared his throat before he spoke. 'While you're with grandma, I think I might take a drive past the house to see how the technicians are getting on. Then, why don't we meet up and take Truffles for a walk along the beach?' His suggestion was met with a nod and smile from Sam and excitement from the twins. 'Okay. I'm going for a quick shower first.' He stroked

Truffles as he passed then shut the hall door behind him. As he stripped off his clothes, he thought about the missing solicitor. She was due to be married today. He hoped she turned up.

Chapter 14

From the moment of Abigail Slater's smile, that day in court, he was obsessed.

He started to invent excuses to be absent from work so that he could go back to the Magistrates' Court and watch her. It was risky, because he couldn't afford to lose his job but she was in his mind from the minute he woke up to when his head hit the pillow. He wanted to see her. Needed to be near her.

Sometimes she was there and rewarded him with another of those smiles which made him tingle. Sometimes she breezed past, in conversation with a scumbag she was defending, or absorbed in thoughts of her next case.

One of the ushers had asked him if he was doing his observations. When he didn't know how to reply she'd continued, 'You know. Your observations before you apply to be a magistrate.'

He'd nodded enthusiastically and always ensured that he carried a notebook after that. It would stop people being suspicious of his frequent visits. Soon, he was acknowledged by Legal Advisers and other solicitors. He felt that he'd joined Abigail's professional family.

He started going to the club more often too. Once, he even took out a payday loan because he had no money for the entrance fee and he just had to be where she was. The repayment amount was scandalous, but it was worth it because that was the night he had the courage to ask her to dance with him. She'd agreed and they were inseparable until closing time.

'Where do I know you from?' she'd asked as they waited to be served at the bar.

'I'm doing my magistrate observations. I've seen you at court.'

'Does my performance meet with your approval?' She flicked her hair back, her smile, alluring and mischievous. He started to fall in love with her.

He spent the last of his loan money on a taxi to take her home and his heart sank at the length of walk he faced to get to his own bed. The driver scowled when he saw how ungenerous his tip was.

'It's all I've got, mate,' he said quietly, hoping she would not hear.

'I hope she's worth it. Don't hang around here, son, it's not safe.'

When the taxi left, he followed Abigail to her doorstep where she was already opening her front door. She turned and kissed him hard. He wondered if he might not be walking home after all. Then, she stopped.

'Early start,' she said. 'Will you be at the club on Friday?'

He nodded.

'I'll see you there.' In contrast to her earlier passion, she planted a chaste kiss on his cheek, stepped through the door, and was gone.

<u>Chapter 15</u>

Monday 10th February

When Morgan got up at 6am on Monday morning he
saw it was frosty outside. He pulled on jeans, thick
socks, and the heavy jumper Sam had packed for him
and tiptoed out of the bedroom to avoid disturbing her.
Truffles greeted him, head up and tail wagging and Nick
smiled as he fussed over him. He shoved his feet into the
rubber boots he always had in his car in case he needed
them at a crime scene and set off into the darkness.

When they got back from their walk Sam had
breakfast ready. Truffles left prints on the floor and
when Nick went to clean them, she said, 'Don't worry,
I'll do it when you've gone to work.'

'Apart from exploring, how are you going to keep the
kids amused?' he asked. They had planned to spend half
term week unpacking and settling into their new home
as well as establishing exactly what needed to be done to
make it habitable again. 'It may take a few days before
they release Cliffside.'

Sam thought for a moment before replying. 'I still
need to shop for uniforms, and Vicky will need new
shoes. This school won't let her wear the ones she's got.
They have a flat heels only policy.'

Nick nodded as he got up from the table and put his
personal mobile in his pocket. 'I expect I'll get the
health and safety lecture today and the allocation of my
new equipment. It's a bit like being the new boy at
school for me too.'

'I'm also going to see Mum again. She seemed a bit off when I took the twins on Saturday.'

'I wouldn't have been able to tell the difference,' he said, 'she's always off with me.'

Samantha's mobile rang. 'Talk of the devil,' she said glancing at the screen. 'Hello, Mum.' Nick leaned over to kiss her cheek as she continued, 'I'm sure it's nothing to worry about. He probably overslept.' Nick whispered his goodbyes, picked up his keys and went to leave. At the door, he turned back and blew her a kiss. Sam half smiled and rolled her eyes and he wasn't sure if it was in response to her mother or the kiss.

Arriving at the station, he pushed the button at the car park barrier and spoke to a voice which sounded as if it came from the next county. 'I'm DI Nick Morgan and it's my first day here so I don't have a code or a pass.' Once he had provided his registration number and mentioned Johnson's name, the barrier lifted. He noticed that the space where DS Spence had parked on Friday was vacant and was tempted, but decided against it and chose one further down the row.

He was about to endure the same security ritual at the staff door when Morgan heard Johnson's voice behind him. 'Tell them I'm here and I'm letting you in.' Morgan stood to the side while Johnson swiped his pass and pushed through the door. He followed him.

They walked down the corridor, Morgan a half step behind as it wasn't wide enough for the two of them to walk comfortably side by side. 'Coffee to start you off,' said Johnson, 'then there are some induction procedures and after that, I'll get someone to update you on our on-going cases.'

'What's happening at Cliffside?' asked Morgan.

'Correction. I'll get someone to update you on our on-going cases, except that one. I'm sure you understand why. You'll have to meet up with DI Patel sometime today. I understand she has some questions regarding the statement you provided on Friday.' Morgan winced. That wasn't a conversation he was looking forward to.

Johnson made the coffees again and carried them to a meeting area in the corner of his office. He started by asking where they were staying and how they were settling in.

'It's early days, sir. My daughter is upset by what's happened at Cliffside, my son, a little less so, unless he's hiding it better. We're staying over at East Gullhaven in a park home which has all we need at the moment but I can see it won't take long for the novelty to wear off. It's half term and the twins will miss the extra TV channels we had at home.'

Johnson took a sip of coffee. 'And what about you?' Before giving Morgan a chance to respond he continued. 'Now that you're here, I can tell you that we had reservations about accepting your transfer. It's no secret that you had a high profile at the Met. Life is quieter here so you won't have the same celebrity status.'

Johnson was watching him and Morgan returned his stare, determined not to react. 'I didn't consider it celebrity, sir,' he replied, 'and it came with its own problems. My children were picked on at school and I was sometimes door-stepped by the tabloids. My wife was threatened and both our cars were vandalised when my name was released as lead investigator in a gang execution case. If we're both being honest, then yes, I'll miss the high profile jobs, but I won't miss what comes with them.' He decided to remind Johnson of his reason for requesting the transfer. 'Anyway, as I explained when we spoke before, my wife needs to be near her mother for a while. Over the years, she's made some personal sacrifices for me and I'm pleased to do this for her.' As he placed his cup and saucer down on the table, his phone rang. Johnson's expression was pained. 'I'll turn it off, sorry.'

For the next half hour Johnson lectured him on the differences between coastal, rural and town centre crime as he presented the latest statistics for the area. He explained that, before the discovery of the body at Cliffside, the area of Gullhaven Cove's fastest growing problem had been internet fraud. The ageing population was targeted in the hope that its members may not have a good understanding of the technology they were using. Also, they were inclined to be more trusting than streetwise youngsters. Johnson said he was also concerned that these crimes were under-reported because the victims felt embarrassed. He told Morgan that he looked forward to learning how the Met were dealing with the problem even though it didn't fall under the remit of the Major Crimes Unit.

There was a timid knock and a young PC came in. 'Sorry to interrupt, sir,' he said, 'Mrs Morgan has rung in. She wants to speak to DI Morgan and won't take no for an answer.'

The pained expression returned to Johnson's face. 'Is this something she does a lot?' he asked with a sigh.

'Definitely not, sir. I'm sorry.'

'Well you'd better find out what she wants, I suppose.'

Nick cursed his wife's timing. Another ten minutes and his meeting with Johnson would have been over. He was sure that the whole of CID would hear about this and if they didn't make fun of him to his face, he was certain they would be doing it behind his back.

Safe in his own office, Morgan rang his wife's mobile and before he had a chance to remonstrate with her, she yelled at him. 'Where have you been and why didn't you take my call? I need you back here now!' She was breathing hard and Truffles was close by, making a noise he hadn't heard before. Somewhere between a bark and a howl.

'What's happened? Where are you?' Morgan knew his wife didn't cope well with stress but he had never heard her sound so panicked. 'Take a deep breath and tell me what's happened. Where are the children?'

'The children are with me. They're okay.' He heard her start to breathe more slowly, the exhalations long and loud before she continued. 'We came out to explore and to let Truffles have a good run round. We planned to go to the lake, but I decided to drive to the woods and walk on the path that cuts through. I thought that if it rained, we could shelter under the trees.'

Nick tried to remember the map. 'Do you mean the path that's closed due to flooding?'

'That's not the issue, Nick,' she snapped. 'I took the lead off when we got into the woods. We must have walked down the path for about ten minutes before we came to a clearing. The sky was black. We were all calling for Truffles so we could get back to the car before the rain. I could hear him howling, but he wouldn't come back, even when the rain started. Then, when he did appear... he had a garter in his mouth.' She started to hyperventilate again.

'A what?' Nick wasn't sure he had heard correctly as the reception on Sam's mobile was poor.

She shouted at him. 'A garter. A blue silk garter thing with lace edging.'

'And on my first day in a new job, you rang me to tell me that?' Even as he said it, he felt a chill creep through him.

'Nick, it's got a date embroidered on it. It's last Saturday's date,' her voice quieted to a whisper, 'it's a bride's garter.'

<u>Chapter 16</u>

Monday 10th February

'Oh, shit.' He sat down heavily and leant his elbow on the desk. 'The missing solicitor was due to marry on Saturday.'

'That's why I rang,' she said. 'It was in the papers. You need to come now. The kids are with me and we're all holding on to Truffles because he's trying to drag us back into the woods.'

'Okay here's what to do.' Morgan tried to balance the preservation of evidence at the same time as keeping his family safe. 'Have you got a bag?'

'Of course I've got a bag. I'm walking the dog so I've got a whole roll of them.'

'Okay, sorry. Put the garter in a bag. Have you handled it much?'

'I'm a policeman's wife, Nick, I understand about evidence. I've handled it enough to get it out of Truffles' mouth and to read the date but I'm wearing leather gloves.'

'That's great. Get everyone back to the car and I'll meet you in that little car park. I don't know how long I'll be, or if I'll be there before uniform can respond, but I'll be on my way as soon as I've spoken to Johnson.'

'I'm beginning to wonder if we've done the right thing, you know, coming here. It's not started well, has it?'

'Let's not think too much about that. Before I go, what was your mother in a flap about when she rang earlier?' He really didn't care what was bugging Dotty but hoped it would give Sam something else to think about before he ended the call.

'God, I'd forgotten all about her. She rang to tell me that Steven hasn't turned up for work this morning. It turns out that my lazy brother hasn't been at work for a while, but whenever she's rung and asked to speak to him, someone has covered for him. She's furious and she rang to ask me to take over from him from today.' At forty-two, Sam was eight years older than her brother and when she had chosen marriage and a new life in London, Steven had buckled under relentless parental pressure to take up the reins of the family business. He was artistic and scruffy, neither of which were ideal attributes for a funeral director, but he was also sensitive, which made him popular with clients.

'Does she not realise it's half term?'

'Don't panic, I've told her I'm not even thinking about the business until we've moved in and the children are back at school.'

'We didn't move here so that you could go back to work.'

'For God's sake, Nick, I'm not having that conversation now. Can you just get here, please?' She ended the call and Morgan made his way back to the DCI's office.

Johnson was incredulous. 'You've not been here four days yet and in that time you've found a body and your wife has found an item of clothing you believe may belong to a missing girl. It's like a TV drama.' He put his glasses on. 'But of course, go and make sure your family are okay. I'll get them to send uniform to secure the site and I'll see if someone from CSI can be freed from the scene at Cliffside House to follow on. For the moment, you'll need to be SIO because I've no one else. Pick up a decision log from the office. I assume you've got whatever else you need?'

'I'll need a radio and mobile, sir.' Morgan carried a grab bag in his car with everything he was likely to want at a crime scene plus a few bits and pieces that he'd found useful as Senior Investigating Officer in the past.

'I'll have them forwarded to the scene. Go and make sure your family is okay and report back as soon as you can.'

<u>Chapter 17</u>

Monday 10th February

When Morgan got back to Gullhaven Park, Sam and the twins were waiting in her car with the windows open a little to stop them fogging. Sam got out, walked round to his door and opened it.

'Nice place you brought us to,' she said.

He ignored the barb. 'Uniform's on the way and there's a dog coming too, so we need to keep Truffles in the car. Which direction did you take?'

She nodded towards an obvious path which led from the east side of the parking area. There was a rustic sign with arrows pointing towards three different walking routes. Morgan took a few photographs with his mobile but their quality was limited by the dark sky. He returned to the cars and sat in Sam's passenger seat unwilling to discuss the significance of the garter in front of the twins. They sat in silence until the arrival of the police dog handler. Morgan got out and greeted him.

'I'm PC Barber, sir. And you've no need to introduce yourself, I know who you are.' When Barber opened the van doors, two dogs in separate cages were pressing their noses through the bars. Both tails were wagging enthusiastically. He unlatched the cage on the left and attached a lead to the collar of a large tan and black German Shepherd. 'We'll take Kaiser. He's more for tracking and cadaver searching.' He pointed to the smaller dog in the neighbouring cage. 'I use Oscar here for drugs, money, firearms, that sort of thing.' Kaiser leapt down and started to drag on the lead until Barber calmed him. 'Now, which direction are we heading in?'

Morgan pointed to the gap between the trees and repeated the details of the walk his family had taken.

Barber asked if Truffles had a blanket in the car to see if his dog might track Truffles' scent back to where he had found the garter. He said it might be a long shot, but with more rain threatening he thought it was worth a try.

'I'll be behind you,' said Morgan. 'Don't worry, I know to keep my distance. I'll fetch my torch.'

The smells of rotting vegetation and wet soil intensified as they advanced through the woods and into the clearing Sam had described. Kaiser's nose was down. He was intent on following whatever scent had grabbed his interest. Morgan could see footprints in the mud. The shelter offered by the trees must have protected the ground from the overnight frost. He thought it likely that the prints belonged to Sam and Victoria as they were clearly defined and there were dog prints alongside. It was Alex's habit to wander off pathways when they walked, so it made sense that his were absent. The Crime Scene Team would want to take their footwear for examination which he knew would upset Sam. It had taken her a while to break-in her walking boots.

Without warning, Kaiser veered off to the left and into rough ground. He was moving faster than before and both men had trouble keeping up as they avoided slippery mud, exposed roots and low branches. The air was still. There was an eerie silence. Morgan looked behind him and wondered how they would find their way out again, but Kaiser was still tracking so he pressed on. Barber spoke over his right shoulder. 'He's not following your dog's scent anymore. He's found something else.'

They came to a holly bush and Kaiser stopped. He stood upright and perfectly still; eyes and nose pointing straight ahead. His mouth was slightly open and he was panting. 'That's his indicator,' said Barber. 'There's something here.'

Morgan didn't need to be told. The woodland smell he had been enjoying was now tainted by the stench of decaying flesh. Although decomposition would be slower in low winter temperatures, nature would still have its way. Through the intertwined branches and prickly leaves Morgan saw a flash of white. He waited while Barber made a fuss of his dog then picked his way round the holly bush to get a better view.

In the light of his torch he saw something was leaning against a wide tree trunk. Ignoring the scratches to his hands, he held the holly branches aside. It was a figure, covered in white fabric which was streaked with mud and other stains, but still sparkled in the beam of light. Was that something in the figure's lap? He wasn't sure.

PC Barber was gripping Kaiser's collar when Morgan returned from behind the holly bush. 'Is it the missing solicitor, do you think?'

Morgan shrugged. 'Can't be sure. If it is, she's not in a good state. It'll be dental records and personal effects... if there are any.'

Barber started to make his way towards the path before calling back. 'Enjoy the rest of your first day and I'll no doubt see you again at some point.' He waved before reaching into his pocket and producing a mangled yellow tennis ball. Morgan heard him tell Kaiser how clever he was and knew that when they had reached a safe distance from the scene, the dog was going to get his reward – ten minutes of fetch the ball.

Now alone, Morgan felt that the peace and stillness had intensified. There was an occasional drip of water on areas of rotting leaves and it reminded him of the death at Cliffside. A slight movement of air disturbed the bare branches of the trees. Then, nothing.

If this was Abigail Slater, what was she doing here? Was this the suicide of a soon-to-be bride who had decided she couldn't go through with it, or had someone made that decision for her?

Tiredness washed over him. This wasn't the way it was supposed to happen. A member of the public usually came across a body, quite often when they were walking their dog. They rang the police who sent a uniformed officer or PCSO to guard the scene. After that, forensics did their bit, and the pathologist and Senior Investigating Officer turned up later. He shouldn't be the first responder. How had that happened? Of course, it happened because the member of the public walking the dog was his wife.

He didn't know how long he waited before he heard footsteps. When he turned, he saw two uniformed officers. The male was carrying a mobile phone and a police radio which he handed to Morgan, and the female had three rolls of blue and white police barrier tape. 'How far back do you want this?' she asked. As they were choosing trees to secure the tape to, he heard more people coming from the direction of the car park. Another body; another circus.

Chapter 18

Samantha Morgan watched her husband disappear into the woods with PC Barber and Kaiser. She was resigned to a long wait and might have sat it out if she had been alone, but with the twins arguing, and the pervasive smell of wet dog in the car, she decided she would make a move as soon as someone came who could take a message to Nick.

A marked police car arrived and two uniformed officers got out. She approached and told them that she had found the garter. Then, she pointed them to where her husband and the dog and handler had gone into the woods. The female officer thanked her and asked her to wait in the car until someone came to take a statement. When Sam replied that she intended to leave the scene, the officers looked at each other with obvious alarm. 'I'm not asking you for permission,' she clarified her position, 'I'm telling you to let DI Morgan know that I'll see him at home this evening.' She stomped back to her car and started the engine. As she turned in a tight circle, the tyres spraying loose chippings, Alexander shouted 'Yey. Go Mum!'

Samantha drove back to the park home and told the twins to wait in the car. She was angry that Nick's priority had been the police investigation, rather than his family. Just because they hadn't actually seen the body didn't mean that they weren't traumatised, particularly so soon after the dead youth at Cliffside. When the dog started to whine, she realised she had been taking her temper out on him and rubbing too hard. She hugged him before settling him into his basket with a chew and a couple of toys.

The twins sensed Samantha's mood and stayed quiet during the drive to Silver Sands House. When they arrived, she hustled them through the front door which was propped open, although there were signs everywhere forbidding it. She led them along the hallway, glancing into the dining room and public rooms before hurrying up to Dorothy's suite. There was no reply when she knocked on the door so she tried the handle. It opened. Her mother was asleep in her armchair, head to one side and mouth open. Samantha went into the small kitchen area and put the kettle on. She found Dorothy's biscuit tin which she handed to the twins. They looked at her in surprise. Chocolate biscuits were a rare treat.

She warmed the pot and spooned what Dorothy called "proper tea" into it before re-boiling the kettle and pouring water over the leaves. The ritual took her back to when she lived with her parents. She used teabags nowadays.

When she returned to the lounge Alex had turned on the television and Dorothy was wakening. 'What a surprise, dear. I must have dropped off.'

'We found a body, Grandma,' Alex shouted as he launched himself into the two-seater settee.

'That's not fair,' said Victoria 'I wanted to tell her.'

'I know about the body,' said Dorothy, 'and strictly speaking, your father found it.'

'No!' they shouted together. 'Another body.'

Dorothy looked to Samantha who was pouring the tea.

'In the woods. Truffles found a garter. I think it may belong to that solicitor, Abigail... whatever her name is. We don't know if she's there, but Nick's gone in with a police dog to look.'

Dorothy took the tea and sighed. 'I really hoped she would be found safe and well. But, dead in the woods? That's not good,' she said. 'For so many reasons, that's not good.'

Chapter 19

Monday 10th February

Dave Spence arrived at DI Maggy Patel's office and knocked on the open door. 'I've got the pathologist's preliminary report on Carl Raynor, ma'am,' he said holding up the large white envelope.

'Have you read it?'

'Skimmed it and read the last few paragraphs. It seems he was stabbed in the back and asphyxiated. The stab wounds are on the right side of the body. A couple of tentative ones and a deeper one, but none of them hit vital vessels or organs. Mackenzie says it wouldn't have taken much to smother him. I wasn't there when he was weighed, but if he was fifty kilos I'd be surprised. Full toxicology will come later.'

Patel shook her head, her expression sad. 'Stabbed and asphyxiated? Is that someone sending out a message? Have we any idea how long he was living there?'

'Not long, I'd say. There were ashes in the fireplace, but not enough for many fires. And you'd need a fire in that draughty dump.'

'You don't think our new recruit, DI Morgan, could have found him and decided to circumnavigate the court eviction process, do you?' Patel was tapping a pen against her chin as she spoke.

Spence wasn't sure if she was being serious. 'There was no car on the drive. Where's DI Morgan's car? I'd say that's very suspicious, wouldn't you?' He checked for a reaction, but her face gave nothing away. 'I brought him in after he found the body. I thought about cautioning him, but I didn't. Are you saying I should have, ma'am?'

Patel smiled. Maybe she had been teasing him? 'I expect we'll find out more when I question him. His statement is basic at best.' She tossed her pen on to the desk, sat back in her chair, and crossed her arms. 'There was drug paraphernalia in one of the bedrooms with two unopened electric toothbrushes and a couple of bottles of perfume so I can't believe it was another druggie robbing Raynor of his cache. They would have taken the lot. Were you there when Mack was at the scene?' Spence was surprised to hear Patel use the pathologist's nickname; she was normally more formal.

'Yes, for some of the time. He said he thought that the fight began in the back bedroom. Thinks it started as Raynor bent over to snort a line off a bedside cabinet. He must have tried to get away, because there are scuffle marks in the dust between there and where he we found him, in the front bedroom.'

Patel searched through the papers on her desk before pulling one out and reading from it. 'CSI's initial report found cocaine residue on that cabinet. It'd been kicked over, so they reckon there must have been a bit of a struggle. They're not sure how many people were involved because the footmarks in the dust aren't clear.' She turned over the page. 'No blood trail from the back to the front bedroom so, he was either stabbed and smothered in the front bedroom, or...'

'The stab wounds aren't all that deep. He might have been stabbed in the back bedroom and his clothes absorbed the blood while the fight moved to the front?'

62

Spence held out the envelope which she took and opened. 'How long is it going to be before Mack uses email do you think?' she asked.

'He says he doesn't trust the system and that the only way he can be sure we'll read his reports is if he gives us hard copy.'

She nodded as she glanced through the pages. 'He might have a point.'

'Have you read the bit about bruising to the chest?' he asked.

'Just got there. Some historical bruising but also two recent bruises, one above each nipple. What do you think? It says possibly knee prints?'

Spence nodded his agreement. 'Mack thought he was knelt on as he's being smothered. There were a few kick marks in the dust at his feet. Forensics took some cushions, pillows and a folded blanket for DNA. They've also photographed what they can of the footprints. We'll need to get DI Morgan's shoes for elimination.'

Patel wagged her forefinger at him. 'You know they call themselves CSI now.'

'I'd like to be called DI Spence, but we can't always get what we want.'

'I don't suppose there's any CCTV? The houses along that road are expensive so you'd think someone would have a top of the range system.'

'A lot of them have been turned into flats, but I can find out.' Spence turned to leave and then changed his mind. 'Just to be clear, ma'am. I am formally assigned to this case, yes?'

'What do you mean?'

Spence felt uncomfortable under her gaze. 'I mean that I think I can bring a lot to this investigation and I want to be part of it.'

'Should I translate that as "I don't want to be working with DI Morgan?"'

'I want to be on the Carl Raynor case and DCI Johnson said it would be your decision.'

If Patel was angered that Spence had spoken to her boss about allocation of duties, she hid it. 'Leave it with me, Dave. And come back to me when you've found CCTV that shows Raynor being followed back to Cliffside, by a face we already know and can arrest before teatime. If you can do that, I'll make sure you're always on my team.'

<u>Chapter 20</u>

Monday 10th February

As SIO, Morgan's first job in the woodland was to brief both the pathologist and crime scene manager. Together, they would agree the strategy for approaching the body and for the collection of evidence. Whilst at the Met, he'd often worked with the same people and they had developed an understanding of how each of them operated. He missed that familiarity and camaraderie.

He watched as each new arrival was added to the log. They struggled into their customary protective coveralls and shoe covers at the outer crime scene boundary. He introduced himself to each group before listing his needs and expectations. Glances passed between colleagues which they did not try to hide.

'I'm sure that when we've worked together for a while, we'll be able to make these briefings shorter but you'll forgive me if I dot i's and cross t's today. This is already a high profile case. Now, who can book this into evidence for me, please?' He held up the black plastic dog poop bag containing the garter and gave details of its provenance to the technician who took it.

A couple of the CSI team had been given the task of clearing a route to the body and they were examining the ground and branches for trace evidence before chopping the coarser greenery into large plastic crates. They stopped to listen when Morgan addressed the group before returning to their task. Although masks covered most of their faces, he noticed an exchange of raised eyebrows. Fuck them, he thought. He didn't have to prove anything and he didn't need them to like him either.

'And you must be the famous Detective Inspector Nick Morgan.' The voice carried from beyond the blue and white tape which was snapping in the wind that was picking up again. The accent was Scottish although softer than the Glaswegian tones of a pathologist Morgan had worked with in London. 'I'm Dr Mackenzie, Hugh Mackenzie. I won't shake hands since we're both gloved up.' The short man had greying facial hair which looked as if it had been red or dark blonde in earlier years. Bushy eyebrows arched over bright blue eyes which had a sparkle of mischief, even in the limited woodland light.

'I'm pleased to meet you, Dr Mackenzie.'

'I believe your wife is Dorothy Cooper's daughter?' Mackenzie was nodding in response to his own question as he continued, 'The funeral director?'

'Yes, she is.'

'And she found the body?'

Morgan braced himself for whatever joke might be coming next. 'Yes, she did; while she was out with our children, walking the dog.'

Mackenzie was nodding again, 'Well, tell her I'm sorry for her trouble, I really am. Now, where would you like me to start?'

Morgan pointed the pathologist to the gap in the bushes and followed him back to the body.

By the time Morgan returned to the car park by the woods, Sam's car had gone. He assumed she would be at their park home but when he drove there, he found Truffles curled up in his basket, asleep and alone. He called her mobile which went straight to voicemail.

'Hi Sam, please call me when you get this message. I need to arrange for someone to take a statement from you while you still have a clear memory of what happened.' He was about to disconnect, then added, 'I hope you're okay, and the kids too. Love you.'

He called into the park home reception office to tell them that the woods were out of bounds to staff and visitors for the foreseeable future. Maisie wasn't there and the sullen man at the desk was only interested in how soon they would be able to get back to normal. This was Morgan's least favourite reaction to the discovery of an unexpected and unexplained death and he was careful to make his reply as unhelpful as possible. 'These things take as long as they take, sir. We'll let you know when we are releasing the site.'

Driving back to the station, he was faced with the prospect of having to choose a team from a group of people whose strengths and weaknesses were unknown to him. This investigation was already being picked over by the media and, as his first case for the Major Crimes Unit, it was attracting the scrutiny of colleagues too. Who could he trust? He missed his team at the Met.

There was a yellow note stuck to Morgan's office door telling him that Johnson wanted to speak to him as soon as he got back. He glanced at his mobile to make sure he hadn't missed any calls then sprinted up the stairs. Johnson beckoned him in as he passed the glazed panels of his office.

'This isn't how I hoped the Abigail Slater business would end,' said Johnson, pointing to the chair facing his desk.

No coffee and comfy sofa now, thought Morgan, before starting the update. 'I've spoken to her parents and they're coming to identify the body. I told her father straight that Abigail isn't suitable for viewing but he insisted they both come so I've arranged for a car to fetch them. They should be here in about an hour and a half. Apparently there are a couple of tattoos on her arms that they can identify. If it's her, Mackenzie can get on with the PM. Because of the media interest he says he will get it done today, even if it goes into the evening.'

Johnson grimaced. 'He'll charge extra for that, you know.'

'There's already speculation out there, and the sooner everyone gets the facts, the sooner we can ask the public for what they might know.'

'On that subject, the local television news would like to interview you for this evening's broadcast. It's something I would normally expect to do but it seems your celebrity status has got them quite excited and they asked for you by name.' Johnson emphasised the 'celebrity' word and Morgan bit his cheek. He looked at his watch.

'That's not possible, sir, unless it's for the late evening broadcast. I can't predict exactly when the Slaters will arrive and I see no point in speaking to the media unless we can at least confirm it's her.'

Johnson sat forward, planting his elbows on his desk and steepling his fingers. 'The news editor has spoken to the Police and Crime Commissioner who rang me herself. She wants this case given absolute priority and the media to be kept informed at every opportunity.'

'Then she'll have to authorise the budget, part of which I've spent on overtime payments for the postmortem.'

'I tend to use the word "autopsy" now,' said Johnson.

'I'm old school, sir. And I'm still adjusting to using CSI instead of SOCO. I've never found anyone struggling to understand me.' He got up to leave.

'The team is putting together an Incident Room for you.'

Morgan stopped. 'What team? I haven't chosen a team.'

Johnson's smile didn't reach his eyes. 'I've done it for you. Your predecessor thought highly of them all so I don't expect you to be disappointed.'

'Thank you, sir. That's very helpful.' This time he got as far as the door and managed to open it before Johnson spoke again.

'And DI Morgan... I'm transferring Dave Spence from Operation Heartwood. He'll be your Deputy SIO. He's gobby and overconfident but there's very little goes on around here that he doesn't know about and that's the background you're lacking.'

'I'm sorry, sir I don't know what Operation Heartwood is.'

Johnson examined Morgan closely as if checking for sarcasm. 'Operation Heartwood is the suspicious death at Cliffside House,' he said, then looked back down at his notes, 'and I can also tell you that your Abigail Slater case has been allocated the name Operation Siren.'

Walking back to his office Morgan mused that in Greek mythology, the Sirens sang to lure their victims on to the rocks. He hoped to avoid the same fate.

Chapter 21

While he was waiting for her parents at the mortuary, Morgan used his phone to access news reports and social media posts about Abigail Slater. The local paper concentrated on her status as a "bride-to-be," and they had put up a modest reward for information leading to her safe return. Social media posts were more brutal. Many implied that Abigail had developed a reputation as a "party girl" who was a regular at the local clubs and who often went straight from the dance floor to interview rooms at the police station when she was duty solicitor. *#shehaditcoming* was trending. Morgan empathised with her parents. If it wasn't bad enough having to identify the body of your daughter, you had to put up with all this shit as well.

He went outside and paced in front of the building. The rain and wind had stopped but the temperature had plummeted. His breath was condensing in the still air. He knew it was wrong to assume that the body in the bridal gown was Abigail, but realistically, who else could it be? Once they had confirmed it, he hoped the Slaters would be able to provide some authentic information about their daughter which would give him somewhere to start. As it was, he had nothing but rumour and speculation. He decided that if it was Abi, he would stay for the postmortem.

When the duty technician came out for a second cigarette, he asked her about the sparkly white dress which the body had been wearing.

'I haven't seen it, DI Morgan,' she said. 'CSI removed it and bagged it at the scene.'

'That's a bit unusual, isn't it?'

'She wasn't actually dressed in it. It's difficult to explain, but I believe her arms had been put through the straps so it might look as if she was wearing it, if you weren't up close.'

'Okay. I understand.' A thought crossed his mind. 'Can you cover up as much of her as possible so that only the tattoos are visible, please?'

The look she gave him was withering. 'This might not be London, but we have done it before.'

His smile was apologetic and he raked his hand through his hair. 'I know and I'm sorry. It's my first day and it's turned out to be quite the baptism of fire.'

She held out a hand which he shook. 'Annie Geeson,' she said, 'and I already know who you are. We dealt with your unwanted lodger on Friday.'

When Mr and Mrs Slater arrived their faces were rigid but their eyes reflected how much crying had been done during the journey. Morgan introduced himself and led them through to the viewing area.

'I want to see her face,' said Mrs Slater the tears now flooding her eyes again. Her husband took her hand but continued to stare straight ahead at the viewing window. When Annie Geeson raised the blind, Morgan saw it had been difficult to present enough of the body to aid identification without exposing the damage caused by decomposition and forest wildlife. The face had been covered completely and another white sheet was draped so that they could see two tattoos: a ring of yellow sunflowers around the bicep of the discoloured left arm and a pair of wrists in handcuffs above the left breast.

71

'It's not her!' Mrs Slater seemed on the point of collapse. Her sobbing got louder.

'I need to see the inside of her right wrist,' said Mr Slater. 'There should be a small red diamond and heart and black symbols for spades and clubs. She had it done in her first year at university. Said the cards were stacked against her.'

Morgan lifted the phone by the window and asked Annie to check the wrist. When she came back to the phone she told him that only two of the symbols remained.

'I need to see for myself.' Mr Slater's resolve stiffened his posture.

'I'd really advise against it, sir,' said Morgan. 'There's damage to the arm.'

'I won't believe it's her until I see it.'

Morgan gave the instruction to Annie who walked back to the trolley and with obvious care, held the arm at the elbow. The right hand had gone and the skin was ragged around exposed bone. In the cold white light of the mortuary, they could all see a small red heart and black club on the inside of the wrist joint.

Mrs Slater howled and punched her husband hard in his side. 'You had to do that, did you? That has to be my last memory?'

'It's her,' said Slater. 'It's Abigail.' He continued to stare at the viewing window after Annie had lowered the blind. He made no move to comfort his wife who was leaning against the wall wringing her hands and moaning softly. When he turned at last to Morgan, his face was grey. 'I don't recognise the flowers and handcuffs, sorry.'

Morgan nodded. 'I'm no expert, but the colours look quite fresh. They may be recent.' He looked at both of them and could see they weren't up to answering any of his questions. 'Have you brought a bag, or are you planning to go home tonight? I can send an officer to get statements in a day or two.'

Slater looked at his wife before replying. 'We're going back tonight. We have people to call and arrangements to make. We'd be better in our own home. When do you think they'll let us take her?'

It was a question Morgan dreaded. He didn't want to tell him that the body would be kept frozen until they caught the murderer whose legal team would want a second postmortem. 'It's hard to predict, sir,' he said. 'And it's quite likely that the media will be on your doorstep when you get back. They may even be there already. Are you sure there's nowhere you can stay where they won't be able to find you?'

The expression on Slater's face hardened again and Morgan caught a glimpse of suppressed anger. 'It's not for us to be hiding away, DI Morgan. We've done nothing to be ashamed of. Anyway, thank you for your concern, but I'm accustomed to dealing with intrusion from the media.' He shook hands and led his wife back out to the waiting car. Morgan watched it exit the mortuary gates and disappear into the darkness.

By the time he returned, Abigail Slater's body had been wheeled into the dissection room and Dr Hugh Mackenzie was adjusting the microphone to suit his height. When he noticed Morgan, he flicked the switch that allowed him to communicate with the viewing gallery.

'I'm impressed DI Morgan. Many of your colleagues would have delegated attending the victim's examination to a lower rank, especially this late in the day. Is this how it's done in the Met?'

73

Morgan shrugged. 'I feel the need to be at this one Dr Mackenzie. There is a lot of interest and I don't want to be wrong footed by not having the answers.'

Mackenzie nodded before completing the recording system sound check and telling Annie Geeson that he was preparing to make the first incision.

Chapter 22

Nick Morgan arrived home, tired and hungry. Everyone had gone to bed without leaving a light on to welcome him. He opened the fridge and poured the remains of a bottle of white wine into an unwashed glass. He would have preferred red, but the bottle at the side of the sink was empty. He glanced at three takeaway containers in the fridge but didn't open them. One of them would contain rice. Abigail Slater's stomach contents showed she had ingested rice a short while before death and it would be a couple of days before he was ready to incorporate it back into his diet.

The door to the hallway opened and Sam padded into the lounge in her bare feet. She was wearing her outdoor coat over the strappy negligee she had packed for their romantic nights at The Riverview Hotel and Spa. She sat beside him and put her hand out for the glass.

'It's late. Where have you been?' she asked swallowing a large mouthful of the wine.

'I met the family who came to ID your body in the woods, then I stayed for the PM.'

'Don't you have staff to do that?'

'Don't start, Sam. Is there anything to eat?'

'There's the remains of a Chinese in the fridge.' She handed back the wine glass.

'Is there anything else?'

'I can boil you an egg and toast you a muffin but that's about it until I get to a supermarket. And by the

75

way,' she pointed to the glass, 'that's the last of the wine.'

He nodded. 'Come on. Bedtime.' He drained the glass and started to get up from the sofa.

'You left me a message,' she said. 'You left me a message about making a statement.'

'Yes, I'll ask one of the team to get in touch tomorrow.'

'You're missing the point, Nick. Your wife and children came across a dead woman today and your first thought was to get a statement.' Morgan's expression would have served as a warning to anyone other than his wife but she continued, undeterred. 'Your second thought... Yes, your second thought was our wellbeing. You promised me that, once we moved, you would prioritise family time. You've been here one day and you've broken that promise already.'

Morgan dropped back on to the sofa and closed his eyes. 'First of all, you discovered a garter, not a body. Secondly, you left the scene before we could get someone to take a statement. If you weren't married to the SIO, then someone would be having a serious word with you about that. Now I'm not looking for an argument, Sam. I'm tired and I'm going to bed. I left that message in work time as the SIO in what could well be a murder. The message was for a witness who had found evidence and then left the scene without my permission. Yes, my priority was a statement, but that's not to say I didn't want to hug and comfort you all. You just didn't wait for me to do that.'

'I went to see Mum after I left the woods.'

'Good for you.'

'She's asked me to manage the business until Steven turns up and I've agreed. I'll take the twins to her tomorrow morning and whoever finishes work first can do the shopping. If I were you Nick, I'd make sure it was you. And don't forget the wine.' She left before he could summon the strength to reply.

Chapter 23

DI Nick Morgan made his way to the briefing room to meet the team he had been given. He was just in time to see DS Dave Spence arguing with the woman he had seen leaving Cliffside on the day he'd discovered Carl Raynor's body. Morgan ducked back into a doorway and listened.

'I want to stay with Operation Heartwood, ma'am. I was at Raynor's autopsy and I know I'll bring a lot to the investigation.'

'You heard what DCI Johnson said at my briefing, Dave. He's calling it tactical team redeployment, but what he means is that he thinks DI Morgan needs your local knowledge more than I do. I don't want to lose you, but I can see his point. Anyway, when he came to tell me he was moving you, he made it clear that there was no room for negotiation. You need to be at the Operation Siren briefing. No excuses. Please make sure you hand over all the enquiries you were making for me when you get back.' When she walked away, Morgan heard Spence follow, continuing to plead his case.

The briefing room was empty. Morgan looked at his watch, exhaling through clenched teeth.

Johnson called from the doorway. 'DI Morgan. I've spoken to DI Patel and she's happy to release DS Spence. He'll be at your briefing.' Johnson looked across at the wall clock. 'Where is everyone? Did you rearrange the time?'

'No, sir, I expect they will be here soon.' Johnson nodded his reply before disappearing. Morgan walked to the door and was closing it when DC Jenny Smart slipped through. She seemed surprised to be first. 'I thought I was late. Sorry. Where is everyone?'

He shrugged, his face expressionless. 'You tell me. Will you close the door please?'

She looked down the corridor before doing as he asked, then sat at the back of the room. Morgan shook his head and pointed to a chair much closer to where he was standing.

'That's where your deputy should sit,' she said 'That's how we do it in this room, sir.'

'I've been told...' he emphasised the last word, 'that DS Spence is my deputy. If he wants to sit with the grownups, he'll have to show better time keeping skills.' He pointed again to the chair nearest to him.

'I have to work with him, sir. If it's all the same to you, I'll sit here.'

Morgan's blue eyes glittered like shards of shattered mirror in the shaft of sunlight coming through the window. He was about to reply when a noisy group of men and women, some in uniform and others not, burst in. They settled into chairs before looking up, their faces expectant. DS Dave Spence was not among them.

'For those of you, who I've not already met, I'm DI Nick Morgan and I'm SIO of Operation Siren which is our investigation into the death of Abigail Slater. Her body was found yesterday in woodland at the edge of Gullhaven Park. I was with her parents when they confirmed the identification and I attended her postmortem last night.' He paused to let those who were taking notes catch up. 'Dr Hugh Mackenzie's initial findings are that she died of manual strangulation, or was throttled, if you prefer. The killer was face to face with her. There are thumb sized bruises on the front of her neck so it's obvious that this is a murder investigation. The pathologist won't commit to a time of death, or even in this case, speculate as to a date of death, but he has indicated that he doesn't think she was alive for long after she disappeared over two weeks ago. He told me that the condition of the body was consistent with being out there for that length of time but that the cold weather and the fact that she was quite protected by the bushes around her would have helped preserve her a little. He also noted damage caused by wildlife to her face and her extremities.' As he spoke, he walked across to the empty chair designated for his deputy and wheeled it into a corner. 'Any questions so far?'

'I heard she was wearing her wedding dress,' Morgan looked in the direction of the speaker who held up his pen. 'I'm Leo Jenson, sir. DC Jenson.'

'Thank you, DC Jenson and you're right... sort of. Abigail, or Abi as she preferred, left the offices of Fletcher, Armstrong and Gault early to pick up her wedding dress. She had a final fitting at 3pm. We'll need someone to go to the shop and take a statement to that effect now that she's been found.' DC Jenson held up his pen again and Morgan nodded his thanks. 'This was on the 23rd of January, according to the informal enquiries carried out, some by us, some by the media. Since then, there have been no sightings and no contact with friends or family. That's nothing seen or heard for over two weeks.'

Brian Bingley, the Crime Scene Manager, caught Morgan's eye. 'I have the initial findings from the scene, if that would help.'

As Morgan nodded and gave him the floor, the door opened and DS Dave Spence entered, his face flushed. All eyes turned to look, first at him and then back at Morgan. Those who had noticed Morgan moving the chair now understood. To get to that chair, Spence would have to walk around the room and cross in front of the projection screen. It would bring a whole new meaning to "the walk of shame." Everyone waited. It was clear that some were enjoying Spence's discomfort but others looked embarrassed.

'Please carry on, Brian,' said Morgan 'I'm sure DS Spence is okay standing at the back.' The atmosphere in the room relaxed again as Brian Bingley's first photograph was projected on to the screen.

'This is the best shot we have of the whole scene. Abigail was leaning against a dead tree trunk which was about five feet high. The wedding dress you mentioned was mostly laid over her body. She was actually dressed in a pale pink jumper and blue denim leggings. The wedding dress was backless and someone, most likely the murderer, put her arms through the shoulder straps. That's why, from the distance the photo was taken, she looks as though she's wearing it.'

There were nods and murmurs around the room and more notes made. Morgan watched Jenny Smart. Her notes were detailed while most of the others jotted headings.

'This closer photo is of the upper torso and her lap.' Bingley used a laser pointer to put the picture into context. 'This is the dress neckline which has crystals and embroidery and this area is her hair, hanging loose across it. The pink area is her jumper. But this is what you need to see.' The red dot of the pointer traced around something darker in colour which was resting in the white folds of the dress.

'Are we any closer to knowing what it is?' asked Morgan who wondered if Brian Bingley might be enjoying the attention of an audience a little too much.

'It's a piece of corrugated cardboard.' The pointer outlined the darkened area again. 'And these are her fingers... or rather, what's left of them. The right hand is missing altogether. From the way the arms are posed here, it looks as if the hands may have both been holding the card when the body was dumped.'

'I don't understand what the cardboard's for?' said Jenson. Others in the room were twisting their heads at different angles in an attempt to make more sense of what they were seeing.

'Couldn't it have just been blowing about in the woods and got trapped there?' asked Smart.

'Could it?' Morgan asked Bingley, expecting the sort of non-committal response for which crime scene managers and pathologists were renowned.

'It could, but I don't think so.' He flicked the switch and the picture was replaced by another which showed the cardboard and an area of Abigail Slater's lap in much greater magnification. 'As you know, the dress has gone to the lab, and it's way too early for any results. But, if you want an early opinion, I'd say that the dark staining on the dress below the cardboard may be ink. It's not mud or dirt because the colours have separated out. Did any of you do that experiment at school where you put ink on filter paper and dropped solvent on top to let the colours run? I think that stain is the separated colours of a dark ink.'

'Print from the cardboard box?' asked Morgan.

'Could be,' said Bingley, 'but most boxes are printed in waterproof inks.'

'Or a message from a murderer.' It was Dave Spence's first contribution to the meeting and it chilled the room.

Chapter 24

'Where's the fiancé in all this?' DC Jenson broke the silence and everyone seemed to exhale together.

Morgan looked at his notes. 'Yes. Mr Joseph Kendrick. He's an American who trades in crude oil futures. I tried his mobile after Abi's parents identified her, but it went straight to voicemail. I left a message but nothing yet. I spoke to his mother this morning. She and her husband have lived in England for nearly ten years.' He skipped a few lines. 'She told me that her son spent the night before the wedding with them. On Saturday, he dressed and went to the Register Office with his best man, in case Abi turned up. When she didn't, he drove to his own flat, packed a bag and rang to tell her that he was going away for a while, to get his head straight. Those weren't her exact words, but that's the gist of it. She told me that her husband thought Abi had met someone and gone off with him instead. Apparently, she had been flirting with the husband when the family invited her to theirs for Christmas. Mum said that she and her husband thought from the start that Abi was a bit of a trollop.'

'That's a word I haven't heard for a while,' said Bingley.

'I think she was giving me the polite version.'

'Did the message you left the fiancé say that she'd been found?' asked Smart and Morgan nodded.

'Found dead or found murdered?' asked Spence.

'I said she'd been found dead under suspicious circumstances and that he needed to contact us urgently so we could give him more information,' said Morgan.

'Surely, if he went to the trouble of turning up at the Register Office, it suggests he thought she was still alive,' said Smart reviewing the notes on her pad.

'Great bluff if he killed her,' argued Jenson.

'He wanted to marry her so why would he kill her?' Smart was looking round the faces for an answer to her question.

'Because she was a trollop.' Spence provided it.

Morgan sensed that they weren't going to get much further in the briefing so he returned to his folder and started to allocate tasks to his new team.

'DS Spence, can you track down Joseph Kendrick, wherever he is, and whatever he is doing. If his parents shared their low opinion of Abi with him, he might have been angry and humiliated enough to kill her, especially if he knew she'd been flirting with his father. Maybe he would think it appropriate to put her in her wedding dress? Who knows how people's minds work?'

DC Smart volunteered to see if there was any CCTV on the street where Abi collected her wedding dress so they could put her departure on the time-line. She said she would also liaise with CSI and report back to the team when analyses had been completed.

'When I was waiting for Abi's parents at the mortuary, I read some of the posts on social media,' said Morgan. 'She seems to have been something of a night owl and well known at the local clubs. I would go myself, but my party clothes are in storage at the moment. Spence, can you take DC Smart to the most likely venues and see what you can find out. Was Abi a regular? When was she last there? Did she go there with

Mr Kendrick, her fiancé? Did anyone see her arguing?' He was counting the questions off on his fingers and when he looked up, Spence's expression was withering. 'Yes, I know. You've done this before. I was thinking out loud, really. If we can't get any joy from speaking to the staff, then I'm afraid you'll need to go during opening hours and speak to the punters. Sorry.'

Morgan pointed to Jenny Smart. 'You and I are going to go and visit Abigail's flatmate. Nobody knows you better than the person you live with.'

The briefing ended and the officers and civilians started to leave. Morgan replaced his papers in their folder and headed for the door.

'DI Morgan. At last!' The same woman who Morgan had seen Spence follow down the corridor was waiting for him and he saw that she was holding a copy of his statement.

He called after Spence. 'Change of plan. Can you and Jenny go and interview the flatmate, Juliet Riddington? See if you can find out a bit more about what Abigail Slater was really like.' He turned his attention back to the woman. 'You must be DI Patel. I'm sorry about yesterday. It all got a bit hectic after... well, you know.' She nodded and held her arm forward indicating that he should lead the way back to her office. Morgan felt like a prisoner under escort.

Chapter 25

Spence led Smart to his car. Her promotion to Detective Constable was recent, but he knew that Jenny Smart was ambitious and already had her eye on the next rung of the ladder.

'Any chance I can lead the interview?' she asked. 'I'm ready.' She delved into her black shoulder bag and produced a notebook which was not police issue. 'I spent last night going through the information we already have on Abigail Slater's disappearance and I've made a list of questions for both the fiancé and the flatmate.'

Spence was dubious but having nothing prepared himself, he agreed. As he drove, Smart went through her list and he suggested a couple of follow-on questions to help the structure and flow of the interview. By the time they got to the flat, they had a plan and he sensed Smart's excitement.

The voice that answered when Spence pressed the buzzer was hesitant and anxious. She told them to come up to the third floor and the door release clicked.

'It's not a very inspiring property for a go-getter solicitor in the making,' grumbled Spence as they reached the second floor.

'What was your first flat like then?'

'You've got a point. It stank of fish and chips from the takeaway underneath, and during rush hour there was enough carbon monoxide coming in the window to fell a horse.'

Smart laughed. 'The stairwell up to my first flat smelt of piss.'

'Oh, nice. Thank you for sharing.' They trudged upwards.

The door to the flat was open and Juliet Riddington was waiting for them. Bloodshot eyes were sunk into black hollows and her nose was red. She was wearing button down pyjamas with a cartoon character on the pocket and her robe hung open.

'I'm sorry. I overslept,' she said and looked down at her clothes. 'I've not slept well since Abi disappeared and then when they told me about finding her, well...' She shook her head and closed her eyes.

'Come and sit down, Juliet.' Jenny Smart guided her into the lounge and towards a worn, grey sofa. She moved a box of tissues on the table nearer. 'How did you find out?'

'A journalist rang me at tea time yesterday and said they found her in the woods.'

Jenny Smart made eye contact with Spence and he nodded.

'That was a little premature,' she said, 'but we do have her identification confirmed now. I'm sorry.' Juliet Riddington shrunk back into the sofa.

'I knew it was her.' She dabbed at her eyes and then blew her nose again.

Spence held back. He was uncomfortable in the presence of crying women. He never knew what to say or do and when he tried, it always seemed to make things worse. A corner of the room served as a kitchen and, spotting the kettle, he asked if he should make tea.

'I've no milk,' said Juliet. 'I'm sorry.' She blew her nose again. 'Abi usually did the shopping on a weekend.' Inwardly, Spence groaned. Yup, he'd made her feel worse. He crossed to the sink and filled a glass with water. This woman was at serious risk of dehydration.

Jenny Smart sat down on the sofa and took her official notebook out of her bag. 'I know this is hard, Juliet, but there may be things you can tell us that'll help us catch whoever has done this. We'll have a chat today and then you can come to the station later in the week to make a proper statement.' Juliet nodded but didn't look up.

'Let's start with how long you've both lived here, shall we?'

Spence leaned back against the kitchen unit and listened. Jenny Smart's patient but persistent questioning technique impressed him and he didn't interrupt. Smart seemed to sense when Juliet was becoming uncomfortable with the direction of the conversation and she changed course to keep the information coming. But she never failed to re-visit the issue until she got what she needed.

Juliet told them that she and Abi got on well from the minute they met at their university Fresher's Ball. Because Abi's course was longer than Juliet's, there were a couple of years when they hadn't seen as much of each other, but when Abi got her job at Fletcher, Armstrong & Gault, they decided to find a modest rental together whilst they saved a deposit for a property.

'She said when we got to the point of buying somewhere, her dad would draw up a contract for us. He's a solicitor too. Does celebrity contracts. Later on, if one of us wanted to move in with a partner, we were going to sell up and split the equity.'

'You couldn't have been expecting Abi to meet someone so soon after moving in together.' Smart's comment was met with a shrug.

'She fell head over heels and suddenly it's all bridal magazines and honeymoon brochures.' Juliet reached for another tissue but her eyes were dry now and her expression, angry. 'She didn't think about anyone apart from herself. I can see that now. She didn't care how other people were affected by her actions. She'd vanished before, you know. Just disappeared for a couple of days without a word to anyone. That's why I didn't contact the police straight away. When it happened before, she would just turn up and say she'd felt like getting away from it all.'

Jenny Smart nodded, jotting down a few notes. 'What about other boyfriends? From what you've said it seems that Abi got engaged quite quickly after meeting her fiancé. Did that upset anyone else in her life?'

'Abi drew men to her. If we went out together she would be the life and soul, always casting around to track her next conquest. She liked men. I stopped asking her who she was with because it changed every time and I couldn't keep up.' Juliet's voice dropped and she leant towards Smart as if sharing a secret. 'I suppose she was a bit of a slapper, really. At least, if she'd not had the posh accent and the expensive clothes, people would have said she was a slapper.'

Spence was reluctant to intervene but needed clarification. 'So, do you think it was male company she craved, or sex?'

Juliet looked startled, as if she had forgotten he was there and turned to him. 'Abi had a difficult relationship with her parents. Whatever she did to please them, it was never enough. They could have given her the

90

deposit for a property out of her mother's clothing budget but no, we had to live in this shitty place and earn the right to get on to the property ladder. I think she craved being wanted and sometimes she confused that with being used. I suppose having sex was the price she paid for that feeling of being wanted.'

'And where did she find these men?' he asked.

'Clubs, bars, on buses and trains and at work. I never asked.' Juliet's answers were quieter now. 'Abi craved love and attention. But it got her into trouble. She told me they had extended her probation period at work. Twice, I think.'

'Was that to do with her disappearances?' asked Smart. 'She wouldn't have been a very reliable employee.'

'She didn't talk to me about it, but I thought it might have been because she had relationships with people she met at work.'

'You mean the other solicitors?' Spence asked.

'I mean the clients.' The look she gave Spence implied that she thought he was stupid.

'Juliet, do you have any idea why anyone might feel anger towards Abi?' asked Smart.

Juliet looked away, avoiding Smart's penetrating stare. 'No, I don't,' she said. She wrapped the robe around herself and got up from the sofa. 'I need to get dressed now. I've got someone coming to see the flat this afternoon and I need to straighten everything up. Did you say you needed to see her bedroom?'

When she opened the door to Abi's room it was obvious that any opportunity to harvest forensic material from boyfriends who had stayed over, had been bleached, polished and vacuumed away. Juliet told them

91

that she'd cleaned up as a nice surprise for Abi when she came home.

'Was she wearing her engagement ring when they found her?' she asked.

Jenny Smart looked at Spence who shrugged. 'I'm sorry, we don't know,' she answered.

'I just wondered where it went. It wasn't in her room. Is that it, now? I really need to get on.'

Smart handed Juliet her card and told her she would be in touch to set up an appointment for them to take a statement. She also said that they would try to arrange a visit to the flat by a forensics team and asked Juliet to postpone the viewing by the potential new flatmate. Juliet gave a resigned nod.

Chapter 26

'Take a seat DI Morgan,' said DI Maggy Patel, 'I believe you've already met DC Greenfield?' He turned to see that Lynn Greenfield had followed them in and was closing the door.

'Yes, I have.' He sat in the chair opposite Patel's, pulling it up closer to her desk where he rested his hands, fingers interlaced.

'I'm not going to lie, when I first read this, I thought you were taking the Mickey.' Patel was pointing to his statement which she'd tossed on her desk as she sat down. 'Then, when you failed to turn up to answer questions about it, I considered a formal interrogation under caution.' Morgan glanced around while he waited to intervene. This office was bigger than his, but it had two desks so she must have to share with someone. 'But I heard you had a pretty full agenda yesterday.'

His smile was rueful. 'You could say that.'

He watched her long thin fingers align the sheets of paper with the edge of her desk before she spoke again.

'I've read your statement – many times in fact because it doesn't take long. You discover a body - a body that's still bleeding - in a house where you've spent the night, and you only have enough information to fill a page and a quarter of an MG11?'

Nick Morgan knew that the raised inflection at the end of her sentence meant that she expected him to respond but he had too much experience to make that mistake. For a fleeting moment, he thought about saying "no comment." He kept his face emotionless and held her gaze. Beside him, Lynn Greenfield cleared her throat.

'Okay, let's go through it, minute by minute, from the time you got in your car in London.' Patel reached into her drawer and pulled out another statement form and a pile of additional sheets. She made a theatrical gesture of clicking her pen and waited for him to speak.

It took almost an hour of questions and answers which jumped backwards and forwards in the time-line of his account before Patel seemed satisfied that she had all the information she needed to draft his new statement. She had been particularly interested in the fact that his car was missing when Spence had arrived at Cliffside House. Morgan told her that he had been drinking and didn't think that being arrested for excess alcohol would be a very impressive start to his new role.

'So, that..,' she tapped on his original statement for emphasis, 'is the result of your embarrassment that you were pissed and may have slept while a man was murdered upstairs.'

'No, that..,' he leant forward and copied her gesture, 'is the result of having a loaded removal van, and my wife, twins and dog, all bearing down on a house I no longer had access to.' Patel stayed silent and he continued. 'And if that wasn't bad enough, the hotel where we had planned to spend the night cancelled my booking, so while my family were thundering down the motorway, I knew we had nowhere to sleep. When I wrote that, I had a lot on my mind.' He sat back in his chair satisfied that he had justified the insufficiency of his first statement.

Patel nodded. 'Okay, I understand. I don't know if there will be other questions, DI Morgan, but I know where to find you.'

He got up. 'Any idea when Cliffside House is to be released?' he asked.

'A day or two at the most. It's a bit of a shambles in there and it's taking time for CSI to convince themselves they've not missed anything. The keys will go back to Dorothy Cooper as she's the named owner at Land Registry. She's your mother-in-law, isn't she?' He nodded. 'Poor you,' she said and smiled. She stood and they shook hands. 'Welcome to the team, Nick. You'll get used to us.'

Chapter 27

Before finishing for the day, Morgan rang round to check progress and to update everyone with the news Spence had given him of the missing engagement ring. He decided there wasn't enough new information to justify holding an evening briefing and went upstairs where he found Johnson packing papers into his briefcase. The DCI did not bother to hide his disappointment.

'She was missing over two weeks and the media were on it every day. Someone must know something,' said Johnson.

'When I spoke to DS Spence, he told me that she accrued quite a list of male friends in the time she's been here.'

'What does "friends" mean? I know what it means to my generation, but what does it mean nowadays?'

Morgan knew exactly how he would have described Abi Slater's lifestyle to his previous boss but then he'd worked with her on hundreds of cases over many years. He still found Johnson hard to read and chose his words with care.

'When Spence and Smart spoke to the flatmate, she confirmed what's been whizzing round online... that Ms Slater was somewhat generous with her sexual favours.'

Johnson looked up, eyebrows raised. 'Have you had this conversation with her parents?'

'No, sir, I was with them for the identification and I spoke to Mr Slater this morning to confirm the findings of the medical examination. They have returned home and, since she wasn't actually living with them, I've decided to let them be for a while.'

'What's tomorrow's plan of action?'

'Spence and I are going to speak to Graham Fletcher. He's a partner at the solicitor's where she worked.'

'I know Fletcher. He's more into family law now but I remember him from years ago. He's the sort of man who could follow you into a revolving door and emerge first. Watch him and don't let him wind Spence up.'

'Sir.' Morgan left Johnson's office and returned to his own. He checked his watch. If he left now, he could do the supermarket shopping and still be back at the park home before Sam and the twins.

After unloading the shopping into the unfamiliar kitchen cupboards, Morgan rang Spence and arranged to meet him next morning in a coffee shop near the centre of town from where they could walk to the offices of Fletcher, Armstrong and Gault.

He poured himself a glass of red wine then fried some bacon lardons, onion, garlic and mince. Spaghetti bolognaise was normally a Friday favourite and having it on a Tuesday would be strange but at the moment, nothing was normal for the Morgan family. He poured a generous amount of the wine into the pot and then cursed. He had forgotten to buy stock cubes and the sauce wouldn't be the same without them. Unsure when his family would get back, he dialled the estate main number and was pleased when Maisie answered.

'I don't suppose you carry emergency supplies for campers, do you?'

'I've got basic first aid stuff, and toothbrushes, toothpaste, tea bags and long life milk. I've also got tampons and condoms. What do you need?'

'Beef stock cubes.'

Her laugh was hearty. 'Only a Londoner would call a beef stock cube an emergency. The condoms are flavoured, but I don't think it's beef.'

He wondered if Maisie turned every conversation to the subject of sex. 'You're okay,' he said, 'I'll go out again when my wife gets back.'

'If I'd have known you were on your own...' she laughed again. 'I'll nip over to my kitchen and get you some stock cubes. Text your wife and tell her to drop in at reception when she's passing.'

'Thanks, Maisie. I owe you.'

'I'll hold you to that, Nick.' He put his phone down on the work surface and noticed that his hand had a slight tremble as he poured red wine from the open bottle into two glasses.

'How was your first day back in the funeral business?' Nick waited until they had eaten and the twins had gone to bed. He had been careful not to react when he heard them talking about their "rubbish day with grandma and her cronies." Now that he was alone with his wife, he felt ready to talk.

Sam cradled the glass of red wine in both hands and swirled its contents. 'This is expensive,' she said, 'I can tell. You must really want to impress me. Shopping, spag bol and expensive wine... I'm guessing you don't want me to be back at work.'

'Your mother wants you back at work and I know she's a force to be reckoned with, so I'm asking how it was to be back at work.'

She curled her feet up beside her on the sofa and took another sip. 'It tastes woody. It's lovely.'

'It's a 2010 Rioja. The label on the shelf said it was silky and there was something about chocolate, coffee, herbs and spices. It was recommended in the paper at the weekend and I went looking for it.' They sat in silence for a few moments and Nick wished for a crackling log fire to complete the ambience.

'I didn't enjoy being back there today.' She spoke softly and he opened his mouth to speak, and then stopped. Listening would be better.

'Have we done the right thing?' She leapt up from the sofa and perched on the coffee table so they were face to face. 'I mean, nothing's gone right since we arrived. You're up to your eyes, I'm back in Mum's thrall, the kids are unhappy and...'

'Truffles is enjoying himself. Woods, clifftops, beaches... he's happy.'

She put her glass down and reached for his hand. 'We're not.'

It was late and Nick felt tired. If he had known there was to be an intense and emotional conversation, he would not have started the second bottle. He was also conscious that he would be facing Sam's old boyfriend, Graham Fletcher, in the morning and he preferred to do that after a good night's sleep and without dark smudges under his eyes.

'When I went to fetch the kids, I could see they were miserable, so I told Mum I wouldn't be going in tomorrow. There are no more funerals this week and only four in storage. Steven might be back by the weekend.'

Nick concentrated hard on keeping any hint of jubilation from his face. 'What's the score about Steven? Has he fallen out with your mother?'

'Not that she's admitting. It's come to a head because there was a call-out on Sunday to collect a bariatric case and it was all hands on deck. Even though Steven usually limits himself to front of house, he's gone out on a couple of similar cases, so they called his mobile. It went straight to messages and he hasn't responded to anything since. Everyone's been covering for him not being there, but the bariatric caused them a problem, so they got in touch with mum and ratted on him. I tried him today, but the number's ringing out so his message store must be full.'

'Have you checked the petty cash?'

'Nick!' She pulled her hand away. 'How could you think such a thing?'

'He must have his reasons. Has anyone been to his flat?'

'I drove round at lunchtime. The curtains are closed and nobody came when I rang the bell. For all I know, he could be dead behind the door.'

'If he is, I hope he's not expecting a discount. Can't see Dotty authorising that.'

Sam didn't want to smile, but it broke through anyway and this time, Nick reached forward and took both her hands in his. 'Once we've moved and the kids have settled in at school, we can get back to what this is all about. We're here for a better lifestyle and a renovation project to die for. It'll sort itself out, you'll see.' He brought her hands to his mouth one by one and kissed them.

'Better not be "to die for,"' she said, 'I can't see Mum authorising a discount for you, either.'

<u>Chapter 28</u>

Wednesday 12th February

Next morning, Morgan arrived at the coffee shop first and purchased two flat whites. He had no idea of Spence's preferences but thought he had picked a safe option. He didn't usually take sugar in coffee but stirred in the contents of the brown sachet figuring it couldn't harm.

It had been a late night and he and Sam had talked freely about everything that had already happened and a few things that might happen once they got access to Cliffside. When they had at last got to bed there had been the added bonus of unexpected sex. Sam had asked him to keep the light on and when he reached to put on pyjama bottoms she had shaken her head. 'Not tonight, Nick. Just get into bed.'

Sitting at the back of the coffee shop, he remembered her lying against him, her head supported by his right arm. She had combed her fingers through the greying hairs on his chest. 'How soundproof do you think these walls are?' she'd asked.

'There's a hall and bathrooms between us and them. Anyway, they should be asleep by now.' He stroked her face, neck and breasts until her breathing became faster and more shallow. She started to grab at him and he'd felt scratching across his torso and thighs. Their need was urgent and he knew he was being less gentle than usual.

Later, when they lay in each other's arms, she'd started to cry. He'd held her tightly to him. 'I'm sorry. I'm so sorry. Have I hurt you?'

She'd shaken her head. 'Jesus Christ, Nick. I know it's been a while, but where did that come from?' He'd kissed the top of her head and stroked her until she fell asleep but he was troubled and lay on his back staring into the darkness. As he'd climaxed, he'd only just stopped himself from crying out Maisie's name. For Christ's sake, what was that about?

'You look like you had your Weetabix this morning.' He was brought back to the present by the arrival of Dave Spence and he pushed the coffee towards him.

'It's a flat white with no sugar.'

'If it's hot and it's wet it'll do me, thank you, sir.' Morgan smiled.

If the outside of the building which housed Fletcher, Armstrong & Gault solicitors had the appearance of 1980's corporate offices, the interior design was pure twenty-first century. The core colour palette was black, white and a soft grey and each of the offices had its own feature colour. Reception was highlighted with acid lime cushions on the black sofas and there was a huge pot containing a healthy weeping fig.

Behind the receptionist hung a picture which comprised of vertical black, white and lime stripes with random silver splash marks from bottom left to top right. Spence nodded towards it whilst they waited for her to finish a call. 'What do you think Dr Mack would make of that splatter pattern?'

Morgan smiled. 'He'd say that the cause of death was lack of artistic merit.'

Replacing her receiver, the receptionist acknowledged them both and glanced at each I.D. in turn. She invited them to sit and offered refreshments whilst she contacted Graham Fletcher. Morgan refused politely on behalf of them both and hovered near her desk. Spence reached out and rubbed a leaf of the plant between thumb and forefinger. 'It's real,' he said so that only Morgan would hear. 'You can get realistic fake ones which would be a lot less bother.'

Morgan continued to watch the receptionist who seemed to be sending a text. He leaned over the desk and placed his hand on the receiver of the receptionist's phone. 'Could I ask you to ring Mr Fletcher, please? To tell him that we're waiting.'

Without looking up, she replied that Mr Fletcher preferred to be contacted by text when visitors were in reception. 'He finds it less intrusive.'

'Ring him, please, Sylvia. Now!' Her silver badge had provided her name and he lifted the receiver and held it out for her. As her gaze met his it was obvious that she was preparing to stand her ground. The look on Morgan's face was persuasive and Sylvia took the receiver and punched a few numbers. The conversation was short. She explained that police officers had turned up without an appointment but that they were most insistent on seeing Mr Fletcher. It also transpired during the exchange that Fletcher's next client had not yet arrived thus opening a "window of opportunity." She gave assurance that the visit wasn't going to take long. Morgan and Spence exchanged a glance. Morgan was of the opinion that these things took as long as they took.

A door opened and a short woman appeared. She was wearing black shoes with dangerously high heels which Morgan thought must be to compensate for her height.

She strode towards them, her demeanour purposeful and businesslike. There were no creases in her black pencil skirt and the white blouse, which buttoned over a full bosom, didn't gape. From years of sitting outside changing rooms waiting for his wife, Morgan knew that both of these were tricky fashion traits to pull off.

'I am Marcia Mulholland, Mr Fletcher's personal assistant. He will be leaving for court very soon and has asked if this can wait.' She assessed the two men for seniority then focused her attention on Morgan who held out his ID for scrutiny.

'I'm DI Morgan and this is DS Spence. We're here to speak to Mr Fletcher about the death of your colleague.' He returned the ID to his inside pocket. 'I heard that there was a "window of opportunity,"' he used the first two fingers of both hands to draw quotation marks around the three words. Mulholland scowled at Sylvia as she led the men to the inner door. Clearly, there would be further conversation between them later.

Following her down the corridor, Morgan clenched and unclenched his fists. One of his reasons for not wanting to move to Gullhaven had been his suspicion that Fletcher had never really accepted that Samantha had chosen him. When they met socially at weddings and funerals of mutual acquaintances, Fletcher was inappropriately informal and physical with Sam and Morgan hated him for it. He inhaled deeply as Mulholland opened the door and braced himself for the encounter.

Chapter 29

Graham Fletcher's office was in a corner of the building and had wide windows which faced the fire station in one direction and had a view of the flyover in the other. The curtains, sofa cushions and coat stand were a muted scarlet. There was a wall with two rows of framed items including photographs and professional certificates. Looking round Morgan could see none of the bookshelves laden with legal volumes and piles of papers which he normally associated with local solicitor practices. This could be a consulting room for an aesthetic surgeon.

Fletcher sat at a black desk and was typing at an open laptop which was cabled to a second large monitor. There was a red desk lamp shining on his work area but the rest of the office was lit only by the muted February light coming through the windows. In spite of the gloom, Fletcher's crisp white shirt seemed to fluoresce as if he was surrounded by an aura.

He stood and held out a hand to Morgan. 'Good to see you Nick. Take a seat, gentlemen, please.' He pointed to the visitor chairs pulled up to his desk. He strode to the office door, each step confident and assertive. When he flicked a couple of switches the room brightened with the glow from a central fitting and modern wall lights. Morgan sat while Spence held back, standing by the wall from where he could watch both men.

Back in his chair, Fletcher wheeled it up to his desk, leant forward and rested his chin on his clasped hands. 'It's good to see you here in Gullhaven, Nick. I know Sammy must be pleased to be home.'

Morgan winced at the pet name which only this man used. 'Thank you Graham. How is Sadie, and Joshua, of course?'

'We divorced three years ago. She's living in Hertfordshire in a six bedroom house with a pool and tennis court and a heart surgeon... and Josh.'

'I'm sorry,' said Nick and Fletcher shrugged.

'Don't be. We had a few happy years, but the rest were pretty miserable. She's okay now and I'm free to search for my happy ever after.' His fleeting smile was predatory. 'So, how can I help?'

The "happy ever after" comment hung in the room like a cloud of toxic gas and Morgan struggled not to react. Sam's previous relationship with this man might be common knowledge at the police station and he didn't want Spence to see that he still considered the solicitor a threat to his marriage.

Fletcher was taller than Morgan and thinner too, as the well tailored shirt demonstrated. His face was tanned, with white areas around the eyes resulting from wearing sunglasses or maybe ski goggles. His hair was darker than Morgan remembered from their last encounter, probably dyeing it, he thought; and blown dry. He had a precisely edged beard which reminded Morgan of the estate agent who had valued their house in London and who had flirted with Sam.

'There's not a lot I can tell you about Abi, Nick. She worked here for about a year and was due to be married last Saturday but I'm sure you know all that.'

Morgan leant back in his chair, his eyes never leaving Fletcher's. 'It's background I'm looking for. What was she like? Was she popular at work? Were you pleased with her work? Did she socialise with colleagues? Did she socialise with you, Graham?'

Fletcher sighed as if humouring small child. 'She was popular at work, both with colleagues and clients. Some of our frequent flyer toerags had begun to ask for her by name so she was building a client list and of course, that is attractive to the partners. She was bubbly, pretty, and excited about getting married. I don't know what else to tell you.'

'She wasn't looking very bubbly and pretty when I saw her,' said Morgan. Fletcher's lips pursed.

Morgan gave a small nod to Spence who stepped forward, inviting himself into the conversation. 'I met with Ms Slater's flatmate yesterday,' he said. 'She told me that you had extended Abi's workplace probation period, not once, but twice or more. Why was that, Mr Fletcher? Oh, and why would you not think that we would find that relevant to our investigation?'

For the first time since their arrival, Graham Fletcher looked uncomfortable. He turned his attention back to Morgan.

'I try not to speak ill of the dead, Nick, and...'

'Force yourself,' Spence interrupted.

Fletcher's eyes flicked between the two men again before he continued. 'As I was saying, I don't like to speak ill of the dead, but, if you feel it may be relevant, I can tell you that there were some issues with Abigail. The partners were uncomfortable with her social life and some of the people she was seen with.'

'We'll need more than that,' said Morgan. 'We'll need names.'

'The substance of the rumour was that Abi sometimes liked the bad boys. She met up with clients outside of the court environment.'

'Her own clients?' Spence asked.

'Hers, mine, others who used the practice and I heard also, friends of clients. I don't have details as such.'

'I see,' said Morgan 'but this stopped when she met her fiancé?'

Fletcher's developing smile was without warmth. 'Again, this is only rumour you understand, but I'm told she had a boyfriend who she was still seeing and by seeing, I mean fucking, even as the wedding banns were being read. The gossip was that it was Steven Cooper, Sammy's brother. Am I right in thinking he has disappeared?'

Neither officer reacted to Fletcher's revelation immediately. When Morgan glanced at Spence, he was flicking through his notebook. 'I'm certain that Ms Slater's flatmate wasn't able to provide any names. I would have remembered that one.'

'I'm surprised you didn't know,' said Fletcher. 'Gullhaven is such a small town, both in size and mentality. I was sure someone would have already mentioned it. Dorothy was against it and I think she and Steven fell out over it. When I told her that Abi had paired up with a futures dealer and they were getting married, she was ecstatic. Now, if we've finished here... He looked at his Hublot watch. 'I'm due in court later.'

Morgan rose from the chair and followed Spence to the door. As Spence opened it, Fletcher called out. 'Oh Nick, do tell Sammy that I'm looking forward to catching up with her on Sunday.'

'Sunday?' asked Morgan.

'Yes, at the youth football sponsors' charity dinner. Now that Steven has done a runner I'm told Sammy's going to be representing the company. Hasn't she told you? Oh dear, I'm sorry if I've put my foot in it.' The smug smile was still on his face as Morgan shut the door behind them.

The officers walked to the car in an uncomfortable silence which Spence broke. 'I'll check with DC Smart, sir, but I'm certain that the flatmate never mentioned your brother-in-law. I remember she said that Abi had met boyfriends through work and we pushed her on that, but she didn't have any names.'

Morgan's reply was almost inaudible over the noise of the passing traffic. 'Perhaps after they extended her probationary period, she decided to keep her relationships secret. It seems there are a lot of secrets in this place.'

Chapter 30

The paperboy who delivered to Doreen and Ronald Bradley's bungalow in Gullhaven Cove each morning, was always careful to close the gate behind him. When they left him a Christmas card at the newsagent, they'd enclosed a twenty pound note and Mrs Bradley had asked him to be sure to secure the gate as they were planning on buying a dog after being recently burgled.

When he reached their home at ten past seven on Thursday morning, he leant his bike against the wooden fence and paused at the wide open gate. He saw a light in the bathroom and walked up the path with their paper and Doreen's monthly craft magazine. Their letterbox was small so he slid the glass porch door open and left them on a shelf inside. When he turned to retrace his steps, he noticed a shadow across their lawn. It looked like something was propped up against the tree in the middle of the garden, but he couldn't make out what it was. He was unsure whether to investigate. If he ignored it, he could complete his round and get home in time to go through some last minute formulae for this morning's maths test. Remembering the twenty pound note, he walked across the grass.

He knew that Mrs Bradley had a difficult life coping with Ronald's arthritis and more recently, his Alzheimer's. The burglary had shaken her because it had happened when they were at home and asleep. Precious photos had been taken for their silver frames as well as Mrs Bradley's handbag containing money, bank cards and house keys. When he knocked on their door on Christmas Eve to give them a card and to thank them for their gift, she told him that the police had caught the burglar but that he had pleaded not guilty at the Magistrates' Court. There was a trial scheduled for March. None of their stolen items had been traced.

He approached the bundle with care and circled round it. He saw legs with trainers on the feet. If it had been November, he might have thought that someone had dumped their bonfire night Guy, especially as it seemed to have a cardboard sign around its neck. It was still too dark to make out any writing on it. He returned to the Bradley's front door and rang the bell.

As the newest member of the Major Crimes Unit, DI Nick Morgan had the smallest caseload and was first choice for a call out. He had been at his desk for an hour when the Control Room Inspector rung through and told him that he was needed to attend a scene at Gullhaven Cove. Uniformed officers had found a slumped body under a tree in the front garden of a bungalow which had been burgled a few months before.

'Down and out?' he asked.

'Unlikely in Gullhaven, sir, and we usually refer to them as rough sleepers.'

Morgan rolled his eyes and took down the address. Having driven past the end of it, he knew it was a cul-de-sac off one of the main roads which ran down to the cliffs.

'Who reported it?'

There was a tapping of keys at the other end of the line. 'Apparently the paperboy found him and got the householder to come and have a look. She rang 999 but when the responders got there, life was extinct. We've got a medic on the way to do the necessary.'

Morgan took a last sip of his coffee then reached for the black leather jacket he had slung over his chair. It was colder here than London and he was pleased he had it with him. He was looking forward to getting more of his clothes out of storage because somewhere, he had a thick wool coat that he would have welcomed on a morning like this. He phoned Spence as he walked to his car and they agreed to meet at the scene.

Samantha Morgan dried her hands and answered her mobile.

'Samantha,' it was her mother, 'I've got the keys and I need you to collect me and take me to Cliffside so I can see the damage for myself. I'll be ready at ten thirty.'

It was ten o'clock and Samantha had planned to do some washing and then take the twins shopping for the remaining items needed for school.

'It's not all that convenient, Mum. We've bought a few more bits and pieces of clothes, but I'm having to do some washing every day until we get moved in and have all our own stuff. Could it wait 'til tomorrow?'

'The sooner we can see what needs to be done before you move in, the sooner you can move in. Of course, if you're too busy then I'm sorry to have disturbed you.' Samantha waited for click which would end the call and put her on the wrong side of the argument, but it didn't come. It seemed her mother was determined to visit Cliffside and may be open to negotiation.

'I'll need to find someone to look after the twins because I don't want them seeing anything that might distress them. Could we make it two o'clock?'

Dorothy sighed dramatically and waited in the hope that Samantha would defer. Her daughter knew the tactic well. She sometimes used it with Nick, albeit with mixed success. Whoever held out the longest before speaking would win and with all the jobs she had to complete today, she was determined it would be her.

Dorothy sighed again, louder this time. 'Very well, I'll see you at two. Before you go, any news from Steven?'

'No, Mum. I'm sure he'll contact you first. He'll need to apologise, won't he?'

'What do you mean "apologise?" Why would he have to apologise?' She sounded agitated.

'I know you two must have had a row, even if you won't admit it. He'll come back when he's had time to think about it.'

Dorothy tutted. 'It's very inconvenient. He knows that winter is our busiest time. You need to be helping us out in the office at the very least.'

'It's half term, Mum, and a funeral home is not the most child friendly place.'

There was a chorus from the dining table where Alexander and Victoria were clearing away their breakfast plates and mugs. 'We're not children.'

Samantha shushed them. 'The staff were doing okay when I was there a couple of days ago. It's not too busy at the moment.'

'We'll discuss it when you come this afternoon,' said Dorothy and this time she did end the call.

'Looking forward to it, mother,' said Samantha, although she wasn't.

Chapter 31

Like many of the roads in Gullhaven Cove, Baxter Close was narrow and ended in a tight turning circle. The properties were all bungalows, set back from the road to accommodate large front gardens, many with mature trees and borders. Spring was still some weeks away but Morgan noticed a few brave snowdrops in flower and a scattering of early crocuses. The boundary, marked by police tape, enclosed the garden of number eighteen and the pavement outside. Across the road, a few neighbours were standing together taking a keen interest in this unprecedented activity.

Morgan recognised some of the CSI team members from Abi Slater's deposition site and a few of them returned his nods of recognition as they went about the task of photographing the body from every angle. Others were on hands and knees combing through damp blades of grass in their search for evidence. He saw an elderly man, wrapped in a thick dressing gown, and with a duvet over his legs, sitting in Spence's car.

'That's Mr Bradley, sir.' It was a woman's voice from behind his left shoulder. Morgan turned to see DC Smart and grimaced by way of greeting. 'He's got Alzheimer's and Dave... that's DS Spence, sir, thought he'd be safest and least confused by all the comings and goings if he sat in the car. He's got the heater on and a cup of tea.'

'Lucky him,' said Morgan wrapping his jacket tighter around him against the biting west wind. 'What do we know... if anything?'

Smart opened her notebook. 'Probably not a lot more that you've already heard. It was called in at half seven this morning after the paperboy found the body. DS Spence has let him go to school because he has a maths test this morning, but we've sent a uniformed officer with him and she'll bring him to the station as soon as he's finished it.' Morgan nodded but wasn't pleased. Witnesses gave their best information when everything was freshest in their minds. God knows what detail would be overwritten by Pythagoras or Venn diagrams.

Dr Mackenzie straightened painfully from his crouching position and walked to Morgan and Smart who were standing on the pavement.

'I'm glad you came here, sonny,' he said to Morgan. 'If you keep this up, my memoirs are going to stretch to three volumes. All money in the bank, you know.'

'Good morning to you, Dr Mackenzie. Glad to be of service.'

Mackenzie chuckled. Morgan had been told that most officers avoided engaging in banter with the pathologist who had a reputation for ferocity. Morgan wasn't scared.

'Time and cause of death, doctor please and...' he looked over the top of the pathologist's right shoulder, 'What's he got in his lap?'

'Round his neck rather than in his lap,' said Mackenzie.

'Okay,' Morgan held his hands up. 'So now I need when, how and what.'

'I'm a man of few words myself, DI Morgan,' said Mackenzie, his soft Scottish accent broader now. 'And

115

as a special offer, I'll add a provisional where.' Smart held her notebook ready in anticipation, but he shook his head. 'Be patient DC Smart, it'll be in the report and that'll come after the postmortem.' Morgan decided that he liked this man even more for staying with the traditional English term rather than the American preference for "autopsy."

'There's bruising round the neck, possibly from smooth cord or a thin belt. Life extinct between twenty four and thirty six hours ago. He wasn't killed here, the body was moved. And there's a piece of cardboard hanging round his neck on string. The technicians will bag it and submit it into evidence but you may wish to know that there's a message on it. It says "Now I'm sorry," and there's what I used to call a smiley face except the mouth is upside down.'

'It's an emoji,' said Smart.

'That's the emoji for sad, not sorry,' said Morgan and Smart's face betrayed her amazement. 'If I say twelve year old twins?' he replied and she nodded, smiling.

'Well, I'll leave you to continue talking like twelve year old twins then,' said Mackenzie. 'It'll be two o'clock at the mortuary. Don't be late.' He walked towards the open gate and then removed the protective booties and coveralls which he handed to the uniformed officer stationed at the scene boundary.

'Do you want me to go to the PM?' asked Smart.

'Spence can go, but if you're working towards your Girl Guides mortuary badge, you can go with him. Can you also organise a team for door to door please, before everyone goes off to work?'

'There's no hurry, sir. This is Gullhaven. Most of the residents in this street will be retired. They'll be sitting up in bed with the day's first cup of tea.'

Morgan looked at the bungalows surrounding them. 'I've already seen a few curtains twitch, and there's an audience,' he nodded at the small group of observers.

'I still don't think there's any hurry, but I'll get in touch with Ops.' He nodded and they both turned their attention back to the body.

'What are you thinking about the sign around the neck?' she asked.

'I'm thinking that I've never seen a piece of cardboard left with a body in all my years, and now I've seen two in four days. Do they all come with labels in this jurisdiction?'

She shook her head. 'Not that I've noticed.'

'Have a word with whoever bags it and ask them to compare it with what was left of the card in Abi Slater's lap.' She made a note.

'What about a comparison of the inks. Wasn't there ink absorbed into the wedding dress?'

'Yes, let's ask for that too, but you're definitely not going to make any friends at the labs. Now, do you know where Mrs Bradley is? I'll have a word with her first and then let's see if we can persuade them to pack a couple of bags and stay away from here for a while.' He glanced again at Mr Bradley who had fallen asleep in Spence's car. 'Poor sod,' he said.

<u>Chapter 32</u>

Thursday 13th February

He hadn't been back to the Magistrates' Court since
Abigail Slater's body had been found and he'd missed
his visits. His employer owed him four hours and
insisted that he take it as time off rather than money, so
he'd gone into town and taken his place at the back of
Court One where the remand cases were being heard.
With no possibility of seeing Abi, the building seemed
dowdier today, the lighting less bright; the staff less
friendly.

When the bench retired, he went back to the waiting
area to see what else was going on. There were more
people milling about than usual, and it was noisy. The
chairs were arranged differently since his last visit; now,
in rows which alternated between facing each other and
back-to-back.

He first noticed them when he came out of the toilets.
Father and son, or maybe old lag and apprentice? They
caught his attention because they looked furtive. Their
heads were close together and they regularly stopped,
looking around as if checking who was listening. Since
childhood, he had always needed to know what people
didn't want him to know. Their behaviour singled them
out. It was just a matter of how to get closer without
scaring them off.

An usher hurried out of Court Three, his gown
billowing out behind him as the difference in air
pressures between the court and the foyer caught it.

'James Weaver to Court Three, please. James Weaver to Court Three.'

Four men rose together and followed the usher. One was wearing a suit which didn't fit and the others had made no effort to smarten up for their outing. They had vacated seats behind his targets and he made for them. Another couple came and took the two furthest away seats. He smiled at the woman and sat next to her. He took out his phone and concentrated hard on the screen whilst his ears scanned the surrounding voices, searching for the conversation behind him.

'The containers are already in the car park and the tools will be delivered on the twenty second. It's all sorts. Drills, saws, grinders, you name it. They're stocking up for the Easter DIY binge in April and there isn't enough room in the warehouse. It'll be the easiest thing we've ever done.' The older man was excited and breathing heavily; the breath of a man who'd smoked a lot of prison roll ups.

'Has to be the Monday after, though, cos I'm at Crawley court the next day an' if I'm goin' down, you an' your mum's gonna need the readies.'

There was a delay and he felt his chair move. The younger man behind him was looking round again. 'I don't know,' he said at last, his voice high pitched. 'Even if we get the stuff, who's gonna take it off our hands?'

'Let me worry about that. We can get it up to Scotland and your mum's cousin can sell the stuff online or at the car boot.'

The conversation ended and they sat in silence until a muffled name was called over the Tannoy. Both men got up and made their way to Court Two.

His eyes pursued them. He waited for proceedings to get started before following them and taking his place at the back of court. He was too late to catch their names and addresses, but he watched them plead not guilty to a number of thefts from student accommodation. Two laptops, a bank card, some jewellery, cash and a bicycle. To his disgust, the scumbags were released on bail. What was wrong with these magistrates?

He was back at work early, but nobody noticed.

Chapter 33

Samantha knew she was going to be late. She'd had no time to do the washing and was forced to add more socks and underwear for everyone to her shopping list. The twins had been difficult because they didn't want to be buying uniforms for a new school they didn't want to go to. They were also sulking because she was going to Cliffside without them. If there was blood, they wanted to see it. Victoria had come to terms with the crime and was keen to be involved.

Her biggest concern was who would babysit while she took her mother to the house. Nick had sent a text telling her he had another new case and with no friends or helpful neighbours to run to, she was stuck. In desperation, she thought of Maisie at the site reception. Their contact had so far been limited to a short conversation about stock cubes and why men were useless at food shopping, but Sam had thought her friendly and kind. She dialled the main estate number while the twins were tucking into scrambled eggs for lunch.

To Samantha's surprise and relief, Maisie told her she was happy to help and that if she dropped the twins off at the office, she would let them watch her TV which had satellite channels. She even volunteered to look after Truffles for which Sam hadn't dared to ask. Upon reaching reception she had hardly stopped the car before Alex and Vicky said hasty goodbyes and raced towards the building's double doors with the family dog bounding after them.

Heavy traffic and some residual flooding added further delay so she was twenty minutes late when she got to Silver Sands. Her mother was standing outside the door, waiting.

Dorothy turned as Samantha drove up. Someone had called out to her. When she looked, Samantha saw a young man run towards her mother. They chatted for a moment before he nodded and ran back in the direction he had come from. For a moment, Samantha thought it was her brother but, when she looked again, she saw that although their features and hairline were similar, this man was a little taller than Steven, longer legs, she thought.

Dorothy got into the car. 'Could you not have rung, I'm frozen.'

'Hi Mum. You should have waited inside. We can always do this another day if you're too cold.' Dorothy was looking at her and Samantha readied herself for a fight but she fastened her seatbelt without further comment.

They got to Cliffside having discussed only the weather and the price of school uniforms. Samantha was unsure what would face them on arrival and superficial conversation seemed inappropriate.

Dorothy handed over the front door key. 'You can do the honours,' she said. 'I had a specialist team come in yesterday. I was told that the deceased was a drug addict so I didn't want to take any chances. They've done something called fogging to kill any pathogens.'

'Good idea, thank you.'

'I'm hoping the house insurance will pay for it. The policy is expensive enough.'

Samantha realised that there were many more expenses that would have to be discussed with Nick and her mother. She hadn't even considered insurance.

The door was reluctant to open. There was a creak as it gave way and both women looked at each other. Neither would be able to confirm later who had laughed first. It was such a cliché. Two women; alone; and opening a creaking door to a property where there had been a recent violent death.

'Who do you think will play me when they make the film?' asked Dorothy.

'Probably Helen Mirren,' said Samantha, 'and me?'

'No idea. Someone with no sense of timekeeping if they're looking for authenticity.'

Samantha detected a faint chemical smell in the hall and she left the front door open to help disperse it. They both looked up to the ceiling to assess the damage to the chandelier.

'Why have they taken it?' asked Dorothy. 'It can't be evidence, can it?'

Samantha shrugged. 'Who knows? Perhaps they need to make sure all the blood belonged to the deceased and not to whoever killed him?' Dorothy snorted her derision.

Next, they scrutinised the black and white tiled floor. There was still no electricity in the house and they relied on daylight coming through the front door. They saw an area of tiles under the missing chandelier which were cleaner than either of the women had ever seen them. The rest of the tiles remained a discoloured pattern of grey and black. Samantha doubted that she would ever manage to merge them.

Upstairs, they started at the back of the house in the room where Carl Raynor had chosen to live. It opened on to the metal fire escape which was added when the house had been a B&B back in the 1990s. There wasn't much to see. The broken window was boarded over and if Raynor had stored any personal property, it had been removed. There were some ashes in the grate and a broken chair which he had been using for firewood. Dorothy picked it up and tossed it to the wall. 'Bloody cheek,' she said, 'that was one of my favourites.' She looked at her fingers which were now coated in black fingerprint powder. 'Oh for God's sake.' She reached into her bag for a wet wipe.

'It couldn't have been a favourite or you'd have taken it with you,' said Samantha. 'He must have been freezing in here, especially with the broken window. Now, shall we go to the bedroom?'

The master bedroom where Nick had found Raynor's body had a large bay window, and even as the light was beginning to fade, they could see that many of the parquet tiles were missing. There were also pieces of sticky tape attached to the remaining tiles. The chemical smell lingered, stronger here than in the hallway.

'This was always my favourite room,' said Dorothy. 'I remember when the estate agent showed us round, your dad and I stood here and I knew that this was the one.' Both women looked out of the window, across to breaking waves topped with the foam which gave them the appearance and name of "white horses." Double glazing and the height of the cliff dulled but did not exclude the crashing of those waves as they battered the shore. It was Samantha's favourite sound and reminded her of childhood.

'I was looking forward to sleeping in this room with the window open in the summer,' said Samantha. She wasn't certain, but she thought she heard her mother say "So was I."

'I'll come back tomorrow and clean the black powder up. Can you take the twins for a couple of hours, please?' Dorothy agreed and suggested, that if Maisie had volunteered to look after the twins for the whole afternoon, they had time to drop in to the pub along the road for a swift gin and tonic. She took a last look out of the window. 'We'd better hurry. It's going to rain. And I also need to talk to you about a charity dinner I'm sending you to on Sunday, dear'

Chapter 34

Morgan looked up from his computer. He welcomed the distraction.

'I've been to the autopsy,' said Spence.

Morgan beckoned to him. 'Come in, Spence, and have a seat. Have we got an I.D. for the garden gnome?'

Dave Spence allowed himself the beginnings of a smile. 'It's another local lad, sir. The appropriately named Wesley Crook. I can tell you, I've seen a few magistrates struggle to keep a straight face when he's turned up. Twenty eight years old with at least a page of previous for every one of those years. On bail for burglary. He pleaded not guilty. Trial was set for next month.'

Morgan nodded as he took in each new fact. 'Drugs?' he asked.

'Mack said that toxicology will take a while but there were no recent track marks and the report will say "well nourished," which doesn't usually indicate a current habit. They'll do the histology to be sure, but Mack says he was strangled. There are marks that show he may have put up quite a fight too, so they might get trace from the clothes and the nails. But the real puzzler is that the burglary he was going to trial for, was at the Bradleys'.'

'What? The bungalow where we found him?'

'Yep. And I'm not much of a one for coincidence, are you?'

Morgan was running a few possibilities through his mind. 'Well it's not likely to have been Mr Bradley as his wife isn't even sure he knows they were burgled. I've met her now and if she weighs in at eight stone it'll be because she was carrying a full shopping bag, so it wasn't her. Any offspring, especially well built, angry offspring?'

Spence said he would get someone to find out. He hadn't seen any family photos in the house because they had been stolen for their silver frames during the burglary.

'Let's get everyone who's in the office together for a late update,' said Morgan and within half an hour, they had all assembled in the briefing room.

'Why would someone put that poor couple through the trauma of dumping a body in their garden when they're still recovering from being burgled?' asked one of the DCs.

Smart was perched on the edge of a desk. 'It's almost like a cat bringing a dead mouse to its owner. "Look what I've brought you, aren't I clever?"'

Morgan was standing by the board where photographs were accumulating. Wesley Crook's criminal record photo had caught him with a hint of a smile. In the crime scene picture, his head hung downwards, face framed by tangled, mousy hair. The picture taken at the mortuary showed the unmistakable marks of a ligature and there were scratches on his neck where he had tried to get his fingers inside the tightening noose. Morgan pointed to the close-up of the cardboard sign around Crook's neck. 'The sign found round his neck says "Now I'm Sorry." Anyone got any thoughts?' he asked.

Spence was quick to respond. 'Obviously, he's sorry about the burglary.'

'If he was that sorry, why not plead guilty and get the discount off his sentence. And I don't think any of us believe this is a suicide, do we?' A few of the team members winced at Morgan's sharpness. 'I'm sorry,' he said, 'that came out harsher than I meant.' Everyone looked to Spence but his face remained stony.

'Two lines of enquiry here,' Morgan drew two arrows on the white board, 'the first is what it says, and the second is where it comes from.'

'How about, now I'm sorry because I've been caught?' suggested DC Leo Jenson who had come into the room having completed his list of tasks for Operation Siren. 'Or even, now I'm sorry because I've been caught and killed?' There were a few murmurs of approval.

'Was he ever done for a burglary before this one?' asked Morgan. One of the other DCs picked up the sheaf of antecedents and read from the front page.

'A lot of shoplifting... and there's a TWOC. Took his mum's car without asking. That resulted in no licence and no insurance. He's stolen bikes from the railway station and sold them online.' She turned the page. 'And there's a street robbery where he grabbed a mobile phone from someone who was walking past. Possession Class B, and later, Class A, non payment of fines, breached by probation when he's missed unpaid work, so no, lots of thefts, but only one burglary.'

'So we need to put some thought to that,' said Morgan. 'I've also asked Jenny to liaise with the lab. They're going to compare the cardboard and ink to what we found in the woods.'

When he looked around the room, some of his team were nodding as if this was an obvious next step. One or two looked surprised.

'I'm sorry. I missed the start of the briefing,' said Jenson 'so, for my benefit, are we saying this is linked to Abigail Slater?'

'Truth is, Leo, I don't know. But two cardboard signs in such a short space of time can't be a coincidence, can it? And remember, we didn't release information about the cardboard we found in the woods. Now, it's late so here's what needs doing from first thing tomorrow.'

Morgan listed half a dozen straightforward tasks which he hoped would progress the investigations into both the Slater and the Crook murders. Finally, he said 'Spence and I will do the death visit. Parents or partner?' he asked, looking straight at Spence who shrugged.

DC Smart answered for him. 'His mother lives locally and he always gives her contact details when he's detained.'

'Right then. Change of plan. You and I will visit Mrs Crook and see what she's got to tell us.'

As they walked away, Dave Spence mumbled, 'She was never married to Wes's dad. If you call her "Mrs," she'll kick your arse. Prick.'

Chapter 35

DC Jenny Smart set off in the direction of the three year old red Renault which was her pride and joy.

'It's okay, I'll drive,' said Morgan. 'You navigate. It'll help me get my bearings'

It was a twenty minute journey to an estate which comprised maisonettes in small blocks connected by walkways between stairwells. He parked by the kerb and followed Smart into a square which was a rubbish tip of abandoned broken toys and parts of bicycles as well as a pile of black bin bags in varying stages of degradation. All that was missing was the ubiquitous settee with floral upholstery which seemed to feature at every fly-tipping site.

'It's that one, in the corner,' said Smart nodding towards the property. 'I've arrested him on warrant a couple of times. His mother can be difficult but, as she's got older, she's been less aggressive and more resigned. She knows me.'

'Have you done a death visit before?' asked Morgan and she nodded. 'Are you happy to lead, then?' She agreed and when they reached the door her knock on the glazed panel was loud and confident. Morgan glanced at his watch and she raised her hand to knock again. He touched her arm. 'It's okay, someone's coming.'

The door was opened by a woman who looked to be in her fifties but could have been younger and had a hard life. A ruddy complexion betrayed her acquaintance with a vodka bottle. Her jumper was covered by a tabard and her black trousers were faded by frequent washing, and frayed at the hem. She looked at him first, before turning her gaze to Smart.

'Oh, it's you. He's not here and I'm leaving for work, so, if you don't mind...' She reached behind her for a bag and keys which were sitting on a narrow hall shelf. She gripped the door handle and yanked it so she could close it with them all on the outside. Morgan extended his arm to hold it open.

'He's not here and you're not coming in without a warrant.' Wesley's mother lifted a fist towards his flexed arm but Smart caught her wrist and gripped it. 'Sharon, we know he's not here. We need to talk to you about him and it'd be better if we did it inside.' Their eyes met and Sharon Crook seemed to realise that this visit was going to be different. Her feistiness drained from her. She dropped her bag and keys as she grabbed at Jenny Smart's shoulders for support. Morgan bent to gather the items and they escorted her back into the flat and to a grubby chair in the living room. He went to the kitchen and put the kettle on, then looked for mugs, tea bags, milk and sugar. Tea making was the role of the number two on a death visit, regardless of rank.

Her howl of anguish pinpointed the exact moment Sharon received the news and he leant on the sink and exhaled. Wesley Crook had brought trouble to his mother's door from a young age but like most parents, her love for him was unconditional. Now, he had broken her heart forever.

When he took the three mugs of tea into the sitting room, DC Jenny Smart was seated at the end of a settee angled towards Sharon's chair. 'I didn't know about milk and sugar,' he said, 'so I put them on the tray.' The women looked at three unmatched mugs, each with a tea bag still floating in the steaming water, a bag of caster sugar and a two pint plastic container of semi-skimmed milk without its green top.

'He's not used to this, then?' asked Sharon.

A weak smile crossed Smart's face when she replied. 'It's not often a requirement of the rank of DI if I'm honest.'

'Just as well.'

Smart rose, took the tray from his hands and nodded at him to show that he should take the seat she had vacated. She asked each how they liked their tea and took the tray to the kitchen.

'I've known her since she was a rookie,' said Sharon Crook. 'You be nice to her, she's a good one.'

'I've not been here long,' he replied, 'but I agree. I'm not sure how far DC Smart got in explaining what's happened.'

'Not much to explain. He was in a garden and even though you lot probably saw more of him than I did, I need to come and identify him. Last time I saw him, he told me he was off the drugs. He looked better too. Had a bit of weight on him and he'd been doing a bit of labouring and got a tan.'

Morgan looked out at the darkening February evening and asked her when she had seen him.

'He was with some girl over Christmas so, not since October. He rang now and again, said he was up in Glasgow with this girl and that he'd see me soon. Never gonna see me now, is he?'

'He was found in a garden,' said Morgan.

'I know. She told me.'

'The circumstances were a bit odd.'

'What do you mean?'

Smart came back with the teas. She sat at the other end of the settee and took out her notebook and pen.

Morgan took a sip before he spoke. 'Ms Crook, he...'

'You can call me Sharon.'

'Okay, thank you, Sharon. I'm sorry to have to tell you that we believe he may have been murdered.'

She looked at him and her jaw slackened, then she looked around him to Jenny Smart as if she trusted her more. 'Murdered? Not an overdose?'

Smart put her mug down on the floor. 'That's what we think. Do you know of anyone who would do that to him?'

She thought for a while. 'I haven't seen him this last five or six months. He was in Glasgow. When did he get back here?'

Morgan told her about the burglary and the upcoming trial and that he had been found in the garden of the bungalow he was accused of breaking into. He asked again if she could think of anyone who would do such a thing.

'Whoever lives there I should think,' suggested Sharon Crook. 'I'd kill anyone who broke in here.' Suddenly, she stood up and made for the door, knocking Jenny Smart's mug over and spilling the tea on the rug. 'Wait there,' she called over her shoulder.

Smart got up and collected a roll of cheap, thin kitchen paper. She was dabbing at the stain when Sharon came back with an envelope. 'This came for him a while back. Someone must have put it through the door. I opened it so I could tell him about it when he next rang.'

'Please put it on the table without opening it again,' said Morgan.

'It's a letter, not a fuckin' bomb.'

133

'Please just do as I ask. Have you a polythene bag for us to put it in?'

Jenny Smart reached into her shoulder bag. 'It's okay. I've got evidence bags here. I always carry a couple.'

'Do you remember what it says?' asked Morgan.

'Not really. Something about his behaviour, I think.'

'Is it signed?'

'Of course it's not signed. Even his name on the front's been stencilled. It was some sort of threat about changing his ways. Something like "change your ways or you'll be sorry," or something. Well he probably is sorry now, don't you think?'

Chapter 36

Friday 14th February

Sam was delighted when Nick handed her a bunch of red carnations and a Valentine's card at breakfast. She had forgotten all about it. She would have to look for something for him while she was shopping.

'Have you seen my keys?' asked Nick.

'I put them in your jacket pocket.' Sam watched him check. 'When will you be back? I want to talk about the move.'

'Not sure. I'll text you.'

Nick was always more distant when he was in the middle of an investigation, but she thought there was more to it this time. He'd barely spoken to her since getting back from work on Wednesday.

'Cliffside is covered in fingerprint powder, but I don't want to wait. I'd like to move in as soon as possible, especially with the kids starting school next week. We're on the wrong side of Gullhaven here and the school run will be a nightmare.'

Nick was reading something on his phone as he replied. 'Just arrange what you want. I'm happy with that.'

'I rang the removal company when Mum and I were in the pub but they'd closed for the night. I'll get on to them first thing. Can you speak to the gas and electric companies?'

He shook his head. 'I'm sorry, Sam. I can't.' He kissed her cheek, ignoring the disapproving comments from the twins. He grabbed his briefcase and headed for the door. 'I'll text you.'

'Oh, before I forget,' she said, 'Mum wants me to represent the company at some charity do on Sunday evening. She asked me yesterday. Apparently, Steven usually goes, but with him vanishing, she told me I'd have to go instead.'

He turned back. 'But you're old enough not to have to do everything she tells you. Besides, we won't have our clothes by then. What would you wear?'

'I've got the dress I packed for dinner at the Spa.' Her tone was defensive.

'Yes, of course.'

'Mum thought it would be a good opportunity for me to catch up with my old friends. Let them know I'm back.'

'Of course she did,' he said, this time leaving without looking back.

The soonest Samantha Morgan could organise the reconnection of services to Cliffside was the following Wednesday and when she rang the removals company they could only offer a smaller van than was ideal for the day after. The man she spoke to told her it would need two trips and that there would be an additional payment to cover mileage. Samantha agreed instantly. She was tired of the park home and of not being surrounded by her own things. She sent a text to Nick to ask if he could put in for a couple of days leave although she already knew what his answer would be.

She took the twins to stay with Dorothy before driving to one of the retail warehouse sites to buy what she needed to make a start on cleaning Cliffside. As she put the key in the front door she remembered that the water had still not been turned on. Her shoulders dropped, the enthusiasm she felt when she'd got up this morning gone now. Another text to Nick.

Any chance you can pop over to get the water running? Xx

She wandered round the rooms, mentally positioning their furniture and pictures but when there was no reply, she stacked her recent purchases in a corner of the hall, closed and locked the squeaky front door, and set off for town.

The receptionist at the Aphrodite Hair and Beauty Spa flicked back and forward between the screens on her computer. 'Friday is one of our very busy days,' she told Samantha. 'We recommend making an appointment.'

'I'm hoping you can help me. I've just moved here and am looking for a beautician. This formal occasion has come up at short notice and I'm a bit of an emergency case.' The receptionist gave her an appraising glance and did not dispute the comment. Samantha scowled and decided that whatever happened, she would never be a regular here.

'Simone can do your hair at 2pm and we have a trainee who can do your nails now. I've nobody available for a facial or a spray tan until the middle of next week.' The girl's smile was patronising but Samantha was desperate. She took a seat and waited for the trainee.

Chapter 37

'All I said was, I'd prefer you not to go.' Nick Morgan looked at his wife, dressed in the outfit she had bought for their dinner together at the Riverview Hotel. His heart sank. She looked stunning and Graham Fletcher would think the same. He had not mentioned that he knew the solicitor would be attending - the topic of Graham Fletcher invariable caused friction in the Morgan household which would inevitably escalate into a full argument.

'Mum needs someone there to represent the company and with Steven still AWOL, that leaves me.'

'Why can't she go herself? I've never known her not be able to do something when she wants to.'

'I asked her and she said she wouldn't be comfortable sitting for that long and that the food is always too rich. She doesn't want to offend by leaving it on the plate.'

'She could shove it in her handbag,' he murmured.

'It's one evening, Nick, and she is giving us the house.'

'I hope that's not what I'm going to be hearing for the rest of my life. I hope that every time she does something that pisses us off, you don't feel obliged to say "she's giving us the house." She's giving us the house so that I will spend my every waking hour fixing it up. Then what? We don't know, do we?'

Sam glanced through the blind. 'My taxi's here. If I don't set off now, I'll be late and it'll get back to her.' She kissed him on his cheek and left.

He sat down on the sofa and Victoria threw herself down beside him.

'I don't understand why Mum has to go. Just cos grandma says.'

He reached an arm around her and pulled her close. 'No, darling, neither do I.'

The Cooper family's involvement with their local youth football team had begun when Steven started playing for them. When he lost interest, his father continued to go along to matches and fund-raising events until a deal was struck and the family business became one of the club's main sponsors. In the absence of her husband, and now her son, Dorothy Cooper had been adamant that Samantha attend the annual dinner.

The taxi dropped her off at the impressive entrance to East Gullhaven Country Club and Samantha regarded the steep steps with trepidation. She took her time, wary of the high heeled shoes she had chosen to compliment her elegant black cocktail dress. Nick had loved this dress when she bought it, although she thought it might be a little too short. This was the first time she had worn it and she knew Nick was right. She looked and felt good in it. She returned the envious glances of a few women with confidence, and held the stares of admiring men.

'I remember those legs.' The familiar voice came from behind but she didn't turn in case she lost her balance. At the top of the stairs, she felt an arm curl around her waist and Graham Fletcher's mouth touched her right ear. 'In fact,' he whispered, 'I remember being between those legs.' Samantha felt her cheeks flush and checked to see if anyone was within earshot.

'That was a very long time ago,' she replied. 'And where is your beard? You had a beard when I saw you at Becka's wedding.' His arm was steering her through the noisy swarm of people greeting each other in the reception hall. She took in the sparkly sequins and smelled expensive perfumes as she was propelled towards the cloakroom. Fletcher leaned in closer and whispered, 'The beard went when I knew you'd be here. You always preferred me clean shaven.' He manoeuvred her in front of him. 'I'll have to follow on behind you, Sammy, because I've got the biggest hard-on just remembering our times together. I don't want to scare the good people of Gullhaven.'

Her face got hotter. 'Stop it,' she whispered but she was excited by his closeness. She felt his breath on her neck and suddenly she was seventeen again and enjoying being with the best looking boy in school. He was a year older, self-assured and experienced and she was the envy of her peer group. She knew he wasn't faithful but he always came back.

The queue at the cloakroom was long and waiting gave her time to regain her composure. She was determined not to look round but wasn't sure whether she was scared he would still be there, or scared he wouldn't.

Having handed her coat in and stashed the ticket in her clutch bag, Samantha made her way to the bar. It took a while as she stopped to talk to friends she had not seen since leaving Gullhaven twenty years ago.

'Gin and tonic with ice and lemon,' Graham Fletcher was back and handing her a glass which was slippery with condensation. 'Always used to be your favourite, even before you were old enough to be drinking it.' She

140

took a large swig and thanked him. 'I've also been to see the seating plan and we're on the same table,' he said.

She sighed, 'No surprises there, then.'

When they were called into the dining room Samantha saw that it had been laid out with round tables, twelve settings at each. She and Graham were seated opposite each other which she hoped was a safe distance. She didn't know any of the others but it didn't take long before everyone had introduced themselves. On her left was a couple who managed a laundry and dry cleaning business on the outskirts of town. They sponsored the team by cleaning the match kit. On her right was a young man who owned a couple of hairdressers in Gullhaven and Hitchfield.

Throughout the meal she felt Graham Fletcher's eyes on her but she didn't look back. The strategy worked until a conversation began which animated the whole table. Samantha had been discussing hair and make-up regimes for the deceased with the hairdresser when the topic had arisen so she didn't know how it had started. Someone must have mentioned divorce and as a specialist in family law, Fletcher had picked up the baton. When asked how divorce could be avoided, he replied that the only foolproof way was not to marry in the first place. During the polite laughter of the other diners Samantha risked a glance. He was watching her.

'You've been married a while now, Sammy,' he said, 'What's the secret?' He paused with the skill and timing of a comedian who was anticipating the punch line. 'Don't tell me... It's because he's married to his work and you never see him.' There was an awkward silence before one of the men sniggered.

'Actually Graham, I believe in the saying "absence makes the heart grow fonder." Over the years there have been times when I've seen very little of Nick. He's often been involved in the sort of cases that make media headlines. But the highlight of my day is when I hear his key in the door and I know he's safe and that we're a complete family again.'

Someone mumbled 'Well said,' and the hairdresser raised his empty glass in a toast. 'Here's to the complete family.' The response was unenthusiastic. All the glasses were empty.

Soon after, tables were cleared and most of the diners took advantage of the break to mix with friends or to grab a cigarette or toilet break. Some looked at phones before excusing themselves to catch up with partners or baby sitters. Fletcher had disappeared from the table at the earliest opportunity and Samantha turned her phone back on to see if Nick had rung, or sent a message. Alexander had texted a joke he had heard on the television and for a moment, she thought of fetching her coat from the cloakroom and calling a taxi to take her home. These weren't her people and this wasn't her responsibility. Nick was right. Her mother was more than capable of attending a charity function.

Fletcher slipped into the hairdresser's chair and placed a large glass of brandy in front of her.

'Peace offering,' he said.

'You can take your peace offering and...'

He interrupted her. 'Drink it myself?'

'I'm not laughing, Graham. What you said was out of order. I'm sorry your marriage didn't work out, but my marriage to Nick is happy. We still love each other.'

His arm was resting across the back of her chair. It was proprietorial and an unknowing observer might have mistaken them for a couple. He was about to reply

142

when the event organiser announced that everyone should take their seats for the auction and presentations.

'How lovely to see you two getting on so well.'

Samantha turned, her face frozen in shock. She moved her head backwards to avoid the kiss that was about to be planted on her cheek. 'Mother! Why are you here?'

Chapter 38

'I said, "Why are you here?"' Samantha deliberated on each word, her jaws clenched and anger adding a sparkle to her eyes.

Dorothy ignored the question, turning her attention to Fletcher who rose and kissed her on each cheek. He held out his arms 'How lovely to see you, beautiful lady. Every man in the room is jealous of me now. I am in possession of the two finest girls in the county.' Dorothy giggled.

'Now that you're here mother, you can represent the company. I'm going home. And Graham, for the record, you have never been in possession of me and never will be.' She picked up her bag and took a step towards the door.

'Stop right there.' Dorothy Cooper's voice was low and menacing. 'How do you think it would look if the company representative disappeared the minute the auction began? I gave you a budget and you will stay to spend it. Now sit down, drink your brandy, and smile as if you're enjoying yourself. I've been invited to present a couple of the trophies, so I'll be at the top table. We can all catch up later.' Dorothy walked towards a local bigwig whose arms were outstretched in welcome.

Samantha struggled to control her fury. The hairdresser returned to the table and was about to sit when Fletcher intervened. 'Would you please swap with me?' he said, already lowering himself back on to the chair. 'I have so much catching up to do with this young lady.'

'No probs,' said the hairdresser and walked around the table to introduce himself to his new dining friends.

After the auction and presentations, Dorothy mingled with dignitaries, smiling, laughing, air kissing and hugging her way around the room. When people were making their way home, she went to the door to make sure that everyone had seen her. Samantha and Graham were among the last dozen to leave the ballroom and Graham invited both ladies to join him in his suite for a nightcap.

'Yes, mother. I think that's the least you can do.' Samantha was unsmiling. Graham's arm was across her shoulders and her body language screamed discomfort.

The three of them went up in the lift to a suite in the recently built Jacklin Wing. Floor to ceiling windows overlooked the golf course and framed the clouds scudding across an almost complete moon. Graham pointed to a bottle of brandy and a couple of bottles of red wine on the dressing table, the 2008 Barolo already half drunk. When offered, both ladies chose brandy and he poured generous measures of the oak aged liquor before half filling his own glass with wine.

Dorothy had always been fond of Graham and they talked like old friends.

'Graham comes to visit me every Wednesday, Samantha. He smuggles my alcohol past the gun turrets.' Dorothy giggled as she patted Graham's knee.

Samantha took another gulp of brandy. 'You're allowed to bring in whatever you want, Mum. You're not in prison. I can bring you booze if you tell me what you want.'

'Graham knows what I like,' said Dorothy and they both broke into conspiratorial laughter.

Samantha's extended absence from the community excluded her from most of the gossiping about mutual friends and local scandal. When she excused herself and disappeared into the bathroom, Dorothy glanced at her watch and feigned surprise at how late it was. She hoisted herself out of her chair and let Graham lead her to the door where he kissed her lightly on both cheeks. 'Thanks Dorothy,' he said.

She waited in the corridor until she heard the toilet flush, before pressing an ear to the door. When she heard him say 'Graham knows what you like too,' she nodded and was contacting the taxi company as she walked to the lift.

The taxi driver had been unwilling to take Samantha to the door of the park home. 'This place is notorious for getting lost and I've never been here before. I might never find my way out.'

They sat in the reception car park and he turned the internal light on to take his fare. Samantha could see the clock on the dashboard. It was 3am and she didn't want to wake Nick up to ask him to collect her. She produced a ten pound note and held it out, but he shook his head. A second ten pounds persuaded him and they drove between the high hedges until she saw moonlight reflected in water. At last, they were at the Lakeside sector. There was a light in the window of A-20 and for a moment, she felt fear. If Nick had waited up for her, he would be worried and angry.

She got out of the taxi and closed the door as quietly as she could but with the extra tip safely tucked away, the driver revved the car and tooted the horn as he departed, spraying her legs with wet gravel.

No point now in trying to be quiet. Samantha unlocked the door and went in. The room was empty, the only light coming from a table lamp which Nick had moved nearer the window. She was touched by his thoughtfulness. She took off her shoes and tiptoed into the kitchen in her bare feet. The tiled floor was arctic cold and it shocked her. She ran the cold tap for a few moments before filling a tumbler and downing the contents greedily. How many brandies had she drunk in the end? She couldn't remember, and although the headache hadn't yet started, she expected it to be bad.

The door to the hallway was closed and she hoped that the taxi driver's attempt to waken her family had failed. She started to undress in the living area, convinced that she could slip into bed without waking Nick. Her black dress was heavily creased. She unzipped it and let it slither to the floor. When she lifted a leg to step out of it, her head started to spin and she knew she was going to be sick. She made it to the kitchen sink before throwing up the four course meal and the accompanying wines and brandy. Coughing and spitting out the thick saliva which had protected the mucosal cells of her mouth, she heard the hall door open.

Nick Morgan stood in navy pyjama bottoms drawn in below his waist with a white cord. Even now, his upper body retained the tan he had developed when building the extension to their south London home last summer. His arms were muscular although he no longer boasted the well defined abdominals of his younger days. When she turned, he was staring at her without moving or speaking.

'I'm sorry, Nick. I know it's late, but Mum turned up and we got chatting. I've had too much to drink.' She was holding on to the edges of the sink for support.

Nick's face softened as she took an unsteady couple of steps in his direction and he reached out to support her upper arms. He inspected her face in the light of the table lamp. She closed her eyes and was about to fall into his welcoming embrace when she felt herself propelled backwards. Her hip collided with the sink unit and she yelped. When she opened her eyes, he was pointing to the congealed mess which was blocking the plughole. 'Clean that up, then sleep on the sofa. You need to be up and showered before taking the twins to school and you'd better do that by taxi. I have a briefing at seven thirty.'

'I'm sorry Nick. I really am.' She reached out to him.

'I can smell him on you.' He left without looking back.

Chapter 39

Monday 17th February

Nick Morgan lay awake until five o'clock then got up, showered, dressed, and took Truffles for a walk. When he returned, he changed into his shirt and suit and kicked Sam's discarded clothes to one side on his way to the kettle.

She was huddled under a pile of outdoor coats and he heard her soft snoring. It was a sound he usually found endearing. Not today. Deciding that he would grab breakfast on his way to work, he took his leather jacket from where it lay across Sam's legs. He put it on and started to shake her, tilting his head to one side to avoid the smell of garlic, stale brandy and vomit.

'Samantha, wake up.' She didn't respond so he shook harder until she started to groan. 'Wake up, Samantha,' louder this time. Her eyes opened and she cowered from him. 'You need to get cleaned up and dressed. It's Monday and you have to take the children to their new school. Whatever you were last night, today you need to pretend you're a loving wife and mother.' He grabbed his keys and left.

The morning was cold and dark and his mood was not improved by having to scrape frost from his windscreen. His car windows had misted up and it took ten minutes with the blowers turned on full before it was safe to drive.

The roads around the estate were dark until he reached the reception building which was bathed in the brightness of a security light. He saw Maisie struggling with an A-board pavement sign He stopped the car to help her.

'Well, thank you. I knew you were a gentleman. Can you put it over by the entrance to the main car park please? We've got a shareholder meeting in the ballroom and they'll need to park there.'

'How many shareholders can this place have?' he asked.

'Not our shareholders. It's a healthcare company. They come every year and we put on a spread for them. The income helps us through our quiet period.'

'I hope my wife's arrival in the early hours of the morning didn't disturb you.' He'd said it before thinking and immediately wondered why he'd even mentioned it.

'No. I sleep the sleep of the innocent,' she replied following it up with a throaty laugh.

'Lucky you. There aren't many can say that.'

'Well, perhaps not all that innocent.' Her right eyebrow arched Was she flirting again?

'Maybe you shouldn't have told me that because I need someone to come and talk to you about Abigail Slater.' It had been in Morgan's mind that finding Abi's body on the estate may not have been entirely random. Whoever left her there might have been familiar with the territory.

She looked puzzled now. 'Come yourself. Save someone the trip. You're here anyway and I don't have a problem with talking to you about Abi Slater.' When he didn't reply, she continued, 'Although you should know that I never really considered her a friend. She was just someone who came here sometimes. I'm going in now. It's bloody freezing out here. Thanks again for helping.'

In the short time he had left his car, the windows had misted over again and he sat in the dark with the engine running. Why had he thought it might be better to have someone else question Maisie? It's not as if there was anything going on between them. He shook his head, put the Volvo into gear and set off towards the main road.

Chapter 40

DI Nick Morgan sat at his desk, his eyes on the computer screen but his concentration on the thought of his wife with Graham Fletcher.

He opened his decision log for Operation Siren and read through his justifications for the way he had steered the enquiry so far. He looked at the photos of Abigail Slater before jotting some notes on the information his team was still chasing. He retrieved his personal mobile from his pocket. No messages. He hoped that Samantha would be able to pull herself together in time to deliver the twins to their new school. He pocketed the phone. In ten minutes, he was due to update DCI Johnson with progress in his cases. At least with two high profile investigations going on and a DCI turning up the heat, his day would be full enough to distract him from brooding over her betrayal.

DI Maggy Patel strode into his office. Since Johnson had moved Dave Spence from Patel's team to his own, he had seen little of her. He told himself it wasn't that he was avoiding her, he just wasn't seeking her out. Anyway, she was still wrapped up in the investigation at Cliffside House and his instructions to keep out of that had been very clear.

'You're due to see Johnson in a minute,' she said. 'He's going to speak to us both together. Come on.'

Morgan frowned. 'Why together?'

'No idea. Come on, he said ten o'clock.'

They walked down the corridor.

'Any news on Cliffside?' Morgan asked.

Patel hesitated before replying. 'Frankly, I'm at a loss where to go next. Nobody seemed to know that Raynor was staying at Cliffside. We can't find who sold him his last fix either. He's not on any of the shops' CCTV. It's as if he didn't exist before you found him. I don't suppose you've had any thoughts?'

Morgan shook his head. 'My wife and I went to the house at Christmas when we were down here visiting Dotty and there was no sign of him then.'

Patel gasped and laughed. 'You call Mrs Dorothy Cooper, venerable aristocrat of this parish, Dotty? I know you have awards for bravery but that's pushing it.'

'She's a card-carrying, class "A" bitch who calls me Plod. Calling her "Dotty" out loud is almost affectionate by comparison to what I call her in my head.'

They were making their way up the second flight of stairs to Johnson's office before Patel spoke again. 'Do you think Johnson sees a link between the cases? I can't say I've spotted one, but why else would he want to speak to us together?'

'I have no idea. MOs are different. Raynor and Crook were into drugs, but Abi Slater has no history of drug abuse. She may have defended them both. She may even have been sexually involved with one or other, or perhaps both. She seems to have been quite a free spirit where sex was concerned.' As he said it, he felt a sharp pain in his gut. 'Anyway, I don't officially know enough about your Raynor case to make connections.'

They arrived at Johnson's office and Morgan followed Patel in. They sat in the two chairs drawn up to his desk. The DCI's face was stony, and although he had a cup of his special coffee beside him, still hot enough to be releasing its aromatic steam, he did not offer refreshment to his subordinates.

'I cannot understand why there is so little progress in the three cases you are both working on. What is taking so long?'

Morgan glanced to his left to check whether Patel was going to speak first. She was fixing Johnson with a glare and he could see the muscles in her jaw twitching before she spoke.

'Operation Heartwood was set back by at least a couple of days after you transferred DS Spence to DI Morgan's team. I had to brief outsiders from scratch. And, being outsiders, they had next to no knowledge of the ground and the drug culture. Where Dave Spence would have known who to speak to and what to ask, the transfers-in had no idea... sir.'

Johnson returned her stare. 'You should have explained the negative effect of my suggestion when I made it.'

'It wasn't a suggestion, sir. It was an order. And I did try, you were very determined.' She continued to stare at him, her lips pursed.

'What's your take on this? Why is Abigail Slater's killer not downstairs?' Johnson's attention was now directed at Morgan.

'I have no take on the operation at Cliffside. I will say that DS Spence's input into both my on-going operations has been invaluable so I can see what a loss he would be to DI Patel. He has his finger on the pulse of the community and he knows where to go for information. I've had an email this morning telling me that Abigail Slater's fiancé, Joseph Kendrick, is coming in later with his solicitor. We are also trawling the local clubs to see if anyone knows what might have happened to her. And DC Smart is working through a list of clients Abigail Slater has defended. We have prioritised those where she lost the case and particularly those where the defendants were imprisoned. There are six of those who completed their sentences and were back in the community in time to have been responsible for her death.'

Johnson continued to glare at him. 'Is that all you've got?'

'She was only found seven days ago.' Patel jumped into the exchange. Morgan held a hand out, palm towards her. He was grateful for her support, but angry enough to fight his own corner.

'DI Patel is correct. It has been seven days and we have uncovered a significant number of individuals who were in personal relationships with her. We are tracing and interviewing them. It seems that every interview generates another half a dozen names. It's taking time.'

'And what about the body in the garden?' Johnson changed the subject again.

Morgan tightened his fists and slowed his speech to retain his patience. 'There's a notice around Wesley Crook's neck and possibly, we believe, the remains of a notice in Abi Slater's lap. Maybe a connection, maybe not. And there was a letter sent to Crook's home address which says something about his offending. As you know, sir, the team has been prioritising the Slater death as you instructed.' Out of the corner of his eye, he saw Patel nod emphatically.

Johnson cleared his throat. He leant back, elbows resting on the arms of his chair, fingers steepled and touching his lips. 'But that's not all, is it DI Morgan?' Morgan waited for him to clarify. 'I understand that there was a close, physical relationship between Abigail

Slater and a certain...' he looked down at a printed sheet on his desk 'Steven Ian Cooper. How far have we progressed with investigating him? Or have you let the fact that he is your brother-in-law cloud your judgement on his potential culpability?'

Chapter 41

'I seem to be waiting for an answer, DI Morgan, so let me ask an easier question. It's my information that nothing has been done to look into this relationship. So, how does an experienced officer such as you, drop the ball in such a high profile investigation?'

Morgan was speechless. He tried to remember who had mentioned Steven Cooper's relationship with Abigail Slater and failed.

Maggy Patel cleared her throat. 'Sir, if you've finished discussing my investigation...' She rose partway out of her chair.

'Please remain seated DI Patel. I've not finished with either of you.'

During that short exchange Morgan remembered Graham Fletcher's words "and by seeing, I mean fucking, even as the wedding banns were being read." He had allowed the smug grin on Fletcher's face when he told him about the charity dinner, to distract him from Steven Cooper's potential involvement. And then, when the body had turned up at the bungalow, it had slipped his mind. It was obvious that someone else knew about the relationship between Abi and Steven and had thought it more appropriate to contact Johnson than to have a quiet word with himself. Of course - the ambitious DS Dave Spence. He'd been at that interview. Traitorous bastard!

'It came up when I interviewed Graham Fletcher and I didn't prioritise it, sir. I can see how that looks, but there was no intention on my part to overlook a potential lead. Fletcher told Spence and me that Ms Slater had formed relationships with a number of clients and that's the route I took the investigation down.'

'So, where is Cooper now?'

'I believe he is away from home at the moment. He's not been at work for a couple of weeks.'

'By my reckoning, that means he must have gone missing at about the time Abigail Slater vanished. A copper in his first days in the job would see that was suspicious.' Johnson's stare was hard and uncompromising. 'Can you give me any reason why I shouldn't just suspend you now, DI Morgan, pending enquiries into your behaviour?'

Morgan felt a chill grip his spine. He had never before been threatened with suspension, but then he'd never before made such a monumental cock-up. 'I've no excuses, sir. I know I can contribute to the successful resolution of these investigations but I understand how my oversight may well have compromised me, and I apologise.'

Johnson sighed. 'I'm short of senior staff as it is so here's what's going to happen. DI Patel, you will continue with Operation Heartwood. We don't know if Raynor's murder is an isolated case or if there may be some loose connection with Abi Slater's death. You will also take responsibility for the investigation into Steven Cooper's involvement with Ms Slater. Find him and bring him in. If he had issues with her engagement, we need to know how resentful it made him. Morgan, you stay out of that line of enquiry. Don't try to contact Cooper and don't speak to your family about it. And stay out of the Cliffside investigation. You will continue to hold separate briefings for the operations and if there is any potential that you may trip over each other out there, you come to me. Do you both understand?'

'Sir.' They rose from their chairs together and Morgan held the door open to let Patel pass through. In the corridor, they looked at each other and exhaled.

'Are you okay?' asked Patel. 'You're very pale.'

'I'm not sure. Bloody Steven Cooper.' He gathered his thoughts. 'I'm sorry that my oversight has added to your workload.'

'I thought we had him, until the Cooper thing came up. We were working well together. Who do you think told him?'

'Spence. He was with me when I interviewed Fletcher.'

'I don't think that's his style. He's belligerent and up-front, not sneaky. Can I borrow him to help find Steven Cooper?'

Morgan agreed. 'As far as I'm concerned, you can keep him. I can't work with someone I don't trust.'

'Don't be too hasty to judge him, Nick. Innocent until proven guilty and all that.'

'He's made no secret of the fact that he was a shoe in for my job and he resents me for blocking his promotion.'

'He's young and in a hurry. We've all been there. Anyway, he wouldn't have got the job this time round because he's not sat the exam. He knows that. Do you want me to speak to him?'

'No, you're okay.' Morgan sighed as he started to walk away.

'Before you go...' she called after him. 'Do you know where Steven Cooper is hiding?'

'No... sorry.' He closed his eyes and shook his head as he spoke. He was overwhelmingly tired.

'Where would you start if you were looking for him?' she asked.

'I'd start with Dorothy Cooper. She's the puppet master in that family. I'd be amazed if he took off without getting her permission.'

'Okay. Thanks for that. I'll get Spence to go and see her. And Nick? Have you thought that it might be Fletcher himself who told Johnson about Abi and Cooper? Has he any reason to make trouble for you?'

'You mean apart from him spending last night fucking my wife.'

Her jaw dropped. 'Oh God,' she said. 'Sorry.'

'So am I, Maggy.' He started to walk away. 'So am I.'

Chapter 42

DS Spence drove DC Lynn Greenfield to Silver Sands House where they were met at the door by a middle aged woman in a navy suit which was a size too small for her. Tendrils of grey hair escaped from a bun and her eye shadow and mascara were smudged. When the officers explained the reason for their visit and produced warrant cards she barely looked at them. 'Mrs Cooper's suite is on the first floor but she may be asleep. The residents have recently had lunch and many of them take a nap before the afternoon's activities. I'll ring up and tell her you're on your way.'

Spence held out a hand. 'Please don't. I'd prefer it if you gave us directions. We'll find it.'

The woman's face registered surprise. 'I hope there isn't a problem.'

'No problem,' he replied, 'We just need the directions.'

She led them to the bottom of the staircase and was about to speak when a young man appeared through a door.

'Oh, there you are, Danny. Can you please show these officers to Mrs Cooper's suite?' she turned to Spence with obvious disdain, 'I assume that will be acceptable?'

'Thank you.'

Danny was wearing well pressed navy overalls with the Silver Sands logo they had seen on the sign at the bottom of the drive. Under the logo was a plastic name badge with his name and "Maintenance." He led them up the stairs, through the fire door at the top, and down a corridor which had no windows. Lighting was triggered automatically by their progress until they reached the end where he pointed to a white door and went to knock on it.

'That's okay, Danny. We'll take it from here,' said Greenfield. Her knock was firm and authoritative and Danny held back, as if waiting to see what was going to happen.

Greenfield knocked again, harder, and Spence noted that Danny flinched. He asked, 'Do you have a master key if we need it?'

Danny's mouth gaped. The very idea of giving strangers access to Dorothy Cooper's suite without her permission clearly terrified him. The light in the corridor went out at the same time as the door was thrown open. 'What's going on?' Dorothy Cooper's eyes showed that she had been sleeping and was unimpressed by being disturbed. 'Who are you?'

Spence and Greenfield held out their identification again. 'What's wrong? Is Samantha okay? You'd better come in.' As they stepped into the light of her lounge, she called her thanks to Danny who was making his way back down the corridor, before closing the door.

The room was a little too fussy for Spence's taste with framed photographs of the Cooper family on most of the available surfaces. There was a black and white wedding photo. A man, who Spence took to be Morgan's father-in-law, had his arm around a young Dorothy Cooper's waist. They were looking into each other's eyes and laughing. Spence found it difficult to believe that this was the same woman who was in front of him now, her face scowling and lips tightly closed.

'I'd offer coffee, but I'm sure you won't be here long,' she said as she sat on the white leather armchair and put her feet up on a stool.

'If you could sit with me at this table please, Mrs Cooper,' Spence was keen to take control of the interview, 'It'll help my colleague take notes and no doubt speed things up so we can get out of your way sooner.'

Dorothy Cooper looked towards the small dining table where Spence had settled. She narrowed her eyes and rose slowly as if it caused her physical pain. She came to the table, sat down and immediately crossed her arms.

'Will this do?'

'Yes. Thank you.' Spence indicated that Greenfield should sit beside him so that both were facing Dorothy. He would have preferred a less confrontational seating arrangement but figured that his hand had been forced by her attitude.

Dorothy gave them both a cold smile. The message was superiority with a touch of tolerance. 'What is it I can do for you Mr Spence?'

Greenfield looked up from the new page of her notebook and intervened. 'Detective Sergeant Spence and I have a few questions for you,' she said. 'DS Spence?'

Dave Spence said, 'Yes, Mrs Cooper, we're here to ask a few questions about Steven Cooper.'

'My Steven?'

'Your son, yes. We understand that he hasn't been at work for a couple of weeks. Is that correct?'

Dorothy looked from Spence to Greenfield and then back again. 'What about it? What's this about? Has he been in an accident?'

Spence sighed, his frustration building. 'Is your son on holiday?'

'I believe so.'

'Where has he gone and when do you expect him back?'

'He didn't tell me and I didn't ask. He's a grown man.'

'He is employed by the family business, is he not? Surely you must know when he will be back at work?' asked Greenfield.

Dorothy seemed unsettled by her interruption. 'My daughter is running the business now.'

'And she'll confirm that when I question her, will she?' said Spence, his eyebrows raised.

Dorothy Cooper didn't respond immediately. 'We haven't completely agreed the terms and conditions of her employment, but in essence, she knows she'll be running the business.'

Spence had to hand it to her. She evaded direct questions with the skill of an expensive defence lawyer.

'Would it be accurate to say that your son is missing?' The question was posed by Greenfield.

'Why ever would you say that?'

'If you could answer DC Greenfield's question, please. I know you're keen to get back to what you were doing.' Spence watched her closely.

'I don't know how to answer that.'

Spence continued. 'Your son's name has come up in a current investigation and we need to speak to him as soon as possible. It's been suggested that he disappeared a couple of weeks ago and that nobody has heard from him since. I'll be frank with you, Mrs Cooper, if you can't or won't tell us where he is, we're going to consider getting a warrant for his arrest.'

The look of horror which crossed Dorothy's face was rewarding. 'If this is about that solicitor tart, I can tell you he knows nothing about it. They broke up... well, they were never really together. I told him to stop seeing her before Christmas.'

'We have some questions for him, Mrs Cooper and it would help everyone if you can tell us where he is; especially him.'

'He's not answering his phone and I think his answer service must be full, because the number rings out now.'

'We'll need that number please.'

Dorothy got up and fetched her handbag from beside the armchair. She took out a phone encased in silver and pink sequins and accessed the contact details. The officers' eyes met, their mutual surprise obvious. This was not the sort of phone case they expected this unsmiling woman to have.

DC Greenfield noted the number and checked it and they thanked her for her co-operation whilst preparing to leave. Dorothy appeared to relax as she opened the door. 'Can you tell him to ring me? I've been worried about him.'

Spence nodded and said they would be in touch if they had any more questions.

'I've got one last one,' said Greenfield. 'Do you have any other property... apart from Cliffside House, I mean? A holiday apartment or somewhere you used to go as a family when Steven was younger? Somewhere that might mean something to him?'

Dorothy's genial expression vanished and her face froze. 'I've answered everything you've asked,' she snapped.

'Just that last one outstanding, then,' said Spence, holding the door.

165

'There's a caravan at Southwold. I haven't been there for thirty years, but I pay the fees and Samantha has taken the twins when her husband has been too busy to give them a holiday.' She spat out the sentence as if the very mention of Nick Morgan was distasteful.

'We'll need the address then, and we'll leave you in peace.'

As they walked back down the corridor to the staircase, Spence turned to Greenfield with the broadest smile and offered a high five. 'Just one last question... Get you, Columbo.'

Chapter 43

Morgan and Spence met Abi's fiancé, Joseph Kendrick, at the reception desk. He was standing beside a small man who was talking excitedly on a mobile phone. They all waited for the call to end before Kendrick introduced the man as his solicitor, Neville Wicks. Spence led them to an interview room.

Morgan watched Kendrick closely. He was tense. He had frown lines in the centre of his forehead which were deep for a man in his late twenties, and his eyes darted round the room.

'Firstly, Mr Kendrick, thank you for coming in, and we're sorry for your loss.' Morgan waited for Kendrick to acknowledge his words, but it was the solicitor who responded.

'My client is here to provide you with any information that'll help with your enquiries.'

'Thank you,' said Morgan before explaining that the interview was not being recorded and that, as Kendrick was not under arrest, he could leave at any time. Again, no response. 'Perhaps we can start by you telling us about Abigail and your relationship with her?' Kendrick looked at his solicitor and sighed. 'I've said all this before: when she went missing... I already told you everything I know.'

'I understand, sir,' said Morgan. 'But sometimes things are overlooked and they only get remembered when we go over the story a few times.' It also helps us catch you out in a lie, he thought.

'I met Abigail at a business networking meeting in September. We had a lot in common. It seemed that no matter how hard we worked, our bosses were on our backs. We'd each had our probation periods extended and we were pissed off about it. We just clicked.' He made eye contact with both officers, as if checking that this was the type of information they sought before continuing. 'We met for coffee a couple of times, a few meals together, walks along the beach and the cliff tops, the usual way a relationship develops, I suppose.'

'When did you decide that she was the one, Mr Kendrick?' asked Morgan.

'We spent her birthday weekend at my flat. That was at the end of November. I gave her a few presents I thought she'd like: books, a bracelet and a cashmere pashmina as well as a couple of silly little extras. When she'd finished opening everything, she said "Where's my engagement ring?" I was surprised. I mean... I loved her, of course I did, but it seemed quite soon to be thinking about being engaged.' Morgan saw that Spence was creating a time line of the relationship in his note book. 'I think I said something a bit flippant like "why don't we skip engagement and go straight to marriage?"

'And she agreed?' asked Morgan. Kendrick nodded.

'It took me a couple of days to get my head round it, but I thought, why not? She was good for me. I'm Mr Conventional; Mr Boring; and she's so full of life and adventure, or she was. Who would do that to her?' His voice broke and he looked down to his hands which were clasped together, his knuckles, white.

Wicks stopped writing and placed a hand on his arm. 'I think that's probably as much information as my client can give you,' he said.

'When you talked about your dating history, you didn't mention clubs, or dancing,' said Spence.

Kendrick's frown lines deepened. 'Abi persuaded me to go a few times in the early days. The music was too loud for me and I was so much older than everyone else. I hated it. Anyway, she was out of hours duty solicitor more often than not, particularly when we were paying all the bills for the wedding, so we didn't get many opportunities for late nights.'

'You mentioned that your relationship with Abi developed quite quickly, Mr Kendrick. Are you aware of any pre-existing relationships Abi may have ended when you and she became an item?' asked Spence.

'I knew she was popular, but...'

Spence interrupted. 'Can you define what you mean by "popular" for us?'

'Wherever we went, people came to say hello. She didn't always introduce me to them and when I asked why, she told me that some of them were clients and it was a confidentiality issue.'

'Clients of both sexes?' asked Morgan.

'Mostly men... or boys, some of them. One or two women. Once, I remember, a man with massively dilated pupils came up to us while we were waiting for a taxi at the station. He thanked her for keeping him out of prison and asked for a business card. He said his mate was in trouble and needed a brief.'

'Were any of these approaches, if I can call them that, were any of them acrimonious?' Morgan watched as Kendrick searched his memory.

'Just the once... I'd forgotten about it. Abi said it came with the job. This lad came up to her in the club; not sure when exactly. He was shouting and I didn't pay much attention because everyone needed to shout to be heard over the music. It was only when the spotlight flashed across his face that I saw he was angry, so I moved closer to Abi and tried to figure out what was happening. When he saw me put my arm around her, he swore at us both, then he went away. I think we left soon afterwards, but only because it was late, not because Abi was scared. I think I was more scared.'

Morgan and Spence exchanged a glance which was interrupted by the solicitor. 'I really think that Mr Kendrick has given you everything he knows.'

'We've one or two more questions for him Mr Wicks. Are you okay to continue Mr Kendrick or do you need to take a break? We can organise tea or coffee,' said Morgan.

'No thank you.' He turned to Wicks, 'I want to help as much as I can, Nev.' His solicitor turned a page in his yellow notepad, seemingly resigned to the continuation of questioning.

'Did Abi speak to you again about that confrontation? At any time?' asked Spence.

'No.'

'Were you not curious? Did you not ask?'

'She said it was nothing and that I shouldn't worry about it.'

'Did you form your own opinion about it?'

Kendrick nodded. 'I wondered if he might be an old boyfriend rather than a client because he was pointing at her engagement ring.' His face became more animated. 'So that helps me put a date on it because I didn't give it to her until the first week of December and then we had to take it to be sized. I'm pretty sure she couldn't wear it until around the end of the third week in December. The jewellers were very busy sizing rings for presents and for couples getting engaged at Christmas.'

'Which club was it Mr Kendrick?'

'The one in Grove Park. I don't know the name.'

'That's Club Europium,' said Spence, making a note and underlining it.

It was dark when Morgan left his office and the car park was nearly empty. He got into the Volvo and sat, unsure where he was going to go. He didn't want to return to the park home because the twins would be there, full of excitement and tales of their first day at the new school. He couldn't face Sam. He felt sick at the thought.

As soon as he reversed on to the drive at Cliffside House, Morgan knew he had made a mistake. This was Sam and Dotty's domain and it would always have memories for his wife that he could never share. She'd probably had sex with Fletcher here too, with or without Dorothy's blessing.

He crashed his fists down on the steering wheel. In the space of twenty four hours a grenade had exploded in his marriage and he had lost control of a high profile investigation as well as the trust and respect of his new colleagues. He'd replayed the meeting in Johnson's office over and over during the day. How had he overlooked that throwaway comment made by Fletcher? Why had he not gone straight back to the office and started investigations into the whereabouts of Steven Cooper? He knew exactly why and he could still hear Fletcher's smooth, well educated tones in his head "Do tell Sammy I'm looking forward to catching up with her on Sunday." Those words were his overwhelming memory from that meeting and when his wife hadn't mentioned the dinner until the last minute, he knew she must be in on the plan. He shouldn't blame Dave Spence for taking it to Johnson. Maybe Spence had tried to remind him that Steven had been mentioned and he hadn't noticed. No wonder he'd escalated it. He rested his elbows on the steering wheel and rubbed his face with his hands. Looking over his shoulder at Cliffside House, soulless and unwelcoming in the darkness, he decided he couldn't spend the night there and headed towards Gullhaven Park Estate.

Chapter 44

Monday 17th February

The lights were on in the reception building when he parked but he could see that the desk was unmanned. Morgan's feet crunched on the gravel and as he approached, he blinked in the sudden blaze of the security lights. The dot of red light on the CCTV camera winked as it followed his progress to the glazed door. When he opened it, Maisie Sangster appeared from nowhere. She was chewing. He must have disturbed her evening meal.

'I'm sorry, Maisie. I'll come back later.'

She swallowed and smiled broadly. 'No matter. Are you okay?'

'I have a few questions, but I can come back later.'

She opened the flap in the counter and beckoned him through. 'Come on, I was grabbing a few of the leftovers from the shareholders' buffet. Thanks again for helping with the board outside, you're a lifesaver. It's like putting up a deckchair in a storm. There's a knack, and I don't have it.' She laughed nervously. 'I'm sorry, I'm going on a bit. Come and get something to eat. Actually, I dreamed about you last night.'

He was caught off guard. 'Did you?'

'No, you wouldn't let me.' She laughed heartily and he returned her smile. His only smile of the day. He barely knew her but she was warm and funny and that's what he needed now.

'You're not old enough to know that joke, and certainly not old enough to crack it with me.' He followed her through the door and into a short corridor which led to her office. She stopped without warning and turned towards him leaving him no time to avoid a collision.

'Sorry... sorry.' He was blushing now. This was ridiculous, he thought. He was a married father of twelve year old twins and a Detective Inspector. He needed to start acting like it.

'Come and sit down.' She took his hand and led him into the office. There was a long black desk under the window which he assumed must overlook the car park, although he could only see darkness. 'I saw you arrive,' she said nodding at a CCTV monitor. 'You looked serious, so I'll be serious.' She pointed towards a wheeled chair and sat beside him in front of a computer screen displaying a complicated spreadsheet. She pushed a tray of assorted sandwiches, chicken wings, sausage rolls and quiche segments towards him. 'Take whatever you want,' she said, smiling brightly.

He sat and swivelled his chair a little away from her. He didn't want her to see that his body was starting to react to her flirtation. He took a deep breath and tried to focus.

'I need to ask you about Abigail Slater.' He spoke slowly, not looking at her. He was straying from police procedure. He shouldn't be alone in this small, hot room with her. He should have waited until tomorrow and brought one of the female DCs with him.

'Aren't you supposed to watch me while you interrogate me? Something to do with body language and eye direction when I answer, isn't it? So you'll know if I'm lying, like.' She cleared her throat and replaced the smile with a theatrically serious expression.

'Abigail Slater,' he persevered. 'How well did you know her? Did she confide in you?'

'Abi wasn't a close friend. She was more of a customer I suppose, but a regular. I miss her.'

'What do you mean, "customer." She had a flat in town.'

'You're really quite naive, aren't you, Nick?' said Maisie. 'She brought men here and I gave her an hourly rate. She said her flatmate didn't approve of her friends so she needed somewhere to be with them. I charged her for the power she used and the laundry and a little bit for my trouble. She paid cash.'

'Did she always use the same property?'

'No. She had to take what I had available. She used to come and tell me about it afterwards. Sometimes gave them grades.' The memory made Maisie smile again, but this time it was tinged with sadness.

'Do you have records of who she brought here?'

'Of course not. I don't even have records of when she came. She would ring, I would tell her which property was available and then I'd go and turn the heating on, if it was needed, and put out laundry, like I did when you arrived. Once or twice, when she'd gone, I'd go to change the sheets and find they hadn't been used. She must have fancied it al fresco those times, but she still paid the full amount. That hadn't happened for a while, mind. It's been too cold.' She waited for his next question and the silence lengthened. 'Look, Nick... or maybe I should say DI Morgan since this is work. You don't look well. I'll still be here tomorrow. We should do this in the morning.' She got up and stood by the door making no effort to give him space as he tried to pass her without touching. 'Or you could stay with me,' she whispered, her voice was hoarse and she cleared her throat again.

He stopped and turned towards her slowly, giving himself time to think. His fingertips gently lifted her chin and their lips met in a long kiss, soft at first but harder as she opened her mouth and pressed her tongue into his. He was shocked by the charge of longing he felt when her painted nails reached inside his jacket and started to pull at his shirt.

'Stop. Stop.' He gently pushed her away. 'Not here.' He pointed to the window.

Maisie's eyes glittered with excitement. 'Move your car behind reception where it can't be seen. I'll open the back door and wait for you there.'

He hurried out, his short, shallow breaths misting in the February night air. A thin layer of frost was developing on the windscreen and as he scraped at it, he felt the cold embrace of common sense. This was madness. This would make him as guilty as Sam. He should get in his car and drive home to his waiting wife and family. Facing Maisie for the few remaining days they were here would be embarrassing, but surely it was preferable to the risk of not meeting her expectations. He was tired and she was confident and obviously, experienced. She must be at least fifteen years younger than him. What if he disappointed her?

He got in his car, started the engine and put the blowers on full blast to demist the windscreen. Selecting first gear, he drove to the car park exit and stopped. He sensed the triumph Graham Fletcher must have felt when he seduced his wife. His outrage was reignited. He felt the ghost of Maisie's kiss on his lips and he thought about all the things he wanted to do to her. His breathing was faster now, the anticipation, unbearable. He turned the car and made for the narrow entrance to the staff car park where light and trouble beckoned him through the door.

Chapter 45

Tuesday 18th February

When Samantha got up next morning she prepared packed lunches for the twins before waking them up for breakfast. Last night they had been disappointed when Nick wasn't there to hear about their first day at school.

'Did Dad come home at all?' asked Victoria.

'Sometimes he comes home very late and leaves before I wake up,' she replied. 'I slept so well last night that I really don't know.' They both accepted her answer.

'Is the car fixed?'

Samantha had lied about the need to take a taxi to school yesterday and almost let herself down by saying there was nothing wrong with her car. 'Yes dear, It's sorted. I'll drive you both to school today.'

The twins were subdued during the journey and walked together through the school gates without looking back. Samantha dialled her mother's mobile number and was relieved when she responded.

'He didn't come home last night.' Dorothy did not reply and Samantha glanced at her phone screen to see if she was still connected. 'Did you hear me? He didn't come home last night.'

'Well that's very tiresome of him, particularly when you'll be moving into Cliffside this week. Have you had an argument?'

'I got home late from the dinner and I was pretty drunk. He was cross.'

Dorothy snorted. 'He has to realise that you have friends here and that many of them will want to link up with you, now that you're back. You're going to have your own life again and he'll have to learn to share you.'

Samantha was puzzled by the comment, but her mother was continuing. 'He'll be tied up with his little detecting. I had a couple of officers here yesterday asking about Steven. Maybe Plod's involved in that and didn't want to talk to you about it.'

'He hardly ever talks to me about his work. And what did they want to know about Steven?'

'They said his name has come up in an investigation and they needed to interview him.'

'What investigation?'

'They wouldn't say. They wheedled the caravan address out of me. He may be there... who knows?'

'Did you and Steven have an argument? Is that why he left?'

'No, dear. Now why don't you come over for a cup of coffee so we can talk about you getting back into the business?'

Nick left Maisie before it got light. When he was clearing the thick ice from his car he felt his body tremble from spent excitement and lack of sleep. First things first, he thought. DS Dave Spence would instantly notice that he was wearing the same shirt as yesterday so he drove to the 24-hour hypermarket on the outskirts of town and bought a new one. He took the battery powered razor he kept in his grab bag to the mall's toilets and did his best to shave in the blue light before changing his shirt and setting off for work.

Morgan was aware of the obvious horizontal creases across his shirt front so when Dave Spence arrived, he

179

told him that the launderette at the park estate was closed and he had run out of shirts. Spence's look told him that he would rather die than come to work in an un-ironed shirt.

The first text arrived at nine forty five. Morgan's personal phone was in the pocket of the jacket he'd slung across the back of his chair. He looked at his watch. Over twenty seven hours since he had walked out of the park home leaving Sam on the sofa. She had been patient. He'd expected the barrage of messages to start when he hadn't gone home last night.

Spence was going through the task list so that they could update the decision log for Operation Siren. He stopped when he heard the vibration. 'Do you need to get that?' he asked.

Morgan shook his head. 'It's my own phone – it'll be something or nothing.'

'If my wife knew I treated her incoming texts like that, I'd lose my privileges.'

Morgan's ignored him. 'Where were we?' he asked.

'We were talking about Club Europium and deciding whether to go back during opening hours to speak to the punters. Like the other clubs, some of the staff remember Abi, but nobody remembered her being involved in anything specific. Problem is, they only open Thursday to Sunday, so we've got a bit of a wait.'

'Okay.' Morgan drummed his pen on the desk for a few beats before continuing. 'And I'm guessing the younger team members are more likely to get information from the clientele. What do you think?'

Spence's expression was rueful. 'I think even I'm too old to make much headway at Europium. How about sending the DCs with a few of the newer uniform bods –

out of uniform, of course. I can go too, to keep a watching brief.'

'Sounds good. Can you fix it up?'

Spence was about to reply when the phone vibrated again. 'Sir... I really think...'

Morgan sighed and reached to retrieve the phone. The first text was brief.

Come home. The children are asking where you are.

So that was how she was going to play it. She was going to use the children.

The second was longer.

Im sorry I was drunk but nothing happened. Absolutely NOTHING happened.

The missing apostrophe annoyed him almost as much as the lie.

'Can you excuse me for a moment, Dave. You're right – I do have to deal with this now.'

Spence nodded and left the office, closing the door behind him. Morgan typed quickly.

I don't know what's worse. Being married to a liar or a whore.

He thought about it before replacing "whore" with "cheat." He reread it, and felt the grip of Maisie's strong thighs; heard her urgent cries of encouragement. He deleted the whole message and put the phone back in his pocket.

Ninety minutes passed before the phone vibrated again. He was concentrating on trying to find any overlooked links between Abigail Slater and Wesley

Crook and it startled him back into the reality of his own problems.

**Come home 4 lunch kids at school need to talk.
NOTHING HAPPENED.**

Spence bounded into his office without knocking.

'The locals have found Cooper at the caravan. He's pissed. They're going to put him in a cell for his own protection and are asking if we're going to send a car for him.'

Morgan looked at his watch. 'It's not even midday yet. Why is he pissed already?'

'Guilty conscience, I expect. I'd turn to drink if I'd killed two people.'

'You're definitely linking the Slater and Crook deaths, then?'

Spence nodded. 'It's the cardboard signs that do it for me. Too much of a coincidence.'

'Abi Slater only had the remnants of a piece of cardboard. I'm not sure I'm completely there with a link yet. Anyway, Cooper had disappeared before Crook was offed.' He looked back at his watch. 'I need to go out for a little while. Can you organise transport for Cooper, please.'

'I expect you'll be glad to move into Cliffside and get back to normal,' said Spence, his eyes lingering on the creased shirt.

'I'm not convinced that life at Cliffside will ever be what you'd call normal,' said Morgan, before heading out.

<u>Chapter 46</u>

Driving past the reception building at the estate Morgan felt a longing for Maisie before steeling himself for the confrontation he was expecting. There was a car coming towards him on the narrow road and he gave it all his attention so they would pass safely. When he glanced over his shoulder, there was a man at the reception desk. Maisie must be having some time off or was behind the scenes.

Sam's car was carelessly parked and he struggled to get into the second space. When he got out, the cold water which had been sitting on the leaves of the evergreen bushes soaked his trousers.

Opening the door he could smell cigarette smoke. Sam was sitting on the sofa with a mug of tea by her side.

'I didn't think you were coming.'

'I'm in the middle of a number of cases. It's difficult to get away.'

'Is that your way of telling me I'll have to deal with the move into Cliffside on my own?'

'Probably.' He touched the side of the kettle, added more water, and flicked the switch.

'Where did you go last night? The children wanted to tell you about their day.' Her voice was low.

'It's not about where I was last night, Sam, it's about where you were the night before. More to the point, it's about who you were with the night before. I've spent time with that man. Did you really think I wouldn't be able to recognise his aftershave all over you? And that's before we even get to the fact that you weren't wearing your tights when you eventually came home.'

'Ever the detective.'

He reached across the breakfast bar and picked up his keys. 'I thought you wanted to talk, not bitch. I've got work to do.'

The kettle boiled and she got up. 'I'll make it. Tea or coffee?'

'Coffee, please.'

'You look rough. That shirt doesn't even fit you.' He didn't answer. She spooned the instant coffee into two mugs. 'At least when we get into Cliffside we can have proper coffee again.'

'Why did you go to that dinner? I asked you not to.'

'Mum said it was important for the business. You know I've felt guilty for not being here to help out, especially since Dad died. Steven isn't up to the marketing and PR stuff and...'

'We've found him.'

His interruption irritated her. 'What do you mean, "We've found him?" Is he okay?'

'He's being brought back here. I don't know if he's under arrest or not.'

'Under arrest for what?'

'I can't tell you. Not yet, anyway.'

She smacked the mug down beside where he was standing, spilling some of the contents, before returning to the sofa and her cigarette.

'You're not supposed to smoke in here,' he said. 'There are enough signs.'

'I went to the dinner. I ate the dinner. Graham wasn't even close by. Then mother appeared out of nowhere. After the speeches, Graham invited us to his suite and we had a few drinks. When I came out of the loo, mum had gone. I went to fetch my bag and coat and he asked me to stay for a bit. Nothing happened. We chatted about school and old times. He sat beside me and put his arm round me, but that's all.'

'I saw the look on his face when he told me about the dinner. It wasn't the look of a man planning a chat.'

'I don't know what he was planning, but what he got was a chat.'

'You reeked of his aftershave when you got back.'

'He saw me out to the taxi and kissed me goodnight.' She was staring at him, daring him not to believe her. 'And, let's face it Nick, even if it had gone further, you're hardly in any position to judge.'

He felt his face and neck flush and the deafening noise of his heart, pounding in his ears. 'Meaning?'

'I haven't forgotten DC Alison Goddard.'

He exhaled, slowly. 'That was fourteen years ago. And it was one night. You agreed at counselling that you wouldn't keep bringing it up.'

She nodded, 'And I've kept to that. I'm only bringing it up now because I was late back from a dinner and you leapt straight to the assumption I had sex with an old boyfriend. You're not being fair.'

'Not being fair! You agree to go to a do, where an ex who has had a hard-on for you for the last twenty five years, will be. You choose not to tell me about it so I have to hear it from him.' His voice was getting louder. 'And then... then... you come home stinking of his aftershave and missing half your underwear and it's me who's not being fair. How do you even begin to justify that?'

'I wasn't missing my underwear!' She was outraged and shouting, 'I laddered my tights so I took them off

185

and put them in my handbag.' She sighed and continued in a softer tone, enunciating each word, 'Nothing. Happened.'

He took a few sips of the coffee then put the mug down. He wanted a cup of real coffee made from ground beans. This tasted thin and bitter.

'If you don't believe me, why don't you ask him?'

'Ask him?' he was shouting now. 'Ask a solicitor whose sole purpose in life is to present a case which shows his client in the best possible light, whether it be truth or fiction? Why would I ever believe a word that comes out of that man's mouth?'

'I don't know how I can convince you, Nick. Yes, I got very drunk and yes, I probably did have the opportunity to have sex with Graham Fletcher, but I didn't. Nothing happened.' She grabbed his hand. 'I value what we have here and I'm sorry that you think I would risk it for a quick tumble with him.' She got up, picked up her mug and took it to the sink. 'I'm going to the house this afternoon to do some more cleaning then I need to get some shopping. Will you come home tonight?'

'How did the kids get on at school?' he asked.

'There were ups and downs, but mostly ups. Vicky's skirt is longer than anyone else's and she wants me to take the hem up this weekend. Alex wants to try out for the school football team and has joined the chess club. You should ask them.'

'I'll ask them tonight,' he said. He left without saying any more.

During the drive back to work, Morgan replayed the conversation again and again. At some point, he started to believe his wife's version of events and that put a new perspective on his night with Maisie. If he had ever held the moral high ground in this mess, he wasn't perched up there now.

Chapter 47

Dave Spence was talking to DC Jenny Smart when Patel approached his desk. 'I expect you already know, but Steven Cooper is downstairs and I'd like you two to interview him,' she said.

'I've heard we'll need respirators,' said Spence. 'Not had a bath since Christmas, and the guys in the car weren't sure which Christmas. In fact, one of them said he once drove the body of a dog that had been dead for three days to the veterinary department for a PM, and Cooper smells worse.' Patel's smile was rueful and she apologised.

'I've heard he's lawyered up,' said Smart.

'Yes, I'm told that Brian Gault is on his way.'

'I don't know him,' said Smart.

'Partner and Solicitor Advocate at Fletcher, Armstrong and Gault. Dorothy Cooper must have got her cheque book out,' said Spence.

'The very same. Don't underestimate him. He's a tiger,' said Patel.

'Or a snake,' Spence replied.

Brian Gault started by demanding time to consult with his client alone. When Gault was ready, Spence led Smart to Interview Room 3 and they took their places. The room was hot and cramped with a pervasive smell of unwashed clothing, nervous sweat and, strangely, cooked onions. Cooper and Gault were both flushed, their faces coated with a thin, oily veneer.

Spence nodded to Smart who started the digital recording system and cautioned Cooper for the record. She opened her book and Spence was about to ask his first question when Gault interrupted. 'I have a prepared statement to read to you and I should advise you that my client has nothing further to say.'

The statement was short. Cooper denied knowing either Carl Raynor or Wesley Crook. He admitted meeting Abigail Slater at a club last year and that they had been in a short relationship which ended before Christmas, after which he had not seen or heard from her. He did not know that she was about to marry or that she had been killed. He was not involved in her murder.

'Why did you run away?' asked Spence as Gault was laying the statement on the desk.

'As I said, my client...' Gault intervened.

'Give him the chance to answer please, Mr Gault,' said Spence. 'The statement makes no mention of Mr Cooper's unexpected trip. We know he's intelligent enough to see how suspicious that trip looks in light of Ms Slater's disappearance. Why did you run away?'

'I'm advised to answer with "no comment."'

'You don't have to take that advice. This is your opportunity to tell us why you took off at around the same time as Abigail Slater vanished. It looks suspicious, right?'

Cooper was picking at his dirty fingernails. He glanced to where Gault had his pen poised over his legal pad. 'I want to answer,' he said.

'I've given you my advice and I suggest you take it.'

'Mr Cooper,' said Spence, 'if you want to answer, you should. Courts tend to be suspicious of "no comment" interviews. If there was a legitimate reason why you decided to visit Southwold and it has nothing to do with the cases we are working on, it would be better to tell us now.' He sat back in his chair anticipating a long story.

Cooper exchanged a look with his solicitor. 'No comment,' he said.

Chapter 48

DI Nick Morgan dropped into his chair when he got back to his office after the morning briefing. He knew he should be at Cliffside to help with the move, but he wasn't ready to spend the day alone with Sam. Over the last couple of days he'd begun to accept that maybe she hadn't slept with Graham Fletcher, and that left him with a guilt that nagged him like a painful tooth. His desk phone rang. 'DI Morgan.'

'Morning, sir, it's PC Eastman here, on the desk. You've got a visitor. A journalist who has information about the "Sorry Slayer" murders.'

Morgan winced at the name given to the case by the tabloids. Recently, their headlines had comprised of fewer words, in larger font. "A Sorry Excuse of an Investigation." "Find the Sorry Slayer." "Who'll be Sorry Next?"

The media had a voracious appetite for information and journalists would try anything to get exclusive access to lead investigators. He wasn't going to fall for their tricks. 'Tell him to email it to me. You can give him the address.'

It's a "her," sir. 'Natalia Kowalowski is a columnist for the local Gazette.'

'Then please tell *her* to email me,' he repeated but, as he went to replace the phone, he heard the woman's raised voice.

'I'll email now. Tell Morgan he has five minutes before I take it to Johnson.' Eastman started to repeat her words but Morgan told him he'd got the message. The last thing he needed was Johnson hauling him into his office to ask why he was overlooking another lead. He replaced the receiver, opened his email account, and waited, wishing he had his own coffee machine in this impersonal and uninspiring office.

When the message arrived, it was a link to a web page. With some trepidation, Morgan clicked on it hoping that he wasn't about to infect the whole team, or worse, the county, with a catastrophic virus. It was a video and at first, he couldn't make out what he was seeing as both pictures and sound were blurred. He could hear chinking of glasses and cutlery on crockery. He checked the video length which was ten minutes. So much for "five minutes before I take it to Johnson," he thought. His email pinged again and then again. He received a total of seven links before he gave in and rang Eastman. 'Tell Ms Kowalowski I'm coming down.'

When he got to the front desk PC Eastman pointed to a tall woman with dark hair swept up into a style reminiscent of the nineteen fifties. She was typing on her phone with a speed and expertise that Morgan associated more with teenagers than women in their thirties. Eastman called her name.

Natalia Kowalowski approached him and they shook hands. Up close, she was younger than he'd first thought. The thick layers of makeup, particularly the black mascara and eye liner, aged and hardened her features. He wondered if that's what it took to be taken seriously in the world of local journalism.

As they walked to his office she asked 'How much have you watched?'

He liked this woman. No time-wasting, straight down to it. 'A couple of minutes,' he replied. 'I thought it would save time if you took me to the specific part of the footage you think is relevant.

At his office, he turned his monitor so they could share. When he clicked on his inbox she said 'It's in link three.'

'Why not just send me link three, then?'

'You'll want to see it in context.'

He asked where she got the material and she told him it had been sent to her by someone who attended the event featured in the recordings, but who wished to remain anonymous. She added that she didn't know where or when the event had happened but she was sure it would be easy to find out.

The third link had the same background noise, but now there were voices in the foreground. They were discussing the recent local deaths and he heard two male voices and one woman's. Carl Raynor's demise was dismissed as another bloody junkie that the world would be better off without. When the woman spoke, she was of the opinion that Abigail Slater's death was very sad. She said she felt sorry for the fiancé. The man whose voice was louder and more confident than the other two had scoffed at that and told her that he thought the fiancé had a lucky escape. 'Liked the bad boys, I heard. Not that I wouldn't have given her one myself,' he said, 'but I don't like queuing.'

'Is that it?' asked Morgan pausing the recording. Kowalowski was typing on her phone and shook her head without looking up. He pressed play and listened again. The picture was still out of focus.

The confident man was getting louder and another male voice had joined in. The discussion moved on to the body outside the Bradley's bungalow and they were empathising with the couple. Confident voice said 'The only good burglar is a dead burglar. If I had it my way, we'd string 'em up. I'd do it myself.'

Morgan stopped the recording again and looked at Kowalowski. 'He's an idiot who's drunk too much at a function and has let his gob run on because people are listening. He probably doesn't even remember saying it, and they won't remember hearing it. Let's hope he got a taxi home.' He stood up to indicate that it was time for her to leave. 'Out of interest, do we know who they are?'

'The loudmouth is Councillor Kenneth Wyatt and I was sent the footage because later on it shows him groping some serving staff. It must be a recent event because the murders were only in the last couple of weeks, so it shouldn't be too hard to trace who all the voices belong to.'

'He was pissed and out of order. We all speak out of turn when we've had too much to drink.'

'He's up for re-election to the council in May so I've rung him for a comment but he's not picking up. He doesn't know I've got this so there's no reason for him to be ducking my calls. Over the last couple of days, I've tried his work, his home and his mobile. I've also sent emails to his council and work accounts.' She threw her hands out. 'And... Nothing. No response. We all know he's a self publicity addict. He's aiming to be mayor and never misses an opportunity. Maybe he's too busy out there stringing up burglars?'

Morgan exhaled loudly through barely open lips. Every major investigation had its share of complications which could end up being the breakthrough, or a time-wasting irrelevance. The trick was to get it right. Senior investigators still shuddered at the thought of falling victim to a hoaxer like "Wearside Jack" who had dragged the Yorkshire Ripper enquiry off track.

'Why would you believe that a local councillor who has his eyes on the mayoral prize would risk everything to see off burglars? It makes no sense.'

Kowalowski put her phone face down on his desk. 'I'm not saying he's doing it himself. I don't think he would be able. I mean he's big enough, but it's all fat. Anyone who broke into a slight trot could get away from him without any difficulty, and I should know. But he has money enough to buy whatever he needs. If he needs to see off a few criminals to clean the streets up and win the election, he could get his wallet out.'

I can't see it being a motive for him to be arranging for burglars to die. It's just not realistic... is it?'

'But you can't risk not having a quick look at him, just to make sure.' She rose and dropped a business card on his desk before picking up her phone and making for the door. 'You know where to find me. And it's my exclusive, okay?'

Morgan escorted her back to reception before returning to play the remaining clips. The last one had been filmed from a different angle and he saw the rotund Councillor Wyatt holding court. But his attention was fixed on the neighbouring table. It was out of focus, but he would recognise his wife anywhere. And, sitting next to her, his arm across the back of her chair, was Graham Fletcher.

Chapter 49

DCI Johnson winced when Morgan told him why he needed to talk to Councillor Kenneth Wyatt. 'He's always been a bit larger than life. I don't think he means anything by it.'

Morgan persevered. 'I believe if you saw the clips, sir, you may feel differently. There are two which show him with his hands on waitresses' thighs and there's a very clear shot where he's got his hand up a skirt. You can see by the look on the young lady's face that she neither encouraged nor welcomed it.'

'Has there been a formal complaint by anyone? Without that, I don't think there's much we can do. How about me having a quiet word next time I see him?' Johnson's look of hope stiffened Morgan's resolve.

'The footage is on the internet and it'll get a lot more attention when the paper is printed. There's already a link to it from the Gazette website. How's it going to look if we don't at least have him in? Anyway, the groping is one thing but it's the "string them up" comment that I want him to clarify.'

Johnson gasped. 'You're not seriously suggesting that Councillor Wyatt is our burglar killer?'

'I'm suggesting that I want to talk to him about his opinions and where he voices them. Then I'd like to ask him who knows about his opinions and who might share them with enough fervour to do something about it.'

'He's going to be Mayor one day, you do know that? I can't imagine how much harder he could make our

196

lives if we don't have a good relationship with him. For God's sake, Morgan, our wives play bridge together twice a week. This is beyond embarrassing.'

'Not for me, sir. I have no pre-existing relationship with him. DS Spence and I can bring him in for a quiet word. He doesn't even have to know that this conversation's taken place so Mrs Wyatt and Mrs Johnson can continue, oblivious of your involvement. If he's contrite, that may be the end of it. We can leave him to deal with the fallout from The Gazette however he pleases.'

Sensing Morgan's determination, Johnson raised his hands in resignation. 'Okay,' he said, 'but keep it to just you and Spence until we know more. Do I make myself clear?'

'Crystal clear, sir. I'll find Spence and we'll get it sorted straight away.'

Spence parked a short walk from the house shared by Councillor Wyatt and his wife. These were 1970s houses thought Morgan as he got out of the car and he was prepared to bet that they were initially marketed as "executive living." The properties were all sited off curved roads with branching cul-de-sacs. Some were fake Georgian whilst the design of others was more modern. Most had been extended in some way; rooms on top of garages; conservatories; and one with an ornate porch, better suited to a steak house restaurant. Wyatt's was at the very edge of the estate and there was a red convertible on the drive. As they approached the property, Morgan felt neighbourhood eyes track their progress.

'Don't worry, Spence, they think we're Jehovah's Witnesses. They will be retreating towards the back of their houses and hiding until they're sure we've gone away.'

Dave Spence feigned personal offence. 'Jehovah's Witnesses! That must be your suit, sir. Mine is designer and cost me a fortune... and the tie is silk.'

They walked up the drive and Spence rang the bell then reached for the door knocker before recoiling. It comprised a flaccid penis hanging between two oversized testicles.

'Very classy,' said Morgan. 'I think that's what's called a novelty knocker. I must be sure to get one for Cliffside. It'll piss my mother-in-law off.'

Spence rang the bell again, this time leaning on it for longer. The men waited before returning partway down the drive and looking back for open windows or other evidence of habitation.

'Perhaps he's seen the footage online and he's keeping a low profile?' suggested Spence.

'More like Mrs Wyatt has seen the footage and those are his hanging on the door. He'll be bleeding to death in the utility room,' said Morgan.

He noted the number of alarm boxes and CCTV cameras on the surrounding houses and deduced that the locals took their security seriously. Without much hope, he tried to open the garden gate. Locked.

'Excuse me!' Both men turned to see a small woman approach from the direction of their car. She had white hair held back by a navy Alice band and was wearing a purple sweatshirt with "Head Gardener" and a picture of a flowerpot and trowel on the front. Her baggy trousers were tucked into black rubber boots which looked too big for her.

'Excuse me!' she repeated pointlessly as they were already giving her their full attention. 'Who are you, please?'

Morgan and Spence looked at each other before retrieving ID from their pockets and waiting for her to get closer. 'It's Miss Marple,' said Spence, hand in front of mouth and looking down. Morgan's smile served to acknowledge the comment and also welcome the woman.

'I'm DI Morgan and this is DS Spence from Central and Southern Major Crimes Unit. Do you know if Mr Wyatt is at home? He's not answering the door.'

She took the wallets from both men and peered at each in turn before handing them back.

'Why do you want him?' she asked.

'And you are, madam?' Spence had stepped forward and now towered over the woman. She held her ground, her face a picture of indignation.

'I am Gladys Granger. I'm the neighbourhood watch co-ordinator for this part of the estate and I'm asking again, why do you want Councillor Wyatt?' She emphasised his title.

Morgan sighed and put on his conciliatory smile. 'Mrs Granger, we're not in a position to discuss why we're here. It would help if you could tell us if you know whether the Wyatts are at home now, or are likely to be back soon. If you can't, then we'll let you get back to your gardening.'

'How did you know I was gardening?' she snapped.

'Lucky guess,' chipped in Spence. 'Now, can you help?'

She looked both men up and down again before speaking. 'She, the wife that is, hasn't shown her face for weeks. There's been a young woman banging on

199

their door for a couple of days. Have you seen that knocker? Completely inappropriate for an executive home. My husband thinks he's got the woman pregnant.'

'Can you describe the woman?' Morgan asked and her response was an accurate representation of Natalia Kowalowski, the journalist from The Gazette.

'When did you last see Councillor Wyatt, madam?' Spence persisted.

She gave him a disapproving look before turning back to Morgan. 'I saw him a couple of days ago when he got out of the car. The wife keeps hers in the garage and if he's at home and she's coming and going, he has to move it off and back on the drive. The car makes a growling noise. It disturbs everybody.'

'So you don't think the car has moved for a couple of days?' Morgan asked since it was obvious she preferred to speak to him. Her response was a shrug.

'Okay, thank you Mrs Granger. We won't detain you any longer,' said Spence and turned back to face the house.

Gladys Granger stepped closer to Morgan and rested her hands on his right forearm. She rose a little on to her tiptoes and spoke in his ear. 'The woman at number twelve has a key. They think nobody knows but I've seen them. Why would she need to be watering the plants when he's inside?' Morgan smiled at her and patted her clasping hands.

'Thank you Mrs Granger, you've been very helpful,' he said.

'I'm thinking about putting the kettle on, if you'd like a coffee.'

'That's kind, thank you, but we must get on.' He smiled again and with obvious reluctance she released him and walked away.

'Remind me never to take you on in a "Grab a Granny" contest,' said Spence. 'I'd stand no bloody chance!'

'I'll remind you not to disrespect our more mature citizens, especially when they tell us where we can get a key.'

'We'll need a warrant.'

'Oh, put the manual away, Spence. No one has seen the man for two days and his wandering hands are all over the internet. If we need an excuse, we'll think of one.'

Chapter 50

The woman who answered the door of number twelve was not happy. She started by flatly denying she had the key, and when Morgan explained that they needed to ensure that Councillor Wyatt was okay, she demanded to know who had told them about the key.

'Does that matter?' asked Spence. 'He may be unwell or injured – we need to check.'

'I'm responsible for the key. I can't just give it to you. I've never seen a police warrant card so I wouldn't know if yours are real.' Morgan thought she had a point. People focused on the word "Police" and it seemed to him that you could show a library card and it would be accepted.

'The best I can offer, and this is against protocol but I need to speed things up, is that you come and open the door for us, and then you stay on the doorstep. You cannot come in, do you understand?' said Morgan.

She nodded and produced the key from the pocket of a coat hanging in the hall.

It took less than a couple of minutes for them to get to the Wyatt's house. She held out the key to Morgan. 'If they're not in, the alarm will be on. The box is on the left, but I'm not telling you the code,' she said.

'Okay, but no further than the control panel. Understood?' She replied with a nod.

Both men put on latex gloves, retrieved from their pockets, and Morgan opened the door. They waited for the alarm breach siren but there was nothing. Some mail lay behind the door and a few newspapers. That morning's Gazette was on top and, as he picked it up, Morgan saw Councillor Wyatt's face was filling a quarter of the front page. The headline was "Local Councillor in sex pest allegation." Brutal but accurate, he thought as he laid it on an antique shipping trunk. He heard the woman choke back a small cry, but she didn't say anything.

'Please wait here,' said Morgan and opened the lounge door. Spence took the stairs, two at a time.

Downstairs, Morgan searched through two reception rooms and a kitchen which had been extended into a conservatory. Behind the front door he found a small toilet and shower room and next to it, a utility area. He checked behind doors and furniture before going back to the hallway.

Spence came back down the stairs and shook his head. 'Four bedrooms, but only the master looks as if it's been recently used. It's very smelly in there. Sweat; whisky and aftershave. The shower in the en-suite's dripping and lime scale in the toilet bowl's stained.'

'But no body,' the woman scoffed, 'so can I get back to the TV? They're going to do a Yorkshire pudding recipe.'

When she had crossed the threshold, Spence whispered that there were no women's clothes in the master bedroom wardrobe, and no cosmetics or toiletries in the en-suite or on the dressing table. Morgan nodded, but when he stepped outside, he paused. 'What about the garage?' he asked. 'Do you have a key for the garage?'

'Why would I need a key for the garage? I've got a front door key so I can water the plants. That's all.' Her voice was firm but her face reddened under their scrutiny.

All three now headed to the kitchen where the back door was locked, but the key was on the kitchen unit by the doorframe. It opened on to a flagged path. In front of them was a separate brick built garage with a partially glazed side door.

'Where are the garage keys?' Spence asked.

'I don't even know if it's locked,' she said. 'His wife put her car in there, so I suppose she has the keys.'

Morgan smoothed his gloves before crossing to the garage. He turned the white handle downwards and pulled the door towards him. He kept his feet outside and leant in. It was much tidier than any garage he had ever owned but that was because his DIY obsession filled every available storage area.

In the limited light, he could see there was no car. Mrs Wyatt must either be enjoying another few rubbers of bridge, or perhaps she really had left him. He screwed up his eyes in the gloom. Was that a punch bag hanging from the wooden beams? Too big for a punch bag, surely? He ran his gloved hand down the wall to the left of the door and found a light switch. Ensuring that the woman had remained at the kitchen door, he flicked it.

Hanging from the beam was something or rather, someone, sheathed in a wheelie bin liner with only two legs visible. Then he could smell it. Urine, faeces and death. Turning the light off, he walked back to the kitchen door and asked Spence to take the woman home.

Wyatt's lady friend was hysterical even though she had seen nothing and neither officer had specified their findings. As Morgan watched Spence walk her back to number twelve, her feral howls of anguish were bringing people to their windows but nobody came to help her.

Morgan was standing in the Wyatt's front garden when Spence got back.

'I waited till she had spoken to her sister on the phone. She's coming over,' he said. 'I made her some tea and she's a bit calmer now.'

A marked police car was parked on the other side of the road and two officers were wrapping crime scene tape around fence posts and street lamp poles.

'That's the Medical Examiner,' said Morgan, pointing to a man in a mud encrusted Range Rover. 'He was also Wyatt's GP, so he's local. I'm waiting for the rest of the team before he goes in. CSI's already going to be upset with us.'

'Is Dr Mack coming?' Spence asked, 'Or have we worn him out?'

'No idea,' said Morgan.

'You're sure he's dead?' asked Spence and then raised both hands submissively in response to Morgan's look.

'He's got no right to smell as bad as that if he's not dead and, come to think of it, we don't know if it's a he. We're assuming...' he accentuated the word, 'assuming that it's Kenneth Wyatt, only because he's missing and that's his garage. It might even be Mrs Wyatt for all we know,' said Morgan.

'Suicide when he heard The Gazette was after him do you think?'

'He's wrapped in a bin bag, Spence. He didn't do that himself.'

They gave their names to the young PC at the door and this time, put on coveralls, gloves and shoe covers before entering. They walked through the house and crossed the paving flags to the garage.

'What are we going to tell CSI,' asked Spence.

'We were concerned for his welfare. At least that's how I remember it. And if it is him, we were right to be.'

A petite woman dressed in the same protective clothing and carrying an aluminium flight case followed them and called out. 'Which one of you is DI Morgan?'

'The one with the grey hair,' said Spence, pointing to his right. Morgan shook hands as she introduced herself as Dr Mackenzie.

'Can't be,' said Spence. 'He's a short, irascible Scottish person with a beard.' She turned to look at him with warm brown eyes which were smiling over her face mask.

'I inherited my height from my father, but not yet his propensity for facial hair. Now where is the deceased please?'

'You're a Home Office Pathologist too?' asked Morgan.

'Yep. My father is soon to go into hospital for a knee replacement and so I have transferred in from the West Midlands for a few weeks or maybe longer.' Her expression and tone evidenced how regularly she had to explain her family connection.

'I'm so sorry, Dr Mackenzie,' Spence reached out and they shook hands 'I'm DS Spence.'

'I know. My father has briefed me,' she replied. 'Now where's the deceased?'

She joined the team of CSIs swarming around the garage. Some carried camera cases and others had plastic or metal crates which contained the paraphernalia needed to collect evidence. Lights were being set up and the second to last in the procession was carrying a step ladder.

'I always think it's important to make a good first impression,' said Morgan with a mischievous grin, 'Particularly when you're going to be working closely together.'

'Oh shit,' Spence sighed. 'I don't even know why I said it. I like Dr Mack and I've never known him be testy.'

'Irascible is the word you used. Great word that.' He paused before continuing. 'You can't think she won't tell him. Good luck getting your PMs to the front of the queue in the future.'

'And how did she know who I was?' continued Spence.

'Must have seen the designer suit before you put the coveralls on. Your wardrobe has its own Twitter feed. Come on! Let's see how they're getting on.'

Chapter 51

Thursday 20th February

'I'm sorry I'm late,' said Spence.

Dr Morag Mackenzie's broad smile was welcoming as he hurried into the mortuary. 'The suit has arrived,' she told Annie Geeson, 'so now we can get on with it. You missed the identification DS Spence. DC Greenfield brought Mrs Wyatt along and Annie tells me she never saw a widow less upset.'

Spence nodded at Annie. 'Did she mention the on-line stuff when she was here?'

'Not to me, but she had quite an animated conversation in the car park with DC Greenfield. You should ask her.'

As the women carried out the last preparations before starting the postmortem, he went to sit in the viewing gallery. Staring down at the pile of flesh that had so recently been Councillor Kenneth Wyatt he found it difficult to see any similarity between the loud, outspoken man who had been filmed at the dinner and what he was now.

When the body was cut down from the rafters of the garage and the huge black wheelie bin liner removed, they'd found a leather dog lead digging into his neck. Dr MoMack, as she was becoming known, had asked for it to be left in place while the body was transported to the mortuary. They now had a number of digital photos of the neck before and after the lead was removed and she had emailed them to Spence's phone. He was swiping through them when she called his name.

'I'm going to start now.' He wished she had made the first cut without him knowing. For Spence, the Y-incision and the removal of the top of the skull were the worst parts of an autopsy and he braced himself.

When she finished the dissection, Dr MoMack suggested to Spence that they meet in her office.

'I've taken tissue samples for completeness,' she said, 'But I believe he was hit on the back of the head, or maybe fell and hit his head. It's a serious laceration so there will be blood and hair where it happened. While he was unconscious, someone put the lead around his neck and pulled it tight. There are no fingernail scratches on his neck, so I don't think he had a chance to try to loosen it. Whoever did it must be quite strong because, even with the pulley attached to the rafters in the garage, they had to heave his full weight up off the ground.' She looked puzzled. 'Why would there even be a pulley system in the middle of the garage?'

'We found a punch bag on a trolley in the corner. We think he must have stored it out of the way, then wheeled it into the middle and hoisted it up when he wanted a workout.'

'Why not just leave it there?'

'His wife kept her car in the garage.'

'You saw the size of him, and if you hadn't kept your eyes closed most of the time, you would have seen how much fat there was. He could have done with wheeling that trolley out more often. His arteries were pretty blocked too. He could have gone at any time.' Dr MoMack looked genuinely saddened, 'But he didn't deserve to go like that. Slow asphyxiation is a bastard of a way to die. Let's hope he stayed unconscious till it was over.'

Spence agreed then asked, 'If you were a betting woman would you say he was hit or fell backwards? It'll help narrow the search for the crime scene team.'

'You heard me mention the ante mortem bruising to his chest. It looks like punches, but not very hard ones. If he stepped back to avoid them and fell, I would be looking for something hard and low; a mantelpiece, fireside kerb maybe, or furniture, like a coffee table. I say that because if he was in a fight, I don't think he would turn his back so someone could smash something down on his head with that degree of force. On the other hand, if he fell, with his weight and height, he would go down like a Douglas fir in a forest.'

Spence thanked her and apologised again for his previous remarks about her father. 'I've got a lot of respect for your dad. I don't know what made me say it.'

'I'd already forgotten it DS Spence, so thanks for reminding me. I'm having dinner with him tomorrow and it'll be good to open with a funny story. He can be so irascible.' She wiggled the two first fingers of both hands as quotation marks and he heard her laughing with Annie Geeson as he made his way down the corridor.

After the last of the furniture and boxes were unloaded at Cliffside, Samantha handed the removal van driver an envelope with a wad of ten pound notes. She stood at the door, listening to the clang of the tailgate being closed and the bolts driven home then watched as the van edged out of the drive and turned on to the cliff top road. Closing the door, she noticed how quiet the house was with nobody else in it.

When she had packed up in south London she had taken time to label each box with its ultimate destination. Having decided not to move into the master bedroom until it had been completely refurbished, her system had unravelled and it was obvious that the removal men had taken advantage. She almost wept when she thought how long it would take to make Cliffside into their new home.

The boiler had performed well overnight and the house was warmer now but she decided that their beds and bedding needed to be aired after being in storage. They would spend one last night in the park home.

When she collected the children from school, they were disappointed but accepted it before starting to argue over bedrooms.

She parked in the reception car park and went in, leaving the twins in the car. Maisie appeared from the back and greeted her cheerily. 'We'll need the extra night after all,' said Samantha. 'The house is nearly ready, but the mattresses and bedding are very cold. I don't know where the storage unit is but it must be freezing in there.'

'That's okay, Mrs Morgan. I'm pleased to have you here.'

Samantha returned Maisie's smile. 'That's kind, thank you. Do you want me to settle up now and then I'll hand the keys in when we leave tomorrow?'

Maisie typed a few commands on her keyboard. 'It's DI Morgan's credit card that the booking is on. I'm afraid I'll need him to come in and sign it off.'

'He's very busy at the moment and I'm named on the account. Can we not do it now to save him the trouble?'

'Sorry. Tell him it won't take long. He can pop in tonight, or tomorrow.' Maisie came round the desk. 'Is that your children outside? I'll just go and say goodbye to them.

At the car, Maisie hugged Victoria and shook hands with Alex who told her he was too old to hug. Samantha's phone rang and she rummaged through her large handbag. When she looked at the screen, she scowled and compressed her lips. The caller spoke briefly before she responded.

'No, Nick. The beds are too cold. Come back to the estate tonight. And it seems you have to sign off on the bill.' The two women locked eyes and Maisie beamed as Samantha glowered back at her. She ended her conversation before thrusting the phone back into her bag.

'He says he'll drop in on his way back tonight if you feel it's really necessary.' The sentence dripped with resentment and maybe a hint of suspicion.

Chapter 52

Thursday 20th February

In his office, Morgan carefully placed his personal phone on his desk as if it might explode. Why was it necessary for him to sign off the bill? Oh God, please don't let Maisie Sangster turn out to be a vengeful bunny boiler. The desk phone rang, making him jump.

'DI Morgan.' He picked up a pen to make notes.

'DI Morgan, it's Andrew Slater... Abigail Slater's father. My wife and I were wondering how the investigation is progressing. It seems to have gone very quiet.'

Morgan winced. He had thought of ringing Slater a number of times but, with nothing to report, had always put it off. Now, the uncomfortable conversation had arrived and there was no way of ducking it.

'The investigation is on-going, Mr Slater. We've spoken to Abi's fiancé, and to a number of people she saw socially. We still have quite a list of those to identify and contact. Do you remember any names she might have mentioned in passing?'

Slater made a noise which sounded like a snort. 'She stopped confiding in us when she was fourteen,' he said.

'Mmm. My sergeant tells me that there has been quite a lot of social media activity since your daughter was found. We have been monitoring that, but nothing has come out of it. Not so far, anyway.' Morgan glanced at his watch, judging how long to continue a conversation that was going nowhere.

'My wife and I would like regular progress reports, please. Nobody is telling us anything... except the journalists.'

Morgan accepted the rebuke. Slater was right. He should have made contact, even with nothing to report. 'Of course, Mr Slater. I'll be in touch.'

The call ended with polite goodbyes, but Morgan felt bad. He put himself in the Slaters' shoes. God only knew what they were going through.

Earlier, he had returned to the office leaving Spence to oversee the despatch of Wyatt's body to the mortuary and to attend the PM. He wanted to tell Johnson about Wyatt's death in person but found his office empty and dark. He collected a paper cup of water from the cooler and took it to his desk where he jotted down a few lines of enquiry in the new decision log. He hadn't received a name for the Operation, but was confident it would be another murder enquiry. It was never too early to start the log.

Spence rang in and outlined the initial findings from the postmortem. 'I wasn't sure if I'd catch you, sir. Aren't you supposed to be moving in today?'

'No. We're spending one last night at the park home while our stuff comes to a temperature which satisfies my wife.'

Spence must have noticed his testy tone as he hesitated before continuing. 'Okay. Are you doing a briefing this evening? I suppose what I'm asking is, do you need me to come back in?'

Morgan looked at his watch and saw that it was half past six. 'No, it's fine. You go home. I'll schedule a briefing for eight o'clock tomorrow. Can you let the team know?'

'Which team?'

'It's getting a bit like that, isn't it? Let's get everyone in the same room and see if we can unravel some of this mess. I'll speak to DI Patel before I leave.'

'Right, I'll ring round and I'll see you tomorrow.'

Morgan piled his case logs on the desk then scooped them into his briefcase. He dialled Patel's mobile and waited, expecting to leave a message. When she answered, she was breathing heavily and he heard that wherever she was, it was windy.

'I'm sorry,' he said, 'Am I interrupting you?'

'I've come out for a run to try and clear my head. I'm getting these cases mixed up. And I hear you dug up another one today?'

'In the interests of accuracy, I'd have to say we cut down another one. Councillor Wyatt.'

'The online guy? Wasn't he going to string up all burglars?'

'The very same.'

Patel whistled and Morgan moved the phone further from his ear.

'Now what?' she asked.

'Now we wait to see who Johnson will appoint SIO and the lucky winner gets the decision log I've already started.'

'It's going to be you. "Multimedia Morgan" we're calling you. TV crews will be on your doorstep first thing so make sure you wash behind your ears and wear your lucky pants.'

'I'm going to tell Johnston that you requested it specially,' he said.

'Piss off. Have you seen my caseload?'

'I'm organising a cross team briefing for tomorrow at eight. Can we meet up at seven and try to collate some of the information that's coming in? I'm struggling to believe that there isn't some sort of link although I can't see it yet.'

'Seven is good. I'll come to your office and you'd better have a flat white waiting for me. See you then. Bye.' She hung up before he could reply.

He made one more call from his personal phone before setting off for his last night in the park home.

Morgan was tired when he walked into the reception building. He'd been stuck in a tail back caused by a collision on the by-pass. Maisie was seated on a stool at the desk and when she glanced up, she looked surprised.

'Oh my God, are you okay? Is eh... everything okay?' He looked over to the CCTV camera and then back at her, hoping she would receive the message that he wanted to hold and kiss her, but didn't want there to be a record of him doing it.

'All is well,' he said. 'I'm just tired. There's a lot going on at work, and I'm not sleeping very well.'

'I know you didn't sleep well on Monday, but you've surely had a chance to catch up by now?' She was being flirty again. He didn't want to hurt her feelings but he wasn't in the mood.

Maisie seemed to sense that something had changed and she reached under the desk. 'I asked for you to come to the office because I wanted to give you this.' She produced an itemised invoice for their stay, 'And also to tell you how much I enjoyed Monday. I haven't stopped smiling all week. Thank you. Now go and help your wife pack.'

He saw the threat of tears in her eyes and wanted even more to hold her and cry with her. 'Thank you, Maisie... for everything,' he said, taking the invoice and leaving without looking back.

Chapter 53

On his way to work the next morning, Morgan stopped for fuel, coffees and the local paper. The headline read "Sex pest found dead at home" and he noted the byline attributed the article to Natalia Kowalowski, Assistant Crime Correspondent. His last call yesterday had been to confirm the identification of Wyatt's hanging body and to give her the go-ahead for submission of the story to her editor. He imagined that the lawyers worked late into the night to agree wording which would get the story published. Natalia must have negotiated hard to get on to the crime team with only one scoop and he was glad for her. It never harmed to have a good relationship with local journalists however much the Press Office tried to discourage it. Excluding the Mackenzie pathologists, she was his first non-police contact in his new post and it helped him feel settled.

When he approached his office he could see that the lights were already on. Maggy Patel had made herself comfortable in one of his visitor chairs and was reading through paperwork. He balanced both coffees precariously in his left palm and opened the door. Without looking up, Patel held out her right hand as if she were already holding a cup. 'Put it there,' she said, 'I'm gasping.' She took a sip and nodded her approval. 'Thanks for this.' Another sip. 'I've had the tox screen back for Carl Raynor.' Patel held out the A4 document. 'You'll never guess.'

'I can't guess, and if it's Raynor we're talking about, I'm not even supposed to guess, but go on.'

'He was snorting a mixture of cocaine and ketamine.'

'He got his wish then.' She looked puzzled. 'I mean... anyone who snorts a cocktail of cocaine and ketamine has got a death wish. And it was granted.'

'It explains the lengths someone had to go to... to kill him, I mean. It must have been like wrestling an amorous gorilla.'

Morgan pointed at the pile of papers he had put on his desk. 'I went through the Slater, Crook and Wyatt cases last night and I'm like you. I see common threads, but nothing that gets us any further. And the HOLMES analysis hasn't thrown up anything we weren't seeing for ourselves. Not yet, anyway.'

'Johnson's not going to be happy,' said Patel.

'He's not been happy since I got here.'

The briefing room was full when Morgan and Patel arrived. Johnson was standing at the back of the room and he beckoned them across. 'What's the progress on the Wyatt case?' he spoke quietly, looking downwards.

Patel looked to Morgan who responded. 'Large laceration to back of the head and found hanging in his garage. Crime scene team have confirmed blood and hair on the edge of a marble hearth so they're pretty confident he fell and hit his head. The wound was too serious for him to have got to the garage by himself, and he was alive when he was strung up. Asphyxia and venous congestion, so whoever put the noose round his neck murdered him.'

Johnson looked nervous. 'Are you linking it to the on-line material?'

218

'I'm keeping an open mind, sir.' Morgan was enjoying the man's discomfort and pushed to capitalise on it. 'DI Patel and I are holding a joint briefing this morning. Some of these recent deaths have similarities. We've decided to make everyone aware of all the cases, even if they aren't specifically investigating them. Cross team communication will ensure that nothing is overlooked,' he paused before adding, 'sir.'

'I can't see how you can throw Councillor Wyatt in with a couple of dead drug addicts and a solicitor with questionable morals,' hissed Johnson.

'The asphyxiation, sir,' Morgan butted in. 'Each of the deaths has involved asphyxiation, in one form or another.'

Johnson wasn't giving up. 'As I understand it, there's no cardboard sign round his neck, so that should exclude him from the other operations.'

'No cardboard round the neck of Carl Raynor either, sir,' said Patel.

Johnson's jaw clenched. 'Listen... both of you. I don't care which Operation you put Wesley Crook in, but I want Wyatt's death investigated as a stand-alone. Apply for an Operation name as soon as this briefing is over.' Morgan agreed and started to follow Patel who was walking to the front of the room. 'And DI Morgan... we'll discuss later how the local paper got on to Wyatt's death so quickly.'

Johnson left without closing the door and Patel, now in position to present to the assembled team, pointed to DC Smart who was nearest. 'If you would, Jenny, please.' The rest of the group took the hint and the room became still.

There were four whiteboards at the front, one for each case, with pictures of the deceased in life and in death. Patel stood on the left of the room beside the Operation Heartwood board and she ran through her information uninterrupted. Carl Raynor; known shoplifter and drug addict; found dead in a bedroom in DI Morgan's house. When she added the results of the toxicology screen, there was a murmur around her audience.

'I thought ketamine wasn't supposed to kill you.' It was one of Patel's DCs from the Heartwood team. Morgan hadn't seen him before. Another voice suggested he should stop using it, just in case.

'That's enough,' said Patel, reaching an open palm across to Morgan, inviting him to continue.

Morgan ran through the cases of Abi Slater and Wesley Crook, highlighting the facts that both had been strangled and also that they may both have had notices left with their bodies. He accepted the possibility that the card in the solicitor's lap may be spurious but told his audience that he did not want it to be overlooked.

DC Jenson caught Morgan's eye before he moved across to the fourth board. 'Yes, Leo. Something to add?'

Jenson looked across to Jenny Smart who nodded. 'Jen and I went to the solicitors' office yesterday.' Morgan closed his eyes as a picture of Graham Fletcher with Sam flashed into his mind. 'They were reluctant to help us, but Jen hinted that she'd have no trouble getting a search warrant, so they came up with the goods. Abigail Slater was duty solicitor the day Crook appeared at the mags court for the burglary. The partners were still discussing whether she was going to defend him at the trial because of his extensive previous. They thought that one of the more experienced solicitors might have to do it. So, it's another link, isn't it?'

220

'Good work, both of you,' Morgan smiled at each of them. 'I'm leaning towards including Wesley Crook in Operation Siren. Any thoughts?'

DS Dave Spence had been standing at the side of the room and took a pace forwards. 'Should we wait for the ink comparison analysis from the wedding dress, sir?'

Morgan glanced across to include Patel whose response was a shrug.

'Okay, let's keep it in mind,' he said and crossed to the fourth board. He wrote "Operation X" at the top. 'And now for Councillor Kenneth Wyatt, our internet star, who was found in his garage yesterday. We're getting an Operation name for this one.'

'Operation Pervert.'

'Operation Groper.'

'Operation Hashtag Me Too.' Everyone seemed to have an idea.

'Okay, okay. Whatever we may think of him, he has still been murdered and we mustn't let our emotions stand in the way of catching who did it. Now, let's start with cause of death.'

Chapter 54

Friday 21st February

After she dropped the twins off at school Samantha Morgan drove back to their park home and packed the last of their belongings into her car. She ran the vacuum cleaner round and cleaned the shower and sinks in the bathroom and kitchen. Standing there, she remembered Nick's fury when she'd returned from the charity dinner. He had been distant ever since. She thought he believed her, but couldn't be sure. She buttoned her coat and locked up for the last time. Her new life was at Cliffside House. She hoped that once the police had found whoever was responsible for these deaths, Nick would have time to get on with the renovations. He was so much happier when he was doing hard, physical stuff. All this cerebral detecting depressed him.

When she parked on the drive at Cliffside she took a moment to look at her new home. It looked dark and unloved under the threatening sky. Rummaging through her handbag, she found the key and headed for the front door. The lock was stiff and reluctant and the door creaked when she pushed it. Some junk mail lay on the floor tiles and as she bent to pick it up, she heard the noise of tyres on the drive. For a moment, she thought that Nick must have made time to help and her spirits lifted. She heard the car door slam and footsteps on the shingle and was smiling as she straightened up and turned.

'What a sight to be greeted by,' the voice came from behind a large patio rose plant in a blue pot. 'I turn into a drive with the expectation of a cup of coffee at best, and I'm rewarded by the magnificent spectacle of Sammy's arse in tight jeans as she bends over to greet me.'

'You can't be here, Graham,' she said, 'I've got to pick the children up soon.'

'School's not out for at least four hours, Sammy, and I've brought you a house warming present. Don't be ungrateful.' He held out the pot and she took it. 'It's called "Sweet Memories," and I have such sweet memories of you. I'm hoping to make some more. How about that coffee to start with?'

'Nick could be here at any minute. He said he'd try to get here for lunch.'

'Come on, Sammy don't be so inhospitable. It's a cup of coffee. Where's the harm?' He had one foot on the doorstep now and she made room for him to pass her. He pushed the door closed and glanced back when it creaked. 'You need a handyman,' he said before taking the plant back from her and placing it on a side table. 'Right at this minute, I'm a very handy man.' He put his hands on her hips and pulled her towards him kissing the tip of her nose before their lips met. He lifted her light frame and she wrapped her legs around his waist. She clung tightly to him and he carried her to the sofa where Nick Morgan had slept two weeks before. As he laid her down and started to unbuckle his trouser belt he said, 'I've been dying to ask... Did we get away with it on Sunday or is DI Plod on the case?'

Chapter 55

Friday 21st February

After another grinding day of dealing with information that got them no further, Morgan was glad of the shorter drive home to Cliffside House. When he got out of his car he was pleased to see welcoming light shining through windows which weren't yet curtained. Sam opened the door as he got to it, her smile warm, her eyes sparkling. He saw that the lined, angry look which had masked her face for months had gone, and when he bent to kiss her he could smell peach shampoo and musky perfume.

Sam was wearing black leggings and a red jumper with a plunging neckline, complimented by a black velvet choker. He loved this outfit. The shiny black stripper heels might have been overkill for a Friday evening family meal, but he appreciated the effort, especially since he'd not been the most supportive of husbands during the last week.

'Welcome home,' she said reaching out a hand for his briefcase. 'I've roasted a chicken with all the trimmings. Once you've had a shower, we'll have a glass of champagne - I've promised the kids they can have a thimbleful - and then we can start our new life in our new house sitting down in the dining room for a proper family dinner.' She closed the creaking front door. 'Can you sort that out before you get involved in anything more complicated?'

In their temporary bedroom, Nick Morgan hung up his suit and stripped off the rest of his clothes before turning on the shower in the en-suite. There were lime scale stains on the tiles and the water drained reluctantly. Everywhere he looked, something needed attention but, seeing Sam's happiness, it would be worth it. The shower came to temperature and as he stepped in, he heard the front doorbell ring.

'I've brought champagne and a special rose. Can you take them, dear, they're quite heavy.' Dorothy's outstretched arms held two carrier bags. 'You didn't think I'd miss this special occasion, did you? In fact, I rather thought you would invite me.'

Samantha took the gifts and kissed her mother's offered cheek. Two roses in one day, she thought, but under very different circumstances. The memory of Graham's visit this morning gave her butterflies. She imagined she could feel him inside her still. She felt her face flush. 'Alex. Vicky. Grandma's here,' she called.

The twins came from the direction of the kitchen and hurried towards Dorothy who opened her arms to embrace them. 'Hello, both of you.' After hugs and kisses were exchanged she turned her gaze back to her daughter. 'You look well, dear.' Samantha's blush intensified. 'Something in this new life by the seaside is definitely doing you good.' As the four of them walked to the kitchen Dorothy stepped closer to her. 'Don't think I don't know what, or rather, who, has got into you,' she said quietly, 'but you need to be careful not to overdo it. Whether I like it or not, you married a detective and he's not completely stupid.' She pointed to Samantha's partially exposed breasts. 'Now, put those away dear, your mother's here.'

DS Dave Spence left his black Vauxhall Astra in the 24 hour multi-storey car park and walked the short distance to Club Europium. He found DCs Jenny Smart, Leo Jenson and Lynn Greenfield waiting round the corner from the main entrance, where a queue was forming.

'It's just as well we aren't meant to be undercover,' he said, 'I have more clothes on when I get into bed than some of those punters are wearing. It's February, for Christ's sake!'

Jenson was hugging himself and stamping his feet to keep warm. 'I've been here half an hour and I'm freezing.'

'You're too keen, Leo,' said Greenfield. 'What's the plan, sir?'

Spence reached into his jacket pocket and took out a wad of photos which had been downloaded from Abi Slater's social media pages. He handed them round. 'I'm sorry we couldn't have a formal briefing, but with everyone involved in different cases, it's been impossible to get us all in one place at the same time. Has anyone from uniform turned up to help?'

'When I was leaving the office, every spare body went out on search warrants. Stolen firearms. Duty Sergeant apologised for not being able to help us,' said Smart.

'Typical,' said Spence, distracted for a moment by a wish that he was involved in the raids rather than trying to extract information from party-loving clubbers. 'The boss has given us an open remit here. Show the pictures; ask if anyone remembers her; what do they remember? Usual drill. Then...' he handed round more pictures, 'do they recognise this guy? Some of you will have seen his picture on the board in the briefing room. It's Abi Slater's fiancé, Joseph Kendrick.'

Greenfield took out her phone and shone its light on the photo. 'I've not seen it,' she explained, 'I need a closer look.'

'No matter,' said Spence. 'He told us he came here with Abi a few times and that during one of those times, Abi was approached by an aggressive male. He wasn't able to give much of a description because it was pretty dark.'

'In the club, or outside?' asked Smart.

'Inside. He caught a glimpse of the face but it didn't leave a lasting impression. That's about all I can tell you, I'm afraid.'

'Can we go in now?' said Jenson. 'I'm freezing.'

Stop moaning, Leo,' said Smart before turning to Spence. 'Are the management expecting us? I mean, are they being co-operative?'

'Yes, they are. They said they would put Abi's picture up in the toilets with the Crimestoppers phone number and they've given us access to an office in the back if we need to speak to someone in a quiet place. I think you should take turns at speaking to the punters in the queue. Show them the pictures and see what you get.' He rifled through the photos he had kept for himself before holding one up. 'This is Abi in her clubbing gear and she looks very different from the ones the newspapers and TV have been running. If they recognise her at all, it'll be from this one.' He looked at his watch. 'Let's all meet up at the front of the Club at say... two o'clock. We can see where we are and decide how much longer we need to be here.'

They agreed and set off towards the entrance.

Chapter 56

Monday 24th February

'Did you have a good weekend, sir?' DC Jennifer Smart came into Morgan's office with a stack of files in her arms. He was unpacking his briefcase and paused to reflect. Friday evening's dinner had been fraught. Dorothy goaded him with regular references to his inability to catch whoever was responsible for the local murders. Sam had been apologetic and tried to make up for it in bed that night but he was tired and he kept remembering the sight of Maisie with tears in her eyes. He'd spent Saturday and Sunday up ladders, surveying, prodding plaster and brickwork, and measuring up what was going to be needed to replace the damage that years of salty sea air and neglect had caused. It had been good to be back in his scruffy jeans and sweatshirts and best of all, the phone hadn't rung.

'I did, thank you Jenny. What about you? How did your evening at Club Europium go?'

'More of a night than an evening, sir. I'm getting too old for double shifts and all nighters. Yesterday was good. I took my nieces to the latest Disney film. It was nice to forget real life for a while and I even managed to catch up on some sleep without them noticing.' She smiled at the memory. 'We all gave our interview notes to DS Spence before we went home from the club on Friday, well, Saturday really. He's checking a few things out with Leo before he comes in to speak to you.'

'What was your gut feel?'

Smart screwed up her features and rocked her hand from side to side. 'There was some interesting stuff, but I wouldn't like to comment on its veracity. I spoke to a young lad who remembered Abi really well. He said she'd taken his virginity in the service alley behind the club.'

Morgan's eyebrows rose. 'Not beyond the realms of possibility, I suppose, given the other stories we've heard about her.'

Smart shook her head. 'He was speaking to me in front of his mates who I think were egging him on. I suspect if we went to visit him at home in the presence of a responsible adult, like his mum, for example, we'd get a different story.'

'Okay, I get the picture. Did anything else come in over the weekend? I didn't get any calls.'

She shook her head. 'Not as far as I know. Do you want me to check?'

'I'm sure they'll be in touch if we're needed. I'm nipping downstairs for a coffee and then I'll speak to Dave before we sort out the briefing.'

On his way back to his office, coffee in hand, his work mobile rang. Unknown caller. Morgan prepared to deal with what he expected would be a desperate journalist whose editor had given an ultimatum.

'DI Morgan,' he answered.

'Is that DI Morgan?' Immediately, he was irritated. Why did people do that?

'Yes, it is, how can I help?' He continued walking, juggling phone and coffee as he manoeuvred through fire doors.

'Sharon Crook gave me your number.' The name didn't register. Then he remembered going with DC

Smart to tell Wesley Crook's mother that her son had been found under a tree with a sign around his neck.

'Okay. And you are..?'

'My son and Wesley were friends. It was a while ago.'

Morgan remembered Sharon Crook's pragmatism. Surely she would not have given his number to a woman who only wanted to chat about her son's schooldays?

'How can I help, Mrs er..?'

'I've had a letter,' she said. 'Or rather, my son's had a letter. I opened it cos he's inside at the moment.' She spoke quickly as if she was frightened he would end the call before she had finished what she wanted to say.

Morgan waited. 'And?' he said.

'Sharon said that Wesley had a letter before he was killed.' He didn't answer. 'Are you still there?' she shouted.

'I'm here. What does the letter say?'

'It says he'll be sorry.' The woman's voice was breaking. 'Sharon told me that's what Wesley's letter said.'

Morgan closed his eyes and nodded. He felt the back of his neck prickle. 'I'm at my office now. If you give me your address, I'll be with you within the hour. Don't touch the letter again.'

Passing through the main office he noted that most of his team had arrived and were preparing their reports for the briefing.

'Grab your jacket, Spence. There's been another letter.'

<u>Chapter 57</u>

Monday 24th February

If Morgan had been expecting to visit a similar property to Sharon Crook's flat, he could not have been more mistaken. Spence drove them north through the forest, before turning into a wide road lined with trees and grassy verges.

'Are those cherry trees?' asked Morgan when they stopped outside a detached 1930's house.

'I don't know. I've never been here before.'

'If they are, this road must look magical when the blossom's in full bloom.'

Morgan pushed the wrought iron gate which squeaked as it opened. He made a mental note to buy some oil on his way home for his own front door, but knew he'd probably forget. As the two men walked up the path they were greeted by an elderly golden Labrador who appeared from the side of the house. Morgan offered the back of his hand and the dog sniffed at it. Spence held back.

The shiny blue front door opened before they had a chance to ring the bell.

'I burnt the toast and had the back door open to get rid of the smell. She must have got out. Get in, Bella and stop annoying these gentlemen.' They stood to one side to let Bella through and watched as she collapsed into a basket in the hall. 'She's thirteen and bothered by arthritis. She's almost blind too. I don't know how I'll manage without her.'

The woman spoke quickly as if unfamiliar with the concept of punctuation.

'I'm DI Morgan and this is DS Spence.' They both held out ID but she waved it away.

'I can tell you're police by the way you walked up my path. It's not the first time I've had police at my door. I'm Mrs Drake. Megan Drake, that is. Harry's mother.' She seemed about to offer a handshake, but changed her mind and continued speaking instead. 'The last lot turned my house upside down and it took me a week to get straight. I hoped Bella might bite them but she just watched.'

'Can we come in, please?' asked Morgan hoping that politeness might help her forget her previous experience.

'Of course. The kettle's boiled.' She pointed towards the back of the house where weak winter sunshine leaked into the hallway through an open door. 'That's the lounge. Have a seat. Is coffee okay? I've only got instant.'

Morgan sensed that coffee was a necessary ritual for Megan Drake and since he had left his first caffeine hit of the day untouched on his desk, he accepted. 'That's very kind of you Mrs Drake, milk and no sugar for us both, please.'

The room was a lounge diner with an arch through to the kitchen. Bi-fold doors led out on to decking which looked green and slippery and a garden which was well tended for the time of year. The officers stood at the doors and took in the view before making eye contact. Spence raised his eyebrows and Morgan replied with a shrug. This wasn't the sort of property they usually visited when following up errant offspring.

Megan Drake came in, carrying a tray with three mugs of coffee and a plate of ginger biscuits. 'I buy them at the farmers' market. I don't have time to make my own nowadays.' She held the tray towards them. 'Either of the green mugs,' she said. The remaining white mug had a picture of a stick figure woman with a big round head and a wide smile. Her short arms with overly large hands were held open for a hug. Written beside her were the words "World's Best Mum." She saw them look at it. 'I've had it a while,' she said, obviously feeling the need to explain before pointing them towards the beige settee.

They sat, and Morgan, who had already planned his questioning strategy, started. 'Mrs Drake, you should know that I've only been on this patch for a couple of weeks and I'm not aware of your son's history. Before we get to the letter, it would help if you could start with some background.'

Spence fiddled with his phone before placing it on the coffee table. 'I hope you don't mind,' he said. The prospect of having her words recorded flustered her, but she nodded her agreement.

'Where should I start?' she asked, still staring at the phone.

'You said that your son is in custody, perhaps you could start there?' said Morgan. He was hoping that Spence hadn't blown it by introducing the recording.

'Harry went to prison two weeks ago for breaching a restraining order his ex took out. He just wanted to see his kids.'

Morgan intervened with a placatory softness in his tone. 'I appreciate how difficult this is for you but what I need is to get an understanding of how your son got to know Wesley Crook. Oh, and if you can tell me of anyone else who might know that they knew each other, that would help too.'

She looked disappointed. 'But you need to know that he's not a bad lad, really.'

'I need to know about his relationship with Wesley, Mrs Drake. And about the letter too, of course.'

'He met Wesley in Portland. Nothing was the same after that.'

'Youth Offenders Institute,' said Spence, in case Morgan hadn't heard of it.

Morgan's phone rang and she jumped. He reached into his pocket and handed it to Spence who disappeared into the kitchen to take the call.

'I'm sorry,' she said. 'Where were we?'

'Harry met Wesley at Youth Offenders,' said Morgan, at the same time, trying to get the gist of the conversation Spence was having in the kitchen.

'They met there and they were released on the same day. Harry wanted Wesley to come here, but I put my foot...'

'Sir,' Spence's head appeared round the kitchen door. He was pointing to the phone.

Morgan excused himself and joined Spence in the kitchen.

'DI Morgan,' he said.

DC Lynn Greenfield sounded excited. 'The forensic report on Councillor Wyatt's clothes has come in. There were marks on his sweat shirt which they have identified as tears and nasal secretions.'

Morgan kept his voice down to avoid being overheard by Megan Drake. 'I might cry a bit myself if someone was putting a dog lead round my neck and about to hang me.'

'It's not his DNA,' she replied.

He looked at Spence who was nodding and indicating that he wanted to speak.

'Hang on a minute, Lynn, Spence wants a word.'

'I saw the state of the bedrooms, sir. That man's clothes have not visited a washing machine in a good few weeks. It could be his wife's if he tried to stop her from leaving, or any other unsuspecting female he had his hands on.'

'I heard what Dave said, sir,' said Greenfield and Morgan heard the rustling of paper as she turned pages. 'The report says that the secretions are from the same person and that person is male.'

Megan Drake appeared at the kitchen door as he ended the call. She was carrying the three empty coffee mugs in her hand. 'I'll put the kettle on again,' she said.

'Mrs Drake, something has come up and we have to be going. I'll need the letter and please tell me why your son is in prison.'

'They activated a suspended sentence for theft in breach of trust. He was selling fake insurance policies. But, it wasn't his fault. Bloody magistrates didn't even listen to all he's been through.'

The officers made their way back through the long reception room and Spence picked up his phone and ended the recording. Megan Drake held out the letter and Morgan opened an evidence bag for her to drop it into. He gave it to Spence who started to fill in the details on the label. As Morgan thanked her again for the information and the coffee she was shaking her head. 'Why did he have to go to prison? He only wanted to see his kids.'

They passed Bella who had fallen asleep in her basket and was snoring.

Chapter 58

Morgan entered the open plan office with Spence close behind him.

Greenfield looked up from her computer screen as they approached her. 'Sorry, sir. No match for the DNA.'

DC Smart crossed the office to where they were congregating. 'I've got bad news too, I'm afraid. The wording of the sign around Crook's neck has been circulating on social media. Eight thousand hits so far but increasing faster than a celebrity scandal.'

For a moment, everyone seemed to hold their breath. Nobody had experienced how well or otherwise DI Nick Morgan took bad news and this was really bad news. He nodded and pursed his lips.

'Well, I don't know if it's good news, or not,' he said, 'but we've picked up another letter. Same words as the letter to Wesley Crook.' He held up the evidence bag before handing it to Jenny Smart. 'Repent or die.'

Smart frowned.

'Okay, I'm paraphrasing.' He headed for the door.

Spence crossed to his desk and picked up a blue folder which had a sheet of paper sitting on top of it before following him, reading from the paper as he walked. He had caught up by the time Morgan reached his office. 'The interviews from Friday, sir,' he called from outside the door.

'Come in, Dave,' Morgan beckoned as he spoke. 'Take a seat.'

Spence sat opposite Morgan and removed a thick sheaf of paper from his folder. 'I came in yesterday and went through the notes. I've tried to put them in some sort of order.' He held them towards Morgan who shook his head.

'You've read them, what do you think?'

Spence pulled a notebook from his pocket and started to read from it. Morgan smiled. It was small, but it was a smile. He had suspected there would be a summary. He had saved himself time by not having to trawl though pages of notes written under dodgy lighting by tired officers who were beyond caring about legibility.

'I've already heard about the virgin in the service alley,' said Morgan.

'I put that one down to wishful thinking,' said Spence, 'but there are a few things we might take a closer look at.' He separated the sheets of paper into two piles. 'Males and females,' he said. 'More males than females remembered Abi, thus the bigger pile.'

Morgan nodded. 'Go on.'

Spence consulted his notes. 'The males told us how pretty she was and that she was a good dancer. Never off the floor when she was at the club. She was seen to chat to everyone and dance with anyone. Leo spoke to a lad who saw an argument outside a different club, a couple of nights before Abi disappeared. Thought it might have been her, but wasn't sure.'

'And he didn't think to mention this sooner?'

Spence looked down at his notes and then pointed to the pile of papers in front of Morgan. 'Number twenty four.'

Morgan flicked through the larger pile and pulled out a page. 'It looks as if Leo didn't ask why this lad kept quiet for so long. That's disappointing.'

'When you go through the pages, you'll see that a lot of them are headed GIR. That means Gave Information Reluctantly. I asked the team to add that where it was relevant to show why they hadn't pushed hard.'

Morgan felt chastened and continued to read. 'So, he wasn't sure that the girl was Abi, but he recognised the male in the picture he was shown.'

'Yes, sir. Joseph Kendrick. Abi's fiancé. And when Leo showed him the picture of Abi in her clubbing gear, he was a bit more sure it was the pair of them he'd seen arguing, and that Kendrick had slapped her.'

'And yet, a day or two later, she picks up a wedding dress, presumably with the intention of marrying him?'

'I hope you're not going to ask me to comment on the psychology of female motivations, sir.'

'Wouldn't dream of it. What was the gist of the interviews with the females?'

'Some of the females were complimentary, especially if they were interviewed in the company of their boyfriends. However, this is a selection of the more typical responses.' He cleared his throat before reading from his personal notes. '"Abigail Slater was an attention seeker. She wore clothes that barely covered her arse and when she was dancing, or chatting, she was constantly looking round to see who was admiring her, or if there was someone more important to be seen with."'

'Meow,' said Morgan.

'It gets worse, sir.' Spence returned to his notes. 'And I quote. "She never left the club with the same man twice. I thought she was on the game until someone told me she was a solicitor. When I heard she was engaged, I felt sorry for the guy."'

Morgan blew air out of his mouth. 'Those comments corroborate what we've heard about her. Useful to know, but doesn't take us any further really.'

'Until this came in while we were out talking to Mrs Drake. It's from Crimestoppers.' Spence indicated the page from the top of the pile. 'It's anonymous, but it's a message left by someone we spoke to on Friday who says they didn't want to be overheard giving us information. He or she says that Abigail Slater was still meeting one of her previous boyfriends at the club, long after she was telling everyone that she was engaged.'

'I don't suppose they left a name for this boyfriend?'

'Sorry, sir.'

Steven Cooper's name was in Morgan's mind and he was certain that Spence was thinking the same. It would also tie up with the rumour Graham Fletcher had told them. Abi was still seeing Sam's brother when the banns were being read. He waited for Spence to speak and when nothing was offered, carried on.

'And it says she was meeting him at the Europium? Didn't the fiancé tell us she'd stopped going to clubs because she was often the overnight duty solicitor?'

'Maybe that's just what she told him. Perhaps she was still going dancing and telling him she was on duty.'

Morgan sat back in his chair and tutted. 'So we've got the fiancé telling us they'd stopped going clubbing, but he's seen arguing with Abi outside a club and slapping her, two days before she disappeared. Did he find out about this other man? We'll have to get him in again.'

'Sir.' Spence headed for the door, but Morgan was still speaking.

'Would she do that? Would she risk her imminent marriage to a successful broker just for some illicit sex? I'm going to struggle to sell it to Johnson, which is what I've got to go and do now.' Morgan looked up at his office clock and compared the time with his watch. He followed Spence through the door and stopped abruptly when he heard a text alert. The message was from Maisie but he couldn't make sense of it.

Come now fnd ring

He frowned at the phone as if that would help. 'I need to make a quick call. Sorry.' He hurried to the doors at the end of the corridor and slipped through them into the stairwell. After listening for footsteps on the concrete steps, he called her and she replied immediately.

'Are you okay?' he asked, his concern obvious. 'I don't understand the message.'

'The papers said that Abi Slater's engagement ring was missing, is that right?'

Morgan hadn't been keeping up with the papers or social media. It was a deliberate choice on his part. He preferred to deal with evidence based facts from investigation rather than supposition. He opened the door to the corridor where Spence was leaning on the wall inspecting his own phone screen.

'Remind me. Is Abi Slater's engagement ring missing?' he called to his DS.

Spence thought for a couple of seconds. 'Yes. I remember her flatmate... Juliet something, she asked if we had it.'

'Okay, hang on.' Morgan returned to the stairwell. 'Yes, it's missing.'

240

'I've got it. Or I should say, I think it's the same one - she only showed it to me once. It's a sapphire with two diamonds on either side of it.'

'I don't think we have a description, unless it's in a statement somewhere. Where did you find it?'

'If you come now, I can show you exactly where. It was next to a bed.' She was using the soft, husky voice he remembered from before their relationship had progressed beyond flirting.

He cleared his throat and tried to lose the image of her naked body and her eyes smiling at him.

'DS Spence and I will be there right away. Where shall we meet you?'

'I'm in A-38,' She gave concise directions in a business-like voice. 'Please hurry, I've got a lot on today.' She ended the call before he could answer.

Spence hadn't moved and was looking expectant. 'Is it the ring?'

Morgan stretched out his arms, palms facing upwards. 'It's *a* ring, whether it's *her* ring is another matter. Looks as if Johnson will have to wait for his update.' They set off back to Spence's car.

Chapter 59

Morgan got out of the car first and approached the open door to the park home with a sense of urgency. It would only take Spence a few moments to park in the tight spot between the bushes and Maisie's service van, but that was long enough to explain why he had come accompanied.

Maisie appeared at the door. 'I thought I heard a car. You made good time.' She looked beyond him. 'On your own?'

'DS Spence is parking. If this is Abigail Slater's ring, then two of us need to see where you found it. We'll need to get a crime scene team here too.'

'Good luck with that,' she scoffed. 'I've been cleaning. I had a call from the owners last week and they're coming on Thursday for a few days. They asked me to tidy up and air the place. It's not one of ours but the owner, Mrs Stockton, uses a walking stick nowadays, so I help her out when I can.'

Spence knocked on the open door and came in without waiting. 'This is really nice. I'd no idea they were so spacious,' he said.

'Where's the ring?' asked Morgan and followed Maisie's pointing finger to the breakfast bar. 'Did you touch it?'

'It was between the bed and the wall in the master. I pulled the bed out to vacuum and there it was.'

'We'll need the vacuum cleaner for forensics,' said Spence.

'How long for? The season is starting soon and I need every vacuum cleaner I've got.'

'Can you make the call please, DS Spence?' Spence nodded and took his phone outside.

'We're going to need a statement, Maisie.'

'I remember what happened last time you said that.'

'I do too. I remember it well, and I think of it often.' Their eyes met and Morgan cleared his throat. 'Can you show me exactly where you found the ring?'

He followed her down the hall to the master bedroom. Through the window he could see across the lake and into the woods. If Abigail Slater had died here, even someone unfamiliar with the territory would have seen there was an ideal place to dump her body right on the doorstep.

'When was Mrs Stockton last here?' he asked.

'The Stocktons don't have to book because this is their property.'

'So, you don't know.'

Maisie looked a little taken aback. She was used to "off duty" Nick Morgan and seemed to find DI Morgan a bit abrasive. She looked uncomfortable.

'I do happen to know, actually. Mrs Stockton popped in to wish me a Happy New Year. They were here for Christmas and drove home on New Year's Eve.'

'Is this one of the homes you allowed Abi Slater access to for her personal assignations?'

'No!' she shouted. 'I told you. This is a privately owned home. I have a master key which gives me access, but I would never allow anyone to use it.'

Morgan heard Spence call for him and he put his head around the door. 'We're in here.'

'Forensics don't have anyone free to send until later this afternoon but I've got a PCSO coming to hold the fort. He will be here in about fifteen minutes and he'll put the tape up. When can you come in to make your statement, madam?' He was looking at Maisie.

'It's not that easy to say. I'll come when I can get someone to cover.'

'Okay,' said Morgan 'But that really needs to be sometime today. Ask for either DS Spence, or DC Smart when you arrive. Please contact Mrs Stockton and explain that they will have to delay their visit, I'm afraid. This could be where Abi Slater was murdered.'

Chapter 60

In the days since overhearing the plans to burgle the DIY store, he used his motorbike to visit a few sites, checking to see which of them had shipping containers in their car park. He narrowed it down to two and picked one at random. If they turned up, he would deal with them, if not, well, he'd never intended this to be about commercial burglars, it was the bastards who invaded homes and turned lives upside down he wanted to make sorry.

He was in position when the store closed at nine o'clock. Most of the staff had left by quarter past getting into vehicles parked up against the back fence. He was out of their line of vision, but ducked down in the front seat of the van anyway. After a while, there was only an estate car and a small hatchback beside it. Management, he thought. They would be more vigilant in looking around when they left. He considered cutting his losses and going to the pub. Dinner felt heavy in his stomach and a couple of pints with a few games of darts would help his digestion. Besides, his friends would be wondering where he was.

Twenty minutes later, the small staff door opened again and a tall thin man appeared followed by a shorter woman. They were laughing and he saw small clouds of condensed breath. The man pushed the woman against the wall and started to kiss her. She was still laughing as the security light faded, leaving them in darkness. Under any other circumstances, he might have enjoyed watching, but not tonight. He needed them to leave.

A white car pulled into the car park and approached the delivery bay. The couple must have moved because the security light triggered again. The car changed direction and drove towards them. From his van, he could see a shield logo on the front passenger door and blue and white chevron markings up the side. Mobile security. He hadn't thought about that. How often did the patrols come?

The couple chatted briefly with the uniformed driver before waving as he reversed into a parking bay to turn the car, and leaving. They snogged again, then the woman got into the estate car and blew a kiss as she drove away. He watched the man get into the hatchback and make a phone call. He guessed he was telling his wife he'd been delayed at work. Liar.

The security car returned about two hours after the first visit. The man got out and flashed his torch at the store's main entrance and the staff door before getting back in and speeding off. As he watched, it crossed his mind that the company would be pissed off if they knew the level of service they were getting for their money.

He had brought a couple of tins of beer and a large bag of crisps to help pass the time and eventually, he needed to pee. When he got out of the van and went round to the back he heard a vehicle approach. It was being driven slowly but it went straight past the entrance. It was a van, dark coloured, not very big. Earlier, articulated and refrigerated lorries from the industrial estate had gone by, but not for a while. God, he really needed to pee but he zipped himself up and crouched down behind his van. If this was them, he didn't want to be caught with his dick in his hand.

The van drove into the parking area for the property opposite. When he popped his head up, he could see the lights were off, but heard the engine running. After a couple of minutes it crossed to the DIY store car park and stopped, facing the storage containers' padlocked doors. The headlights came on again – full beam. He ducked back down behind his van.

Fuck it! Everything he needed was on the passenger seat but, if he opened the door, the internal light would come on. It would either scare them away or, more likely, they would come for him and he didn't think that would end well.

There was another delay before he heard the van doors open and when he looked again he saw they were both wearing balaclavas. Short Man was carrying what looked like a cordless angle grinder and the other one had bolt cutters. He couldn't see what they were doing at the front of the containers, but he saw a shower of sparks and it wasn't long before the doors of the first one swung open. Short Man disappeared inside and he started to pile big boxes between the container and their van.

Tall Man started to load the boxes into the back of their van. He heard him say that they should have brought help. It was the higher voice and, remembering it from the court waiting area, he knew now that he was the younger guy. That made it easier to plan how he would tackle them.

As he crept around the back of the container he heard Short Man say 'Pack 'em in tight. We'll get as much as we can.'

The open door hid him from view as he tiptoed up the side of the container. He saw the discarded bolt cutters. They would have to do.

Short Man was taking longer to make each trip into the container and he could hear laboured breathing.

He waited.

Tall Man jumped down from the back of the truck and he arced the bolt cutters down on his head like an executioner's axe. A loud crack, then his knees buckled and he fell forwards, knocking over the pile of boxes he had been reaching for.

He heard a voice call 'Mickey?' It was no louder than a whisper. Then, 'Mickey? Are you alright?' followed by a stream of curses.

He could hear that Short Man wasn't pleased. 'Fuck's sake, Mickey. What have you done?' He waited until Short Man was bending over Mickey then delivered the same fate. He went down like a felled tree across the top of Mickey's body.

He leant against the shipping container for a moment to catch his breath before hurrying to the Transit and turning off the lights and ignition. The next security patrol might come any minute and he wanted to be sure that the car park was in darkness. He rubbed the handles of the bolt cutters on his jeans and threw them into the back of the open container. Then, he went back to his van for gloves and a Sharpie pen. He ripped the top off one of the cartons. There was just enough light for him to see what he was writing before he tucked the card between the layered bodies and went back to his van. As the wind picked up across the car park he felt chilled and realised that at some point, he must have wet himself.

Chapter 61

The Ops Room inspector was apologetic when he woke Morgan up at 4.30am. 'It's a messy one, DI Morgan. Two men in a DIY outlet car park, both with head injuries. Life pronounced extinct and pathologist in attendance.'

Morgan rubbed sleep from his eyes. 'I'm not the Duty DI. You should be contacting DI Patel.'

'I did, DI Morgan, and she attended. Dr Mack told her there were similarities to a case you're working on and said he thought it appropriate for you to attend.'

'Since when do pathologists get an input into our duty rota?' Tiling a shower until the early hours of the morning had done nothing to improve Morgan's amenability. 'Sorry. Late night. Can you give me the details?'

A PCSO logged him in at the scene. He directed Morgan over to the area furthest from the floodlit activity where he parked, locked up, and thrust his hands into a pair of blue nitrile gloves retrieved from a box in his boot. Wind was swirling litter around the area and a crime scene technician was chasing after it with long handled tongs. He pulled up the collar of his thick wool coat, thankful that at last, he had access to his full wardrobe. He strode across to where people in white hooded overalls were working.

'Dr Mackenzie. I understand you put in a special request for me to attend?'

249

Mackenzie nodded and beckoned him towards the white crime scene tent. He held the flap open and Morgan saw that he would have to wait before getting a closer look. There were CSI technicians taking photos and collecting evidence under lights which made the tent glow like an alien craft, recently landed.

'It's two men. One draped over the other. Looks like blunt force trauma to the head. Both of them. Of course, I'll know more after the examinations.'

'And why's it for me?' asked Morgan.

Mackenzie called over to one of the white suited technicians who produced a flat evidence bag from a plastic crate.

'We found this, tucked between the bodies. I believe you're collecting them?' He produced a small torch from his pocket and shone it on the piece of brown corrugated cardboard, sealed in plastic.

Morgan read aloud. "'Now I'm sorry and Mickey's sorry too.'"

Morgan was at the front of the briefing room talking to Spence when the door flew open and crashed into the wall behind. They looked up to see DC Jenny Smart struggling to manoeuvre another white board into the room. 'No, please don't anyone help, I'll manage.' Some of the men looked embarrassed but most laughed. 'This is the last spare board. I've stolen it from the lecture room,' she continued. 'If we don't catch this one soon, we'll have to draw on the walls.'

Spence helped her wheel the board past randomly scattered tables and chairs. He aligned it with the other boards at the front and taped two photos to the top, taking care to ensure they were level. 'This is Angus and Michael Maguire. Father and son.'

'We just need the Holy Ghost now,' said one of the DCs who had been drafted in. It earned him a scowl from both senior officers.

'Gus and Mickey are well known to us,' continued Spence, 'In fact both were in court recently for thefts from the student halls in the town centre. They pleaded not guilty and were on bail pending trial. Father should have been at Crawley for sentencing today. He was likely to go down, or to be remanded for sentencing at the Crown Court, depending on which magistrates he got.' He picked the next photograph from the top of the file open on the table in front of him. 'This is today's message. It was sandwiched between the bodies.' He taped it under the men's pictures and stepped back to look at the board.

'We can't read the sign at this end of the room,' said DC Leo Jenson.

'It says "Now I'm sorry and Mickey's sorry too,"' said Morgan. 'And I have to applaud the grammar. It's not everyone who's mastered the correct use of the word "too."' There were a few nods of acknowledgement around the room and Morgan saw Smart make a note. She looked up and caught his eye. 'Go ahead, Jenny,' he said.

'I'm wondering what happened to the concept of M.O. If we're grouping all these cases together, it's all over the place. Drugs, stabbing, suffocation, strangulation and now blunt force trauma.'

'Times two,' chipped in a voice. 'Two PPOs. One on top of the other. A real shit sandwich.'

'Whether these men were Prolific and Priority Offenders or ministers of the church, they didn't deserve to die like that,' said Morgan. 'Nobody deserves to die like that, so let's remember what it is to be professional and if you've nothing to say that moves us nearer catching them, please keep quiet. And Jenny, I'm not sure we are grouping them together at this stage.' Jenny Smart shrugged her shoulders and Morgan continued.

'Father and son appear to have been disturbed while breaking into a couple of shipping containers in the car park of DIY Deals on the outskirts of town. The store has a contract with a mobile security company but it seems that the guard was twenty minutes late on his rounds. When he arrived, there was a Transit van beside the two containers, one of which had been forced open. The two bodies were to one side, laid, one on top of the other, with the cardboard sign sandwiched between them. Apparently the containers were being used to store high end garden and DIY tools ready for the Easter trade. Some of those boxes were already stashed in the Transit, and some were scattered across the car park.'

'Any of the stock missing, sir?' asked Jenson.

'The store manager will let us know for definite, but he didn't think so,' said Morgan.

'So we're not looking for a gang who planned to knock off another gang's loot?'

'We shouldn't rule anything out at this stage,' said Spence, looking across the room for Morgan's reaction.'

'I agree.' He started to jot down some of the things they already knew about the case on the whiteboard. Each of the Maguire men had an extensive criminal history in which theft featured predominantly. Neither record mentioned drugs. Both had been hit from behind and Mackenzie's provisional examination had neither included nor excluded the bolt cutters left at the scene, as the weapon. There was little chance of any witnesses and not much to go on until the lab reported back. The technicians had also found tyre marks in an area of mud which looked fresh, but offered no way to confirm that they were from a vehicle used by the killer.

When the briefing was over, some of the team left to get on with tasks from previous cases whilst others came to the front of the room and stood with Spence and Morgan staring at the white boards, searching for inspiration.

'For what it's worth, I don't think Councillor Kenneth Wyatt links to any of this,' said Spence throwing an arm out in the direction of the board from which Wyatt's veined red face smiled confidently. 'No drugs, no letter, no connection with theft. I think we're looking for a father, or brother, or maybe boyfriend who saw the footage from that dinner and went round to have a word.'

'Okay,' said Morgan. 'I'm open to all ideas.'

'Had Abigail Slater defended either of the Maguires?' asked DC Smart.

'Don't know,' said Morgan. 'Can you get in touch with the solicitors again and ask please, Jenny?'

'Wesley Crook's tox screen isn't back yet, but if his mother's right and he's clean then the only mention of drugs is Carl Raynor,' offered Spence. Morgan's mobile rang and he moved away from the group to answer it.

When he finished the call, he rejoined his colleagues. 'Forensics say they've got prints. There's a partial thumb and even more partial index finger on the Transit key and the same finger on the van light switch. They've done a comparison with the Maguire records and there's no match. They'll let us know if it puts anyone in the frame.'

They exchanged glances. If the prints were already known it might be the breakthrough they needed.

The briefing room emptied leaving only Morgan and Smart who was looking at her notes. 'After I've spoken to the solicitors to check if Abi defended the Maguires, I'd like to speak to the lab about the bolt cutters.' She looked up as if suddenly aware that she was speaking out loud rather than thinking. It flustered her. 'Unless there's something else you had in mind for me to do?'

Morgan nodded his approval and his eyes followed her out of the room. He knew she had only been a DC for a few months but her confidence impressed him. He didn't remember having that level of self-assurance when he was new to the rank of Detective Constable. He hoped it wouldn't come back to bite her.

Chapter 62

When he got back to his office he closed his door and took out his personal phone. The dialled number rang out. 'For God's sake, Andy, get Voicemail,' he said and was about to end the call when it was answered.

'Andy Gillingham.'

'Andy, Nick Morgan.'

'Hi Nick. I'm late for a psych assessment. Can I ring you back?' Morgan could hear that his friend was hurrying.

'Okay. I know from the ring tone that you're in this country, for once. Fancy a few days by the sea?'

'Work or pleasure?'

'Work... but you might get a case paper out of it, and I know that Sam would love to see you.'

'Let me get back to you in two and a quarter hours. Bye.'

And that was typical of Dr Andrew Gillingham, thought Morgan. When anyone else would say "later," Gillingham would say "two and a quarter hours" and Morgan knew that was when to expect his call.

Morgan was aware that he was pre-empting confirmation of Gillingham's availability but he emailed DCI Johnson anyway. He suggested that the opinion of a criminal psychologist might be of value to the current cases which had both commonalities and discrepancies. He was sure that the words "budget" and "overspend" would feature in the response but by documenting the request, he could add it to his decision log. 'CYA,' he murmured as he pressed the send button. 'Cover Your Arse.'

Johnson's immediate reply invited Nick to his office to discuss where the investigations were going. When he read it, Morgan smiled. He had been outsmarted by a senior officer whose years of playing police politics had taught him how to swerve the traps. Now the response to his request would not be documented and could not be proven.

Morgan delayed his discussion with Johnson until he had taken Gillingham's call, a surprising four minutes ahead of its expected time slot.

'I thought I'd try to catch you out,' said Gillingham. 'What do you need?'

Morgan summarised the cases.

'And your DI gut feel says what?'

'Every time I get that, another body turns up with another couple of anomalies and I'm back to the drawing board.'

'I did simplex optimisation as part of my first degree. You should try that.'

'I really don't want you to tell me, but I need a favour, so I'll ask as if I'm interested,' said Morgan, looking at his watch in anticipation of a lecture he did not have time for.

'You plot variables in multi-dimensional vector space to find the minimum or maximum of an objective function and...'

'Stop! Just stop... or I may have to kill you.'

'You'd have to innumerate the variables, of course,' Gillingham was laughing.

'Can you come? Even a couple of hours would be better than nothing. I need a friend.'

'How *is* your mother-in-law?'

Morgan sighed, 'I've tried tampering with the brakes on her broomstick, but she's still here. If anything, having Sam back here has added a new spring to her step. When she came for dinner on Friday, she looked ten years younger. They're like naughty schoolgirls when they're together.'

'I'll come, if only to redress the testosterone balance. Is Thursday lunchtime okay?'

'I can't promise the budget.'

'I'm sure we can work something out,' said Gillingham. 'I must go. I'm having dinner this evening with the producer of my next series.'

They said their goodbyes and Morgan hurried upstairs for his meeting with Johnson. When he got there, the DCI was leaving his office, briefcase in one hand and turning out the lights with the other.

'I've got a Rotary dinner so I need to get home to change. Can you walk with me, or will it wait till tomorrow?' Morgan opted for the former.

'I need these cases concluded,' said Johnson. 'Especially the solicitor and the Councillor. I get a lot of phone calls from... well, I'm sure you can guess. And have you seen what the papers are saying about the investigations? I need these cases solved immediately.' Morgan thought it imprudent to reply. Why did senior officers say they needed cases to be solved immediately? Did they think their demands had any effect on the time it took to investigate a murder? Had they worked their way up through the ranks or arrived from another planet? Johnston had stopped talking and was waiting for a response to a question he had missed.

'I'm sorry sir, I didn't catch that.'

'I asked how many hours of consultant time you would need me to pay for.'

'I don't know. I can't know until they have a look at what we've got already.'

'And you believe it'll speed things up?'

'I can hope,' said Morgan. They were at the door to the car park and Johnson gave him the name of someone they had used before. Morgan replied that he had worked with Dr Andrew Gillingham on half a dozen cases and that he valued and respected his opinions.

'My budget won't stretch to TV personality rates.' Johnson's tone was clipped.

Morgan nodded. His friend Andy Gillingham was something of a polymath. He lectured at venues around the world, wrote both fiction and non-fiction, and appeared as a consultant on true crime programmes across terrestrial and satellite channels. When they'd last worked together, he was co-writing a film script which had nothing to do with crime or psychology and was enjoying the challenge. Although he was contractually obliged to deliver a number of lectures at universities in England each year, Gillingham was now in a position of financial security which allowed him to choose the work he took on. 'I'll have a word, sir. He won't do it for nothing, but if his curiosity is piqued, he may give us a bit of a discount.'

Johnson told him it had better be a hell of a discount.

Chapter 63

Two days later, Joseph Kendrick sat in Interview Room 2, again with his solicitor, Neville Wicks. He had attended voluntarily, but he looked wary. Morgan and Spence took their seats opposite and Morgan led by telling Abi's fiancé that he was to be interviewed under caution this time. The recording system was started and, after the words of formal caution, Morgan started the questioning.

'Can you remind us when it was you last saw Abigail please, Mr Kendrick?'

Kendrick looked towards his solicitor. 'I think I answered that when I was here before.'

'If you could answer it again, for the recording, please.'

'I met up with Abi at the Magistrates' Court, the day before she disappeared. We had a sandwich together in town, then she went back to work.'

'So you weren't at work that day?' asked Morgan. 'Because you work in London, don't you?'

'I had holiday owing and I took it to help with the wedding. Abi had done most of it, but I wanted to take a share.'

'Did you see her after the sandwich break?' asked Morgan.

'I'm not sure what you mean. I walked her back to the court and watched her go in. I think I sat on the wall outside for a bit, before going in myself. I asked an usher which court Abi was in but he wasn't sure, so I

259

wandered round and looked through the glass windows in the court room doors. When I found her, I went in and sat at the back.'

'Had you watched her at work before?'

'A couple of times maybe? I'm not sure. Look... where is this going, and why am I under caution?'

'Are you telling us that the last time you saw your fiancé, Abi Slater, was when she was defending a client in the Magistrates' Court?'

'Yes.'

'You didn't wait until she'd finished work and leave with her?'

'No.'

'You didn't meet up later?'

'No, I er... I don't think so. Why are you asking?'

'Yes, DI Morgan,' the solicitor interrupted, 'why are you asking?'

Spence opened a document wallet and produced a photograph which he placed on the table in front of Kendrick. 'For the recording, I'm showing Mr Kendrick a still, taken from CCTV outside the Golden Palm Club. Is this you, Mr Kendrick?'

Kendrick reached into his pocket and took out a pair of metal rimmed glasses. He picked up the photograph and studied it closely. 'It could be anyone,' he said, handing it to Neville Wicks.

'We believe it's you. And it's the first of a series.' Spence opened the wallet again and counted as he laid six photographs on to the desk with the skill of an experienced croupier. 'We believe it's you, and we believe that the woman you are with is Abigail Slater. The second last photo shows you with a raised open hand and the final one shows Abi holding her face.'

'Why did you hit your fiancée, Mr Kendrick?' Morgan asked. 'Why would you want to hurt the woman you were about to marry?'

Kendrick looked up from the photographs. 'I loved her,' he said quietly.

'You won't be the first man to kill the woman he loved,' said Morgan.

'I didn't kill her. We argued, and I lashed out. I was sorry the minute it happened. It was the wedding... the pressure... I didn't mean to hit her.'

'The CCTV shows you walking away and leaving her on her own, in a dodgy area, in the middle of the night. You don't look sorry, you look angry. Were you angry enough to hunt her down two days later and kill her?'

'No!'

Spence reached again into the wallet, this time producing an evidence bag.

'Is this the ring you gave Abigail Slater to celebrate your engagement?' asked Morgan.

'May I?' Kendrick reached out for the bag which Spence handed over.

'It's difficult to tell through the plastic, but yes, I think it is. It was left to me by my grandmother. I've never looked really closely at it, but I think this is the one.' He looked up at Spence who was holding out his hand for its return. 'Where was it? Can I not keep it? It's mine again, now.'

'For the moment, it's evidence, Mr Kendrick, so we'll be keeping it. Tell me, did you ever visit Gullhaven Park with Abi. It's an estate of park homes over in East Gullhaven?'

Kendrick shook his head before turning to his solicitor. 'Never been there. Never even heard of it,' he said.

'I think Mr Kendrick and I need to have a consultation, gentlemen,' said Wicks, closing his binder. Spence stood and made the announcement for the recording before closing it down and making for the door. Morgan followed him out.

Spence was waiting in the corridor. 'He's going "no comment" when we go back, isn't he? But we can see he's got a temper. God, I hate men who hit women.'

'Hitting her doesn't mean he killed her. We'll see what he says once he's had a bit more legal advice. Meantime, can you have a word with CPS and make sure we can charge him with the assault. That'll show him we mean business.' Spence started to walk away but Morgan was still speaking. 'I can't get past the fact that he turned up to marry her. I know he could have done that to try and cover his tracks, but I just...'

'I'll speak to the CPS,' said Spence. 'He lied about when he last saw her. He could easily be lying about killing her.'

Chapter 64

Dr Andy Gillingham drove to Gullhaven and booked into a small bed and breakfast, just off the cliff road. He left his car there and took a taxi to the police station. When he arrived, he pinned the security pass to his jacket and followed a PCSO to the briefing room which was locked.

The uniformed officer mumbled her embarrassment and left him outside where he lowered his backpack to the floor, retrieved his phone, and proceeded to work his way through texts and emails which had arrived during the drive.

When DC Lynn Greenfield arrived with the key she found the tall, thin, athletically built Gillingham leaning against the wall. 'Excuse me,' she said. He raised his eyes without moving his head. 'DI Morgan asked me to offer you tea or coffee. I've got Hobnobs too - the proper ones, not the cheap ones.' He shook his head without speaking then murmured a distracted and barely audible thanks as she entered the room.

Other team members arrived in ones and twos, unaccustomed to a mid-afternoon briefing and hoping for the announcement of a breakthrough. The arrival of Brian Bingley, the Crime Scene Manager for many of the recent deaths, added to their speculation.

Jenny Smart sat beside Lynn Greenfield and nodded towards the door. 'Who's the newbie?'

'Don't know. He's not lifted his head from his phone.'

'He's doing a lot of swiping on that phone. What do you think? Tinder or Grindr?'

Both women looked out into the corridor and watched as Gillingham looked up, his attention caught by Morgan's approaching voice. As the men shook hands and spoke for a moment, Greenfield leant over and whispered in her friend's ear, 'Tinder, I think. Definitely Tinder.'

The room quietened as Morgan spoke. 'Listen up everyone. Before we start, let me introduce Dr Andrew Gillingham who is here in his capacity as forensic psychologist. I'm hoping he can shed some light on what's going on.' He extended his arm towards the row of white boards at the front of the room. 'Some of you will recognise him from his TV appearances or you may have read his books. Please provide any information he needs while he's with us.' Gillingham responded with a very brief smile. He sat at a table at the back of the room, turned his mobile to silent and removed an iPad from his backpack.

Morgan started the briefing by confirming that the engagement ring found in the park home had been identified by Abi's fiancé as the one he'd given her. 'He also said he'd never been to the park homes estate, so if Abi was there with a man, he says it wasn't him. Now... Brian.'

Brian Bingley nodded and unfurled a roll of paper he was holding. Morgan thought he looked like an Ancient Roman about to speak to the Senate.

'We've checked the thumb and two fingerprints from the Transit van against IDENT1 and there's no match so this person has never been in a UK prison, but the good news is that we think we have enough points of comparison from the samples to confirm an assailant when we get him.'

There was a murmur of approval around the room.

'Okay everyone, unless anyone has any new lines of enquiry they want to mention, I'll close the briefing.' Morgan looked around like an auctioneer searching for a higher bid. No takers. One by one they got to their feet and made for the door, some nodding to Gillingham on their way past.

Morgan's work mobile alerted him to the arrival of a text.

'It's a call to Johnson's office,' he said to Gillingham. I expect he's written a cheque for you.' Gillingham snorted and turned his attention back to the information on the boards.

Morgan's meeting with Johnson had been difficult. As expected, the "budget" word featured frequently in the lecture, as well as "Police and Crime Commissioner and the Chief Constable." The latter had apparently expressed his disappointment at the lack of progress in finding Councillor Wyatt's murderer. Returning to his office Morgan wondered why Abigail Slater's murder had stopped attracting the scrutiny of the senior staff. He assumed it must be the salacious newspaper and social media stories about her sexual exploits. He felt sorry for her parents and realised he should have rung them with an update. Something else to add to his task list.

When he got to his office, Maggy Patel was sitting in his chair writing on a message pad. She looked up and Morgan thought she looked tired and dejected; very different from the bright, confident officer who had interviewed him two weeks before.

'Hi Maggy. Everything okay?'

'I was leaving you a note,' she replied waving the small sheet of paper at him.

'You could have sent an email,' he said reaching out for the paper. 'I was upstairs sitting on the naughty step again.'

'Any special reason this time?'

'"Spending too much money; overtime budget unacceptable; PCC and Chief Constable disappointed with progress;" the usual.'

'You forgot "eye watering amount spent on forensic analysis which could have been covered by old fashioned policing."'

'Mmm. I expect the bill hasn't come in yet. Anyway, what does the note say?' She crumpled it and aimed it successfully into his bin.

'I've had word from the street,' she said, 'About Raynor.' Morgan nodded. 'I thought you'd like to know.'

'Okay, but I need to speed this up, I'm afraid. I've got someone waiting in the briefing room.'

'I heard there was a celebrity in the building. Can you get me an autograph?'

Morgan took a step towards his bin.

'Okay DI Impatient,' said Patel, 'word is that Carl Raynor was involved in a bit of bottom of the barrel drug dealing. The real lowest of the low. He was dealing at school gates. It seems that Raynor stepped up to work with one of our notorious dynastic crime families... or stepped down, depending on your opinion.'

'Are you saying that some pissed off parent stalked Raynor to my mother-in-law's house to kill him? In Gullhaven?'

She shrugged. 'I don't know. But bad people are losing their lives so perhaps we've got a vigilante on the loose.' She made a gun shape with her right hand, 'Bang.'

'Raynor wasn't shot, he was stabbed, and smothered,' said Morgan.

'If I'd known we were playing charades... Anyway, "bang" is more dramatic.'

'How reliable is the source?' asked Morgan.

'Very reliable, I'd say. They've given me decent stuff in the past.'

'And what about Abi Slater? Are we saying that promiscuity can get you killed too? If that's the case, then as retribution, it's almost biblical.'

'I didn't say I'd brought the picture on the lid,' said Patel, 'just another couple of pieces of the jigsaw.'

'Christ! Let's hope these pieces fell out of the wrong box.'

Chapter 65

'I'm sorry I wasn't able to spend more time with you today.' Morgan held the boot of the Volvo open to let Gillingham throw his backpack in. 'Still travelling light I see.'

'My overnight bag is at the B&B and anyway, I don't expect to be here more than a couple of days.'

'And?'

'And I have to be back in London for Monday. I'm giving evidence at The Bailey.'

'That's not what I meant. I meant have you solved it yet?'

'Them. It's not an it. I'm sure it's a them. At least two and maybe even three separate clusters. But I don't think I'm telling you anything you don't already know. I've seen the HOLMES printouts.'

Morgan slammed the boot shut and opened the passenger door for his friend. He sat and folded his long legs into the foot well. 'Can I move the seat back?'

'Of course. It's only so far forward because I had plasterboard in the back at the weekend.'

'How are the renovations going?'

'I haven't really started yet.' They sat in companiable silence as Morgan negotiated his way out of the car park and into the queuing traffic on the main road.

'It's kind of Samantha to invite me for dinner,' said Gillingham reaching into his pocket and retrieving his phone. There had been four alerts to incoming messages in the short walk to the car and Morgan was starting to realise how much in demand his friend was.

'I can't imagine the hard time she would give me if she knew you'd been here all day and I hadn't brought you home to eat.'

'Can we stop off so I can buy some wine?'

'It's all taken care of.'

The conversation for the rest of the drive returned to the cases until Morgan swung across the coastal road and backed the Volvo on to the driveway at Cliffside. The house was in darkness this evening and he wished Sam had made the place look more welcoming for their guest.

'I bet it looks great in daylight,' said Gillingham, but Morgan could tell he didn't mean it. This was an ugly property and no amount of compliments would change that.

When Dorothy gifted the house, she provided only one key for the front door which she'd ceremoniously presented to her daughter. It was an obvious and deliberate slight to Morgan but he had got his own key cut as soon as the shop opened the next day and had raised two metaphorical fingers to his mother-in-law. He was reaching into his pocket for it when the door opened and Sam was there to greet them. She switched on the hall light and squealed with excitement when she saw Gillingham. 'Andy! It's been such a long time. How are you?'

Andy Gillingham bent down and tolerated her hug without returning it. 'You're looking well, Samantha. The sea air agrees with you.' He looked around, 'Where are the twins?'

'They've gone to the cinema with a classmate and his family. I know I'm substituting one screen for another

269

but at least they will have to look up to see the film instead of poring over their phones and tablets. It'll be good for their posture. Are you staying with us tonight? It's easy for me to make a bed up.'

'Thanks, but no thanks. I'm booked in at the B&B along the bay.'

She looked disappointed but Morgan knew she would be relieved. Their guest bedroom was currently a dumping ground and in no state to offer a comfortable night to visitors.

'Why don't you take Andy to the pub for an hour, Nick? By the time you get back, the kids'll be here, and I'll have had a chance to throw something edible on the table.'

'D'you fancy a pint?' asked Gillingham.

'You can get all the shop talk out of the way before dinner,' said Sam taking Gillingham by the arm and guiding him to the door.

'Steady on, Samantha,' he said. 'We're going. Anyone would think you had a man upstairs.' Only Gillingham laughed.

Chapter 66

Thursday 27th February

The pub was a ten minute walk across the cliff top but the recent rain had made the ground boggy so they chose the longer route along the pavement. The strong west wind made conversation between them difficult to maintain.

When they arrived, the landlord at The Smuggler's View welcomed Nick Morgan with a broad smile. 'We thought you must have gone back to London,' he said. 'Two pints of best, is it?'

Nick looked towards Andy, remembering that he had never seen him with a beer in his hand.

'I'll have a diet tonic with ice and lemon, please.'

'Got that,' said the landlord making a mock salute, 'and a pint for you, Nick?'

'Please.'

'I'll bring them over.'

They sat at a table by the window although there was nothing to see apart from street lights and the darkness of the bay beyond. These seats were furthest from the music speakers and slot machines; ideal for a quiet chat.

'Not many people in,' said Gillingham.

Morgan looked at his watch. 'It's early yet, and out of season too.'

The landlord brought the drinks and placed the tonic in front of Gillingham with exaggerated care. When he had gone, Morgan noticed that there was a cocktail cherry on a stick in the glass, as well as the slice of lemon. Gillingham's thin lips formed a small, lop-sided smile as he placed it on a beer mat to drain. 'Does he do a comedy turn on alternate Fridays?' he asked raising one eyebrow.

Morgan shook his head and shrugged. When he looked back from the window, Gillingham was appraising him, poker faced; brown eyes penetrating. Under this scrutiny Morgan felt uncomfortable and looked back to the window.

'Are you going to tell me what's going on?'

'What do you mean "going on?" You've seen the crime boards and read what we've got so far. There's not a great deal more I can tell you.' He looked around, aware that his voice was too loud and his tone, defensive.

Andy Gillingham had been about to take another sip of his drink but replaced it on the mat and leant in. 'We've known each other too long, Nick. Don't give me the bullshit. All is not well on Planet Morgan. And I don't think it's the caseload, either.' He sat back in his chair again and waited.

Morgan stayed silent, still avoiding his eyes.

'If you haven't brought me here to share the burden, we can walk back and I'll help Samantha prepare the meal.'

Morgan sighed. 'We should never have come to Gullhaven. I knew it was a bad idea. I don't know what possessed me.' Gillingham was completely still, his attention focused on his friend.

'I've been with Sam over twenty years and we have two lovely kids together. I thought that living closer to her mother would lift some of the pressure off her. She was up and down that motorway two and three times a week.' He gulped more of the beer and lifted the glass. 'Can I get you another?'

'No, because we've barely touched these and you would be using a trip to the bar as an avoidance tactic. You've started now so you may as well tell me everything.'

'I don't come out of the story well.'

'We know a lot about each other where we don't come out of the story well. It hasn't affected our friendship, has it?'

Morgan picked at a spot on his beer mat before continuing. 'I accused Sam of shagging her old boyfriend. It's a longer story than that, but that's the punch line.'

'And had she?'

Morgan returned Gillingham's unflinching stare for a long time. 'Only you would ask that. No one else would think that Saint Samantha could do such a thing.' He spat the words out.

'But you think she did.'

'I did at the time, then I didn't... don't. God's sake. I don't know what to think. She was so pissed when she got home, anything might have happened.'

'Have you had a conversation about it since she sobered up?'

'No, I feel too guilty.' Gillingham looked puzzled and Morgan shook his head, eyes closed. 'I took revenge. I was made an offer I couldn't refuse. So I didn't.'

'So, you had a one night stand that started off as Sam's fault, and now you're blaming your mystery woman. None of it is anything to do with you. Is that what you want me to believe?'

'I knew you'd say that. I know I'm in the wrong. I don't need you to tell me.'

'If you want my advice...' said Gillingham.

'Can I afford it?'

'...keep your trousers and your mouth zipped. No good will come from telling Samantha. Stay out of temptation's way and don't go near your mystery woman. Get on with solving the cases and if you've got any spare time, fix something at the house, then take a cold shower. That should cover it. Christ, Nick. How old are you anyway?'

Morgan took another gulp of beer and smiled for the first time since they had sat down but Gillingham was looking concerned as he continued. 'Is it possible that the embers of that night with the mystery woman are still glowing? She's trouble, and you know it.'

'I know,' Morgan was nodding as he got up to go to the bar. 'But it may not be that easy. Same again?' he asked, holding up his glass.

Gillingham nodded, 'But put a gin in it this time. Now that I know about all this I don't think I can face Samantha sober.'

Chapter 67

'Settle down quickly, please. There's quite a bit to get through.' Morgan had to shout to be heard over the noise of two teams squeezing into the briefing room. He saw Maggy Patel in close conversation with Andy Gillingham at the back. She was talking quickly, arms and hands gesturing something Morgan could not interpret. As ever, Gillingham was standing completely still, his concentration on her, absorbing every detail of what she was saying as if she was the only person in the room.

Morgan thought that Gillingham had no right to look as unscathed as he appeared. After Sam and the twins had gone to bed last night, they'd sat up till three o'clock, using sticky notes and coloured sheets of paper to represent the cases and the commonalities between them. Gillingham's new eyes on the evidence helped Morgan drill down to the basics of each investigation and he felt he was seeing things more clearly. Well, he would be seeing things more clearly if he didn't have this headache. At midnight, Gillingham had gone to the kitchen and returned with a two litre bottle of sparkling water. Morgan remembered screwing up his face and opening another bottle of red. He wondered if it was this restraint that helped his friend look at least ten years younger than his age.

The room quietened and faces turned towards him. 'For those of you who weren't at yesterday afternoon's briefing, let me introduce Dr Andy Gillingham who's a forensic psychologist I've worked with him on a number of cases.' Morgan didn't mention the Met in case inter-force rivalries and misconceptions clouded the issue at hand. 'He's here to help us get some insight into what we've got here. But before that, I want to share some intel that has come to light.'

The door opened and Johnson came in, nodding his permission for Morgan to continue. He remained at the back of the room like a dark cloud threatening rain on the family barbeque.

Morgan referred to his notes then started the briefing by relaying Patel's information. When Johnson did not react to him knowing details of Operation Heartwood, he pressed on.

Nobody in the room seemed surprised that Carl Raynor was involved in dealing drugs – one or two nodded as if long held suspicions were now confirmed. Their reaction turned to anger when they heard he'd been dealing to school children as many of the officers were parents or had younger siblings. But comments were regulated by the presence of DCI Johnson. Morgan avoided eye contact with Patel who had specified that he must not identify her as the source of the information.

When they moved on from Operation Heartwood to Operation Siren it was obvious that information about Abi Slater's engagement ring and the prints from the Transit van were widely known. One of the advantages of open plan offices, Morgan thought.

Andy Gillingham was sitting at the side of the room. He had picked a good place from where he could observe the teams as well as have a clear view of the white boards. Morgan could see that when he wasn't typing notes on his iPad his brown eyes were scanning the room, monitoring and appraising. To make notes, he put on a pair of black framed glasses which Morgan hadn't seen before. Each time he needed them, Morgan saw the fleeting expression of irritation of a man who no longer has twenty-twenty vision. Welcome to the club, he thought before standing to address the teams again.

'Yesterday evening Dr Gillingham and I spent some time categorising the evidence we have on our current five major cases and I'd like him to share with you some of his thoughts so far. Andy?'

Gillingham strode to the front of the room with the confidence of a man accustomed to holding the attention of a large group of people when he spoke. His face was expressionless. Morgan knew that this was the self protection mechanism his friend had developed during the thousands of hours he had spent in the company of murderers, torturers and rapists. Morgan remembered him saying 'If they can't see that they are in your head, then they aren't in your head.'

There was a change of atmosphere in the room and many of the occupants fidgeted in their chairs. Gillingham cabled his iPad to the projector and moved a couple of the white boards to one side so that the image appeared on the wall mounted screen. He waited for the room to settle again and when he looked up, Johnson was leaving. He looked towards Morgan who shook his head and shrugged.

'I'm going to start by telling you what I'm not going to do,' he said. 'I'm not going to tell you that you are looking for a five foot ten male who is unemployed, has dandruff, lives on his own and plays Abba music. It's that sort of speculation that gives my profession a bad reputation, and anyway, profiling is more in the remit of criminal psychology. But I am going to play in that playground for a while, because I hope I can give you some insight into what I think is going on with some of your cases.'

Morgan hoped that this introduction would help overcome any suspicion or negativity towards forensic psychology that might be in the room.

'I've based my analysis on postmortem findings, photos taken of the bodies in situ, evidence, and the results of your investigations up to now. DI Morgan asked me to use this information to see if I could identify how many perpetrators you might be looking for, and that's what I've done. So, starting with Carl Raynor...' He walked to the white board and pointed to the photo taken from his criminal record. 'I can't link this death to any of the others. Firstly, there are no marks of strangulation. Also, he was never represented in court by Abigail Slater, and although there's evidence of shoplifting, he wasn't due in court. I'm aware of the speculation of there being a commonality of retribution against criminality across most of these cases but, for Raynor, it doesn't fit for me. In the absence of any other evidence, I see this as a standalone case. This is your case DI Patel? Do you have any observations?'

Her lips formed a moue and she shook her head. 'Nope, nothing comes to mind,' she said.

'I'm not going to surprise anyone when I link Wesley Crook's murder with what happened to father and son Maguire. I know that the wording of the sign around Crook's neck was floating around social media by the time the Maguires were killed and also, that they don't share an MO but I think this is the same individual. And I agree with those of you who are linking Abigail Slater with these cases. In fact, I think what links them is the legal profession.'

Although he had already heard Gillingham's hypothesis when he first suggested it in the early hours of that morning, Morgan listened carefully.

Gillingham was pointing to the copy of the letter which had been delivered by hand to Wesley Crook's home address. '"Offending behaviour" is wording I associate with the legal profession,' he said tapping the board. 'You hear it used by judges, the CPS, and defence solicitors. You don't hear members of the public saying "did you read about that guy's offending behaviour?" do you?'

'And Abi Slater was a defence solicitor who was often at the Magistrates' Court,' said DC Leo Jenson. Everyone turned to look at him. 'Sorry, just thinking out loud.'

'What about magistrates? They would hear the expression a lot. Maybe some of them use it routinely?' Jenny Smart added.

'I agree,' said Gillingham. 'I don't think we can rule magistrates out.' Morgan groaned. He had quite liked the odds when the suspects were limited to the legal profession. The addition of magistrates added at least a couple of hundred more people to the mix, and that was if they limited it to their local courts.

'Any questions so far?' Gillingham's eyes scanned the room but nobody spoke. 'Okay, then here's where I'm going to put forward a couple of suggestions rather than absolute theories. Wesley Crook was killed while he was waiting for his burglary trial. The Maguires were killed while they were stealing power tools. Harry Drake was stealing from people who thought they were buying legit insurance policies. Crook and Drake received letters telling them to stop their offending behaviour, which in their cases, was stealing, or they would be

279

sorry. I think that, one, you're looking for someone who has been directly or indirectly the victim of a theft of some sort and two, that this person also killed Abigail Slater, possibly because she defended individuals who were up for theft, when they appeared at court.'

Someone in the room whistled, but apart from that, there was silence. Gillingham held their gaze his face as ever, impassive. 'Any questions?' he asked again.

'Where does Councillor Kenneth Wyatt fit?' asked DC Lynn Greenfield. 'You've not mentioned him.'

'I don't know where he fits,' said Gillingham, 'Or even, if he fits. No sign round the neck and no connection with theft apart from a published desire to string burglars up. I don't think there's evidence that links him with Abigail Slater either. Based on what you've uncovered, I can't see anything to link him to the others apart from the fact he was strangled.'

'Unless we go back to the retribution theory,' said Leo Jenson. 'We could be looking for the relative of a girl who has been sold or offered drugs by Raynor, and been groped by Wyatt. It's enough to make any father or brother go on a spree. I've got daughters myself.'

There were soft murmurs of agreement and Morgan was glad that Johnson had already left. Gillingham looked over to where Morgan was standing. 'That's all I've got, for now,' he said.

Morgan looked around the room but there was no further input. 'Thank you Dr Gillingham. You've given us a lot to think about. Now, we're going back to my office to go through some action points. DI Patel?'

'I'll be right there,' she said pausing to have a word with a couple of members of the Operation Heartwood team.

'What do you think, Dave?' DC Jenny Smart asked Spence. She had glanced over at him a few times while Gillingham spoke.

'I didn't want to like him. I thought he'd be too clever by half. Penny watches his programmes on TV and she's read some of his books. He talks sense,' he sighed, 'but actually, whatever he says, we're not going to know if it's accurate until we catch the bastard. And we're no nearer to that. I think I might have preferred it if he'd told us that he was five foot ten, living alone, unemployed and whatever else he said.'

'With dandruff and plays Abba music,' said Smart and they left the briefing room together.

Chapter 68

Samantha was enjoying the excitement of her renewed relationship with Graham. She checked her phone constantly for a text or email. Once, he sent her a clip from a piece of music they shared as teenagers. The anticipation and fluttery feeling she got when she thought about him made her feel young again. Yesterday, while she was vacuuming the bedrooms, he'd sent her a text telling her to come to the door in ten minutes with a dress on – just a dress – nothing else. Her heart pounded as she stripped off and stood looking in her wardrobe. Difficult to decide but she'd settled on a knee length, sleeveless, navy crepe dress, very clinging and showing every curve. The hard work she had done in the south London gym had been worth it.

She waited in the hallway until she heard his tyres on the drive, the slam of the car door, and his footsteps. When she opened the door he'd pushed her inside and against the wall, kissing her with passion and urgency. He'd run his hands up the back of her legs and gripped her buttocks, pulling her in to his hardness. Struggling to grab her breath she'd whispered 'Close the door.'

'I can't stay,' he'd replied, taking a deep breath in and exhaling through his mouth. 'I'm on my way to a client visit and I wanted you to know that I was thinking about you.' As he hurried to his car he called back, 'Wear that next time, I like it.' And he was gone.

Letting herself be led on like that and then disappointed; letting him exert that power over her;

made her angry. She was snappy with the twins when they got home from school and had gone to bed early to avoid Nick. And always, at the back of her mind, was the problem. Her mother knew about her affair.

In the early hours of Friday, she resolved to find out how big a threat her mother might be and, after breakfast, she called to invite her for coffee at the East Gullhaven Country Club. She could still hear the smug smile in her mother's voice. 'That would be nice dear, but why there? Does it have special memories for you?'

Driving up to Silver Sands House to collect her, she saw that her mother was talking to the same man who reminded her of her brother. Dorothy was laughing, and reached out to touch his arm. Maybe she was settling in at last?

Samantha stopped the car and her mother got in, immediately adjusting the seat. 'How lovely of you to invite me,' she said. 'Such a treat. How are you and how are things?'

Samantha glanced over to assess her mother's sincerity. 'We're all okay, thank you. The twins are settling in well at school and seem to be making new friends. They still complain about missing their old ones, but we expected that. Alex...'

'And Plod? How is his detecting going? Is he involved in the Kenny Wyatt case?'

'Please don't call him Plod. I've asked you before. Nick is working on some of the murders that have been on the news. He goes to work early and gets home late, and knackered. He doesn't say much about his detecting, and I don't ask. Why do you care?'

'No reason. Just curious.'

'He brought Andy Gillingham home for dinner last night and they stayed up till the small hours.'

'So Nick needs help again, does he?'

'Everyone wants to find who's behind all this and lock them up.' Dorothy gave a little laugh which Samantha would describe as musical but it contained no humour. They drove the rest of the short journey to the country club in an uneasy silence.

Chapter 69

After the briefing, Gillingham and Morgan walked together to the car park. They talked about how the team had reacted to the analysis and Morgan apologised for Johnson leaving the meeting early.

'I don't see it as my problem,' Gillingham replied. 'I came to do a job and I've done it. It's up to you and Maggy to either use the information, or not.' With the parting advice 'Stay away from your mystery woman,' Gillingham shook hands with Morgan and got into his car. Morgan swiped his security pass to raise the barrier and waved before heading back to Maggy Patel's office. She looked up as he got to her open door.

'I'm starting to recognise your footsteps,' she said.

Without waiting to be invited, Morgan sat. 'What did you think?'

'Nice bloke,' she replied. 'Not at all full of himself or show bizzy. Yeh, nice bloke.'

Morgan paused, staring at her 'I meant what did you think about his findings.'

Patel laughed and Morgan thought he detected a hint of embarrassment. 'I thought he made a lot of sense,' she said. 'Some of it... we were already there, but that bit about the wording of the letters; he's got a point. You do hear that at court and not many other places. Police don't use it, I don't think. It's far too respectful for the scumbags. He's right, it's legal profession wording.'

'And magistrates?'

'I don't know. Was Kenneth Wyatt a magistrate? He was on the Council and once people get into the habit of volunteering it can get addictive.'

'Wyatt was dead before the Maguires. If we're connecting the warning letters to the signs left on the bodies, that rules him out from killing them himself? I suppose you could argue he may have already paid someone to do it, before he was strung up. Anyway...' he got up and walked to her office window, 'I think I'm with Andy. I don't think Wyatt's part of the pattern.'

'So, are we saying Carl Raynor's not one of the ones who's sorry?'

'Well I'm sure he's sorry, but maybe not in the same way.' He sat down again, 'I'm a bit restless, sorry.'

She nodded, 'I don't suppose this was how you thought your first weeks were going to pan out down here.'

He shook his head. 'I haven't even unpacked my stuff yet.'

Patel's computer pinged. She pointed at the screen, 'Email from Johnson. Why do you suppose he left before the meeting ended?' She clicked the mouse button and screwed up her face. 'I think I need glasses,' she said.

Morgan waited while she read. 'He's sent you the same message. He wants to see us at two this afternoon. I still have Operation Heartwood, but now I have the Kenneth Wyatt case as well – Operation Artemis.'

Morgan snorted. 'Where does he get these names anyway?'

'There's a list and you get the next one on that list. Anyway, did you just drop in to take the piss out of my new operation name? We've got five murders to solve before two o'clock.'

Morgan frowned, 'it's six.'

'What?' Patel was irritated now and not bothering to hide it.

'You must have missed one out. There are six murders.'

'Get out of my office and think of something to say that'll appease Johnson at two o'clock.'

There was a large envelope waiting on Morgan's office desk. He opened it while he waited for his computer to boot up. Reading the first page put a smile on his face and he dialled Patel's mobile.

She answered her phone with 'Now what?'

'I've got the forensic report from the park home,' he said. 'Abigail Slater's hair from the contents of the vacuum cleaner and a fingerprint match.'

'Whose are they?' asked Patel.

'I don't know.'

He heard her exasperated sigh.

'If you've not got a name, you can sod off and let me get on with my work. And don't forget Johnson at two.'

'I don't know who they belong to, but I know that they were also found in the van that the Maguires were driving.'

'Well, lucky you. So we're categorically linking Abi Slater to the "Now I'm Sorry" signs.'

'I'd say so, yeh. You're going to have to pull a pretty big rabbit out of the hat to beat that when we see Johnson.'

'Mmm. What are you going to do now?'

'I'm bringing Maisie Sangster in to make a statement. Please God the vacuum cleaner she used when she cleaned that home was empty before she took it up there.

I need Abi Slater, with her engagement ring, in that park home, with this guy and his prints.'

'Sounds like a game of Cluedo,' she said. 'Be back by two.' Patel ended the call without saying goodbye.

<u>Chapter 70</u>

Friday 28th February

Dorothy chose a table near the door of the club. It gave her the best view of arrivals and Samantha was surprised by how many people came to hug her mother and share their gossip. Dorothy introduced her to everyone. 'This is my daughter. She's been in London for a while, but she's back with family now.' Nick and the twins were never mentioned.

The waiter brought a silver cafetière on a tray with two white coffee cups, a jug of cream and a bowl of brown sugar cubes. There were four small ginger biscuits on a plate, just uneven enough to be made in-house. When he left, Dorothy caught Samantha off guard by asking her what she wanted to talk about. As she tried to put her words in order, Dorothy continued with her own agenda.

'Because the twins are back at school now, and you promised to run the business.'

Samantha sighed, 'I didn't promise, mum, you know I didn't. And anyway, that's Steven's job. I'm not going to take away his livelihood.'

'I can't rely on Steven any more, especially not after his recent disappearing act. A funeral business can't just be put on hold while the manager goes off in a huff. You know, he hasn't even been to see me since he got back. Not a hint of an apology. I suppose he's been in touch with you.'

'I haven't had any contact with Steven since I got here. I thought he was back at work.'

'The business is spiralling out of control and if your father was alive, he'd be appalled.'

'I've asked you before but, did you two argue again? I can't see any other reason why he would just head off.'

Dorothy looked away. She reached out for a ginger biscuit and bit down hard on it.

'What did you row about?' Samantha persevered.

'I've always treated you both equally,' said Dorothy.

'What happened? What did you say?'

'I didn't get a chance to say anything. He did all the saying.' She pointed to the cafetière. 'Do the honours dear, I'm parched.'

Samantha leant forward and pushed the plunger down. She poured the coffee; added one cube of sugar to her mother's; stirred the cup and held it out.

'Just put it on the table, thank you. My arthritis is playing up a bit today.' Samantha pushed the cup across to within easy reach.

'What did you argue about?'

'I told him that I'd given you Cliffside and he wasn't pleased.'

Samantha frowned. 'It's nearly six months since we talked about that. When did you tell him?'

'A couple of weeks before you were moving in.'

'A couple of weeks!' Samantha was incredulous. 'No wonder he's angry. Please don't say you told him I was going to be managing the business at the same time.'

'It was a good opportunity to put things straight with him. He needed to be told.'

'Is that when he disappeared?'

'He shouted at me, Samantha. Then he stormed out. Steven has never shouted at me. You were always the drama queen; he just used to go off in a sulk.'

Samantha tutted and gulped her coffee.

Dorothy leant towards her. 'He accused me of being vengeful,' she hissed.

Inwardly, Samantha applauded her brother. It was time he stood up for himself. 'And had you been?' she asked.

'He had a fling I didn't approve of and I told him to put an end to it. But that was before Christmas. He should have got over it.'

'He's thirty four... nearly thirty five, he's old enough to have flings without your approval. You don't get to decide who he has sex with,' said Samantha. Dorothy's smile was smug and Samantha braced herself. She had stupidly invited a comment about her relationship with Graham.

'His fling was with that solicitor you found in the woods.'

The two women looked at each other and Samantha started to count on her fingers. 'Are you saying that Steven went missing at the same time as the solicitor... that Abigail whatever her name is?'

'He had nothing to do with that.'

'How do you know he had nothing to do with it?' The volume of Samantha's voice was raised enough to attract the attention of a couple sitting nearby.

'Shhh,' said Dorothy. 'This is about money. It's nothing to do with that tramp.' She reached out for a second biscuit. When I told him about Cliffside, and you coming back to the business, he was pleased. Said he could go to France now, and join the art school he'd read about.'

'That doesn't sound like an argument.'

'He wanted me to pay for the art school, and to set him up in France. He had the nerve to tell me he was entitled to it.'

'What happened?'

'I refused, and he flounced out in a huff. Stopped turning up for work. Disappeared.' She bit down hard on the biscuit. Samantha waited, certain that there was more. 'He came to see me the day before you were supposed to be moving into Cliffside. Had the nerve to present me with an ultimatum. Shouted at me. Frightened me. He said I had to hand over my shares in the business, or give him the house. He wanted to move in that night. He looked terrible. He was dirty and he'd lost weight. I told him to grow up and get back to work.'

'Well that worked. He hasn't been back there since. When did he go to the caravan?' asked Samantha.

'I don't know. He has keys, the same as you do. Anyway, I'm sure you didn't invite me to coffee to discuss my little tiff with Steven. What was it you wanted to talk about?'

'Nothing really,' Samantha replied although her brain was screaming 'Are you going to tell Nick about Graham and me?'

'I don't think you've ever asked me to coffee to discuss "nothing,"' said Dorothy.

Samantha's mouth was dry and she couldn't put the right words in the right order to get the information she needed.

'So, tell me more about the cases then,' said Dorothy. 'I heard about the engagement ring. It belonged to that solicitor, didn't it? They found it in a park home near where you were staying.'

'I haven't been following the case in the papers and I try not to have the radio on when the kids are in the car in case it upsets them. It's a bit close to home.'

Dorothy nodded. 'And you've got a lot on your plate at the moment too.' She paused long enough for

Samantha to feel uncomfortable, 'I mean unpacking and getting the house the way you want it.'

Samantha shoved a whole biscuit into her mouth and softened it with a slug of coffee. 'I know that Nick's working on the solicitor case, but he hasn't said much about it.'

'The caravan where they found the ring belongs to the daughter of one of my fellow inmates, you know. The maintenance man, Danny, was just telling me.'

'Oh, don't call them inmates, Mum. I thought you liked it there.'

'It'll do for now, at least until I get a bit more mobile and you settle into Cliffside.' As Samantha met her mother's eyes, the price of her silence on the subject of Graham Fletcher began to dawn on her.

Chapter 71

Friday 28th February

The persistent rain which fell on the clubbers queuing outside Club Europium did not dampen their high spirits. It was the first Friday after pay day and they were here to enjoy themselves. Once inside, they were absorbed into a world of pounding music, flashing lights and overpriced alcohol. The management insisted that there was a strict "no drugs" policy, but everyone knew it was not enforced.

Just after one in the morning, the music was paused and there was an announcement that the bar profits for the next hour were going to be sent to the parents of Abigail Slater who were setting up a charity in her name to promote the safety of young women in the town. There was cheering and applause before the music and the intricate, erotic writhing of the dancers resumed.

'Her parents are rich enough to fund the bloody charity on their own.' The man shouted his opinion at the young girl who was serving him at the bar. She ignored the comment as she handed him his change and turned to serve the next customer.

A few minutes later, he felt a tap on his shoulder and turned to face the barrel chest of one of the doormen. 'I hear you've got a problem with us collecting for Abi,' he said. He glanced back to the bar where the girl who had served him was watching.

'Not a problem,' he said, 'I was just surprised that her parents need donations when they are as well off as they are.'

'The club wants to donate,' the doorman replied, 'and if you don't want to donate, then it's time for you to leave.'

'I paid to get in and I don't see why I should leave.'

The doorman took his arm in a vice-like grip and guided him to the door. 'You need to learn a bit of respect for the dead, mate,' he growled as he hurled the man out on to the wet pavement. There was giggling and applause from the clubbers who were waiting patiently for their turn to enter.

'I need my jacket,' the man shouted to the door keeper.

'Come back for it on Monday when you've learned some manners,' the door keeper replied before turning back to the couple at the front of the queue.

The man got up and peeled his wet trousers away from his legs. He looked confused as he walked away, periodically glancing over his shoulder to see if anyone was watching, but he was already distant memory for the excited crowd and doorman.

Chapter 72

Penny Spence answered her husband's phone and asked the caller to wait while she went to get him out of the shower.

'DS Spence,' he said, picking the phone up, 'and this had better be good because I'm not on duty this weekend.'

There was a delay before the caller spoke. 'DS Spence, this is DCI Johnson and I'm sorry to call you out on a Saturday but I'm going to need you at the station to interview a suspect. He was arrested last night and they are deciding whether to charge with ABH or GBH. It seems he hit a bouncer with a brick, after a bit of an argument.'

'Sir, I...'

'His fingerprints have come back as a potential match for the unknown prints on the Maguires' van and keys but you need to keep that to yourself for the moment.'

'The Maguire case is DI Morgan's Op and I believe he is the duty officer this weekend.' Spence moved his phone from one ear to the other.

'I'm calling you because DI Morgan cannot interview this suspect. He's Morgan's brother-in-law, Steven Cooper.' Johnson paused to let Spence assimilate the information. 'I'm confident that you can interrogate Mr Cooper with your usual competence. DC Smart is already on her way in. Ring me when the interview is complete.' The line went dead. Spence wrapped the bath towel tighter and dialled Jenny Smart's mobile. She

296

responded on hands free. He ran through the information he'd received from Johnson about the alleged assault. After some thought, he added the information about the fingerprint, swearing her to secrecy. She was sceptical.

'We've already interviewed Steven Cooper and ruled him out of everything we're working on. What's going on?' she asked.

'Right on both counts,' he said. 'When we spoke to him on the day they brought him back from Suffolk, he didn't strike us as being able to batter a fish, never mind two blokes intent on robbing DIY gear.'

'Was he even here when the Maguires were killed?'

'Uniform drove him back here about a week before. I don't know where he's been since then. How soon can you drive in? I'd planned to go clothes shopping with Penny.'

'For you? Or for her?'

He laughed. 'I always make sure she thinks we're looking for her and then I have a quick browse while she's trying stuff on. Is that not what's meant to happen?'

'Not so much,' she said. 'I'll be there in about half an hour.'

'Okay. I won't start without you.'

Spence and Smart sat together at her desk in their designated area of the open plan office. There were a few officers at desks, but it was quieter than on a weekday.

'How are we going to approach this?' asked Smart. 'Did Johnson have any suggestions?'

'I don't need any suggestions from him,' said Spence. 'I bet he can't even remember the last time he interrogated a suspect.' He pursed his lips as he thought.

297

'We're just going in with the assault initially. Johnson wants the fingerprints kept quiet. If we get the go-ahead, we can build up to them later. There's plenty time. We've still got about sixteen hours on the custody clock.'

'Will he not think it's a bit odd that a DS and a DC from Major Crimes would come in on a Saturday for an assault outside a club?'

'The door guy is in a coma. It's pretty serious.'

Spence's phone rang and he wheeled his chair over to his desk 'DS Spence.'

'Duty solicitor's here,' said the desk sergeant, 'and there's a young lady from Club Europium. She's brought your guy's jacket.'

'I'll be right down.' He opened his desk drawer and pulled out a box of disposable gloves. 'I might need some evidence bags. Someone's brought Cooper's jacket in.' He crossed to a cupboard in the main office and took out a large bag and a couple of smaller ones.

'If he wasn't wearing the jacket when the assault happened,' said Smart. 'Is it evidence?'

'I'm not taking any chances with this one. If it all pans out, we're about to charge our new boss's brother-in-law with two murders, and maybe two more.'

When he got downstairs, the desk sergeant beckoned Spence closer and spoke quietly. 'Don't look round but both these women are here for you, you lucky boy. The one nearest the door is Harriet Lees-Langham, your guy's duty solicitor. I've called someone to take her downstairs. The other one is from the club.'

Spence thanked him before turning to face the visitors. Lees-Langham was standing by the side of a large briefcase. Unlike some of her colleagues who dressed down for weekend callouts, she was immaculate in a dark grey suit, cream jumper and soft leather boots which added two inches to her height. She was tapping her right foot and concentrating on her phone screen. She didn't look up.

The second woman wore jeans and a padded jacket. She was clutching a battered carrier bag to her chest. When Spence approached her, she looked alarmed.

'They asked me to bring the jacket on my way to the university library this morning,' she said.

'I'm DS Dave Spence,' he replied holding up identification which hung from his MCT lanyard. 'And you are?'

'Tina Smith. I work behind the bar at the Europium.' She awkwardly raised a hand as if unsure whether a handshake was correct etiquette.

Spence smiled his encouragement and held out his hands for the jacket.

'It's all my fault,' said Tina. 'If I hadn't been so upset about the comment he made when I served him, he wouldn't be here.'

A voice called out 'Ms Lees-Langham,' and the smartly dressed woman clip-clopped her way across the tiled floor towards the door which led to the cells. It seemed to distract Tina who stopped talking whilst she watched.

Spence looked back at the desk sergeant and nodded towards two doors which led off reception.

'Be my guest,' said the uniformed officer, 'both free, at the moment.'

Spence led Tina into a small interview room and put the light on. 'Have a seat. Do you want any water?' She shook her head. 'What happened at the club?'

Tina Smith recounted her story about the announcement at the club and how most of the punters were pleased. She said that some had asked who Abi Slater was because not everyone was aware of what had happened to her. When she'd served the man who had been ejected from the club, he had been narked by the donation, and that upset her.

'What happened then?'

'Tommy came inside.' Spence was about to ask who Tommy was, but she pre-empted him. 'Tommy's one of our door keepers. I pointed out the man to him. He went across and had a word and I saw them walk to the door together. The next thing I knew was police and ambulance were outside. It's my fault Tommy got hurt.'

'You didn't hit him, Tina, so you aren't to blame. How come you got the jacket to bring in?'

'We were tidying round and it was in the corner... where that man had been sitting. I said I'd bring it in on my way to the library. I've got my finals this year. That's my life; work; eat; study; sleep.'

Spence noted her contact details and thanked her. He warned her that they would need a formal statement at some time, but he wasn't going to ask her to wait. This time, they did shake hands before he showed her out of the small room and to the revolving door at the front of reception.

When he returned to the carrier bag in the interview room, he snapped his gloves on and reached inside. It was tricky, but he managed to remove a black leather wallet from the breast pocket without taking the jacket out of the bag. He opened the wallet and his shoulders slumped. 'Fuck's sake,' he mumbled before slipping it into one of the small evidence bags. He gathered everything together and sprinted towards the stairs calling his thanks to the desk sergeant as he went past.

Chapter 73

The custody clock continued to tick down.

Spence rang Johnson with the news that the man in custody was not Steven Cooper, in spite of that being the name he had provided when arrested. He also suggested that it might be more appropriate for DI Morgan to lead the interrogation for his own Operation. Spence could hear tango music playing in the background. 'I hope I'm not interrupting you, sir.'

Johnson reluctantly agreed that Morgan should be called in but he ignored Spence's reference to the music. When he ended the call, Jenny Smart told him that Johnson was an enthusiastic ballroom dancer and attended classes every Saturday morning.

'With his wife?' asked Spence.

'With a neighbour. While his wife plays bridge, I think.' Smart smiled at the expression on Spence's face. 'No really, I don't think there's any more to it than that. Just dancing.'

'Well I hope it's not Argentine tango,' he said. 'DCI Johnson dancing the Argentine tango is a picture I don't want to have in my head.'

Spence set about making the call that would scupper Morgan's renovation plans for the day.

When Morgan arrived at the station, he sent Jenny Smart home. 'No point in buggering up everybody's weekend plans,' he grumbled.

'DS Spence and I prepared the disclosure for the solicitor,' said Smart, slipping her arms into her jacket. 'He's got hard copies and so has the solicitor. Oh, and they are ready for interview.'

Morgan glanced through the details of the assault that the police were willing to share with the defence. They were obliged to disclose enough information for an advocate to provide their client with appropriate legal advice. He read that there was CCTV and at least twenty witnesses prepared to provide evidence of the man hitting the door keeper with what looked like a brick or a piece of concrete. Surely a guilty plea, he thought.

Morgan and Spence had barely entered the interrogation room before Lees-Langham started. 'Is this everything you have on my client?' She was waving the sheet of paper. 'I find it hard to believe a DI and DS would be here on a Saturday to interview someone, who I'm sure was recorded on CCTV, assaulting a doorman. Care to give me more?'

Dave Spence sat on Morgan's left and flicked the switch to start the recording. Morgan identified himself and his sergeant before inviting the solicitor and her client to do the same. He completed the rest of the standard procedure whilst watching them both.

Morgan leaned back in the hard upright chair before speaking. 'Well Danny, let's start by establishing for the recording that you are not Steven Cooper and that you are, in fact, Daniel Francis Easton.'

Lees-Langham looked confused. 'Who is Steven Cooper?' she asked.

'It's the name your client gave to the officers who arrested him,' said Morgan 'earning him a charge of obstructing a police officer in the execution of his or her duty under Section eighty-nine brackets two of the

Police Act 1996. We'll be adding that to the assault charge.' The solicitor frowned but gave no reply.

'Are you Daniel Francis Easton?' asked Spence.

'Yes.'

'Then I'm going to caution you in your correct name.' Spence recited the words. At least this time, he wasn't holding down a wriggling body which was all arms, legs, biting teeth and foul language.

Morgan fixed his grey blue eyes on Easton and started the questioning. 'Before we talk about what happened outside the club, I'd like you to tell us why you said you were Steven Cooper.'

'No comment.'

'It's not a name you made up on the spot, is it?'

'No comment.'

'How well do you know Mr Cooper?' Danny looked down and shook his head.

'For the recording please, Danny. How well do you know him?'

'He's the son of one of the residents at Silver Sands. That's where I work.'

Harriet Lees-Langham leant across and whispered into Easton's ear.

No surprises that she's asking him to stick with "no comment," thought Morgan.

'Why that name?' growled Spence. His tone startled Morgan and it must have had the same effect on Easton because he looked up, eyes wide.

'I've been with Mrs Cooper when he's come to visit. He gave her a hard time last time he came, shouting and swearing at her. Really upset her, and I don't like to see her upset. And after all she's done for him. Job on a plate; good money; and a fantastic inheritance when she dies.' A sly grin crossed his face. 'I thought I'd make some trouble for him. Show him what life was like for the rest of us.'

'And instead, it's added to your trouble. Tell us what happened last night at Club Europium,' said Morgan.

Easton looked back and forward between the officers. Lees-Langham leant in again and spoke softly to him. 'Remember my advice.'

'Whatever Ms Lees-Langham has advised, Danny, this is your opportunity to tell us what really happened when you were at Club Europium?'

'The bouncer threw me out. I'd only been in there five minutes, and it's expensive to get in. He came up behind me, grabbed me, and threw me out. It was right in front of the queue as well. I hurt my arm when I landed, and my arse. They were all laughing at me. He was out of order.'

'Then what happened?' Spence continued without looking up from the notes he was making. Lees-Langham reached out a hand and touched Easton's arm as if physical restraint might stem the flow of his words.

'He needed to learn a lesson,' he smiled as if the memory satisfied him. 'I wanted to hit him. He was a big fucker, bigger'n me, so I looked for something to hit him with. Found a brick and I used that. He wasn't laughing then.' Lees-Langham's Montblanc pen paused. She looked at him, her frustration obvious.

'What?' he said returning her glare. 'It's on CCTV, they know I did it.'

'The door supervisor is in an induced coma until they can assess the bleed on his brain,' said Morgan. 'Admitting the offence now will reduce your sentence, but you must know you're going to serve time for this. So again, for the record, you admit hitting Thomas Earl Finch, a door supervisor at Club Europium over the head

305

with a weapon, namely a brick, in the early hours of this morning?'

Danny glanced once more at Lees-Langham before speaking. 'Yes.'

'Okay,' said Morgan tapping his papers into a neat pile. 'You'll stay here while we speak to the custody sergeant and the Crown Prosecution Service. Then we can all be clear what the charges are going to be. I'll warn you now that I'm going to ask for you to be held in custody until the next bail court at the magistrates which...' he looked at his watch, 'will be Monday now.'

Morgan and Spence left Easton with his solicitor and made their way back upstairs.

Chapter 74

At four o'clock, Spence called CPS Direct for an update and got the go-ahead to charge Easton with grievous bodily harm and remand him in custody.

Spence, Lees-Langham and Easton grouped at the custody sergeant's desk while she told Danny Easton that the officer would read out the charges and that he should listen but it was obvious that he only heard a few words before he switched off. Morgan watched.

'Do you understand the charges?' the sergeant asked and Easton nodded. 'Do you have any reply to make to the charges?' He shook his head. 'Sign the pad then and we'll get you a copy.'

Harriet Lees-Langham stepped forward. She pleaded that Daniel Easton was not a flight risk and that his mother relied on his income and support since the death of her husband six months before.

The uniformed officer looked as if she'd heard it all before, but she waited until the solicitor stopped speaking before replying. 'I've listened to and understood your representations and I've weighed them against my responsibility to keep the public safe. He's going to stay with us until he goes to the Magistrates' Court on Monday.'

'This is outrageous,' said Lees-Langham narrowing her eyes as she pointed at Morgan. 'It's an assault outside a club. He'd been drinking. Keeping him in custody is an over-reaction.'

A middle-aged male officer stepped forward and took hold of Easton's arm to take him back to his cell. Morgan moved to block the solicitor's exit. When Dave Spence saw his expression he ducked back.

'I've heard a lot about you DI Morgan. I even Googled you before I came in today. I must say, I'm disappointed by your lack of empathy. Anyone can see he's not a flight risk.' She was up close and invading his personal space.

'Ms Lees-Langham, my empathy is with the victim who is lying unconscious because your client hit him with a brick. If you familiarise yourself with Sentencing Guidelines, use of a weapon is the first aggravating factor.' He was counting on his fingers. 'Under the influence of alcohol is the second and offence committed against someone providing a service, the third... I could go on. Your client is a dangerous man who needs to be in custody.' He stood to one side. 'Thank you for your help today and I have no doubt we'll meet again very soon.'

The custody sergeant made eye contact with Spence. She gave a small nod of approval before disappearing behind the bank of screens which displayed the live feed from surveillance cameras around the suite.

Spence caught up with Morgan who was making his way to the stairs. He didn't want to speak first in case Morgan hadn't completely vented his anger.

'I know what you're thinking,' said Morgan without slowing his pace or looking back. Spence remained silent. 'I've decided to keep the fingerprints thing under wraps for now. I figure he's in custody until Monday and the magistrates will have to send him to Crown Court for sentencing. Meantime, if they bail him, we can arrest him at the court and start another twenty-four hour custody time clock. If they keep him, we'll wait till we have the full fingerprint analysis, then we'll arrest him on suspicion of the Maguires. By that time, with any luck, we can link Wesley Crook in by the "sorry signs."

Spence was forced to recognise that it was a good plan. 'And Abi Slater?'

'Not sure yet. Let's not get ahead of ourselves.'

Chapter 75

Monday morning bail court was busy. Morgan and Spence queued at security with people who were appearing on summons and their supporting family and friends. When they got to the waiting area, Spence found the usher for Court One and asked when Daniel Easton's case would be called on. The tall, blonde man in a black gown referred to his clipboard then glanced at his watch. 'About half an hour I'd say. There are three on before him. He's already spoken to his solicitor.'

Spence thanked him and returned to Morgan who was standing near the exit. 'Thirty minutes, if all goes to plan.'

Morgan nodded, then got his phone out and started reading through emails. When he looked up again, he thought that a documentary maker would find rich pickings in a court waiting area. There were smartly suited professionals who he thought were probably here to plead their case against being disqualified from driving. He saw a young couple leaning on each other. Her head was resting on the man's shoulder and her eyes were vacant. Morgan guessed at drug possession or shoplifting to fund their habit. A dishevelled man with a baggy suit and thick glasses bustled across the waiting room acknowledging a few people. Defence solicitor, he decided, as the Tannoy crackled into life.

'The case of Daniel Easton is about to be heard in Court One. Daniel Easton, Court One.' Spence joined him and they went through the heavy wooden door into the courtroom.

The magistrates, two women and a man, were talking together as they waited for Easton to be brought up from the cells. The unsmiling woman who was chairing the court watched them as Morgan and Spence took seats in the area allocated to the public.

Harriet Lees-Langham came into court and sat in the front row facing the bench. The unsmiling woman greeted her by name. When she had sorted her papers into individual piles, she leant across to speak to a statuesque black woman who was prosecuting. They both turned to Morgan and Spence. When Lees-Langham shuffled back along the wooden seating to her place near the dock, the CPS solicitor rose and came to the back of the court. She introduced herself without offering a handshake. 'I've read through the case a couple of times and I can't see a justification to remand in custody. He's not a flight risk, he's previously of good character, and he lives at home with his mother. I've also just been told that the victim of the assault is conscious now and awaiting further assessment.' Morgan didn't hide his disappointment. 'Look, I know you want him in custody and I'll do my best, but I don't see them keeping him.' She gestured towards the magistrates with her head before returning to the front of the court.

There was a noise of footsteps and a jangle of keys. The door at the back of the dock opened and a custody officer preceded Danny Easton into the area which was triple glazed from a height of about three feet to the ceiling. There were small gaps between the thick glass panels to allow passage of documents and to facilitate communication between the court and the defendants.

Easton looked towards the public area then quickly away again when his eyes fell on the officers. He acknowledged Lees-Langham with a nod as the single handcuff which joined him to the custody officer was removed. She returned his greeting with a wan smile.

The Legal Adviser who sat at her desk in front of the magistrates asked Easton to give his full name, date of birth, address and nationality before reading out the charges. Morgan held his breath when she asked for a plea. It was always possible that Easton might have changed his mind about admitting the offences of grievous bodily harm and obstruction. He was pleased to hear the pleas of guilty to both charges. Now he only had to worry about whether the magistrates would grant bail before the sentencing hearing at the Crown Court.

The CPS solicitor read from her tablet computer. She opposed bail due to the seriousness of the offence and how it might be dealt with at sentencing. As he listened, Morgan felt the likelihood of custody slip away. When Lees-Langham stood and gave her performance of barely controlled outrage, he leant towards Spence and said, 'He's getting out.'

The defence suggested bail conditions which restricted Easton to living and sleeping at home and a curfew from eight at night until six in the morning. After a short discussion, the magistrates agreed, adding a stern warning about what would happen if he broke the conditions. Then it was over. Easton put out his arm for the single cuff to be replaced and followed the officer back through the door and down to the cells from where he would be released.

The court room door opened and two women almost fell through. Everyone turned towards the commotion and Morgan was astounded to see that one of them was his mother-in-law. The usher hurried across to speak to them and Morgan heard him apologise. 'I'm sorry, Mrs Easton, you've just missed him, but he'll be coming back up to the waiting area to speak to his solicitor.' Dorothy Cooper put her arm around the other woman and escorted her back through the door. As she passed him, she looked straight at Morgan and her eyes narrowed. She mouthed something at him and although he wasn't sure, he thought it might have been "bastard."

Morgan turned to his sergeant. 'Let's wait for the full fingerprint report. We know where to find him.' He followed the usher to the front of the court and crouched down to speak to the prosecutor. The usher was talking to the legal adviser and Morgan heard him say 'GBH! That's gonna put an end to his ideas of being a magistrate, isn't it? Anyway, there are two more cases ready and they're both with Ms Lees-Langham. Did you want Mohammed or Bishop up next?'

When he finished his conversation with the prosecutor, Morgan returned to where Spence was waiting at the back of the court. 'I just want a quick word with the usher before we go,' he said.

Chapter 76

Tuesday 3rd March

Sheila Turnbull, the officer in charge of exhibits taken from the DIY store car park rang Nick Morgan, just as he was thinking about lunch.

'Thanks for your patience, Nick,' she said. 'Your predecessor was on to us every ten minutes when it was a hot one. But things take longer when you keep having to answer the phone.'

'It's okay, I know you're busy. I need to be sure it's him before we go all out to nail him. So don't keep me in suspense. Is it him? Is it Danny Eaton's prints on the Transit?'

'I'd say there are enough points of comparison to question him, at least. There are only partials on the van keys and light switch, but we've found eleven points in total. Some experts say that twelve is enough and some want more than twenty. As I say, I think you're justified in questioning him.'

'Cheers Sheila, I owe you.'

Morgan replaced the receiver and almost skipped the short distance between his office and the briefing room. The case boards had been stacked, one behind the other, as if filed away to make the room look tidy. One by one, he wheeled them out again, in order of when the bodies had been found. The living faces of the victims stared back at him and he was struck by the contrast between them. Raynor was scowling and Crook had that strange half smile on the photo taken for police records. Slater and Wyatt both grinned broadly from pictures published on their social media pages. Each living photo was accompanied by a second, taken at the mortuary. In these, the victims' eyes were closed, but Morgan found them more reproachful.

He was here to look at the Maguire case board, but was distracted by Wesley Crook's photo. He couldn't pinpoint why, but to him, it all seemed to come back to this case. The body was found at a bungalow Crook had allegedly burgled. Morgan unpinned the photocopy of the sign from round Crook's neck. "Now I'm Sorry." Sorry for what? He'd posed the question at every briefing but nobody had an answer. He unpinned a copy of the letter which Crook's mother had given them and held it in his other hand. "Stop your offending behaviour or you'll be sorry."

Morgan remembered Andy Gillingham's opinion that the writer of the letters had an awareness of terms used in law courts. The usher at yesterday's hearing had told him that Daniel Easton was often at court. He was doing observations in preparation for applying to be a magistrate. Morgan's pulse quickened as the evidence started to connect together. Easton's prints on the Maguire van keys and lights; the signs left with the Maguires and Wesley Crook; a letter to Crook written using court legalese; Danny Easton as a regular observer of the activities of the Magistrates Court.

He took out his mobile and searched his contacts for the number of Silver Sands House. His call confirmed that Danny Easton had turned up for work on time and that he wasn't due to leave until five. The clock on his phone told him it would be another skipped lunch. He also knew he would be late home and sent a text to Sam to tell her. His next interview with Danny Easton was going to be lengthy.

He glanced back at the boards. Doubt began to nag. His theory didn't account for Carl Raynor or Kenny Wyatt and the link to Abi Slater's inky wedding dress was tenuous, at best. He ran through the connections again and nodded emphatically before heading for the main office.

When he couldn't find Dave Spence, Morgan approached DC Jenny Smart. 'We're going to go and bring Daniel Easton in.'

'Are we? Why?'

He lowered his voice, mindful of the Exhibits Officer's caution. 'Easton's prints may be a match for the prints on the van at the DIY store.'

She looked surprised. Morgan didn't guess that she already knew about the prints. 'If we think he's a murderer, are we taking backup?'

'Nah, it'll be fine. Let's go.'

Chapter 77

There were no available parking spaces when Morgan and Smart arrived at Silver Sands so he left his Volvo on the driveway. He made sure there was room for emergency vehicles to pass and he wasn't going to be long.

They walked purposefully towards the main building. The main door was locked and he nodded to Smart who was nearer the bell. A harassed young woman in black trousers and a blue tabard opened the door. 'We prefer that visitors don't come at mealtimes,' she said. 'Can you come back after two please?'

Morgan put his hand against the door to prevent her closing it. He produced his identification. 'I'm DI Morgan and this is my colleague DC Smart. Where will we find Daniel Easton please?'

The woman stared at each of them in turn. 'Danny? Why do you want him?'

'Where will we find him, please?' asked Smart. Morgan watched her decide whether or not to be helpful.

'He'll be in his workshop around the back. His mum sends him to work with a flask and a sandwich and he gets a bit of peace if he eats it there.'

'Thank you,' said Morgan and released his pressure on the door.

It started to drizzle as they walked around the building and it took the edge off Morgan's anticipation. During the drive to Silver Sands he had considered reasons Easton might have for his prints being in the

317

Maguires' van. He still could not come up with any that didn't put him at the scene of the murders. As he and Smart approached the maintenance area they heard a radio playing.

'It's a workshop,' said Smart as they got closer. 'He'll have tools. We should call for backup?'

Morgan shook his head. 'Get the cuffs ready and stay here. If I shout, slam the door shut so he can't get out.' He marched ahead of her and disappeared through the open doorway. She waited and listened.

'Hello again, Danny. I'm sure you remember me. DI Nick Morgan. Turn the radio off, please.'

There was a click and the music stopped.

'Face the wall and put your hands out behind you. Daniel Francis Easton, I am arresting you on suspicion of the murder of Angus Maguire and Michael Maguire between the hours of 8pm on Monday 24th February and 6am on Tuesday 25th February this year. You do not have to say anything but it may harm your defence if you do not mention when questioned something which you later rely on in court. Anything you do say may be given in evidence. Come and cuff him please, DC Smart.'

Morgan stood to one side so that Smart could snap the cuffs on. Easton was standing in front of a wall, staring at a work schedule as if choosing a slot for a new task. He was a couple of inches shorter than Morgan and not quite as wide although his arm muscles bulged through the overalls. Smart looked relieved that he hadn't resisted arrest and Morgan knew he should have waited for backup. It wasn't like him to be reckless. 'Are we going to need a van, Danny, or are you going to come with us?' he asked.

'I didn't do anything,' said Easton. 'Why are you picking on me?' Morgan thought there was a little boy inside this man's body and he wasn't surprised to see tears in his eyes. They led him to Morgan's car and apart from Easton asking for the cuffs to be loosened, they completed the journey to custody in silence.

Chapter 78

It took three hours for Harriet Lees-Langham to arrive and take instructions from Danny Easton. By the time Morgan and Spence were ready to start the interview, street lights were dotted in the darkening sky. Descending the concrete steps to the cells, Spence asked his boss how the house renovations were progressing.

He glowered. 'They're not. The windows are letting in a gale force wind that comes straight from Siberia and I've no idea when I'm going to get time to do something about it. I've got scaffolding coming this week and the rental on that would make a hole in the national debt.' The conversation ended when they got to the door.

Spence entered the interview room first and sat opposite the solicitor. Her floral perfume saturated the room. Morgan settled into his chair and opened his folder. He nodded at Spence who started the recording. After they had covered the preliminaries, Morgan repeated the caution. Before he could continue, the solicitor put out her right hand, palm upwards and said 'Disclosure, please. I've seen nothing which justifies this arrest. This is harassment of my client.' She turned to Easton. 'They are obliged to tell me what they've got so I can advise you properly.'

'I know what disclosure is,' he mumbled.

'There's no disclosure for you today Ms Lees-Langham,' Morgan replied before looking at Danny Easton. 'During this interview I'm going to talk to you about the 24th and 25th of February this year. I'd like to start by you telling me where you were and what you were doing.'

'I don't even know what days of the week they were. I was probably at work,' said Danny.

'Please follow the advice I gave you, Danny.' Lees-Langham spoke on autopilot and without looking up from her notepad.

'As I said when I cautioned you at Silver Sands earlier, the 24th was a Monday and the 25th, a Tuesday. Where were you, Monday before last?'

'Monday night is my darts night. I was probably there.'

'And there will be witnesses to say you were there and when you left?' Spence intervened. In the bright light of the oppressive little room, the first beads of sweat sparkled on Easton's upper lip.

Morgan and Spence fired a salvo of questions at Daniel Easton for the next fifteen minutes and were rewarded with the response of "No comment" to each round. Lees-Langham did not try to repress her smile as she continued her note taking. She intervened, 'If I had some disclosure, I'm sure my client would be happy to provide a statement which would assist you with your enquiries. As far as I can tell from your questions, you are on some fishing expedition. I suggest you row to another part of the lake and try your luck there.'

Morgan decided it was time to wipe the smile from her face.

He started, his voice low, his eyes down on the papers in front of him. 'It's unfortunate that you're unable or unwilling to account for your movements on those dates, Danny. We'll certainly follow up with the darts club. You should know that I'm also applying for warrants for your home and any vehicles you have access to. I don't need a warrant for your workshop, but we'll be searching there too. Of course, it'll be distressing and inconvenient for your mother who I believe is not long widowed. It's correct that you've recently lost your father?'

Easton shot to his feet. 'You keep her out of this. She's been through enough.' His metamorphosis from sulky, uncommunicative boy to combat-ready warrior startled both officers who rose to their feet to restrain him.

'Danny.' Lees-Langham's voice was almost tender. She stretched her hand out and held his arm, pulling him gently back down on to his chair. 'How many more times? Please follow my advice.'

The officers sat down again. Until that moment, Morgan had wondered if they might have the wrong man. His upper body strength was obvious, but his demeanour did not suggest he was capable of bludgeoning two men to death. This flash of passion in defence of his mother changed his opinion and he felt a frisson of excitement as he anticipated Easton's reaction to the question he was building towards.

'Well, just a couple more things and then we'll take a break and we'll get some tea for you.'

It was one of Morgan's signature techniques. Make the coming questions sound unthreatening. Promise a break and refreshments. Everyone fell for it, even battle hardened criminals. They anticipated the break and relaxed, them bam! The killer question. He kept his voice soft and calm. Under other circumstances, it might have been described as seductive. He locked his steely blue eyes on to Easton's.

'Can you tell us Danny, please... just how does it come about that your fingerprints are on the keys of the vehicle that Michael and Angus Maguire drove to the car park of the DIY outlet? The same car park they could not drive away from because they were both dead.'

Lees-Langham's jaw dropped open. She glanced at Easton before speaking. 'DI Morgan, this is …'

Morgan's gaze was still fixed on Easton. 'And how come there is also one of your prints on the headlight switch for that vehicle? The lights were off when we found the bodies and I believe you turned them off. So we have you in that car park when those men were murdered and there's no evidence that puts anyone else there at that time. Why did you kill them? Did you fall out over your share of the tools you were stealing?'

'No!' Danny Easton's howled in outrage. 'I'm not a thief.'

'This is exactly why I wanted disclosure before you started your questioning, DI Morgan,' shouted Lees-Langham, her cheeks flushed now. 'I thought the days of pulling rabbits out of hats in police interviews had long gone.'

'Is that what you thought, Ms Lees-Langham?' Morgan smiled thinly at her. 'We'll take a break now and I'll check on progress of the warrants. You may want to take further instructions from Mr Easton.'

'Magistrates' Court has finished for the day so I'm going through the out of hours procedure to get the warrants.' DC Lynn Greenfield called across the office as Spence returned. 'Is he giving us anything useful?'

Spence was chewing on a cold sausage roll he'd got from the minimarket on the other side of the road. 'Solicitor's about to implode. She and the boss have taken a dislike to each other and I'm not sure that's helping.'

'Are you going to do the searches tonight while he's still in custody?'

'Up to the boss, I suppose, but I think so.'

Two hours later, Morgan beckoned Spence and Greenfield into his office. His face was pale and there were dark shadows under his eyes.

'We've got warrants for the home address, his bike, and the garage he keeps it in, and his mother's car. Everything except the work vehicle,' said Spence and pointed to Lynn Greenfield. 'She's done a grand job, sir.'

Greenfield asked 'Are you going in tonight, sir?'

Morgan looked at his watch and took a moment to consider. 'We can hold Easton until tomorrow afternoon so I think we should all go home and get some sleep. We'll start with a briefing at seven tomorrow morning. I'll try to rustle up a second team but if I can't, we'll do the home first and see where that gets us before we move on to the other sites.'

'I'd like to be in on the searches,' said Greenfield.

'Speak to DI Patel and if she can spare you, I'm okay with that.' He stood up slowly and stretched before packing a few loose papers into a blue wallet.

Spence and Greenfield wished him goodnight before filing out of the office. 'Do you think he's okay?' Greenfield spoke softly as they made their way down the echoing corridor.

'No idea, and I'm not going to risk asking him. I think he's pissed off that he can't play with his DIY tools. Come on. Let's get out of here before he changes his mind.'

Chapter 79

Once the briefing was over it took less than an hour to get two teams together. Morgan was taking the first to search the Easton family home and car and the second one headed for the Silver Sands workshop and Danny's motorbike and garage.

Gillian Easton answered on the second ring of her doorbell. Her eyes were dead and she held a crumpled tissue in her hand. 'He's not here,' she shouted and went to close the door. DS Dave Spence blocked her, handed her a copy of the search warrant, and explained the procedure. He also told her that her son was in custody. They stood to one side as a team of uniformed and plain clothed officers filed past them. DI Nick Morgan was last to enter.

'You!' Gillian Easton shouted and pushed at his chest. 'I remember you from court. If this is about Kenny Wyatt, then Danny had nothing to do with it. I asked him.'

Morgan stopped, unsure if he had heard correctly.

Spence looked puzzled too. 'Shall I contact DI Patel? he asked. 'Wyatt is her case.'

Morgan agreed. 'Get her to join us,' he said. 'And we'll need your car keys please, Mrs Easton,' he called over his shoulder. 'Constable Ferguson, please stay with Mrs Easton in the lounge.'

From the kitchen, Morgan could hear Gillian Easton shouting at the constable. 'How many of you are there? It's a shame you weren't so fuckin' interested when we were burgled. Maybe if you had been, my husband would still be here.'

He saw keys sitting on a breakfast bar and picked them up in gloved hands. On the ring was a gilded letter "G," two house keys and a car key.

He wanted the car searched by someone he knew and trusted. He called up the stairs to DC Greenfield.

Her head appeared through a doorway. 'Sir?'

He held up the keys. 'Can you search the car? Make sure that the one on the drive belongs to Mrs Easton. I don't want any cock ups with us searching the wrong vehicle. The car park where we found the Maguires is about eight miles from here. Easton must have used some sort of transport to get there. I know he rides a motorbike, but it was a cold night and I'm fancying the car.'

Spence went into the lounge where Gillian Easton was distracting the young constable from his search. He crossed to the settee and sat opposite her, waiting for a pause in the tirade. When she noticed him, she screwed up her face. 'I remember you too. You were at court with that other one. Well, my Danny walked away a free man that day, and he'll walk away from this. You'll see.'

Spence continued to look at her without speaking.

'What?' She was shouting again. 'What are you lookin' at? You gonna to accuse me too?'

'What can you tell me about Danny?' asked Spence with no real expectation of a reply.

'What d' you mean?'

'From where I'm sitting, I see photos of him with awards and I see cups and medals in a cabinet. I see family photos of him with you and your husband on holidays and I know that until last week, we had never heard of him. So, I'm asking you... what can you tell me about Danny?'

She glared at him and wrapped her thin cardigan tighter around herself. Spence looked up at Constable Ferguson who was shaking his head, indicating he'd not found anything in this room. Spence nodded and told him he should continue elsewhere.

'Maybe Danny needs help,' he said, his attention now returned to her.

'Danny lost his dad six months ago. They were very close. Since it happened, he's gone in on himself. Up in his room all the time. Hardly talks to me.'

'Was it an accident?' Spence waited patiently while she decided how much to tell him.

'Danny's father committed suicide,' she paused, 'I'm sorry, I don't know your name.'

'It's Dave. DS Dave Spence.'

'He killed himself, DS Spence, and Danny found him.' She was crying quietly, dabbing at her eyes with a shredded tissue. 'Danny hasn't gotten over it. They promised him counselling, but they can't get funding. I can't afford private. I'm doing two and three jobs at a time just to pay the bills.'

'Was there no insurance policy for your husband?'

'They won't pay for a suicide,' she said.

The door burst open and Morgan came in. 'DS Spence, a moment please.'

Spence was reluctant to go. He looked apologetic. 'I'll be back,' he said but she was already out of her seat and shouting at Morgan. The moment had passed.

DC Lynn Greenfield came back into the hallway through the open front door. 'We're starting to get a bit of attention from the neighbours,' she told Morgan before holding up a crumpled supermarket carrier bag she'd brought in. 'Found it in the boot inside a first aid kit which had a couple of sticking plasters and a roll of cotton bandage. I wanted a closer look without everyone watching. It's worth mentioning that the front seats of the car are a bit grubby, but the back seat and the boot look as if they've been vacuumed to within an inch of their lives.' She placed the bag on the table in the hallway and pulled it open with exaggerated care before peering inside. 'That's worth a look,' she said to Morgan who leant over. He could see a small jumble of disposable gloves and a couple of single-use face masks. As Greenfield watched, he reached into the bag and produced a black permanent marker.

'I know what I'm thinking, said Morgan, 'What do you think?'

'It's not quite "bang to rights," but it needs an explanation,' said Spence who had been watching from a few steps away.

'What did you get out of the mother?'

'Son's not been right since he found the father's body. Suicide.'

'Oh Christ,' said Morgan. 'What with that, and her comment about Councillor Wyatt, we should bring her in. Invite her to help with our enquiries. And good work DC Greenfield. The car's going to need a closer look, so can you arrange to have it taken in please? Oh, and ring DI Patel again. If she hasn't already left, ask her to wait. We'll be bringing Mrs Easton to her.'

Spence was frowning. 'I don't think she'll give us anything in the state she's got herself into at the moment.'

Morgan was surprised. 'And your reasons?'

'We'll get more out of her when she's had time to think.

Morgan disagreed, but didn't show it. 'Okay. Make arrangements for her to come in later today. You and DI Patel should speak to her. I want to know why Daniel Easton, who has no criminal record, has suddenly started killing people.'

Chapter 80

Back in his office, Morgan rang to check on the progress of the second search team. When he heard they were on their way back from Easton's workshop he went to the briefing room and took a few minutes to consider his next move. The contents of the carrier bag from Gillian Easton's car could be significant but they could also be completely innocent. Danny Easton worked in a building where surgical gloves and masks were used every day. Not uncommon for an employee to nick a few for personal use. The marker pen was generic. It was unlikely that the ink would tie it uniquely to the signs left with Wesley Crook and the Maguires, let alone to the stain on Abigail Slater's wedding dress. He looked up in response to a knock on the open door. Sergeant Booth, who had led the second team, came in without invitation.

'Anything?' asked Morgan.

'We bagged up some tools at his workshop behind Silver Sands, but nothing to get excited about. There aren't any obvious blood stains or signs of cleaning up either at the workshop or the garage. There was a shredder at the workshop which we thought was unusual, so we've brought that in. I hope you don't need to reassemble the contents because it was pretty full. There was also a planner. When we took it down, there were a couple of envelopes pinned up behind it.'

Morgan frowned. 'Containing...?'

'The open one had a note from his dad. Looked like a suicide note. The other was sealed and addressed to a "Gill." It was in the same handwriting.'

'What about the bike and the garage?'

'Nothing to report from there, sir.' Sergeant Booth checked his notebook before snapping it closed. 'Everything's being booked into evidence and they'll let you know when you can get hold of it.'

'I don't suppose anyone took pictures of the planner, and the letters, did they?'

'No sir, they weren't my instructions.'

'Okay. Thank you Sergeant Booth.'

Morgan was frustrated. His gut told him that those letters would seal Danny Easton's fate, but he would have to wait for them. There was less than an hour left of relevant time on Easton's custody clock. After that they would either have to release him, or apply to the superintendent for an extension. He set off to talk to Johnson.

Spence held the door open for DI Maggy Patel before taking the seat next to her, and opposite Gillian Easton. She leant forward, tapping the desk as she spoke. 'When are you letting my Danny go? He hasn't done anything.'

Spence ignored her question. 'Mrs Easton, this is DI Patel. She is leading investigations into the death of Kenneth Wyatt. I am part of a team involved in a separate investigation in which Danny is a person of interest. I'd like to remind you that you are attending the station voluntarily to help us with our enquiries. Our conversation is not being recorded. You can refuse to answer any question and you can leave at any time. Are you okay to proceed?' He deliberately hadn't said "happy to proceed."

Gillian Easton stayed silent, resentment radiating from her.

'When we came to your house yesterday...'

'You mean when you and your bullies ransacked my home,' she interrupted.

'... we had a short conversation about your son, Daniel...'

'Danny.'

'... and you were telling me how the death of his father has affected him.'

Both officers watched her and Spence hoped she would pick up from where she had been interrupted during the search.

She didn't.

He tried again. 'You told me that your husband had committed suicide and that Danny had found his body. How did that come about?'

She opened her mouth to speak but tears came before words. She plucked a plastic pack of paper hankies from her scuffed handbag and used one to dab at her eyes. 'He's getting better now. He got a girlfriend, and that helped for a while. They've split up now. He's grieving for his dad. We all deal with that differently.'

'I agree,' said Spence, 'but it's important we get to the bottom of what happened... if we're going to be able to help Danny.' He knew he was deceiving her, but he needed the information.

She took a deep breath which developed into a hiccup.

'Frank had been gardening... getting things ready for winter. He'd always hated winter but when he got diagnosed as clinically depressed, it was worse. He'd recently stopped work because the drugs they gave him made him tired and he didn't feel safe to drive. We started to get short of money, so I was picking up bar work and waitress jobs where I could. He hated that. He got more withdrawn. Moody, even. I thought he was going to hit me once!' She shuddered at the memory looking anxiously at Patel and Spence in turn. 'I know he wouldn't have, but he wasn't himself anymore.' The crying became more persistent and Spence offered to fetch her some water. She shook her head.

'When I got in from work that day, he wasn't in the house. I was glad. I'd had a busy day and was starting a headache. I put a lasagne in the oven. It was Frank's favourite and I bought it often, just to please him. I was bloody sick of lasagne. When Danny came in, he asked where his dad was and I realised I hadn't even cared where he was. Danny looked down the garden and said that Dad's shed was open and he was off out the door before I even thought. I hear that howl every night when I turn my bedside light off.'

'He was in the shed?' asked Spence, feeling the need to say something.

'Antidepressants, whisky and a supermarket carrier bag over his head. Rubber band holding it tight to his neck. "Suicide while the balance of his mind was disturbed," or so the coroner said. I still can't believe he didn't care who found him like that. Danny is destroyed.'

The three of them sat in silence and Spence felt that the oxygen had been sucked out of the room.

'Did he leave a note?' asked Spence.

'He left a note for Danny. I've never seen it.'

'Did the coroner's office not return it to you?'

'Danny said it was written for him and he didn't want anyone else to see it. He said nobody had come when we were burgled and we weren't going to help them now. I

333

never saw the note and I've never told anyone about it. Is there anything else? I have to get to work.' She bent down to pick up her bag and stood up.

DI Patel had stayed silent until now. 'When we came to your house yesterday, you mentioned that you had spoken to your son about Kenneth Wyatt. Can you tell me how that came about?'

Gillian Easton sunk back into her seat as if an invisible force had pushed at her chest.

Chapter 81

In the short time he had worked with him, Morgan felt he had the measure of his senior officer. Johnson was a safe pair of hands who would never step out of line. He would also never achieve the impossible by stretching or bending the rules. He knew before he asked that Johnson would not speak to the Superintendent about extending Danny Easton's detention, but that wasn't going to stop him asking.

Johnson listened when Morgan explained the need for more time to look at what had been seized from the family home and Easton's workshop. He continued to listen when Morgan said they had more questions for Easton about his prints being found on the keys to the Maguires' van. When Morgan fell silent, Johnson asked the one question he'd been afraid of.

'What does the CPS say?'

'They say that, as it stands, we haven't got enough.'

'Release him under investigation for the Maguire case. He's still on court bail. We know where to find him.' He turned back to his laptop screen and jiggled the wireless mouse to reactivate it.

Morgan took this as a dismissal and left without saying anything else. He saw there were only ten minutes remaining on Easton's custody clock and hoped that Patel and Spence were getting something out of the mother.

Gillian Easton sighed. She seemed resigned now.' I told Danny something about Kenny and he got angry. It was something or nothing. Not important.'

'Kenny?' Spence picked up on the familiarity.

'That's what he was called at school. Kenny.'

'You were at school with Kenneth Wyatt?' asked Patel.

'Yes, but only primary. I've not seen him since.'

Patel's brow furrowed. 'Then why have a conversation with Danny about him? I don't understand.'

'He was at the football club dinner... you know, the one that's all over the papers.'

'And..?' Spence was getting impatient. He wanted to speak to Morgan about the suicide note before Danny Easton had to be released.

'It can't harm him now, I suppose.' She dropped her bag back on the floor and faced them. 'I was waitressing. I need the money. I didn't notice Kenny until he followed me outside when I went for a fag break. He was drunk and he said some horrible stuff about my husband. He groped my boobs. Stuck his hand between my legs. He told me I needed a man.' Her face flushed and tears of outrage sparkled in her eyes. I stubbed my fag out on his pudgy little hand and he ran away.'

'Who did you tell?' asked Patel.

'I wasn't going to tell anyone, but Danny saw I was upset and he wouldn't let it go. He's been very protective of me since his dad died.' Patel's head sank and she nodded. 'I spoke to Danny when I saw Kenny'd been found like that. He swore it wasn't him. Swore on his dad's life, and I believed him.' She looked back and forward between the officers. 'That's all I know. Now, I really need to get back to work.'

The officers escorted her to the main desk and Spence arranged for a patrol car to drive her. When he came back in, Patel was waiting. 'They let him go fifteen minutes ago.'

Chapter 82

Thursday 5th March

Morgan convened with Spence and Patel in his office to discuss yesterday's progress.

'I've asked the lab to prioritise the DNA work on Wyatt's shirt,' said Patel. 'If it's Danny Easton's, I'm bringing him in.'

Morgan grunted. Sam had told him at breakfast that she was visiting her mother this morning and that her return to work was likely to be discussed. They had argued.

'We've seen him leap to the defence of his mother,' said Spence, pointing at Morgan and himself, 'but I still don't see how it connects to targeting criminals.'

'Me neither,' said Morgan, reaching to pick up his ringing phone. The conversation was short and when he ended it, they were looking at him expectantly.

'Danny Easton didn't go home last night, and he's not turned up at Silver Sands today. His mother rang in to ask if we'd re-arrested him after she spoke to you. Apparently, she's beside herself with worry.'

After dropping the twins off at school Samantha Morgan picked up a couple of chocolate croissants at the new artisan bakery and headed for home. She was cross with Nick's reaction at breakfast. It wasn't as if she really was visiting her mother, so the argument had been pointless, but she could hardly tell him, could she?

She was expecting Graham at ten. There just time to shower and put on the dress he'd specifically requested. As she walked past the elderly residents who were chatting outside the library, she felt a delicious shiver of anticipation. A small woman who was well wrapped up against the cold looked at her with concern. 'You need a thicker coat, dear,' she said disapprovingly.

She got back to her car and was removing her resident's parking clock from the windscreen when her phone rang. Please God, don't make it my mother, she thought. The screen showed it was Graham. 'Please don't be cancelling,' she whispered.

'Change of plan,' he said. 'Can you come to my flat?'

'I'm on my way home to get ready,' she said. 'I've bought croissants.'

'Just come as you are... you won't be in your clothes for long. And bring the croissants.'

'I don't even know where you live.'

He gave her the address and a pass code to open the security barrier. 'Park in bay seven,' he said. 'It's my neighbour's but she's away at the moment.'

There was a knock on Morgan's door and Jenny Smart appeared, carrying a brown envelope. 'Morning, sir. This has been dropped off. Photos of the evidence collected during yesterday's searches.' Spence retook his seat and Patel held the door open.

'Christ, was it only yesterday?' said Morgan, reaching out for the envelope.

'I'll leave you to it,' said Patel and followed DC Smart out.

Morgan tipped the sheaf of photos on to his desk and split them into two piles, handing one to Spence. 'I'm particularly interested in the suicide note if you find it,' he said. He squinted at the photograph of Easton's wall planner but the print was too small to read. They would need the original.

'I've got it,' said Spence holding out a photograph of a letter. Morgan took it and began to read.

Danny,

I'm sorry to do this to you both, particularly after what you went through with the burglary, but I can't take any more. It is a husband and dad's duty to protect his family and when they ransacked our lovely home I knew I'd failed you both. Since then, a little bit of me dies every day. I can't stand it when you look at me and it's worse when your mum cries.

When you were little you wanted to be a policeman and I hope it's not too late for you to try. Victims like us need a voice. We need justice, not a crime number for the insurance. If the thieving bastards aren't made to be sorry, nothing will change. Join the police and make them sorry.

Your mother will need you more than ever now and I trust you to protect her.

Be a better man than I was.

Love

Dad

'"Join the police and make them sorry,"' quoted Spence. 'I wish it was that easy.'

'Tell them to change their ways or they'll be sorry, and when they don't, make them sorry by killing them. Is that what it's about?' asked Morgan.

Spence took the photo back and read it again. 'Seems a bit drastic, doesn't it?'

'You said his mother told you he was distraught and was struggling to get over it. Maybe he decided that he

340

couldn't be bothered to do the police training and he'd take a short cut to fulfil his dad's wishes.'

'You mean police, judge and executioner?'

Morgan gathered the photos together. 'We need to compare his days off with times when Crook and the Maguires were at court. And that other one who got a letter, the one in prison. I've forgotten his name.'

Spence thought for a moment. 'Drake, but I can't remember his first name. The nice house with the old dog.'

'I'll have it in my notes. Let's find out when he was at court.'

Morgan's phone rang again. 'DI Morgan,' he snapped at the unwelcome interruption. He listened and then looked up at his office clock. 'How long's it been going on?' There was unmistakeable panic in his voice.

Morgan's eyes met Spence's and he saw the alarm in the DS's face. 'Okay, Spence and I will get over there now. Who's in charge of the situation? No, don't worry, I'll find out when I get there.'

He ended the call and immediately rang Sam's mobile which diverted to Voicemail. 'Ring me, Sam, the minute you get this message. It's important.' He faced Spence his voice now even and controlled, 'We need to get to Silver Sands House. It seems Danny Easton has turned up taken my mother-in-law hostage. He's asking for me.'

Morgan got to his office door before glancing back to see that Spence had not moved. 'Come on, Dave. We'll go in my car. He's got my wife as well.'

Chapter 83

Thursday 5th March

Samantha backed her car into the parking bay. Her phone rang. It was Nick. She looked up at the windows of the apartment block and saw Graham watching. She rejected the call and turned her phone off.

Her heart was beating hard by the time the lift stopped on the third floor. She sucked in a large breath of air and exhaled through pursed lips. She wiped her clammy hands on her jeans and wished she'd insisted on going home to shower first.

Graham opened the door before she reached it. He was wearing black low waist jeans which were tighter than the current fashion. He looked good in them. His hair was wet and his torso and feet were bare.

'You've had a shower then,' she said. 'Why wouldn't you wait for me to have one?'

'You can shower here while I shave,' he replied.

She dragged her nails slowly through the bristles on his cheeks. 'Shave afterwards. I fancy you a bit rough.'

'Not a good idea. Your skin is so soft, you'll get a rash and Plod will get suspicious.'

She tutted. 'He's rung already this morning. I wonder if he's checking up on me.'

Graham looked taken aback but didn't say anything. He took her hands in his and raised them to his mouth. He kissed her knuckles, his soft brown eyes looking up at her. 'He wouldn't check up on you if you left him and came to be with me.'

She pulled her hands away. 'This is a fling, Graham, for you and for me. It's a trip down memory lane until one of us gets bored, so don't spoil it. Show me round, and put the kettle on while I shower.'

The flat was an ultra modern bachelor pad. The living area was open plan with use of space designated by differences in the flooring; sparkly tiles for the kitchen, and parquet for the living and dining areas. The latter reminded her of Cliffside and made her think of Nick and the hard work he was doing to make a home for his family. Why he had rung her that morning? Especially after their argument.

'Penny for them, Sammy.' He took her hand and led her to a large room with a king sized bed in the middle. The room was dimly lit by purple and blue wall lights. Samantha screwed up her eyes. There was something strewn across the bed but she couldn't make out what it was. She bent down, unzipped and removed her boots, then padded across the deep pile carpet.

'Are these real?' she asked, picking up a few of what she now could see were rose petals scattered across a black bed cover. She rubbed a few between her fingers and inhaled their fragrance.

'They are. They represent that your life with me would be a bed of roses.'

She stared at him. 'I'm going to need a sick bucket,' she said and he laughed.

'I might too.' He gathered up the cover and tossed the bundle to the corner of the room. 'This was how the younger me was going to propose marriage to you until you came home from university wearing an engagement ring. It's all here as I envisioned it. Me, freshly showered, and low lighting too, although today's effect is a bloody sight more expensive than I could have afforded back then. And my best idea of all was using the petals and that line. You would have been putty in my hands.'

He wrapped her in his arms and held her until she pushed him away. 'Where's the shower?' she asked. 'I need to be back by two for the scaffolders.'

Winter sun filtered through the bare branches of the trees surrounding Silver Sands House. The scene reminded Morgan of childhood visits with his mother to the cemetery where her parents were buried. The memory was invaded by disjointed voices from police radios. A uniformed officer appeared from behind the marked police van which blocked the drive.

'I'm DI Nick Morgan,' he said holding out his ID. 'And this is DS Spence.' The officer stared at Spence until he produced his own ID wallet.

'Who's Bronze Command?' asked Morgan. The officer pointed to a slender woman with cropped auburn hair which framed a serious face. She was deep in conversation with four other officers, two of whom were wearing bullet proof vests, heavy boots and police baseball caps. They were armed. Morgan heard Spence swear under his breath.

'DI Nick Morgan,' he said again as he caught the female officer's attention.

'Inspector Bairstow,' she replied, extending a hand, 'Fiona.' Spence introduced himself and Bairstow guided them away from the other officers. 'You understand that you have no role here, DI Morgan? This Operation is under my command. You are here only because the subject asked for you when he made contact with us.'

'What state is he in?' asked Spence.

'I have not spoken with him, so I don't know.'

'And he's got Dorothy Cooper and my wife with him?'

Bairstow nodded. 'Affirmative to the first but not sure about your wife. The staff heard shouting coming from Mrs Cooper's suite. They fetched the manager who used her pass key. She saw that Easton was holding something shiny at Mrs Cooper's neck before he yelled at her to get out. Then he shouted to her to fetch you, DI Morgan. Any idea why?'

Morgan explained the family connection then asked again if the manager had seen Sam.

'She didn't mention her,' said Bairstow. She pointed up at a curtained window. 'If they haven't moved, they're in that sitting room.'

'Jesus Christ,' said Morgan. He looked down and massaged his head. 'Can we at least kill the lights on these cars? If he looks out, this is not a calming scene.' The LED bars of the police and ambulance vehicles were flashing out of sequence. Bairstow nodded and gave the instruction using her radio.'

'I'll need a stab vest,' said Morgan taking off his jacket.

'You're not going in.' Bairstow moved to stand between him and the building. It was a token gesture as he was significantly taller and heavier.

'I believe he's asked for me,' said Morgan.

'That's not the point. He's already got at least one hostage and I'm not about to approve sending in another one.'

'You won't be sending me in. I'll be going in. My wife's in there and I'm not standing here whilst she's in danger.' He held out his hand. 'I need a vest, please.' He turned away from her and took his personal phone out of his pocket. Sam's number diverted again to Voicemail. He'd already left four messages.

Spence walked across to one of the Armed Response Vehicles. 'Have you a spare vest for DI Morgan, please?' The officer at the back of the vehicle looked over to where Morgan and Bairstow were standing. Bairstow nodded and he handed a vest to Spence.

'Do we know what he's armed with?' asked Morgan as he put the vest on and secured the Velcro straps.

'Something shiny. That's all I know.'

'Okay. Can you arrange for me to speak to him from out here? I want him to see me.'

'Are you even qualified to go in there?' Bairstow sounded anxious.

'I was in the Hostage and Crisis Negotiation Unit a while back, before it became part of SC&O. But what really qualifies me Fiona, is I'm married to a woman who's in there. Surely you understand?'

Morgan took the phone offered by a uniformed officer who had appeared from nowhere. The ring tone on hands free was loud and the surrounding officers fell silent. He moved forward to a part of the drive which was visible to anyone looking through Dorothy Cooper's window.

'Answer the fucking phone,' he snarled. The ringing continued until the call cut off. He pressed redial and waited. He thought he might have seen a small movement of the curtain at the window but wasn't certain. He carried on walking towards the building, aware that Bairstow was shouting, but not listening to her words.

<u>Chapter 84</u>

Thursday 5th March

The front door to Silver Sands House was open and he walked through the deserted hallway. He wondered where the other residents had been taken. He took the stairs and strode along the hallway, lights illuminating as he passed the movement sensors. The vest was heavy and sweat trickled down his back. He considered exploding through the door to catch Easton unawares but decided that the twitching curtain probably meant that the stage was already set for his arrival. Three knocks on the door with a short gap between each - just as he'd been taught by his sergeant when he'd first been a beat bobby. 'Loud and controlled,' Sergeant Gavin Rhodes had said. 'It shows them you're in charge and you're not taking "No" for an answer.'

'It's DI Morgan, Danny. I'm coming in.' The manager's pass key was still in the door. He turned it and went in.

Dorothy Cooper sat in her usual chair at the window and was facing him, her feet up on her footstool, arms resting in her lap. She was staring at him, her face stonier than usual. He thought she looked smaller today; older.

Danny Easton stood behind her, the blade of a Swiss Army Knife at her neck. 'I'm not scared to do it,' he said pointing to the knife. His voice was shaky, but he looked determined.

Morgan held his arms out from his sides. 'You asked me to come and I'm here. I'm not armed and I'll listen to what you want to tell me. But before we do that, where's my wife?' he asked, looking around. 'What have you done with her?'

Danny's expression changed to confusion. 'What's your wife got to do with this?'

'Where is she?' Morgan raised his voice. He heard a soft sound and looked downwards. His mother-in-law's shoulders were trembling. She was laughing.

'Samantha's not here. She never was here. She tells you she's coming to see me, but she meets up with Graham.' She sneered at Morgan. 'You're not enough for my daughter and never have been. You might as well pack your things and go back to London.'

And with those words, Morgan's world shattered. He heard crashing in his ears and the thudding of his fast heartbeat. He thought he was going to faint or be sick, maybe both. He took a couple of strides towards Dorothy Cooper, his right hand clenched into a tight fist.

'Get back!' Easton shouted. The volume of his own voice seemed to surprise him and he jumped. The knife nicked Dorothy's skin and a teardrop of blood seeped into the neckline of her cream sweater. 'And you can shut your mouth. This is bad enough already.'

Easton's aggression ignited his captive's outrage. 'Don't speak to me like that. I've been nothing but a friend to you.'

'I'll do it,' said Easton pressing the blade harder against her thin, wrinkled skin.

'Do it.' she said, 'You don't scare me.' Her eyes were fixed straight ahead, her expression defiant. For the first time since Nick Morgan had met his mother-in-law, he was in complete agreement with her. Yes, Danny, do it, he thought, and waited.

Easton's eyes darted round the room, then closed. Morgan exhaled. He reverted back to police officer mode. 'Don't make this worse than it is already, Danny. And what are you doing here, anyway. You didn't clock on this morning, and you're not dressed for work.'

Easton sneered. 'I had a bit of business to sort with Mrs Cooper. Shouldn't have taken long, but she started shouting. That's when the nosy manager bitch turned up.'

'What business? asked Morgan.

'It doesn't matter what business. Just sort this out,' said Dorothy, waving her hands around.

'You. Sit still and keep quiet?' Morgan's voice was cold. 'I'm going to get a chair from the table and bring it over. Is that okay, Danny?'

With Morgan seated, Danny relaxed. He took the knife away from Dorothy's neck and wiped the blood on his trousers. 'I'm sorry, Mrs Cooper. I must have cut you.' She wiped her neck with her fingers and tutted.

'How does this end, Danny?' asked Morgan. 'I know you've seen the officers outside and I can confirm that some of them are armed. I don't think you're a suicide by cop sort of a man. It'd kill your mother.'

Dorothy moved in her chair trying to turn round and face her captor as she spoke. 'Yes, how does it end, Danny? I've been sitting here for ages and I need to go to the toilet.' Her sudden movement startled Easton and he brought the knife back to her neck. She squealed as he clamped the cold metal against her skin again.

'You were doing really well, Danny. I'm sorry she's upset you,' said Morgan remembering his negotiation training. Use his name and recognise any effort he makes to de-escalate the situation. The next thing would be to get food and drink brought in but it wasn't time for that yet.

'You should let her go, Danny,' Morgan pointed at Dorothy and spoke softly. 'For all her bravado, she's just a twisted bitch who gets her kicks by controlling her children and fooling herself that they still love her. I don't think you want to hurt her and I don't think your mum would want you to hurt her, either.' He let the thought sink in.

Danny Easton's head and shoulders dropped together and he withdrew the knife. Morgan was almost certain that he was no longer a threat and he considered lunging for him before deciding to play the situation out to its natural end. He did a rapid risk assessment. What was the worst that could happen? There was always the chance that his mother-in-law might get her throat cut. Should it worry him that he was unaffected by the thought?

'Can she go? Please, Danny?' Easton nodded and turned back to peep through the curtains. 'Move it Dotty,' said Morgan.

Dorothy wobbled. 'My stick,' she said.

'You only use it to get attention. Get yourself out of this room now and drop the dramatics.' Morgan got to his feet so he could counter any sudden moves Easton might be planning. When Dorothy drew level with him she leant in. He heard her words but didn't register them immediately. 'She's never loved you like she loves Graham. A mother knows.'

Morgan heard the click of her opening the door and waited for it to close. Instead, he heard a gasp followed by a thud. When he looked round he saw a pile of limbs and clothing blocking the doorway. He hurried over, getting out his phone and turning it on.

Chapter 85

Thursday 5th March

Samantha made it back to her car before she started crying. The tingling excitement she had felt for the last three weeks had evaporated. Now, she felt cheap and grubby. Sex with Graham today had been perfunctory at best. And it would be the last time.

They hadn't eaten the chocolate croissants and she was hungry. She should have picked them up before she left. She turned her phone on and was appalled to see six missed calls from Nick. When she tried to ring him back, both his phones diverted to Voicemail. She looked back up at the apartment block. No sign of Graham now. Samantha started her car and nosed her way out through the gates and on to the main road. She still had over two hours before the scaffolding was due and she decided she needed her mother.

When she pulled up at Silver Sands, a police van was blocking the driveway and a uniformed officer told her that nobody was being allowed access due to an ongoing incident.

'I can see DI Morgan's car over there. He's my husband,' she tried. 'My mother is a resident here. Please tell me what's going on. DI Morgan's been trying to ring me.' The icy hand of terror gripped her heart. She struggled to breathe.

The officer looked at her without emotion. 'As long as you're not from the press, I'll tell you. All I know is that DI Morgan is in there and it's some sort of hostage situation. I don't know any more than that. You'll have to leave now. We need the entrance freed up for emergency vehicles.'

'Stop,' said Easton. 'No calls. Nobody else is coming in.' Morgan ignored him as he knelt beside his mother-in-law and felt her neck for a pulse. He rang Spence and told him to send the waiting paramedics up. After regularly wishing her dead, he was trying to save her life and the irony was not lost on him. He was aware of Danny's continuing chatter in the background and when he ended the call he looked over to him.

'Sit down and be quiet while I try to keep her alive. This is on you.' He felt her neck again then rolled her on to her back and started to pump her chest. After twenty compressions, he formed a seal around her mouth with his own lips and breathed air into her.

Danny was watching, mesmerised. 'She hates you and you hate her. Why would you save her?'

Morgan continued his resuscitation efforts until he heard footsteps running down the corridor and saw two paramedics. He backed away from Dorothy and let them take over.

'Okay Danny, you're done here. I'm arresting you on suspicion of common assault and the false imprisonment of Mrs Dorothy Cooper...' He delivered the remainder of the caution whilst monitoring the efforts to resuscitate his mother-in-law. Two uniformed ambulance staff arrived and were preparing to move her on to a stretcher. He handcuffed Danny Easton's wrists to his front and pushed him down into Dorothy's chair. They weren't going anywhere until Dorothy Cooper was moved from the doorway; dead or alive.

He called Sam's mobile although he didn't want to hear her voice. With everything else under control, he'd started to assimilate the information. His wife really had been screwing Graham Fletcher. God, what a fool he'd been. Had there been signs he'd missed?

Sam's phone rang only once and when she spoke she was breathing heavily. Morgan almost laughed. Had he caught them at it?

'Are you okay?' she asked. 'What's going on? They won't let me into Silver Sands and they said you're in there. Are you okay?'

Like you even care, he thought. You're upset because I've disturbed your little tryst.

'Nick! Are you there? Can you hear me?'

'I'm watching ambulance staff trying to resuscitate your mother. She collapsed as she was coming out. You should get to the General and wait for them to bring her in.'

The paramedic looked up at him and he nodded. Morgan took that to be an assurance that Dorothy was still alive and was going to make it. 'And Samantha...' he rarely called her by her full name and knew it would ring alarm bells, 'Before she collapsed, your mother and I had a chat about where you were really going this morning.' He paused. 'I won't be home until late, but I'd like you to wait for me because we need to have a long talk about it.' He drew the word "long" out as if it had many syllables and then cut the call before she could speak.

Chapter 86

DI Maggy Patel was leafing through a sheaf of papers when Morgan entered her office. 'You took a chance,' she said. 'I was waiting for the DNA results before arresting him.'

'Don't worry. I haven't stolen your thunder. I arrested him for cutting Dorothy Cooper and holding her against her will.'

'It's piling up, isn't it? He's like a one-man crime wave.' She held up the papers. 'Results are in. It's Easton's DNA on Councillor Kenneth Wyatt's shirt.'

Morgan smiled. 'Johnson's going to wet his pants. This month's clear up figures will be amazing. I believe they're ready for interview. Shall we?' He extended his arm towards the door.

Custody reception was busy when Morgan and Patel arrived. The custody sergeant beckoned them to her desk.

'If you're here for Daniel Easton, I warn you that he's brought in the big guns this time.'

'Who?' asked Morgan.

'Brian Gault. He's a senior partner at...'

'Oh, I know who he is,' said Morgan and turned to Patel. 'What do you think? Do you want to change the interview plan?'

'No, I'm happy with it. Let's go.'

Morgan held back. 'Who do you suppose is paying for Gault. He won't come cheap, and that family can't

354

even afford counselling, never mind top of the range legal representation.'

'Perhaps Gault's doing the case pro bono?' said Patel, but Morgan was doubtful.

'They're in the consultation room at the end of the corridor,' said the custody sergeant nodding towards the navy painted security gate.

Patel went in first and took the chair opposite Brian Gault who smiled at her with teeth that were too white to be natural. He reminded Morgan of a crocodile he had seen in a reptile park in Singapore before he was married. He saw Patel start the recording. She returned Gault's smile, showing no signs of being distracted or intimidated.

They each identified themselves for the recording and Morgan kept his eyes on Danny Easton throughout. Experience had taught him that appearances meant nothing when it came to criminality. Easton struck him as unremarkable as he sat beside his smartly dressed and even smarter mouthed brief. But he had seen him with a knife at Dorothy Cooper's neck and suspected he would have used it if pushed.

'Danny, you've been arrested on suspicion of common assault and false imprisonment and I am further arresting you on suspicion of the murder of Kenneth Wyatt,' Patel completed the arrest caution.

Gault looked confused. He opened his mouth but Morgan interrupted him.

'It seems that Mr Gault has replaced Ms Lees-Langham as your legal representation. For his benefit, I'll remind you that you are currently on court bail pending sentencing for GBH, and were released only yesterday under investigation for the murders of Angus and Michael Maguire. Where would you like to start, Danny?'

Gault looked up from his yellow legal pad. 'My client has nothing to say to you at this stage, DI Morgan, nor to you DI Patel.'

The officers exchanged a glance and Morgan made a slight gesture with his hand which signalled the go-ahead to his colleague.

'How well did you know Councillor Kenneth Wyatt?' asked Patel.

'No comment.'

Patel ran through her list of questions. She asked if Easton had ever met Wyatt. Had he ever visited the Wyatt family home? Was Wyatt a family friend? Throughout these questions and many others, Easton stared straight ahead, waiting politely for his turn before saying 'No comment.' Gault's expression never altered as he continued to take notes.

'Here's what puzzles me, Danny,' said Patel. 'If you don't know Kenneth Wyatt, have never met him, and never been to his house, why are there stains of body fluids, identified by the lab as lacrimal fluid and nasal mucus, containing your DNA, on the clothing he was wearing when he was found hanging in his garage?' Morgan saw a small frown appear on Easton's face before Patel continued. 'Tears and snot, if that helps.'

Easton's mouth opened, then closed again. He looked to Gault at his side, then straight ahead at Morgan whose face was impassive. 'No comment,' he said.

'You see, Danny, our pathologist tells us that Wyatt had injuries consistent with hitting his head. If you were there when he fell, and were crying when you leant over him, your tears and snot would have fallen exactly where we found them and, I'm told...' she looked back at the report '... in pretty much the exact same splatter pattern.'

Gault looked up. 'My client has nothing to say and hasn't had anything to eat since breakfast. We should take a break.'

Chapter 87

Danny Easton stuck with his "no comment" responses through a further four hours of questioning until Brian Gault suggested they break and start again the next day. Morgan and Patel stood in the corridor, too weary to climb the stairs to their offices.

'What do you think?' asked Morgan.

'I've got DNA,' said Patel. 'I'm ringing the CPS first thing. What are you going to do about the false imprisonment?'

'It's a serious offence, although I'm not sure his heart was in it. I don't know why he went to see her, but when she started to shout, I think he panicked. Let's prioritise getting the murder charge for the Councillor, then follow up with the McGuires and Wesley Crook. Then we'll take a view.'

'You look tired,' said Patel, resting her hand on his arm.

'So do you.'

'Let's call it a day.'

'I wish I could,' he murmured.

When he parked at Cliffside, Morgan was disappointed but not surprised to see that the house was in darkness. It was late and maybe he had to accept that Sam didn't care enough about their marriage to wait up and discuss her infidelity. He sat in the dark listening to the metallic clunks as the car cooled. How could she betray him so easily, and with Fletcher, of all people? She knew how he felt about that man. Then he thought about Maisie and how his night with her made him equally as guilty. He pulled his jacket closed and got out of the car.

He opened the front door and made another mental note to oil it. That was the trouble with squeaky front doors. You only noticed them on the way in and out when you were busy doing something else. He laid his house and car keys on the hall table and saw light under the kitchen door. Sam was already on her feet and walking towards him when he opened it. She reached out and wrapped her arms around him, burying her face in his chest. 'I'm not long back from the hospital,' she said. 'Mum's going to be okay. They said it was you that did the CPR?'

He eased her away, not wanting her gratitude. 'Is there any of that left?' he pointed to the glass of red wine on the breakfast bar.

She took a glass from the cupboard and filled it. 'I'm on my second,' she said. 'Are you charging him with attempted manslaughter? He cut her neck.'

'What happened today will be the least of his problems. As it stands, he's lawyered up and going "no comment" to everything we put to him. It's going to take a while.'

He took off his jacket and slung it across the back of a chair before gulping a mouthful of wine. He knew he couldn't go to bed without addressing the Graham Fletcher issue but didn't know how to start. His inner voice was taunting him. 'You're not innocent, either.'

'Have you eaten? I could do some scrambled eggs for us both.' Sam was watching him. 'Are you okay? Maybe you just want some wine and then we'll go to bed.'

'Your mother told me I'm not enough for you and never have been. She also told me that since we moved here you've been spending quite a lot of time reviving your past with Graham Fletcher.' He took his phone from his pocket and brandished it at her. 'I believe I've still got a number of texts here where you assured me that nothing happened after the charity dinner. Now would be a good time to tell the truth.'

Samantha froze. The calmness of Nick's voice was in stark contrast to his words. He was looking at her, his head tilted to one side.

'My mother has tried to come between us before. She's never made any secret of the fact that she would have preferred me to marry Graham. This isn't front page news for you.'

Morgan clamped his lips together until they almost disappeared. 'You need to tell the truth right now Sam, or I'm going upstairs and packing you a bag.'

When she responded her voice was low and she spoke quickly, her right forefinger pointing towards his chest. 'It's not as if you've never strayed. We'd hardly been married five minutes before you were all over DC Alison Goddard.'

Morgan stared at her then shook his head. 'This isn't about me. This is about you. All about you. You, your mother, and Graham Fletcher. Tell me the truth right now.'

Sam held his gaze and he watched her as she weighed up her options. She took a sip of wine, playing for time. Her shoulders dropped and she sighed. 'He made me feel young again and I was stupid enough to fall for it. I felt desirable and wanted for more than "what's for tea and where are my trainers?"'

'So it's my fault, is it? Mine and the twins?'

She continued as if he had not spoken. 'He made me laugh and he looked at me when I spoke. I've felt more alive for these last few weeks than I have felt for years and so, I won't say I'm sorry, but I will say that it's over. It's inevitable that we'll come across each other in a place this size, but I won't seek him out and I won't have sex with him again. It was great, but it's over.' She braced herself for his reaction.

Morgan heard Dorothy Cooper's spiteful words repeated over and over in his head. He thought of Maisie and the fun they had shared that night. The pleasure and the laughter. He remembered that there were twelve year old twins asleep upstairs whose lives he could splinter with a single sentence. He got up, came around the breakfast bar and pulled her into his arms.

'When did I stop looking at you when you spoke?'

She bent back from his hold. 'You don't have to look so guilty. We've both been busy. I've had Mum, and the planning of the move, and you've had your cases. We just forgot about each other.' She rested her head on his chest and closed her eyes.

Morgan stared across the kitchen remembering the excitement he had felt when he last held a woman this close. But that had been Maisie.

Chapter 88

Spence joined Morgan and Patel in the briefing room. 'I spoke to the CPS while we were waiting for Brian Gault to arrive. We're good to charge Danny Easton for the Maguire murders,' he said.

'We weren't on Wednesday,' said Morgan.

'We didn't have the wording of the father's suicide note and the connection to the signs left with the bodies on Wednesday.'

Morgan turned to Patel. 'What about Wyatt?'

She waved her phone at him. 'Waiting to hear back.'

Patel's phone rang and she left the room. She returned moments later and tossed the phone on to a desk. 'That's disappointing.'

Morgan and Spence waited.

'Charge and remand for manslaughter of Kenneth Wyatt. They'll review if we uncover anything else which shows he planned to murder him. Oh, and Brian Gault's arrived. He's with Easton.

'Okay,' Morgan eased off the edge of the desk where he had been perched. 'Let's go and make Mr Gault's day by charging his client with two counts of murder and one of manslaughter. With any luck, he'll persuade him to cough to Wesley Crook too. The cardboard signs on the bodies link them.'

'Leaving Carl Raynor and Abi Slater,' said Patel.

'I don't think Easton is involved with Carl Raynor,' said Morgan. 'It doesn't fit. And I'm still not sure about Abi Slater.'

'I've no reason to be in this interview,' said Patel. 'I've got my charge. Why don't you and Spence speak to him today?'

'Okay.' Morgan unpinned the premortem photos of Wesley Crook and Abi Slater from their boards and followed Spence out.

Danny Easton looked as if he hadn't slept. His eyes were rimmed with red and bloodshot.

Once the recording software was running, Brian Gault told them that he had a prepared statement in which Danny had admitted to being with Kenneth Wyatt when he fell and hit his head, but denied hanging his body in the garage. He passed the A4 sheet of paper across to Morgan who read it and put it aside.

'Noted, Mr Gault, thank you, but we're pretty confident we can make that charge stick,' said Morgan. 'We'll be coming back with more questions for your client about Kenneth Wyatt and also Angus and Michael Maguire, but today, I'm more interested in this man.' He opened the folder and pushed the photograph of Wesley Crook across until it lay in front of Easton. 'We believe you killed him because he didn't stop burgling after you told him to, Danny? What would you like to say about it?'

'Never seen him before,' Easton barely glanced at the photograph.

'Oh, I think you have,' said Morgan. 'I think you saw him at the Magistrates' Court when he was up for burglary, and you made a note of his address. You sent him a letter telling him to stop burgling or, as you so eloquently put it, to stop his offending behaviour, or he would be sorry. When he was up again for burglary, you killed him.'

Morgan watched Easton for any twitch or tick, but there was nothing.

'You dumped him outside the bungalow he had burgled to ram the message home, didn't you? Did you not think that couple had suffered enough?'

The silence was lengthy, broken only by voices in the corridor and the clang of a security gate.

'How many more letters have you sent?' asked Spence.

That small, sly smile they had seen before crossed Easton's face. 'I'm doing your job for you,' he said.

'What do you mean?' asked Spence.

'You don't have to speak to them,' said Gault. 'We talked about this.'

Easton looked at both detectives. 'There are no consequences when you deal with burglars. I give them consequences.'

'Where did you kill him, Danny?' Morgan pointed to the photograph of Crook again.

Easton crossed his arms and leant back in the chair, his eyes on fire; triumphant. 'He won't burgle anyone else, will he?' he shouted.

Brian Gault leant towards him, but Easton pushed him away.

'How many more letters have you sent?' Spence repeated.

'Dorothy Cooper thinks you're a complete wanker,' Easton pointed first at Morgan, then at Spence, 'and you. You all are. Every fucking police officer, because you're all the same. Stick to the rules, don't rock the boat and when the little people are robbed, add it to the statistics, hand out a crime number and have another cup of tea. We just couldn't get your attention. Your complete lack of interest killed my father and destroyed my mother. Have we got your attention now?' He hammered his fist on the desk to accentuate each word of his last sentence.

Morgan tapped on Wesley Crook's photograph. 'Where did you kill him and how did you transport him to the bungalow?'

'Have we got your attention?' Easton was still shouting and Morgan saw Brian Gault cringe.

'You have my undivided attention, Danny,' said Morgan. 'Now, this guy. Tell me what happened.'

Easton snorted. 'He was one of the ones I sent a letter to and when I was at the court, there he was again. Bold as brass. Still thieving. And he had the nerve to plead not guilty!' Easton's flushed face showed his outrage.

'Go on,' said Morgan.

'We started chatting when he came up from the cells to wait for his solicitor. He said he was looking for work and I arranged to meet him outside one of the park homes up on the estate. One of the Silver Sands residents... her daughter owns it and it needed some work. Her mum recommended me.

'I was giving him a chance to go straight, but when he turned up, all he did was boast about how much he was gonna make when he sold off all the jewellery he'd knicked. I was angry. My mum never had much jewellery and when we were burgled, she lost everything, even her engagement ring. She never got any of it back. Me 'n him,' he tapped Crook's photo, 'We were measuring wood for new steps outside the park home. When he turned his back I threw an extension lead round his neck and pulled tight. He was strong, but I caught 'im off guard. It took ages before I was sure he was dead. It's quicker in films, isn't it? Anyway, good riddance.'

'How did you get him to the bungalow? Morgan persisted.

'I signed out the Silver Sands van overnight. Said I had to buy some bits from the cash and carry. Nobody cared.'

Morgan asked Spence to make a note to raise another search warrant for the van and silently cursed the magistrate who had refused their initial request.

'How many more letters?' Spence persisted.

'Ten... twelve... Not sure. Everyone else stopped, especially after the papers started calling it the "Sorry Slayer murders." I'm doing your job for you.'

'Where did you get the contact details? You couldn't be at court every day.'

Easton took a long time to answer that question. His face was troubled before it changed back to that look of triumph again.

'My girlfriend helped me.'

Morgan drummed his short nails on the folder before opening it and removing a photograph.

'Is this her?'

Danny Easton's lips pouted and he reached out to caress Abi's smiling face with the back of his fingers. 'I loved her,' he said. 'I would have done anything for her.' Brian Gault frowned and his posture stiffened. He looked across at Easton, his pen paused.

'So why did you kill her?' Morgan and Spence watched as Easton closed his eyes and shook his head.

'For the recording, Mr Easton is shaking his head,' said Spence.

Morgan persevered. 'Why did you kill her, Danny?'

'I wanted to marry her. I took out a loan and bought a ring and everything.' Tears formed in his eyes and started to run down his cheeks. He looked from Morgan to Spence and back again before wiping his tears with his sleeve. The room was silent. Gault's pen was waiting.

'I used to see her at court. She started to smile at me, and then say hello when she walked past. I saw her at a couple of the clubs. She danced like a demon. We danced together a lot. Then we got closer...' a smug smirk crossed his face. 'A lot closer, if you know what I mean. She could fuck like a demon too. I was gonna keep her forever.

Chapter 89

Danny Easton tilted his head back and closed his eyes before he spoke again. 'We arranged to meet at the Golden Dragon in town. We had a Chinese. She rang her mate up at the estate to get a caravan for a couple of hours but some bloke answered who she didn't know. I had keys to the one I'd been working on, so I drove her up there in my mum's car. She was carrying this big bag and insisted she took it in with us. I thought it was her dry cleaning. There was something about her that night. She was more beautiful than ever. Her eyes were bright, she was flushed and she was sort of pulsating with excitement. I wanted her so much, it hurt. I was gonna be with her forever, and I was gonna tell her.' He gulped back a sob and Brian Gault reached out and touched his arm.

'Are you able to go on, Danny?' asked Morgan. 'I'd prefer not to take a break at this stage.'

Easton continued without acknowledging his words. 'Then, she fiddles in her handbag and I thought it was for johnnies... you know, condoms. When she holds her hand out to show me, it's got this fucking great big diamond on it. Told me she's been engaged for ages but it was getting near to her wedding now so it would be the last time we'd be together. She opens the bag and it's got her fucking wedding dress in it! I couldn't believe it. She wanted to wear it while we had sex. I told her I didn't want to and she got sulky because she wasn't getting her own way. She took the ring off and

368

threw it on the bed. Then she starts to taunt me. Told me that sex with her fiancé was better than me. I got angry then, and I put my hands round her neck. I'd done it before and she'd liked it. She started laughing again and put her hands down my trousers. I remember her saying she could tell I wanted it, and I didn't, so I gripped her neck tighter and tighter until she stopped laughing.' His head sunk down. 'I wanted to be with her forever.'

'How did she end up in the woods?' asked Morgan.

'Well, I couldn't leave her where she was, could I?' He looked at Gault who was staring down at his legal pad. He had stopped writing.

Easton wiped tears again and sniffed. 'I spent all night with her; just holding her close. It was really cold. I had to get mum's car back to her before she needed it for work so, when it got light, I moved her. I couldn't get her in the boot cos she was a bit stiff and I didn't want to break her, so I put her in the back; across the seats, like. I put the frock back in the bag and threw it in after her. I took her to the little car park and carried her into the woods. She liked it in there. We'd been there together. I laid her down and put her handbag and the frock beside her.'

Nobody spoke and Easton looked at each of the officers in turn.

'I had to get mum's car back and get to work,' he insisted.

'But that's not how we found her,' said Spence.

Easton was crying freely now, and shaking his head. Gault reached into his pocket and handed him a neatly folded cotton handkerchief. Easton looked at it as if he had never seen one before.

'When I got to work, I remembered she'd plugged her phone and computer in at the park home. And they were still there.'

'And so?' said Morgan, keen to get all the details and to get out of this airless room.

'I went back on my bike in my lunch break.'

'There's no sign of you either in your mum's car, or on your bike. We've checked all the vehicles entering and leaving from the day Abi went missing,' said Morgan. 'How do you account for that?'

Easton snorted. 'CCTV only reaches the entrance to the reception car park. The roads around the estate aren't covered. As long as you don't go near the reception building, no-one knows you're there.' Morgan struggled to mask his exasperation.

'So you went back the next day...'

'I went and collected the phone and computer.'

'But you left the engagement ring,' said Spence.

'I took them up to the woods and used her fingerprint to get into them. Computer didn't care if it was a live finger or a dead one but the phone was harder to fool. I went back a few times and when the batteries ran down, I dumped them in the woods. I never thought about the ring.'

'And that's where you got the contact records of her clients,' said Spence nodding his understanding.

Easton was looking as if he had started to enjoy himself. He made a gun gesture with his hand and pointed it at Spence with a clicking noise.

'What about the dress?' asked Spence.

'One of the times I went back, I saw it just lying there and I thought, if she wanted to wear it so much, she could. I put it over her. Then, I saw I could get her arms into it. She looked good in it. I took a couple of pictures.'

Morgan screwed up his nose, his distaste obvious. 'When we found her, the ink had washed off the sign you left with her. What did it say?' he asked. He knew it may not be relevant, but he was curious.

Easton looked pained and he spoke quietly. 'It said "I'm sorry," and I was. Then his demeanour changed again. He picked up the picture of Abi Slater and brandished it at the detectives.

'I watched her defend the thieving bastards. In fact, I think she did that one,' he pointed to the picture of Crook, 'Yes, I'm sure she got him out so he could rob more people. Solicitors are as bad as crooks.'

'Cheers,' said Brian Gault quietly without looking up.

'Interview terminated at twelve fifteen,' said Spence and both officers rose from their chairs.

'Not bothered about the other one, then? Is that cos he's a junkie?' asked Easton.

Chapter 90

'You don't have to tell them anything,' said Gault, now looking distinctly rattled.

'You see, I'm right,' said Easton. 'You're all wankers. You hadn't even sussed that there's another one. Nyah nyah.' He raised his thumb to his nose and waggled his fingers at them. Morgan and Spence exchanged a look then resumed their seats and let the recording continue.

'Tell us, Danny,' said Morgan.

'And PC Plod here slept right through it.'

'I think we should take a break,' said Gault.

'I don't want to take a break. These tossers need to know how useless they are.'

'And you're the man to tell us, eh Danny?' said Spence.

'Why not? Someone has to.' He waited for the officers to respond but neither spoke. 'I was walking past Mrs Cooper's house and I saw this bloke sneak up the drive. He looked as if he was up to no good, so I followed him. I thought he was a burglar.'

'When was this?' asked Morgan, although he already knew.

'Day you were moving in; about midnight, or soon after.'

'What were you doing there at that time?'

Easton thought before he replied. 'If I'm out of an evening, I always take a loop past Mrs Cooper's house. Can't trust the police to look out for it.'

'Then?' asked Morgan.

'I followed him up the fire escape. He was quick; I'll give him that. I stopped and watched him through the window for a while, then I went in and stabbed him.'

'What did you stab him with?' asked Spence.

'I had my pocket knife with me.' He smiled as if he'd answered a trick question successfully.

'Is that the same knife you threatened Mrs Cooper with?'

'I already said I was sorry for doing that. I like Mrs Cooper. She's been kind to me.'

Morgan thought they must both know different Mrs Coopers. 'Is it the same knife?' he repeated his question. 'We'll be able to tell when forensics look at it.'

'I doubt it. I gave it an hour in the ultrasonic bath at the home.' Sly grin again.

'You say you stabbed him. Where did you stab him? How many times?'

'Do you not believe me, or something?' Easton crossed his arms. 'No wonder you lot can't lock people up. You don't believe them, even when they admit something.' He gave a dramatic sigh. 'I crept up behind him while he was bending over and stabbed him a couple of times in the back. What more do you want? I'm getting tired now.'

'Okay, we'll take a break,' said Morgan and nodded at the recording unit. Spence made the announcement and pushed the button. 'Are you going to take further instructions, Mr Gault, or shall we arrange for Danny to be returned to his cell?'

Gault looked at his watch. 'I think I need to contact the office,' he said.

They waited for the arrival of a custody officer who escorted Easton to the cells while Gault packed his pad and papers into his briefcase. 'I'm not even sure he's fit to plead.' he said.

Spence shrugged. 'Some of them put on an act when they see the evidence mount up, but he seems proud of what he's done. There's a righteousness about him.'

'I'm no expert,' said Morgan. 'But it doesn't look like an act to me. We'll see what a psych assessment comes back with.'

The men shook hands and Gault headed for custody reception and the fresh air of the car park while Morgan and Spence went upstairs to tell DI Patel she had a confession for Carl Raynor's murder.

Morgan and Patel were drinking coffee in Morgan's office.

'Johnson's happy,' said Patel. 'It won't last, but he's happy for now.'

Morgan shook his head. 'I know I should be too, but I'm having doubts. He looks like my brother-in-law, so I see how people thought it was Steven in a relationship with Abi Slater, right up to her murder. I can also see how killing Crook and the Maguires fits with his so called mission, and now that I've seen he has a temper, I can go along with him losing it and killing Wyatt and Abi Slater. But Raynor doesn't fit. He was a junkie, there's no sign left with him and he didn't get a warning letter. He was stabbed and suffocated, not strangled. He just doesn't fit.'

'You're looking for reasons to make him not fit,' she replied. 'He'd already killed Abi, but Raynor was his first avenger killing. It doesn't fit the modus operandi because he hadn't developed one by then. He followed a dodgy looking burglar into your mother-in-law's house and stabbed him with what he had to hand. His pocket knife. With everything else he's done since then, he must have forgotten he had to smother Raynor too. The CPS are happy. Don't be such a party pooper.'

Morgan was shaking his head. 'We're missing something.'

Chapter 91

Four weeks later.

The door was open, and Nick Morgan was waiting in Dorothy Cooper's lounge when she returned from her morning walk. He saw she was startled, but she recovered quickly.

'Nicholas, this is a surprise. I'd offer coffee, but you probably won't be staying long.' He hadn't imagined that saving her life would improve their relationship, and it hadn't.

She hung her jacket behind the door 'What can I do for you?'

Morgan waited until she had made herself comfortable in her usual chair.

'I've come to update you about Danny Easton.'

'Ah, yes. Poor Danny. I believe he's undergoing psychiatric evaluation to see if he's fit to plead?'

Morgan's smile was without warmth or humour. 'Of course, you'll be getting your updates from Brian Gault since you're paying his fees.'

Dorothy Cooper closed her eyes and stretched her neck backwards. 'I knew it was a mistake to tell Samantha. She always was one to tell tales.'

'When she told me, it didn't make sense. Why would you be paying for Easton's solicitor after he held a knife at your neck?'

'That's none of your business,' she rasped.

'Then, I got to wondering why he came to see you that morning. The morning he held a knife at your neck, I mean.'

'You don't have to keep saying it, I know what happened.'

'The manager said she heard an argument. Was that because he wanted something from you? Money to pay a solicitor, for example?'

'And why would he come to me? That's just preposterous.'

Morgan nodded his agreement. 'I thought that... at first.' He leant his shoulder on the wall so that she had to turn in her chair to see him. 'He's pleaded guilty to the murder at Cliffside,' he said.

'Has he? My goodness.' Her face betrayed that she already knew.

'It's interesting. Forensics found Danny's DNA on a cushion used to smother Raynor, but no trace of Raynor's blood on Danny's pocket knife.'

'So? I couldn't be less interested.'

'So, and here's where you should get interested, Dotty. The pathologist has excluded Danny's pocket knife as the weapon used to stab Raynor. The blade isn't long enough.' Morgan saw a flicker of something cross her face. Doubt? Fear? It vanished before he could be sure.

'We know that Danny was at Cliffside and that he smothered Carl Raynor. We also know that he carries a knife which doesn't fit the stab wounds in Raynor's body. It's a puzzle.'

She smiled with saccharin sarcasm. 'You're the detective.'

He stepped towards her and brought his face down to hers. 'And I'm good at it,' he said. She averted her face, but not before he registered her distaste.

'Steven came to help me install the new insulation at the house on Sunday.' Her head snapped back. He had her attention now. 'He was using a folding knife which was just like the example the pathologist said we should look for. In fact, he let me borrow it. It was really, really clean which was odd, because he told me he'd had it for years.'

'Steven isn't involved in any of this,' she hissed. 'He doesn't have it in his nature.'

'And if you were the detective, Dotty, you would know that people often act out of character when they're angry.' Her eyes narrowed. 'And Sam told me that Steven was angry when he left you, the day before we were supposed to move in. He told you he was going to move in himself that night, didn't he?'

She looked frightened now.

'This is why you should be interested,' he repeated. 'Because, you see, I believe Danny Easton did see a dodgy man going into Cliffside, but it wasn't the addict he saw, it was Steven. Danny followed Steven up the fire escape and watched him go into the back bedroom where Carl Raynor was bending over the cabinet preparing lines of drugs. Steven was still smarting about us getting the house and Sam taking over the business. He was still raging after the argument he'd had with you and he needed to take it out on someone. He pushed his way in and he stabbed Raynor. And that's where I think you're right – it's not in his nature – so he botched it.

'This is the bit where I have to use my imagination a little, or even my experience as a detective. We know that a fight ensues from the disturbance to the dust on

378

the floor, so maybe Raynor starts to get the better of Steven.' He pointed his forefinger at her. 'Danny's been watching from the fire escape and that's when he piles in to help. Raynor tries to escape, but Danny follows him into the master bedroom and finishes it by smothering him.'

'Why would he do that? You're talking shit.'

Morgan had never heard his mother-in-law swear. Not ever. He was sure now that he was close to the truth.

'Danny likes you. He wouldn't want to see your son hurt, or worse. But now he has something on you. I don't know when he told you what he'd done... what he'd done to help your Steven, I mean, but I think it was when he came for money and you argued. How much are you paying, Dotty, apart from Brian Gault's fees? It must be quite a lot because he's going away for a long time and his mother will need looking after.'

'He's not fit to plead,' said Dorothy. 'He's not right in the head. Anyone can see that.'

'He's taking a risk if that's the game he's playing. I know people who've ended up in high security psychiatric hospitals because they think it's an easier option than prison. They can end up as damaged as the rest of the inmates.'

'That's not my worry.' Her smile returned.

'Maybe not.' He buttoned his jacket and got to the door before turning. 'Has Sam told you that we're staying together? That your little plan to puppet master her away from me and fix her up with your smarmy, posh solicitor friend hasn't worked. Has she told you that?' He shook his head, 'No? I didn't think so.' His turn to smile. 'Do you know why I'm so determined to save my marriage?' He waited but got no response. 'Because it pisses you off so much, it's worth it.'

379

'We can talk about it when I come for tea on Sunday.'

'I don't ever want to see you in our house again,' he said.

'But it's not your house, is it? It's my house and when I've gone, it will be Samantha's house. You'll just be the live-in maintenance man.'

He came back and rested his knee on the arm of her chair so he could get closer to her. She was looking away from him and he raised her chin forcing eye contact, their noses only a couple of inches apart. 'Don't make the mistake of thinking that I'll forget about Steven. I can't prove it at the moment, but you haven't won anything here.'

Her face twisted and she snarled, '"Won anything?" I haven't even started competing.'

He whipped his hand away and strode to the door slamming it shut behind him. At top of the staircase, his phone rang. 'DI Morgan.'

'DI Morgan, its Sergeant Ramsay from Ops. We've got a couple of officers on the beach at Gullhaven Cove. They've reported a death. Body in a beach hut.'

'I'm on my way,' he said and quickened his pace.

DI Nick Morgan Readers' Club

Free Download

I hope you've enjoyed reading "Make You Sorry"

If you'd like to know why DI Nick Morgan agreed to move to Gullhaven, sign up now to access your free download of "FIRE FARM" the prequel to "Make You Sorry."

This download is exclusive to Reader's Club Members ONLY and is <u>absolutely free</u>

You'll also receive news of upcoming publications in the DI Nick Morgan series and priority access to any discounted availability.

Visit
<u>https://www.christinerae-jones.com</u>

and tell us where to email your download link
If you change your mind,
you can unsubscribe at any time

See you there!

DI Nick Morgan Crime Thriller Series Book 2

MAKE YOU BEG

HE KNEW SHE WAS A MISTAKE. HE WAS RIGHT

By CHRISTINE RAE-JONES

A midnight rendezvous.
An irresistible temptation.
He knew she was a mistake. He was right

Simon Dennison is Forest-Fox's top salesman but his success generates rivalry and resentment. When his body is found in a dilapidated beach hut, wrists secured by pink fluffy handcuffs, Detective Inspector Nick Morgan and his team are drawn into the shady world of a man with a dark secret.

A new arrival at the Major Crime Unit creates turmoil in the Morgan marriage that has unforeseen and far reaching consequences. Nick faces a stark decision which will change the lives of those he loves forever. Family loyalty or personal happiness?

Which would you choose?

Make You Beg is the eagerly anticipated sequel to Make You Sorry, also featuring DI Nick Morgan and DS Dave Spence.

Available now from Cliffside house Publishing

DI Nick Morgan Crime Thriller Series Book 3

MAKE YOU CHOOSE

YOU LOVE YOUR BROTHER. HE WANTS YOU DEAD

By CHRISTINE RAE-JONES

Available Autumn 2021

Join the Reader Club at

https://www.christinerae-jones.com

for discounted pre-launch availability

Author's Note

Like DI Nick Morgan, I too have relocated to the south coast of England following a varied career in forensic toxicology, scientific instrumentation sales and professional skills development.

The pivotal role played by the Magistrates' Courts in *"Make You Sorry"* is inspired by a period of over ten years I served as a criminal court magistrate.

Throughout the novel I have used U.K. English spellings and colloquialisms and have taken a few liberties with the geography of Hampshire and Dorset as well as police structure of these two counties.

<u>Acknowledgements</u>

I completed the first draft of "Make You Sorry" during the first nine months of 2018 and then spent more time than was healthy editing and tweaking. My thanks to Eve Seymour; Author and Hannah Bond; Publishing Executive at Bookouture, for their positive and valuable contributions to the process.

I must also thank the pathologist (who wishes to remain anonymous) who advised me where to stab my first victim to ensure his blood would drip down the chandelier, and all the other individuals who gave me insight into police service procedure and politics.

When I chose my route to publication I turned to Debbie at The Cover Collection whose 'can do' attitude to customer service made a difficult decision very easy.

There are numerous friends and family members who have listened patiently while I have droned on about plot problems and writer's block but I especially want to recognise Joyce and Mark. Joyce took Nick Morgan's life down a path I hadn't planned, but for which Maisie is eternally grateful. Mark, my Synopsis Superhero, spent hours of his life honing my words, offering suggestions and encouragement and wasn't afraid to scold me when I needed it. Brave man!

Finally, my thanks to my mum who never stopped believing, even when I did.

CRJ